Fenton's Quest

By

M. E. Braddon

The Author of "Lady Audley's Secret,"
"Aurora Floyd," Etc. Etc. Etc.

The Echo Library 2006

Published by

The Echo Library

Echo Library
131 High St.
Teddington
Middlesex TW11 8HH

www.echo-library.com

Please report serious faults in the text to complaints@echo-library.com

ISBN 1-84702-840-3

CHEAP UNIFORM EDITION OF MISS BRADDON'S NOVELS.

Price 2s. picture boards; 2s. 6d. cloth gilt; 3s. 6d. half parchment or half morocco; postage 4d.

MISS BRADDON'S NOVELS

INCLUDING

"LADY AUDLEY'S SECRET," "VIXEN," "ISHMAEL" ETC.

"No one can be dull who has a novel by Miss Braddon in hand. The most tiresome journey is beguiled, and the most wearisome illness is brightened, by any one of her books."

"Miss Braddon is the Queen of the circulating libraries."—*The World.*

N.B.—There are now 45 Novels always in print; For full list see book of cover, or apply for a Catalogue, to be sent (post free),

LONDON: J. AND B. MAXWELL,
Milton House, 14 and 15 Shoe Lane, Fleet Street;
AND
35 St. Bride Street, Ludgate Circus, E.O.
And at all Railway Bookstalls, Booksellers' and Libraries.

CONTENTS

I.	The Common Fever	1
II.	Marian's Story	11
III.	Accepted	22
IV.	John Saltram	27
V.	Halcyon Days	36
VI.	Sentence Of Exile	44
VII.	"Good-Bye"	51
VIII.	Missing	56
IX.	John Saltram's Advice	64
X.	Jacob Nowell	69
XI.	The Marriage At Wygrove	74
XII.	A Friendly Counsellor	82
XIII.	Mrs. Pallinson Has Views	87
XIV.	Father And Son	94
XV.	On The Track	100
XVI.	Face To Face	109
XVII.	Miss Carley's Admirers	119
XVIII.	Jacob Nowell's Will	126
XIX.	Gilbert Asks A Question	132
XX.	Drifting Away	135
XXI.	Father And Daughter	140
XXII.	At Lidford Again	149
XXIII.	Called To Account	154
XXIV.	Tormented By Doubt	160
XXV.	Missing Again	164
XXVI.	In Bondage	174
XXVII.	Only A Woman	180
XXVIII.	At Fault	186
XXIX.	Baffled, Not Beaten	192
XXX.	Stricken Down	199
XXXI.	Ellen Carley's Trials	209
XXXII.	The Padlocked Door At Wyncomb	213
XXXIII.	"What Must Be Shall Be"	219
XXXIV.	Doubtful Information	224
XXXV.	Bought With A Price	234
XXXVI.	Coming Round	238
XXXVII.	A Full Confession	244
XXXVIII.	An Ill-Omened Wedding	253
XXXIX.	A Domestic Mystery	259
XL.	In Pursuit	271
XLI.	Outward Bound	282
XLII.	The Pleasures Of Wyncomb	291
XLIII.	Mr. Whitelaw Makes An End Of The Mystery	298

XLIV.	After The Fire	308
XLV.	Mr. Whitelaw Makes His Will	314
XLVI.	Ellen Regains Her Liberty	319
XLVII.	Closing Scenes	324

CHAPTER I.
THE COMMON FEVER.

A warm summer evening, with a sultry haze brooding over the level landscape, and a Sabbath stillness upon all things in the village of Lidford, Midlandshire. In the remoter corners of the old gothic church the shadows are beginning to gather, as the sermon draws near its close; but in the centre aisle and about the pulpit there is broad daylight still shining-in from the wide western window, across the lower half of which there are tall figures of the Evangelists in old stained glass.

There are no choristers at Lidford, and the evening service is conducted in rather a drowsy way; but there is a solemn air of repose about the gray old church that should be conducive to tranquil thoughts and pious meditations. Simple and earnest have been the words of the sermon, simple and earnest seem the countenances of the congregation, looking reverently upwards at the face of their pastor; and one might fancy, contemplating that grand old church, so much too spacious for the needs of the little flock gathered there to-night, that Lidford was a forgotten, half-deserted corner of this earth, in which a man, tired of the press and turmoil of the world, might find an almost monastic solitude and calm.

So thought a gentleman in the Squire's pew—a good-looking man of about thirty, who was finishing his first Sunday at Lidford by devout attendance at evening service. He had been thinking a good deal about this quiet country life during the service, wondering whether it was not the best life a man could live, after all, and thinking it all the sweeter because of his own experience, which had lain chiefly in cities.

He was a certain Mr. Gilbert Fenton, an Australian merchant, and was on a visit to his sister, who had married the principal landowner in Lidford, Martin Lister—a man whose father had been called "the Squire." The lady sat opposite her brother in the wide old family pew to-night—a handsome-looking matron, with a little rosy-cheeked damsel sitting by her side—a damsel with flowing auburn hair, tiny hat and feather, and bright scarlet stockings, looking very much as if she had walked out of a picture by Mr. Millais.

The congregation stood up to sing a hymn when the sermon was ended, and Gilbert Fenton turned his face towards the opposite line of pews, in one of which, very near him, there was a girl, at whom Mrs. Lister had caught her brother looking very often, during the service just concluded.

It was a face that a man could scarcely look upon once without finding his glances wandering back to it afterwards; not quite a perfect face, but a very bright and winning one. Large gray eyes, with a wonderful light in them, under dark lashes and darker brows; a complexion that had a dusky pallor, a delicate semi-transparent olive-tint that one seldom sees out of a Spanish picture; a sweet rosy mouth, and a piquant little nose of no particular order, made up the catalogue of this young lady's charms. But in a face worth looking at there is always a something that cannot be put into words; and the brightest and best attributes of this face were quite beyond translation. It was a face one might almost call "splendid"—there was such a light and glory about it at some moments. Gilbert Fenton thought so to-night, as he saw it in the full radiance of the western sunlight, the lips parted as the girl sang, the clear gray eyes looking upward.

She was not alone: a portly genial-looking old man stood by her side, and accompanied her to the church-porch when the hymn was over. Here they both lingered a moment to shake hands with Mrs. Lister, very much to Gilbert Fenton's satisfaction. They walked along the churchyard-path together, and Gilbert gave his sister's arm a little tug, which meant, "Introduce me."

"My brother Mr. Fenton, Captain Sedgewick, Miss Nowell."

The Captain shook hands with Gilbert. "Delighted to know you, Mr. Fenton; delighted to know any one belonging to Mrs. Lister. You are going to stop down here for some time, I hope."

"I fear not for very long, Captain Sedgewick. I am a business man, you see, and can't afford to take a long holiday from the City."

Mrs. Lister laughed. "My brother is utterly devoted to commercial pursuits," she said; "I think he believes every hour wasted that he spends out of his counting-house."

"And yet I was thinking in church this evening, that a man's life might be happier in such a place as this, drifting away in a kind of dreamy idleness, than the greatest successes possible to commerce could ever make it."

"You would very soon be tired of your dreamy idleness," answered his sister, "and sigh for your office and your club."

"The country suits old people, who have played their part in life, and made an end of it," said the Captain. "It suits my little girl here very well, too," he added, with a fond glance at his companion; "she has her birds and her flowers, and her books and music; and I don't think she ever sighs for anything gayer than Lidford."

"Never, uncle George," said the girl, slipping her hand through his arm. And Gilbert Fenton saw that those two were very fond of each other.

They came to the end of a shady winding lane at this moment, and Captain Sedgewick and Miss Nowell wished Mrs. Lister and her brother good-evening, and went away down the lane arm-in-arm.

"What a lovely girl she is!" said Gilbert, when they were gone.

"Lovely is rather a strong word, Gilbert," Mrs. Lister answered coldly; "she is certainly pretty, but I hope you are not going to lose your heart in that direction."

"There is no fear of that. A man may admire a girl's face without being in any danger of losing his heart. But why not in that direction, Belle? Is there any special objection to the lady?"

"Only that she is a nobody, without either money or position and I think you ought to have both when you marry."

"Thanks for the implied compliment; but I do not fancy that an Australian merchant can expect to secure a wife of very exalted position; and I am the last man in the world to marry for money."

"I don't for a moment suppose you would marry any one you didn't like, from mercenary considerations; but there is no reason you should make a foolish match."

"Of course not. I think it very doubtful whether I shall ever marry at all. I am just the kind of man to go down to my grave a bachelor."

"Why so, Gilbert?"

"Well, I can hardly tell you, my dear. Perhaps I am rather difficult to please—just a little stony-hearted and invulnerable. I know that since I was a boy, and got over my schoolboy love affairs, I have never seen the woman who could touch my heart. I have met plenty of pretty women, and plenty of brilliant women, of course, in society; and have admired them, and there an end. I have never seen a woman whose face impressed me so much at first sight as the face of your friend, Miss Nowell."

"I am very sorry for that."

"But why, Belle?"

"Because the girl is a nobody—less than nobody. There is an unpleasant kind of mystery about her birth."

"How is that? Her uncle, Captain Sedgewick, seems to be a gentleman."

"Captain Sedgewick is very well, but he is not her uncle; he adopted her when she was a very little girl."

"But who are her people, and how did she fall into his hands?"

"I have never heard that. He is not very fond of talking about the subject. When we first came to know them, he told us that Marian was only his adopted niece; and he has never told us any more than that."

"She is the daughter of some friend, I suppose. They seem very much attached to each other."

"Yes, she is very fond of him, and he of her. She is an amiable girl; I have nothing to say against her—but——"

"But what, Belle?"

"I shouldn't like you to fall in love with her."

"But I should, mamma!" cried the damsel in scarlet stockings, who had absorbed every word of the foregoing conversation. "I should like uncle Gil to love Marian just as I love her. She is the dearest girl in the world. When we had a juvenile party last winter, it was Marian who dressed the Christmas-tree—every bit; and she played the piano for us all the evening, didn't she, mamma?"

"She is very good-natured, Lucy; but you mustn't talk nonsense; and you ought not to listen when your uncle and I are talking. It is very rude."

"But! I can't help hearing you, mamma."

They were at home by this time, within the grounds of a handsome red-brick house of the early Georgian era, which had been the property of the Listers ever since it was built. Without, the gardens were a picture of neatness and order; within, everything was solid and comfortable: the furniture of a somewhat ponderous and exploded fashion, but handsome withal, and brightened here and there by some concession to modern notions of elegance or ease—a dainty little table for books, a luxurious arm-chair, and so on.

Martin Lister was a gentleman chiefly distinguished by good-nature, hospitable instincts, and an enthusiastic devotion to agriculture. There were very few things in common between him and his brother-in-law the Australian merchant, but they got on very well together for a short time. Gilbert Fenton pretended to be profoundly interested in the thrilling question of drainage, deep or superficial, and seemed to enter unreservedly into every discussion of the latest invention or improvement in agricultural machinery; and in the mean time he really liked the repose of the country, and appreciated the varying charms of landscape and atmosphere with a fervour unfelt by the man who had been born and reared amidst those pastoral scenes.

The two men smoked their cigars together in a quietly companionable spirit, strolling about the gardens and farm, dropping out a sentence now and then, and anon falling into a lazy reverie, each pondering upon his own affairs—Gilbert meditating transactions with foreign houses, risky bargains with traders of doubtful solvency, or hazardous investments in stocks, as the case might be; the gentleman farmer ruminating upon the chances of a good harvest, or the probable value of his Scotch short-horns.

Mr. Lister had preferred lounging about the farm with a cigar in his mouth to attendance at church upon this particular Sunday evening. He had finished his customary round of inspection by this time, and was sitting by one of the open windows of the drawing-room, with his body in one luxurious chair, and his legs extended upon another, deep in the study of the *Gardener's Chronicle*, which he flung aside upon the appearance of his family.

"Well, Toddlekins," he cried to the little girl, "I hope you were very attentive to the sermon; listened for two, and made up for your lazy dad. That's a vicarious kind of devotion that ought to be permitted occasionally to a hard-working fellow like me.—I'm glad you've come back to give us some tea, Belle. Don't go upstairs; let Susan carry up your bonnet and shawl. It's nearly nine o'clock. Toddlekins wants her tea before she goes to bed."

"Lucy has had her tea in the nursery," said Mrs. Lister, as she took her seat before the cups and saucers.

"But she will have some more with papa," replied Martin, who had an amiable knack of spoiling his children. There were only two—this bright fair-haired Lucy, aged nine, and a sturdy boy of seven.

They sipped their tea, and talked a little about who had been at church and who had not been, and the room was filled with that atmosphere of dulness which seems to prevail in such households upon a summer Sunday evening; a kind of palpable emptiness which sets a man speculating how many years he may have to live, and how many such Sundays he may have to spend. He is apt to end by wondering a little whether life is really worth the trouble it costs, when almost the best thing that can come of it is a condition of comfortable torpor like this.

Gilbert Fenton put down his cup and went over to one of the open windows. It was nearly as dark as it was likely to be that midsummer night. A new moon was shining faintly in the clear evening sky; and here and there a solitary star shone with a tremulous brightness. The shadows of the trees made spots of solemn darkness on the wide lawn before the windows, and a warm faint sweetness came from the crowded flower-beds, where all the flowers in this light were of one grayish silvery hue.

"It's almost too warm an evening for the house," said Gilbert; "I think I'll take a stroll."

"I'd come with you, old fellow, but I've been all round the farm, and I'm dead beat," said good-natured Martin Lister.

"Thanks, Martin; I wouldn't think of disturbing you. You look the picture of comfort in that easy-chair. I shall only stay long enough to finish a cigar."

He walked slowly across the lawn—a noble stretch of level greensward with dark spreading cedars and fine old beeches scattered about it; he walked slowly towards the gates, lighting his cigar as he went, and thinking. He was thinking of his past life, and of his future. What was it to be? A dull hackneyed course of money-making, chequered only by the dreary vicissitudes of trade, and brightened only by such selfish pleasures as constitute the recreations of a business man—an occasional dinner at Blackwall or Richmond, a week's shooting in the autumn, a little easy-going hunting in the winter, a hurried scamper over some of the beaten continental roads, or a fortnight at a German spa? These had been his pleasures hitherto, and he had found life pleasant enough. Perhaps he had been too busy to question the pleasantness of these things. It was only now that he found himself away from the familiar arena of his daily life, with neither employment nor distraction, that was able to look back upon his career deliberately, and risk himself whether it was one that he could go on living without weariness for the remainder of his days.

He had been at this time a little more than seven years in business. He had been bred-up with no expectation of ever having to take his place in the counting-house, had been educated at Eton and Oxford, and had been taught to anticipate a handsome fortune from his father. All these expectations had been disappointed by Mr. Fenton's sudden death at a period of great commercial disturbance. The business was found in a state of entanglement that was very near insolvency; and wise friends told Gilbert Fenton that the only hope of coming well out of these perplexities lay with himself. The business was too good to be sacrificed, and the business was all his father had left behind him, with the exception of a houseful of handsome furniture, two or three carriages, and a couple of pairs of horses, which were sold by auction within a few weeks of the funeral.

Gilbert Fenton took upon himself the management of the business. He had a clear comprehensive intellect, which adapted itself very easily to commerce. He put his shoulder to the wheel with a will, and worked for the first three years of his business career as it is not given to many men to work in the course of their lives. By that time the ship had been steered clear of all rocks and quicksands, and rode the commercial waters gallantly. Gilbert was not a rich man, but was in a fair way to become a rich man; and the name of Fenton stood as high as in the palmiest days of his father's career.

His sister had fortunately married Martin Lister some years before her father's death, and had received her dowry at the time of her marriage. Gilbert had only himself to work for. At first he had worked for the sake of his dead father's honour and repute; later he fell into a groove, like other men, and worked for the love of money-making—not with any sordid love of money, but with that natural desire to accumulate which grows out of a business career.

To-night he was in an unusually thoughtful humour, and inclined to weigh things in the balance with a doubtfulness as to their value which was new to him. The complete idleness and emptiness of his life in the country had made him meditative. Was it worth living, that monotonous business life of his? Would not the time soon come in which its dreariness would oppress him as the dulness of Lidford House had oppressed him to-night? His youth was fast going—nay, had it not indeed gone from him for ever? had not youth left him all at once when he began his commercial career?—and the pleasures that had been fresh enough within the last few years were rapidly growing stale. He knew the German spas, the pine-groves where the band played, the gambling-saloons and their company, by heart, though he had never stayed more than a fortnight at any one of them. He had exhausted Brittany and the South of France in these rapid scampers; skimmed the cream of their novelty, at any rate. He did not care very much for field-sports, and hunted and shot in a jog-trot safe kind of way, with a view to the benefit of his health, which savoured of old bachelorhood. And as for the rest of his pleasures—the social rubber at his club, the Blackwall or Richmond dinners—it seemed only custom that made them agreeable.

"If I had gone to the Bar, as I intended to do before my father's death, I should have had an object in life," he thought, as he puffed slowly at his cigar; "but a commercial man has nothing to hope for in the way of fame—nothing to work for except money. I have a good mind to sell the business, now that it is worth selling, and go in for the Bar after all, late as it is."

He had thought of this more than once; but he knew the fancy was a foolish one, and that his friends would laugh at him for his folly.

He was beyond the grounds of Lidford House by this time, sauntering onward in the fair summer night; not indifferent to the calm loveliness of the scene around him, only conscious that there was some void within himself which these things could not fill. He walked along the road by which he and his sister had come back from church, and turned into the lane at the end of which Captain Sedgewick had bidden them good night. He had been down this lane before to-night, and knew that it was one of the prettiest walks about Lidford; so there was scarcely anything strange in the fact that he should choose this promenade for his evening saunter.

The rustic way, wide enough for a wagon, and with sloping grassy banks, and tall straggling hedges, full of dog-roses and honeysuckle, led towards a river—a fair winding stream, which was one of the glories of Lidford. A little before one came to the river, the lane opened upon a green, where there was a mill, and a miller's cottage, a rustic inn, and two or three other houses of more genteel pretensions.

Gilbert Fenton wondered which of these was the habitation of Captain Sedgewick, concluding that the half-pay officer and his niece must needs live in one of them. He reconnoitred them as he went by the low garden-fences, over which he could see the pretty lawns and flower-beds, with clusters of evergreens here and there, and a wealth of roses and seringa. One of them, the prettiest and most secluded, was also the smallest; a low white-walled cottage, with casement windows above, and old-fashioned bow-windows below, and a porch overgrown with roses. The house lay back a little way from the green; and there was a tiny brook running beside the holly hedge that bounded the garden, spanned by a little rustic bridge before the gate.

Pausing just beside this bridge, Mr. Fenton heard the joyous barking of a dog, and caught a brief glimpse of a light muslin dress flitting across the little lawn at one side of the cottage While he was wondering about the owner of this dress, the noisy dog came rushing towards the gate, and in the next moment a girlish figure appeared in the winding path that went in and out among the flower-beds.

Gilbert Fenton knew that tall slim figure very well. He had guessed rightly, and this low white-walled cottage was really Captain Sedgewick's. It seemed to him as if a kind of instinct brought him to that precise spot.

Miss Nowell came to the gate, and stood there looking out, with a Skye terrier in her arms. Gilbert drew back a little, and flung his cigar into the brook. She had not seen him yet. Her looks were wandering far away across the green, as if in search of some one.

Gilbert Fenton stood quite still watching her. She looked even prettier without her bonnet than she had looked in the church, he thought: the rich dark-brown hair gathered in a great knot at the back of the graceful head; the perfect throat circled by a broad black ribbon, from which there hung an old-fashioned gold cross; the youthful figure set-off by the girlish muslin dress, so becoming in its utter simplicity.

He could not stand there for ever looking at her, pleasant as it might be to him to contemplate the lovely face; so he made a little movement at last, and came a few steps nearer to the gate.

"Good-evening once more, Miss Nowell," he said.

She looked up at him, surprised by his sudden appearance, but in no manner embarrassed.

"Good-evening, Mr. Fenton. I did not see you till this moment. I was looking for my uncle. He has gone out for a little stroll while he smokes his cigar, and I expect him home every minute."

"I have been indulging in a solitary cigar myself," answered Gilbert. "One is apt to be inspired with an antipathy to the house on this kind of evening. I left the Listers yawning over their tea-cups, and came out for a ramble. The aspect of the lane at which we parted company this evening tempted me down this way. What a pretty house you have! Do you know I guessed that it was yours before I saw you."

"Indeed! You must have quite a talent for guessing."

"Not in a general way; but there is a fitness in things. Yes, I felt sure that this was your house."

"I am glad you like it," she answered simply. "Uncle George and I are very fond of it. But it must seem a poor little place to you after Lidford House."

"Lidford House is spacious, and comfortable, and commonplace. One could hardly associate the faintest touch of romance with such a place. But about this one might fancy anything. Ah, here is your uncle, I see."

Captain Sedgewick came towards them, surprised at seeing Mr. Fenton, with whom he shook hands again very cordially, and who repeated his story about the impossibility of enduring to stop in the house on such a night.

The Captain insisted on his going in-doors with them, however; and he exhibited no disinclination to linger in the cottage drawing-room, though it was only about a fourth of the size of that at Lidford House. It looked a very pretty room in the lamplight, with quaint old-fashioned furniture, the freshest and most delicate chintz hangings and coverings of chairs and sofas, and some valuable old china here and there.

Captain Sedgewick had plenty to say for himself, and was pleased to find an intelligent stranger to converse with. His health had failed him long ago, and he had turned his back upon the world of action for ever; but he was as cheerful and hopeful as if his existence had been the gayest possible to man.

Of course they talked a little of military matters, the changes that had come about in the service—none of them changes for the better, according to the Captain, who was a little behind the times in his way of looking at these things.

He ordered in a bottle of claret for his guest, and Gilbert Fenton found himself seated by the open bow-window looking out at the dusky lawn and drinking his wine, as much at home as if he had been a visitor at the Captain's for the last ten years. Marian Nowell sat on the other side of the room, with the lamplight shining on her dark-brown hair, and with that much-to-be-envied Skye terrier on her lap. Gilbert glanced across at her every now and then while he was talking with her uncle; and by and by she came over to the window and stood behind the Captain's chair, with her clasped hands resting upon his shoulder.

Gilbert contrived to engage her in the conversation presently. He found her quite able to discuss the airy topics which he started—the last new volume of poems, the picture of the year, and so on. There was nothing awkward or provincial in her manner; and if she did not say anything particularly brilliant, there was good sense in all her remarks, and she had a bright animated way of speaking that was very charming.

She had lived a life of peculiar seclusion, rarely going beyond the village of Lidford, and had contrived to find perfect happiness in that simple existence. The Captain told Mr. Fenton this in the course of their talk.

"I have not been able to afford so much as a visit to London for my darling," he said; "but I do not know that she is any the worse for her ignorance of the great world. The grand point is that she should be happy, and I thank God that she has been happy hitherto."

"I should be very ungrateful if I were not, uncle George," the girl said in a half whisper.

Captain Sedgewick gave a thoughtful sigh, and was silent for a little while after this; and then the talk went on again until the clock upon the chimney-piece struck the half-hour after ten, and Gilbert Fenton rose to say good-night. "I have stayed a most unconscionable time, I fear," he said; "but I had really no idea it was so late."

"Pray, don't hurry away," replied the Captain. "You ought to help me to finish that bottle. Marian and I are not the earliest people in Lidford."

Gilbert would have had no objection to loiter away another half-hour in the bow-window, talking politics with the Captain, or light literature with Miss Nowell, but he knew that his prolonged absence must have already caused some amount of wonder at Lidford House; so he held firmly to his good-night, shook hands with his new friends, holding Marian Nowell's soft slender hand in his for the first time, and wondering at the strange magic of her touch, and then went out into the dreamy atmosphere of the summer night a changed creature.

"Is this love at first sight?" he asked himself, as he walked homeward along the rustic lane, where dog-roses and the starry flowers of the wild convolvulus gleamed whitely in the uncertain light. "Is it? I should have been the last of men to believe such a thing possible yesterday; and yet to-night I feel as if that girl were destined to be the ruling influence of my future life. Why is it? Because she is lovely? Surely not. Surely I am not so weak a fool as to be caught by a beautiful face! And yet what else do I know of her? Absolutely nothing. She may be the shallowest of living creatures—the most selfish, the falsest, the basest. No; I do not believe she could ever be false or unworthy. There is something noble in her face—something more than mere beauty. Heaven knows, I have seen enough of that in my time. I could scarcely be so childish as to be bewitched by a pair of gray eyes and a rosy mouth; there must be something more. And, after all, this is most likely a passing fancy, born out of the utter idleness and dulness of this place. I shall go back to London in a week or two, and forget Marian Nowell. Marian Nowell!"

He repeated the name with unspeakable tenderness in his tone—a deeper feeling than would have seemed natural to a passing fancy. It was more like a symptom of sickening for life's great fever.

It was close upon eleven when he made his appearance in his sister's drawing-room, where Martin Lister was enjoying a comfortable nap, while his wife stifled her yawns over a mild theological treatise.

He had to listen to a good deal of wonderment about the length of his absence, and was fain to confess to an accidental encounter with Captain Sedgewick, which had necessitated his going into the cottage.

"Why, what could have taken you that way, Gilbert?"

"A truant fancy, I suppose, my dear. It is as good a way as any other."

Mrs. Lister sighed, and shook her head doubtfully. "What fools you men are," she said, "about a pretty face!" "Including Martin, Belle, when he fell in love with your fair self?"

"Martin did not stare me out of countenance in church, sir. But you have almost kept us waiting for prayers."

The servants came filing in. Martin Lister woke with a start, and Gilbert Fenton knelt down among his sister's household to make his evening orisons. But his thoughts were not easily to be fixed that night. They wandered very wide of that simple family prayer, and made themselves into a vision of the future, in which he saw his life changed and brightened by the companionship of a fair young wife.

CHAPTER II.
MARIAN'S STORY.

THE days passed, and there was no more dulness or emptiness for Gilbert Fenton in his life at Lidford. He went every day to the white-walled cottage on the green. It was easy enough to find some fresh excuse for each visit—a book or a piece of music which he had recommended to Miss Nowell, and had procured from London for her, or something of an equally frivolous character. The Captain was always cordial, always pleased to see him. His visits were generally made in the evening; and it was his delight to linger over the pretty little round table by the bow-window, drinking tea dispensed by Marian. The bright home-like room, the lovely face turned so trustingly to his; these were the things which made that fair vision of the future that haunted him so often now. He fancied himself the master of some pretty villa in the suburbs—at Kingston or Twickenham, perhaps—with a garden sloping down to the water's edge, a lawn on which he and his wife and some chosen friend might sit after dinner in the long summer evenings, sipping their claret or their tea, as the case might be, and watching the last rosy glow of the sunset fade and die upon the river. He fancied himself with this girl for his wife, and the delight of going back from the dull dryasdust labours of his city life to a home in which she would bid him welcome. He behaved with a due amount of caution, and did not give the young lady any reason to suspect the state of the case yet awhile. Marian was perfectly devoid of coquetry, and had no idea that this gentleman's constant presence at the cottage could have any reference to herself. She liked her uncle; what more natural than that he should like that gallant soldier, whom Marian adored as the first of mankind? And it was out of his liking for the Captain that he came so often.

The Captain, however, had not been slow to discover the real state of affairs, and the discovery had given him unqualified satisfaction. For a long time his quiet contentment in this pleasant, simple, easy-going life had been clouded by anxious thoughts about Marian's future. His death—should that event happen before she married—must needs leave her utterly destitute. The little property from which his income was derived was not within his power to bequeath. It would pass, upon his death, to one of his nephews. The furniture of the cottage might realize a few hundreds, which would most likely be, for the greater part, absorbed by the debts of the year and the expenses of his funeral. Altogether, the outlook was a dreary one, and the Captain had suffered many a sharp pang in brooding over it. Lovely and attractive as Marian was, the chances of an advantageous marriage were not many for her in such a place as Lidford. It was natural, therefore, that Captain Sedgewick should welcome the advent of such a man as Gilbert Fenton—a man of good position and ample means; a thoroughly unaffected and agreeable fellow into the bargain, and quite handsome enough to win any woman's heart, the Captain thought. He watched the two young people together, after the notion of this thing came into his mind, and about the sentiments of one of them he felt no shadow of doubt. He was not quite so clear about the feelings of the other. There was a perfect frankness and ease about Marian that seemed scarcely compatible with the growth of that tender passion which generally reveals itself by a certain amount of reserve, and is more eloquent in silence than in speech. Marian seemed always pleased to see Gilbert, always interested in his society; but she did not seem more than this, and the Captain was sorely perplexed.

There was a dinner-party at Lidford House during the second week of Gilbert's acquaintance with these new friends, and Captain Sedgewick and his adopted niece were invited.

"They are pleasant people to have at a dinner-party," Mrs. Lister said, when she discussed the invitation with her husband and brother; "so I suppose they may as well come,—though I don't want to encourage your folly, Gilbert."

"My folly, as you are kind enough to call it, is not dependent on your encouragement, Belle."

"Then it is really a serious case, I suppose," said Martin.

"I really admire Miss Nowell—more than I ever admired any one before, if that is what you call a serious case, Martin."

"Rather like it, I think," the other answered with a laugh.

The dinner was a very quiet business—a couple of steady-going country gentlemen, with their wives and daughters, a son or two more or less dashing and sportsmanlike in style, the rector and his wife, Captain Sedgewick and Miss Nowell. Gilbert had to take one of the portly matrons in to dinner, and found himself placed at some distance from Miss Nowell during the repast; but he was able to make up for this afterwards, when he slipped out of the dining-room some time before the rest of the gentlemen, and found Marian seated at the piano, playing a dreamy reverie of Goria's, while the other ladies were gathered in a little knot, discussing the last village scandal.

He went over to the piano and stood by her while she played, looking fondly down at the graceful head, and the white hands gliding gently over the keys. He did not disturb her by much talk: it was quite enough happiness for him to stand there watching her as she played. Later, when a couple of whist-tables had been established, and the brilliantly-lighted room had grown hot, these two sat together at one of the open windows, looking out at the moonlit lawn; one of them supremely happy, and yet with a kind of undefined sense that this supreme happiness was a dangerous thing—a thing that it would be wise to pluck out of his heart, and have done with.

"My holiday is very nearly over, Miss Nowell," Gilbert Fenton said by and by. "I shall have to go back to London and the old commercial life, the letter-writing and interview-giving, and all that kind of thing."

"Your sister said you were very fond of the counting-house, Mr. Fenton," she answered lightly. "I daresay, if you would only confess the truth, you are heartily tired of the country, and will be delighted to resume your business life."

"I should never be tired of Lidford."

"Indeed! and yet it is generally considered such a dull place."

"It has not been so to me. It will always be a shining spot in my memory, different and distinct from all other places."

She looked up at him, wondering a little at his earnest tone, and their eyes met—his full of tenderness, hers only shy and surprised. It was not then that the words he had to speak could be spoken, and he let the conversation drift into a general discussion of the merits of town or country life. But he was determined that the words should be spoken very soon.

He went to the cottage next day, between three and four upon a drowsy summer afternoon, and was so fortunate as to find Marian sitting under one of the walnut-trees at the end of the garden reading a novel, with her faithful Skye terrier in attendance. He seated himself on a low garden-chair by her side, and took the book gently from her hand.

"I have come to spoil your afternoon's amusement," he said. "I have not many days more to spend in Lidford, you know, and I want to make the most of a short time."

"The book is not particularly interesting," Miss Nowell answered, laughing. "I'll go and tell my uncle you are here. He is taking an afternoon nap; but I know he'll be pleased to see you."

"Don't tell him just yet," said Mr. Fenton, detaining her. "I have something to say to you this afternoon,—something that it is wiser to say at once, perhaps, though I have been willing enough to put off the hour of saying it, as a man may well be when all his future life depends upon the issue of a few words. I think you must know what I mean, Miss Nowell. Marian, I think you can guess what is coming. I told you last night how sweet Lidford had been to me."

"Yes," she said, with a bright inquiring look in her eyes. "But what have I to do with that?"

"Everything. It is you who have made the little country village my paradise. O Marian, tell me that it has not been a fool's paradise! My darling, I love you with all my heart and soul, with an honest man's first and only love. Promise that you will be my wife."

He took the hand that lay loosely on her lap, and pressed it in both his own. She withdrew it gently, and sat looking at him with a face that had grown suddenly pale.

"You do not know what you are asking," she said; "you cannot know. Captain Sedgewick is not my uncle. He does not even know who my parents were. I am the most obscure creature in the world."

"Not one degree less dear to me because of that, Marian; only the dearer. Tell me, my darling, is there any hope for me?"

"I never thought——" she faltered; "I had no idea——"

"That to know you was to love you. My life and soul, I have loved you from the hour I first saw you in Lidford church. I was a doomed man from that moment, Marian. O my dearest, trust me, and it shall go hard if I do not make your future life a happy one. Granted that I am ten years—more than ten years—your senior, that is a difference on the right side. I have fought the battle of life, and have conquered, and am strong enough to protect and shelter the woman I love. Come, Marian, I am waiting for a word of hope."

"And do you really love me?" she asked wonderingly. "It seems so strange after so short a time."

"I loved you from that first evening in the church, my dear."

"I am very grateful to you," she said slowly, "and I am proud—I have reason to be proud—of your preference. But I have known you such a short time. I am afraid to give you any promise."

"Afraid of me, or of yourself, Marian?"

"Of myself."

"In what way?"

"I am only a foolish frivolous girl. You offer me so much more than I deserve in offering me your love like this. I scarcely know if I have a heart to give to any one. I know that I have never loved anybody except my one friend and protector my dear adopted uncle."

"But you do not say that you cannot love me, Marian. Perhaps I have spoken too soon, after all. It seems to me that I have known you for a lifetime; but that is only a lover's fancy. I seem almost a stranger to you, perhaps?"

"Almost," she answered, looking at him with clear truthful eyes.

"That is rather hard upon me, my dear. But I can wait. You do not know how patient I can be."

He began to talk of indifferent subjects after this, a little depressed and disheartened by the course the interview had taken. He felt that he had been too precipitate. What was there in a fortnight's intimacy to justify such a step, except to himself, with whom time had been measured by a different standard since he had known Marian Nowell? He was angry with his own eagerness, which had brought upon him this semi-defeat.

Happily Miss Nowell had not told him that his case was hopeless, had not forbidden him to approach the subject again; nor had she exhibited any involuntary sign of aversion to him. Surprise had appeared the chief sentiment caused by his revelation. Surprise was natural to such girlish inexperience; and after surprise had passed away, more tender feelings might arise, a latent tenderness unsuspected hitherto.

"I think a woman can scarcely help returning a man's love, if he is only as thoroughly in earnest as I am," Gilbert Fenton said to himself, as he sat under the walnut-trees trying to talk pleasantly, and to ignore the serious conversation which had preceded that careless talk.

He saw the Captain alone next day, and told him what had happened. George Sedgewick listened to him with profound attention and a grave anxious face.

"She didn't reject you?" he said, when Gilbert had finished his story.

"Not in plain words. But there was not much to indicate hope. And yet I cling to the fancy that she will come to love me in the end. To think otherwise would be utter misery to me. I cannot tell you how dearly I love her, and how weak I am about this business. It seems contemptible for a man to talk about a broken heart; but I shall carry an empty one to my grave unless I win Marian Nowell for my wife."

"You shall win her!" cried the Captain energetically. "You are a noble fellow, sir, and will make her an excellent husband. She will not be so foolish as to reject such a disinterested affection. Besides," he added, hesitating a little, "I have a very shrewd notion that all this apparent indifference is only shyness on my little girl's part, and that she loves you."

"You believe that!" cried Gilbert eagerly.

"It is only guesswork on my part, of course. I am an old bachelor, you see, and have had very little experience as to the signs and tokens of the tender passion. But I will sound my little girl by and by. She will be more ready to confess the truth to her old uncle than she would to you, perhaps. I think you have been a trifle hasty about this affair. There is so much in time and custom."

"It is only a cold kind of love that grows out of custom," Gilbert answered gloomily. "But I daresay you are right, and that it would have been better for me to have waited."

"You may hope everything, if you can-only be patient," said the Captain. "I tell you frankly, that nothing would make me happier than to see my dear child married to a good man. I have had many dreary thoughts about her future of late. I think you know that I have nothing to leave her."

"I have never thought of that. If she were destined to inherit all the wealth of the Rothschilds, she could be no dearer to me than she is."

"Ah, what a noble thing true love is! And do you know that she is not really my niece—only a poor waif that I adopted fourteen years ago?"

"I have heard as much from her own lips. There is nothing, except some unworthiness in herself, that could make any change in my estimation of her."

"Unworthiness in herself! You need never fear that. But I must tell you Marian's story before this business goes any farther. Will you come and smoke your cigar with me to-night? She is going to drink tea at a neighbour's, and we shall be alone. They are all fond of her, poor child."

"I shall be very happy to come. And in the meantime, you will try and ascertain the real state of her feelings without distressing her in any way; and you will tell me the truth with all frankness, even if it is to be a deathblow to all my hopes?"

"Even if it should be that. But I do not fear such a melancholy result. I think Marian is sensible enough to know the value of an honest man's heart."

Gilbert quitted the Captain in a more hopeful spirit than that in which he had gone to the cottage that day. It was only reasonable that this man should be the best judge of his niece's feelings.

Left alone, George Sedgewick paced the room in a meditative mood, with his hands thrust deep into his trousers-pockets, and his gray head bent thoughtfully.

"She must like him," he muttered to himself. "Why should not she like him?—good-looking, generous, clever, prosperous, well-connected, and over head and ears in love with her. Such a marriage is the very thing I have been praying for. And without such a marriage, what would be her fate when I am gone? A drudge and dependent in some middle-class family perhaps—

tyrannised over and tormented by a brood of vulgar children."

Marian came in at the open window while he was still pacing to and fro with a disturbed countenance.

"My dear uncle, what is the matter?" she asked, going up to him and laying a caressing hand upon his shoulder. "I know you never walk about like that unless you are worried by something."

"I am not worried to-day, my love; only a little perplexed," answered the Captain, detaining the caressing little hand, and planting himself face to face with his niece, in the full sunlight of the broad bow-window. "Marian, I thought you and I had no secrets from each other?"

"Secrets, uncle George!"

"Yes, my dear. Haven't you something pleasant to tell your old uncle—something that a girl generally likes telling? You had a visitor yesterday afternoon while I was asleep."

"Mr. Fenton."

"Mr. Fenton. He has been here with me just now; and I know that he asked you to be his wife."

"He did, uncle George."

"And you didn't refuse him, Marian?"

"Not positively, uncle George. He took me so much by surprise, you see; and I really don't know how to refuse any one; but I think I ought to have made him understand more clearly that I meant no."

"But why, my dear?"

"Because I am sure I don't care about him as much as I ought to care. I like him very well, you know, and think him clever and agreeable, and all that kind of thing."

"That will soon grow into a warmer feeling, Marian; at least I trust in God that it will do so."

"Why, dear uncle?"

"Because I have set my heart upon this marriage. O Marian, my love, I have never ventured to speak to you about your future—the days that must come when I am dead and gone; and you can never know how many anxious hours I have spent thinking of it. Such a marriage as this would secure you happiness and prosperity in the years to come."

She clung about him fondly, telling him she cared little what might become of her life when he should be lost to her. *That* grief must needs be the crowning sorrow of her existence; and it would matter nothing to her what might come afterwards.

"But my dear love, 'afterwards' will make the greater part of your life. We must consider these things seriously, Marian. A good man's affection is not to be thrown away rashly. You have known Mr. Fenton a very short time; and perhaps it is only natural you should think of him with comparative indifference."

"I did not say I was indifferent to him, uncle George; only that I do not love him as he seems to love me. It would be a kind of sin to accept so much and to give so little."

"The love will come, Marian; I am sure that it will come."

She shook her head playfully.

"What a darling match-making uncle it is!" she said, and then kissed him and ran away.

She thought of Gilbert Fenton a good deal during the rest of that day; thought that it was a pleasant thing to be loved so truly, and hoped that she might always have him for her friend. When she went out to drink tea in the evening his image went with her; and she found herself making involuntary comparisons between a specimen of provincial youth whom she encountered at her friend's house and Mr. Fenton, very much to the advantage of the Australian merchant.

While Marian Nowell was away at this little social gathering, Captain Sedgewick and Gilbert Fenton sat under the walnut-trees smoking their cigars, with a bottle of claret on a little iron table before them.

"When I came back from India fourteen years ago on the sick-list," began the Captain, "I went down to Brighton, a place I had been fond of in my young days, to recruit. It was in the early spring, quite out of the fashionable season, and the town was very empty. My lodgings were in a dull street at the extreme east, leading away from the sea, but within sight and sound of it. The solitude and quiet of the place suited me; and I used to walk up and down the cliff in the dusk of evening enjoying the perfect loneliness of the scene. The house I lived in was a comfortable one, kept by an elderly widow who was a pattern of neatness and propriety. There were no children; for some time no other lodgers; and the place was as quiet as the grave. All this suited me very well. I wanted rest, and I was getting it.

"I had been at Brighton about a month, when the drawing-room floor over my head was taken by a lady, and her little girl of about five years old. I used to hear the child's feet pattering about the room; but she was not a noisy child by any means; and when I did happen to hear her voice, it had a very pleasant sound to me. The lady was an invalid, and was a good deal of trouble, my landlady took occasion to tell me, as she had no maid of her own. Her name was Nowell.

"Soon after this I encountered her on the cliff one afternoon with her little girl. The child and I had met once or twice before in the hall; and her recognition of me led to a little friendly talk between me and the mother. She was a fragile delicate-looking woman, who had once been very pretty, but whose beauty had for the most part been worn away, either by ill-health or trouble. She was very young, five-and-twenty at the utmost. She told me that the little girl was her only child, and that her husband was away from England, but that she expected his return before long.

"After this we met almost every afternoon; and I began to look out for these meetings, and our quiet talk upon the solitary cliff, as the pleasantest part of my day. There was a winning grace about this Mrs. Nowell's manner that I had never seen in any other woman; and I grew to be more interested in her than I cared to confess to myself. It matters little now; and I may freely own how weak I was in those days.

"I could see that she was very ill, and I did not need the ominous hints of the landlady, who had contrived to question Mrs. Nowell's doctor, to inspire me with the dread that she might never recover. I thought of her a great deal, and watched the fading light in her eyes, and listened to the weakening tones of her voice, with a sense of trouble that seemed utterly disproportionate to the occasion. I will not say that I loved her; neither the fact that she was another man's wife, nor the fact that she was soon to die, was ever absent from my mind when I thought of her. I will only say that she was more to me than any woman had ever been before, or has ever been since. It was the one sentimental episode of my life, and a very brief one.

"The weeks went by, and her husband did not come. I think the trouble and anxiety caused by his delay did a good deal towards hastening the inevitable end; but she bore her grief very quietly, and never uttered a complaint of him in my hearing. She paid her way regularly enough for a considerable time, and then all at once broke down, and confessed to the landlady that she had not a shilling more in the world. The woman was a hard creature, and told her that if that was the case, she must find some other lodgings, and immediately. I heard this, not from Mrs. Nowell, but from the landlady, who seemed to consider her conduct thoroughly justified by the highest code of morals. She was a lone unprotected woman, and how was she to pay her rent and taxes if her best floor was occupied by a non-paying tenant?

"I was by no means a rich man; but I could not endure to think of that helpless dying creature thrust out into the streets; and I told my landlady that I would be answerable for Mrs. Nowell's rent, and for the daily expenses incurred on her behalf. Mr. Nowell would in all probability appear in good time to relieve me from the responsibility, but in the mean while that poor soul upstairs was not to be distressed. I begged that she might know nothing of this undertaking on my part.

"It was not long after this when our daily meetings on the cliff came to an end. Mild as the weather was by this time, Mrs. Nowell's doctor had forbidden her going out any longer. I knew that she had no maid to send out with the child, so I sent the servant up to ask her if she would trust the little one for a daily walk with me. This she was very pleased to do, and Marian became my dear little companion every afternoon. She had taken to me, as the phrase goes, from the very first. She was the gentlest, most engaging child I had ever met with—a little grave for her years, and tenderly thoughtful of others.

"One evening Mrs. Nowell sent for me. I went up to the drawing-room immediately, and found her sitting in an easy-chair propped up by pillows, and very much changed for the worse since I had seen her last. She told me that she had discovered the secret of my goodness to her, as she called it, from the landlady, and that she had sent for me to thank me.

"'I can give you nothing but thanks and blessings,' she said, 'for I am the most helpless creature in this world. I suppose my husband will come here before I die, and will relieve you from the risk you have taken for me; but he can never repay you for your goodness.'

"I told her to give herself no trouble on my account; but I could not help saying, that I thought her husband had behaved shamefully in not coming to England to her long ere this.

"'He knows that you are ill, I suppose?' I said.

"'O yes, he knows that. I was ill when he sent me home. We had been travelling about the Continent almost ever since our marriage. He married me against his father's will, and lost all chance of a great fortune by doing so. I did not know how much he sacrificed at the time, or I should never have consented to his losing so much for my sake. I think the knowledge of what he had lost came between us very soon. I know that his love for me has grown weaker as the years went by, and that I have been little better than a burden to him. I could never tell you how lonely my life has been in those great foreign cities, where there seems such perpetual gaiety and pleasure. I think I must have died of the solitude and dulness—the long dreary summer evenings, the dismal winter days—if it had not been for my darling child. She has been all the world to me. And, O God!' she cried, with a look of anguish that went to my heart, 'what will become of her when I am dead, and she is left to the care of a selfish dissipated man?'

"'You need never fear that she will be without one friend while I live,' I said. 'Little Marian is very dear to me, and I shall make it my business to watch over her career as well as I can.'

"The poor soul clasped my hand, and pressed her feverish lips to it in a transport of gratitude. What a brute a man must have been who could neglect such a woman!

"After this I went up to her room every evening, and read to her a little, and cheered her as well as I could; but I believe her heart was broken. The end came very suddenly at last. I had intended to question her about her husband's family; but the subject was a difficult one to approach, and I had put it off from day to day, hoping that she might rally a little, and would be in a better condition to discuss business matters.

"She never did rally. I was with her when she died, and her last act was to draw her child towards her with her feeble arms and lay my hand upon the little one's head, looking up at me with sorrowful pleading eyes. She was quite speechless then, but I knew what the look meant, and answered it.

"'To the end of my life, my dear,' I said, 'I shall love and cherish her—to the end of my life.'

"After this the child fell asleep in my arms as I sat by the bedside sharing the long melancholy watch with the landlady, who behaved very well at this sorrowful time. We sat in the quiet room all night, the little one wrapped in a shawl and nestled upon my breast. In the early summer morning Lucy Nowell died, very peacefully; and I carried Marian down to the sofa in the parlour, and laid her there still asleep. She cried piteously for her mother when she awoke, and I had to tell her that which it is so hard to tell a child.

"I wrote to Mr. Nowell at an address in Brussels which I found at the top of his last letter to his wife. No answer came. I wrote again, after a little while, with the same result; and, in the mean time, the child had grown fonder of me and dearer to me every day. I had hired a nursemaid for her, and had taken an upper room for her nursery; but she spent the greater part of her life with me, and I began to fancy that Providence intended I should keep her with me for the rest of her days. She told me, in her innocent childish way, that papa had never loved her as her mamma did. He had been always out of doors till very, very late at night. She had crept from her little bed sometimes when it was morning, quite light, and had found mamma in the sitting-room, with no fire, and the candles all burnt out, waiting for papa to come home.

"I put an advertisement, addressed to Mr. Percival Nowell, in the *Times* and in *Galignani*, for I felt that the child's future might depend upon her father's acknowledgment of her in the present; but no reply came to these advertisements, and I settled in my own mind that this Nowell was a scoundrel, who had deliberately deserted his wife and child.

"The possessions of the poor creature who was gone were of no great value. There were some rather handsome clothes and a small collection of jewelry—some of it modern, the rest curious and old-fashioned. These latter articles I kept religiously, believing them to be family relics. The clothes and the modern trinkets I caused to be sold, and the small sum realised for them barely paid the expense of the funeral and grave. The arrears of rent and all other arrears fell upon me. I paid them, and then left Brighton with the child and nurse. I was born not twenty miles from this place, and I had a fancy for ending my days in my native county; so I came down to this part of the world, and looked about me a little, living in farm-house lodgings here and there, until I found this cottage to let one day, and decided upon settling at Lidford. And now you know the whole story of Marian's adoption, Mr. Fenton. How happy we have been together, or what she has been to me since that time, I could never tell you."

"The story does you credit, sir; and I honour you for your goodness," said Gilbert Fenton.

"Goodness, pshaw!" cried the Captain, impetuously; "it has been a mere matter of self-indulgence on my part. The child made herself necessary to me from the very first. I was a solitary man, a confirmed bachelor, with every prospect of becoming a hard, selfish old fogey. Marian Nowell has been the sunshine of my life!"

"You never made any farther discoveries about Mr. Nowell?"

"Never. I have sometimes thought, that I ought to have made some stronger efforts to place myself in communication with him. I have thought this, especially when brooding upon the uncertainties of my darling's future. From the little Mrs. Nowell told me about her marriage, I had reason to believe her husband's father must have been a rich man. He might have softened towards his grandchild, in spite of his disapproval of the marriage. I sometimes think I ought to have sought out the grandfather. But, you see, it would have been uncommonly difficult to set about this, in my complete ignorance as to who or what he was."

"Very difficult. And if you had found him, the chances are that he would have set his face against the child. Marian Nowell will have no need to supplicate for protection from an indifferent father or a hard-hearted grandfather, if she will be my wife.

"Heaven grant that she may love you as you deserve to be loved by her!" Captain Sedgewick answered heartily.

He thought it would be the best thing that could happen to his darling to become this young man's wife, and he had a notion that a simple, inexperienced girl could scarcely help responding to the hopes of such a lover. To his mind Gilbert Fenton seemed eminently adapted to win a woman's heart. He forgot the fatality that belongs to these things, and that a man may have every good gift, and yet just miss the magic power to touch one woman's heart.

CHAPTER III.
ACCEPTED.

MR. Fenton lingered another week at Lidford, with imminent peril to the safe conduct of affairs at his offices in Great St. Helens. He could not tear himself away just yet. He felt that he must have some more definite understanding of his position before he went back to London; and in the meantime he pondered with a dangerous delight upon that sunny vision of a suburban villa to which Marian should welcome him when his day's work was done.

He went every day to the cottage, and he bore himself in no manner like a rejected lover. He was indeed very hopeful as to the issue of his wooing. He knew that Marian Nowell's heart was free, that there was no rival image to be displaced before his own could reign there, and he thought that it must go hard with him if he did not win her love.

So Marian saw him every day, and had to listen to the Captain's praises of him pretty frequently during his absence. And Captain Sedgewick's talk about Gilbert Fenton generally closed with a regretful sigh, the meaning of which had grown very clear to Marian.

She thought about her uncle's words and looks and sighs a good deal in the quiet of her own room. What was there she would not do for the love of that dearest and noblest of men? Marry a man she disliked? No, that was a sin from which the girl's pure mind would have recoiled instinctively. But she did like Gilbert Fenton—loved him perhaps—though she had never confessed as much to herself.

This calm friendship might really be love after all; not quite such love as she had read of in novels and poems, where the passion was always rendered desperate by the opposing influence of adverse circumstances and unkind kindred; but a tranquil sentiment, a dull, slow, smouldering fire, that needed only some sudden wind of jealousy or misfortune to fan it into a flame.

She knew that his society was pleasant to her, that she would miss him very much when he left Lidford; and when she tried to fancy him reconciled to her rejection of him, and returning to London to transfer his affections to some other woman, the thought was very obnoxious to her. He had not flattered her, he had been in no way slavish in his attentions to her; but he had surrounded her with a kind of atmosphere of love and admiration, the charm of which no girl thus beloved for the first time in her life could be quite proof against.

Thus the story ended, as romances so begun generally do end. There came a summer twilight, when Gilbert Fenton found himself once more upon the dewy lawn under the walnut-trees alone with Marian Nowell. He repeated his appeal in warmer, fonder tones than before, and with a kind of implied certainty that the answer must be a favourable one. It was something like taking the fortress by storm. He had his arm round her slim waist, his lips upon her brow, before she had time to consider what her answer ought to be.

"My darling, I cannot live without you!" he said, in a low passionate voice. "Tell me that you love me."

She disengaged herself gently from his embrace, and stood a little way from him, with shy, downcast eyelids.

"I think I do," she said slowly.

"That is quite enough, Marian!" cried Gilbert, joyously. "I knew you were destined to be my wife."

He drew her hand through his arm and took her back to the house, where the Captain was sitting in his favourite arm-chair by the window, with a reading lamp on the little table by his side, and the *Times* newspaper in his hand.

"Your niece has brought you a nephew, sir," said Gilbert.

The Captain threw aside his paper, and stretched out both his hands to the young man.

"My dear boy, I cannot tell you how happy this makes me!" he cried. "Didn't I promise you that all would go well if you were patient? My little girl is wise enough to know the value of a good man's love."

"I am very grateful, uncle George," faltered Marian, taking shelter behind the Captain's chair; "only I don't feel that I am worthy of so much thought."

"Nonsense, child; not worthy! You are the best girl in Christendom, and will make the brightest and truest wife that ever made a man's home dear to him."

The evening went on very happily after that: Marian at the piano, playing plaintive dreamy melodies with a tender expressive touch; Gilbert sitting close at hand, watching the face he loved so dearly—an evening in Paradise, as it seemed to Mr. Fenton. He went homewards in the moonlight a little before eleven o'clock, thinking of his new happiness—such perfect happiness, without a cloud. The bright suburban villa was no longer an airy castle, perhaps never to be realized; it was a delightful certainty. He began to speculate as to the number of months that must needs pass before he could make Marian his wife. There was no reason for delay. He was well-off, his own master, and it was only her will that could hinder the speedy realization of that sweet domestic dream which had haunted him lately.

He told his sister what had happened next morning, when Martin Lister had left the breakfast table to hold audience with his farm bailiff, and those two were together alone. He was a little tired of having his visits to the cottage criticised in Mrs. Lister's somewhat supercilious manner, and was very glad to be able to announce that Marian Nowell was to be his wife.

"Well, Gilbert," exclaimed the matron, after receiving his tidings with tightly-closed lips and a generally antagonistic demeanour, "I can only say, that if you must marry at all—and I am sure I thought you had quite settled down as a bachelor, with your excellent lodgings in Wigmore Street, and every I possible comfort in life—I think you might have chosen much better than this. Of course, I don't want to be rude or unpleasant; but I cannot help saying, that I consider any man a fool who allows himself to be captivated by a pretty face."

"I have found a great deal more than a pretty face to admire in Marian Nowell."

"Indeed! Can you name any other advantages which she possesses?"

"Amiability, good sense, and a pure and refined nature."

"What warrant have you for all those things? Mind, Gilbert, I like the girl well enough; I have nothing to say against her; but I cannot help thinking it a most unfortunate match for you."

"How unfortunate?"

"The girl's position is so very doubtful."

"Position!" echoed Gilbert impatiently. "That sort of talk is one of the consequences of living in such a place as Lidford. You talk about position, as if I were a prince of the blood-royal, whose marriage would be registered in every almanac in the kingdom."

"If she were really the Captain's niece, it would be a different thing," harped Mrs. Lister, without noticing this contemptuous interruption; "but to marry a girl about whose relations nobody knows anything! I suppose even you have not been told who her father and mother were."

"I know quite enough about them. Captain Sedgewick has been candour itself upon the subject."

"And are the father and mother both dead?"

"Miss Nowell's mother has been dead many years."

"And her father?"

"Captain Sedgewick does not know whether he is dead or living."

"Ah!" exclaimed Mrs. Lister with a profound sigh; "I should have thought as much. And you are really going to marry a girl with this disreputable mystery about her belongings?"

"There is nothing either disreputable or mysterious. People are sometimes lost sight of in this world. Mr. Nowell was a bad husband and an indifferent father, and Captain Sedgewick adopted his daughter; that is all."

"And no doubt, after you are married, this Mr. Nowell will make his appearance some day, and be a burden upon you."

"I am not afraid of that. And now, Belle, as this is a subject upon which we don't seem very likely to agree, I think we had better drop it. I considered it only right to tell you of my engagement."

On this his sister softened a little, and promised Gilbert that she would do her best to be kind to Miss Nowell.

"You won't be married for some time to come, of course," she said.

"I don't know about that, Belle. There is nothing to prevent a speedy marriage."

"O, surely you will wait a twelvemonth, at least. You have known Marian Nowell such a short time. You ought to put her to the test in some manner before you make her your wife."

"I have no occasion to put her to any kind of test. I have a most profound and perfect belief in her goodness."

"Why, Gilbert, this is utter infatuation—about a girl whom you have only known a little more than three weeks!"

It does seem difficult for a matter-of-fact, reasonable matron, whose romantic experiences are things of the remote past, to understand this sudden trust in, and all-absorbing love for, an acquaintance of a brief summer holiday.

But Gilbert Fenton believed implicitly in his own instinct, and was not to be shaken.

He went back to town by the afternoon express that day, for he dared not delay his return any longer. He went back regretfully enough to the dryasdust business life, after spending the greater part of the morning under the walnut-trees in Captain Sedgewick's garden, playing with Fritz the Skye terrier, and talking airy nonsense to Marian, while she sat in a garden-chair hemming silk handkerchiefs for her uncle, and looking distractingly pretty in a print morning dress with tiny pink rosebuds on a white ground, and a knot of pink ribbon fastening the dainty collar. He ventured to talk a little about the future too; painting, with all the enthusiasm of Claude Melnotte, and a great deal more sincerity, the home which he meant to create for her.

"You will have to come to town to choose our house, you know, Marian," he said, after a glowing description of such a villa as never yet existed, except in the florid imagination of an auctioneer; "I could never venture upon such an important step without you: apart from all sentimental considerations, a woman's judgment is indispensable in these matters. The house might be perfection in every other point, and there might be no boiler, or no butler's pantry, or no cupboard for brooms on the landing, or some irremediable omission of that kind. Yes, Marian, your uncle must bring you to town for a week or so of house-hunting, and soon."

She looked at him with a startled expression.

"Soon!" she repeated.

"Yes, dear, very soon. There is nothing in the world to hinder our marriage. Why should we delay longer than to make all necessary arrangements? I long so for my new home, Marian, I have never had a home in my life since I was a boy."

"O Mr. Fenton—Gilbert,"—she pronounced his Christian name shyly, and in obedience to his reproachful look,—"remember how short a time we have known each other. It is much too soon to talk or think of marriage yet. I want you to have plenty of leisure to consider whether you really care for me, whether it isn't only a fancy that will die out when you go back to London. And we ought to have time to know each other very well, Gilbert, to be quite sure we are suited to one another."

This seemed an echo of his sister's reasoning, and vexed him a little.

"Have *you* any fear that we shall not suit each other, Marian?" he asked anxiously.

"I know that you are only too good for me," she answered. Upon which Gilbert hindered the hemming of the Captain's handkerchiefs by stooping down to kiss the little hands at work upon them. And then the talk drifted back to easier subjects, and he did not again press that question as to the date of the marriage.

At last the time came for going to the station. He had arranged for Mr. Lister's gig to call for him at the cottage, so that he might spend every possible moment with Marian. And at three o'clock the gig appeared, driven by Martin

Lister himself, and Gilbert was fain to say good-bye. His last lingering backward glance showed him the white figure under the walnut-trees, and a little hand waving farewell.

How empty and dreary his comfortable bachelor lodgings seemed to him that night when he had dined, and sat by the open window smoking his solitary cigar, listening to the dismal street-noises, and the monotonous roll of ceaseless wheels yonder in Oxford-street; not caring to go out to his club, caring still less for opera or theatre, or any of the old ways whereby he had been wont to dispose of his evenings!

His mind was full of Marian Nowell. All that was grave and earnest in his nature gave force to this his first love. He had had flirtations in the past, of course; but they had been no more than flirtations, and at thirty his heart was as fresh and inexperienced as a boy's. It pleased him to think of Marian's lonely position. Better, a hundred times better, that she should be thus, than fettered by ties which might come between them and perfect union. The faithful and generous protector of her childhood would of necessity always claim her love; but beyond this one affection, she would be Gilbert's, and Gilbert's only. There would be no mother, no sisters, to absorb her time and distract her thoughts from her husband, perhaps prejudice her against him. Domestic life for those two must needs be free from all the petty jars, the overshadowing clouds no bigger than a man's hand, forerunners of tempest, which Mr. Fenton had heard of in many households.

He was never weary of thinking about that life which was to be. Everything else he thought of was now considered only in relation to that one subject. He applied himself to business with a new ardour; never before had he been so anxious to grow rich.

CHAPTER IV.
JOHN SALTRAM.

THE offices of Fenton and Co. in Great St. Helens were handsome, prosperous-looking premises, consisting of two large outer rooms, where half-a-dozen indefatigable clerks sat upon high stools before ponderous mahogany desks, and wrote industriously all day long; and an inner and smaller apartment, where there was a faded Turkey-carpet instead of the kamptulicon that covered the floor of the outer offices, a couple of capacious, red-morocco-covered arm-chairs, and a desk of substantial and somewhat legal design, on which Gilbert Fenton was wont to write the more important letters of the house. In all the offices there were iron safes, which gave one a notion of limitless wealth stored away in the shape of bonds and bills, if not actual gold and bank-notes; and upon all the walls there were coloured and uncoloured engravings of ships framed and glazed, and catalogues of merchandise that had been sold, or was to be sold, hanging loosely one on the other. Besides these, there were a great many of those flimsy papers that record the state of things on 'Change, hanging here and there on the brass rails of the desks, from little hooks in the walls, and in any other available spot. And in all the premises there was an air of business and prosperity, which seemed to denote that Fenton and Co. were travelling at a rapid pace on the high-road to fortune.

Gilbert Fenton sat in the inner office at noon one day about a week after his return from Lidford. He had come to business early that morning, had initialed a good many accounts, and written half-a-dozen letters already, and had thrown himself back in his easy-chair for a few minutes' idle musing—musing upon that one sweet dream of his new existence, of course. From whatever point his thoughts started, they always drifted into that channel.

While he was sitting like this, with his hands in his pockets and his chair tilted upon its hind legs, the half-glass door opened, and a gentleman came into the office—a man a little over middle height, broad-shouldered, and powerfully built, with a naturally dark complexion, which had been tanned still darker by sun and wind, black eyes and heavy black eyebrows, a head a little bald at the top, and a face that might have been called almost ugly but for the look of intellectual power in the broad open forehead and the perfect modelling of the flexible sensitive mouth; a remarkable face altogether, not easily to be forgotten by those who had once looked upon it.

This man was John Saltram, the one intimate and chosen friend of Gilbert Fenton's youth and manhood. They had met first at Oxford, and had seldom lost sight of each other since the old university days. They had travelled a good deal together during the one idle year that had preceded Gilbert's sudden plunge into commerce. They had been up the Nile together in the course of these wanderings; and here, remote from all civilized aid, Gilbert had fallen ill of a fever—a long tedious business which brought him to the very point of death, and throughout which John Saltram had nursed him with a womanly tenderness and devotion that knew no abatement. If this had been wanting to strengthen the tie between them—which it was not—it would have brought them closer together. As it was, that dreary time of sickness and peril was only a memory which Gilbert Fenton kept in his heart of hearts, never to grow less sacred to him until the end of life.

Mr. Saltram was a barrister, almost a briefless one at present, for his habits were desultory, not to say idle, and he had not taken very kindly to the slow drudgery of the Bar. He had some money of his own, and added to his income by writing for the press in a powerful trenchant manner, with a style that was like the stroke of a sledge-hammer. In spite of this literary work, for which he got very well paid, Mr. Saltram generally contrived to be in debt; and there were few periods of his life in which he was not engaged more or less in the delicate operation of raising money by bills of accommodation. Habit had given him quite an artistic touch for this kind of thing, and he did his work fondly, like some enthusiastic horticulturist who gives his anxious days to the budding forth of some new orchid or the production of a hitherto unobtainable tulip. It is doubtful whether money procured from any other source was ever half so sweet to this gentleman as the cash for which he paid sixty per cent to the Jews. With these proclivities he managed to rub on from year to year somehow, getting about five hundred per annum in solid value out of an income of seven, and adding a little annually to the rolling mass of debt which he had begun to accumulate while he was at Balliol.

"Why, Jack," cried Gilbert, starting up from his reverie at the entrance of his friend, and greeting him with a hearty handshaking, "this is an agreeable surprise! I was asking for you at the Pnyx last night, and Joe Hawdon told me you were away—up the Danube he thought, on a canoe expedition."

"It is only under some utterly impossible dispensation that Joseph Hawdon will ever be right about anything. I have been on a walking expedition in Brittany, dear boy, alone, and have found myself very bad company. I started soon after you went to your sister's, and only came back last night. That scoundrel Levison promised me seventy-five this afternoon; but whether I shall get it out of him is a fact only known to himself and the powers with which he holds communion. And was the rustic business pleasant, Gil? Did you take kindly to the syllabubs and new milk, the summer sunrise over dewy fields, the pretty dairy-maids, and prize pigs, and daily inspections of the home-farm? or did you find life rather dull down at Lidford? I know the place well enough, and all the country round about there. I have stayed at Heatherly with Sir David Forster more than once for the shooting season. A pleasant fellow Forster, in a dissipated good-for-nothing kind of way, always up to his eyes in debt. Did you happen to meet him while you were down there?"

"No, I don't think the Listers know him."

"So much the better for them! It is a vice to know him. And you were not dull at Lidford?"

"Very far from it, Jack. I was happier there than I have ever been in my life before."

"Eh, Gil!" cried John Saltram; "that means something more than a quiet fortnight with a married sister. Come, old fellow, I have a vested right to a share in all your secrets."

"There is no secret, Jack. Yes, I have fallen in love, if that's what you mean, and am engaged."

"So soon! That's rather quick work, isn't it, dear boy?"

"I don't think so. What is that the poet says?—'If not an Adam at his birth, he is no love at all.' My passion sprang into life full-grown after an hour's contemplation of a beautiful face in Lidford church."

"Who is the lady?"

"O, her position is not worth speaking of. She is the adopted niece of a half-pay captain—an orphan, without money or connections."

"Humph!" muttered John Saltram with the privileged candour of friendship; "not a very advantageous match for you, Gilbert, from a worldly point of view."

"I have not considered the matter from that point of view."

"And the lady is all that is charming, of course?"

"To my mind, yes."

"Very young?"

"Nineteen."

"Well, dear old fellow, I wish you joy with all heartiness. You can afford to marry whom you please, and are very right to let inclination and not interest govern your choice. Whenever I tie myself in the bondage of matrimony, it will be to a lady who can pay my debts and set me on my legs for life. Whether such a one will ever consider my ugly face a fair equivalent for her specie, is an open question. You must introduce me to your future wife, Gilbert, on the first opportunity. I shall be very anxious to discover whether your marriage will be likely to put an end to our friendship."

"There is no fear of that, Jack. That is a contingency never to arise. I have told Marian a great deal about you already. She knows that I owe my life to you, and she is prepared to value you as much as I do."

"She is very good; but all wives promise that kind of thing before marriage. And there is apt to come a day when the familiar bachelor friend falls under the domestic taboo, together with smoking in the drawing-room, brandy-and-soda, and other luxuries of the old, easy-going, single life."

"Marian is not very likely to prove a domestic tyrant. She is the gentlest dearest girl, and is very well used to bachelor habits in the person of her uncle. I don't believe she will ever extinguish our cigars, Jack, even in the drawing-room. I look forward to the happiest home that ever a man possessed; and it would be no home of mine if you were not welcome and honoured in it. I hope we shall spend many a summer evening on the lawn, Jack, with a bottle of Pomard or St. Julien between us, watching the drowsy old anglers in their punts, and the swift outriggers flashing past in the twilight. I mean to find some snug little place by the river, you know, Saltram—somewhere about Teddington, where the gardens slope down to the water's edge."

"Very pleasant! and you will make an admirable family man, Gil. You have none of the faults that render me ineligible for the married state. I think your

Marian is a very fortunate girl. What is her surname, by the way?"

"Nowell."

"Marian Nowell—a very pretty name! When do you think of going back to Lidford?"

"In about a month. My brother-in-law wants me to go back to them for the 1st of September."

"Then I think I shall run down to Forster's, and have a pop at the pheasants. It will give me an opportunity of being presented to Miss Nowell."

"I shall be very pleased to introduce you, old fellow. I know that you will admire her."

"Well, I am not a very warm admirer of the sex in general; but I am sure to like your future wife, Gil, if it is only because you have chosen her."

"And your own affairs, Jack—how have they been going on?"

"Not very brightly. I am not a lucky individual, you know. Destiny and I have been at odds ever since I was a schoolboy."

"Not in love yet, John?"

"No," the other answered, with rather a gloomy look.

He was sitting on a corner of the ponderous desk in a lounging attitude, gazing meditatively at his boots, and hitting one of them now and then with a cane he carried, in a restless kind of way.

"You see, the fact of the matter is, Gil," he began at last, "as I told you just now, if ever I do marry, mercenary considerations are likely to be at the bottom of the business. I don't mean to say that I would marry a woman I disliked, and take it out of her in ill-usage or neglect. I am not quite such a scoundrel as that. But if I had the luck to meet with a woman I *could* like, tolerably pretty and agreeable, and all that kind of thing, and weak enough to care for me—a woman with a handsome fortune—I should be a fool not to snap at such a chance."

"I see," exclaimed Gilbert, "you have met with such a woman."

"I have."

Again the gloomy look came over the dark strongly-marked face, the thick black eyebrows contracted in a frown, and the cane was struck impatiently against John Saltram's boot.

"But you are not in love with her; I see that in your face, Jack. You'll think me a sentimental fool, I daresay, and fancy I look at things in a new light now that I'm down a pit myself; but, for God's sake, don't marry a woman you can't love. Tolerably pretty and agreeable won't do, Jack,—that means indifference on your part; and, depend upon it, when a man and woman are tied together for life, there is only a short step from indifference to dislike."

"No, Gilbert, it's not that," answered the other, still moodily contemplative of his boots. "I really like the lady well enough—love her, I daresay. I have not had much experience of the tender passion since I was jilted by an Oxford barmaid—whom I would have married, by Jove. But the truth is, the lady in question isn't free to marry just yet. There's a husband in the case—a feeble old Anglo-Indian, who can't live very long. Don't look so glum, old fellow; there has been nothing wrong, not a word that all the world might not hear; but there are signs and tokens by which a man, without any vanity—and heaven knows I have no justification for that—may be sure a woman likes him. In short, I believe that if Adela Branston were a widow, the course would lie clear before me, and I should have nothing to do but go in and win. And the stakes will be worth winning, I assure you."

"But this Mr. Branston may live for an indefinite number of years, during which you will be wasting your life on a shadow."

"Not very likely. Poor old Branston came home from Calcutta a confirmed invalid, and I believe his sentence has been pronounced by all the doctors. In the mean time he makes the best of life, has his good days and bad days, and entertains a great deal of company at a delightful place near Maidenhead—with a garden sloping to the river like that you were talking of just now, only on a very extensive scale. You know how often I have wanted you to run down there with me, and how there has been always something to prevent your going."

"Yes, I remember. Rely upon it, I shall contrive to accept the next invitation, come what may. But I can't say I like the idea of this prospective kind of courtship, or that I consider it quite worthy of you, Saltram."

"My dear Gilbert, when a fellow is burdened with debt and of a naturally idle disposition, he is apt to take rather a liberal view of such means of advancement in life as may present themselves to him. But there is no prospective courtship—nothing at all resembling a courtship in this case, believe me. Mrs. Branston knows that I like and admire her. She knows as much of almost every man who goes to Rivercombe; for there are plenty who will be disposed to go in against me for the prize by-and-by. But I think that she likes me better than any one else, and that the chances will be all in my favour. From first to last there has not been a word spoken between us which old Branston himself might not hear. As to Adela's marrying again when he is gone, he could scarcely be so fatuous as not to foresee the probability of that."

"Is she pretty?"

"Very pretty, in rather a childish way, with blue eyes and fair hair. She is not my ideal among women, but no man ever marries his ideal. The man who has sworn by eyes as black as a stormy midnight and raven hair generally unites himself to the most insipid thing in blondes, and the idolater of golden locks takes to wife some frizzy-haired West Indian with an unmistakable dip of the tar-brush. When will you go down to Rivercombe?"

"Whenever you like."

"The nabob is hospitality itself, and will be delighted to see you if he is to the fore when you go. I fancy there is some kind of regatta—a race or two, at any rate—on Saturday afternoon. Will that suit you?"

"Very well indeed."

"Then we can meet at the station. There is a train down at 2.15. But we are going to see something of each other in the meantime, I hope. I know that I am a sore hindrance to business at such an hour as this. Will you dine with me at the Pnyx at seven to-night? I shall be able to tell you how I got on with Levison."

"With pleasure."

And so they parted—Gilbert Fenton to return to his letter-writing, and to the reception of callers of a more commercial and profitable character; John Saltram to loiter slowly through the streets on his way to the money-lender's office.

They dined together very pleasantly that evening. Mr. Levison had proved accommodating for the nonce; and John Saltram was in high spirits, almost boisterously gay, with the gaiety of a man for whom life is made up of swift transitions from brightness to gloom, long intervals of despondency, and brief glimpses of pleasure; the reckless humour of a man with whom thought always meant care, and whose soul had no higher aspiration than to beguile the march of time by such evenings as these.

They met on the following Saturday at the Great Western terminus, John Saltram still in high spirits, and Gilbert Fenton quietly happy. That morning's post had brought him his first letter from Marian—an innocent girlish epistle, which was as delicious to Gilbert as if it had been the *chef-d'oeuvre* of a Sevigné. What could she say to him? Very little. The letter was full of gratitude for his thoughtfulness about her, for the pretty tributes of his love which he had sent her, the books and music and ribbons and gloves, in the purchase whereof he had found such a novel pleasure. It had been a common thing for him to execute such commissions for his sister; but it was quite a new sensation to him to discuss the colours of gloves and ribbons, now that the trifles he chose were to give pleasure to Marian Nowell. He knew every tint that harmonised or contrasted best with that clear olive complexion—the brilliant blue that gave new brightness to the sparkling grey eyes, the pink that cast warm lights upon the firmly-moulded throat and chin—and he found a childish delight in these trivialities. There was one ribbon he selected for her at this time which he had strange reason to remember in the days to come—a narrow blue ribbon, with tiny pink rosebuds upon it, a daring mixture of the two colours.

He had the letter in the breast-pocket of his coat when he met John Saltram at the station, and entertained that gentleman with certain passages from it as they sped down to Maidenhead. To which passages Mr. Saltram listened kindly, with a very vague notion of the writer.

"I am afraid she is rather a namby-pamby person," he thought, "with nothing but her beauty to recommend her. That wonderful gift of beauty has such power to bewitch the most sensible man upon occasion."

They chartered a fly at Maidenhead, and drove about a mile and a half along a pleasant road before they came to the gates of Rivercombe—a low straggling house with verandahs, over which trailed a wealth of flowering creepers, and innumerable windows opening to the ground. The gardens were perfection, not gardens of yesterday, with only the prim splendours of modern horticulture to recommend them, but spreading lawns, on which the deep springy turf had been growing a hundred years—lawns made delicious in summer time by the cool umbrage of old forest-trees; fertile rose-gardens screened from the biting of adverse winds by tall hedges of holly and yew, the angles whereof were embellished by vases and peacocks quaintly cut in the style of a bygone age; and for chief glory of all, the bright blue river, which made the principal boundary of the place, washing the edge of the wide sloping lawn, and making perpetual music on a summer day with its joyous ripple.

There was a good deal of company already scattered about the lawn when John Saltram and his friend were ushered into the pretty drawing-room. The cheerful sound of croquet-balls came from a level stretch of grass visible from the windows, and quite a little fleet of boats were jostling one another at the landing by the Swiss boat-house.

Mrs. Branston came in from the garden to welcome them, looking very pretty in a coquettish little white-chip hat with a scarlet feather, and a pale-gray silk dress looped up over an elaborately-flounced muslin petticoat. She was a slender little woman, with a brilliant complexion, sunny waving hair, and innocent blue eyes; the sort of woman whom a man would wish to shelter from all the storms of life, but whom he might scarcely care to choose for the companion of a perilous voyage.

She professed herself very much pleased to see Gilbert Fenton.

"I have heard so much of you from Mr. Saltram," she said. "He is always praising you. I believe he cares more for you than anyone else in the world."

"I have not many people to care for," answered John Saltram, "and Gilbert is a friend of long standing."

A sentimental expression came over Mrs. Branston's girlish face, and she gave a little regretful sigh.

"I am sorry you will not see my husband to-day," she said, after a brief pause. "It is one of his bad days."

The two gentlemen both expressed their regret upon this subject; and then they went out to the lawn with Mrs. Branston, and joined the group by the river-brink, who were waiting for the race. Here Gilbert found some pleasant people to talk to; while Adela Branston and John Saltram strolled, as if by accident, to a seat a little way apart from the rest, and sat there talking in a confidential manner, which might not really constitute a flirtation, but which had rather that appearance to the eye of the ignorant observer.

The boats came flashing by at last, and there was the usual excitement amongst the spectators; but it seemed to Gilbert that Mrs. Branston found more interest in John Saltram's conversation than in the race. It is possible she had seen too many such contests to care much for the result of this one. She scarcely looked up as the boats shot by, but sat with her little gloved hands clasped upon her knee, and her bright face turned towards John Saltram.

They all went into the house at about seven o'clock, after a good deal of croquet and flirtation, and found a free-and-easy kind of banquet, half tea, half luncheon, but very substantial after its kind, waiting for them in the long low dining-room. Mrs. Branston was very popular as a hostess, and had a knack of bringing pleasant people round her—journalists and musical men, clever young painters who were beginning to make their mark in the art-world, pretty girls who could sing or play well, or talk more or less brilliantly. Against nonentities of all kinds Adela Branston set her face, and had a polite way of dropping people from whom she derived no amusement, pleading in her pretty childish way that it was so much more pleasant for all parties. That this mundane existence of ours was not intended to be all pleasure, was an idea that never yet troubled Adela Branston's mind. She had been petted and spoiled by everyone about her from the beginning of her brief life, and had passed from the frivolous career of a school-girl to a position of wealth and independence as Michael Branston's wife; fully believing that, in making the sacrifice involved in marrying a man forty years her senior, she earned the right to take her own pleasure, and to gratify every caprice of her infantile mind, for the remainder of her days. She was supremely selfish in an agreeable unconscious fashion, and considered herself a domestic martyr whenever she spent an hour in her husband's sick-room, listening to his peevish accounts of his maladies, or reading a *Times* leader on the threatening aspect of things in the City for the solace of his loneliness and pain.

The popping of corks sounded merrily amidst the buzz of conversation, and great antique silver tankards of Badminton and Moselle cup were emptied as by magic, none knowing how except the grave judicial-looking butler, whose omniscient eye reigned above the pleasant confusion of the scene. And after about an hour and a half wasted in this agreeable indoor picnic, Mrs. Branston and her friends adjourned to the drawing-room, where the grand piano had been pushed into a conspicuous position, and where the musical business of the evening speedily began.

It was very pleasant sitting by the open windows in the summer twilight, with no artificial light in the room, except the wax candles on the piano, listening to good music, and talking a little now and then in that subdued confidential tone to which music makes such an agreeable accompaniment.

Adela Branston sat in the midst of a group in a wide bay window, and although John Saltram was standing near her chair, he did not this time engage the whole of her attention. Gilbert found himself seated next a very animated young lady, who rather bored him with her raptures about the music, and who seemed to have assisted at every morning and evening concert that had been given within the last two years. To any remoter period her memory did not extend, and she implied that she had been before that time in a chrysalis or non-existent condition. She told Mr. Fenton, with an air of innocent wonder, that she had heard there were people living who remembered the first appearance of Jenny Lind.

A little before ten o'clock there was a general movement for the rail, the greater number of Mrs. Branston's guests having come from town. There was a scarcity of flys at this juncture, so John Saltram and Gilbert Fenton walked back to the station in the moonlight.

"Well, Gilbert, old fellow, what do you think of the lady?" Mr. Saltram asked, when they were a little way beyond the gates of Rivercombe.

"I think her very pretty, Jack, and—well—yes—upon the whole fascinating. But I don't like the look of the thing altogether, and I fancy there's considerable bad taste in giving parties with an invalid husband upstairs. I was wondering how Mr. Branston liked the noise of all that talk and laughter in the dining-room, or the music that came afterwards."

"My dear fellow, old Branston delights in society. He is generally well enough to sit in the drawing-room and look on at his wife's parties. He doesn't talk much on those occasions. Indeed, I believe he is quite incapable of conversing about anything except the rise and fall of Indian stock, or the fluctuations in the value of indigo. And, you see, Adela married him with the intention of enjoying her life. She confesses as much sometimes with perfect candour."

"I daresay she is very candid, and just as shallow," said Gilbert Fenton, who was inclined to set his face against this entanglement of his friend's.

"Well—yes, I suppose she is rather shallow. Those pretty pleasant little women generally are, I think. Depth of feeling and force of mind are so apt to go along with blue spectacles and a rugged aspect. A woman's prettiness must stand for something. There is so much real pleasure in the contemplation of a charming face, that a man had need rescind a little in the way of mental qualifications. And I do not think Adela Branston is without a heart."

"You praise her very warmly. Are you really in love with her, John?" his friend asked seriously.

"No, Gilbert, upon my honour. I heartily wish I were. I wish I could give her more by-and-by, when death brings about her release from Michael Branston, than the kind of liking I feel for her. No, I am not in love with her; but I think she likes me; and a man must be something worse than a brute if he is not grateful for a pretty woman's regard."

They said no more about Mrs. Branston. Gilbert had a strong distaste for the business; but he did not care to take upon himself the office of mentor to a friend whose will he knew to be much stronger than his own, and to whose domination he had been apt to submit in most things, as to the influence of a superior mind. It disappointed him a little to find that John Saltram was capable of making a mercenary marriage, capable even of the greater baseness involved in the anticipation of a dead man's shoes; but his heart was not easily to be turned against the chosen friend of his youth, and he was prompt in making excuses for the line of conduct he disapproved.

CHAPTER V.
HALCYON DAYS.

IT was still quite early in September when Gilbert Fenton went back to Lidford and took up his quarters once more in the airy chintz-curtained bedchamber set apart for him in his sister's house. He had devoted himself very resolutely to business during the interval that had gone by since his last visit to that quiet country house; but the time had seemed very long to him, and he fancied himself a kind of martyr to the necessities of commerce. The aspect of his affairs of late had not been quite free from unpleasantness. There were difficulties in the conduct of business in the Melbourne branch of the house, that branch which was under the charge of a cousin of Gilbert's, about whose business capacities the late Mr. Fenton had entertained the most exalted opinion.

The Melbourne trading had not of late done much credit to this gentleman's commercial genius. He had put his trust in firms that had crumbled to pieces before the bills drawn upon them came due, involving his cousin in considerable losses. Gilbert was rich enough to stand these losses, however; and he reconciled himself to them as best he might, taking care to send his Australian partner imperative instructions for a more prudent system of trading in the future.

The uneasiness and vexation produced by this business was still upon him when he went down to Lidford; but he relied upon Marian Nowell's presence to dissipate all his care.

He did find himself perfectly happy in her society. He was troubled by no doubts as to her affection for him, no uncertainty as to the brightness of the days that were to come. Her manner seemed to him all that a man could wish in the future partner of his life. An innocent trustfulness in his superior judgment, a childlike submission to his will which Marian displayed upon all occasions, were alike flattering and delightful. Nor did she ever appear to grow tired of that talk of their future which was so pleasant to her lover. There was no shadow of doubt upon her face when he spoke of the serene happiness which they two were to find in an existence spent together. He was the first who had ever spoken to her of these things, and she listened to him with an utter simplicity and freshness of mind.

Time had reconciled Isabella Lister to her brother's choice, and she now deigned to smile upon the lovers, very much to Gilbert's satisfaction. He had been too proud to supplicate her good graces; but he was pleased that his only sister should show herself gracious and affectionate to the girl he loved so fondly. During this second visit of his, therefore, Marian came very often to Lidford House; sometimes accompanied by her uncle, sometimes alone; and there was perfect harmony between the elder and younger lady.

The partridges upon Martin Lister's estate did not suffer much damage from his brother-in-law's gun that autumn. Gilbert found it a great deal pleasanter to spend his mornings dawdling in the little cottage drawing-room or under the walnut-trees with Marian, than to waste his noontide hours in the endeavour to fill a creditable game-bag. There is not very much to tell of the hours which those two spent together so happily. It was an innocent, frivolous, useless employment of time, and left little trace behind it, except in the heart of one of those two. Gilbert wondered at himself when, in some sober interval of reflection, he happened to consider those idle mornings, those tranquil uneventful afternoons and evenings, remembering what a devoted man of business he had once been, and how a few months ago he would have denounced such a life in another.

"Well," he said to himself, with a happy laugh, "a man can take this fever but once in his life, and it is only wise in him to surrender himself utterly to the divine delirium. I shall have no excuse for neglecting business by-and-by, when my little wife and I are settled down together for the rest of our days. Let me be her lover while I may. Can I ever be less than her lover, I wonder? Will marriage, or custom, or the assurance that we belong to each other for the rest of our days, take the poetry out of our lives? I think not; I think Marian must always be to me what she has seemed to me from the very first—something better and brighter than the common things of this life."

Custom, which made Marian Nowell dearer to Gilbert Fenton every day, had by this time familiarised her with his position as her future husband. She was no longer surprised or distressed when he pleaded for a short engagement, and a speedy realization of that Utopian home which they were to inhabit together. The knowledge of her uncle's delight in this engagement of hers might have reconciled her to it, even if she had not loved Gilbert Fenton. And she told herself that she did love him; or, more often putting the matter in the form of a question, asked herself whether she could be so basely ungrateful as not to love one who regarded her with such disinterested affection?

It was settled finally, after a good deal of pleasant discussion, that the wedding should take place early in the coming spring—at latest in April. Even this seemed a long delay to Gilbert; but he submitted to it as an inevitable concession to the superior instinct of his betrothed, which harmonised so well with Mrs. Lister's ideas of wisdom and propriety. There was the house to be secured, too, so that he might have a fitting home to which to take his darling when their honeymoon was over; and as he had no female relation in London who could take the care of furnishing this earthly paradise off his hands, he felt that the whole business must devolve upon himself, and could not be done without time.

Captain Sedgewick promised to bring Marian to town for a fortnight in October, in order that she might assist her lover in that delightful duty of house-hunting. She looked forward to this visit with quite a childlike pleasure. Her life at Lidford had been completely happy; but it was a monotonous kind of happiness; and the notion of going about London, even at the dullest time of the year, was very delightful to her.

The weather happened to be especially fine that September. It was the brightest month of the year, and the lovers took long rambles together in the woodland roads and lanes about Lidford, sometimes alone, more often with the Captain, who was a very fair pedestrian, in spite of having had a bullet or two through his legs in the days gone by. When the weather was too warm for walking, Gilbert borrowed Martin Lister's dog-cart, and drove them on long journeys of exploration to remote villages, or to the cheery little market-town ten miles away.

They all three set out for a walk one afternoon, when Gilbert had been about a fortnight at Lidford, with no particular destination, only bent on enjoying the lovely weather and the rustic beauty of woodland and meadow. The Captain chose their route, as he always did on these occasions, and under his guidance they followed the river-bank for some distance, and then turned aside into a wood in which Gilbert Fenton had never been before. He said so, with an expression of surprise at the beauty of the place, where the fern grew deep under giant oaks and beeches, and where the mossy ground dipped suddenly down to a deep still pool which reflected the sunlit sky through a break in the dark foliage that sheltered it.

"What, have you never been here?" exclaimed the Captain; "then you have never seen Heatherly, I suppose?"

"Never. By the way, is not that Sir David Forster's place?" asked Gilbert, remembering John Saltram's promise.

He had seen very little more of his friend after that visit to Rivercombe, and had half forgotten Mr. Saltram's talk of coming down to this neighbourhood on purpose to be presented to Marian.

"Yes. It is something of a show-place, too; and we think a good deal of it in these parts. There are some fine Sir Joshuas among the family portraits, painted in the days when the Forsters were better off and of more importance in the county than they are now. And there are a few other good pictures—Dutch interiors, and some seascapes by Bakhuysen. Decidedly you ought to see Heatherly. Shall we push on there this afternoon?"

"Is it far from here?"

"Not much more than a mile. This wood joins the park, and there is a public right of way across the park to the Lidford road, so the gate is always open. We can't waste our walk, and I know Sir David quite well enough to ask him to let you see the pictures, if he should happen to be at home."

"I should like it of all things," said Gilbert eagerly. "My friend John Saltram knows this Sir David Forster, and he talked of being down here at this time: I forgot all about it till you spoke of Heatherly just now. I have a knack of forgetting things now-a-days."

"I wonder that you should forget anything connected with Mr. Saltram, Gilbert," said Marian; "that Mr. Saltram of whom you think so much. I cannot tell you how anxious I am to see what kind of person he is; not handsome—you have confessed as much as that."

"Yes, Marian, I admit the painful fact. There are people who call John Saltram ugly. But his face is not a common one; it is a very picturesque kind of ugliness—a face that Velasquez would have loved to paint, I think. It is a rugged, strongly-marked countenance with a villanously dark complexion; but the eyes are very fine, the mouth perfection; and there is a look of power in the face that, to my mind, is better than beauty."

"And I think you owned that Mr. Saltram is hardly the most agreeable person in the world."

"Well, no, he is not what one could well call an eminently agreeable person. And yet he exercises a good deal of influence over the men he knows, without admitting many of them to his friendship. He is very clever; not a brilliant talker by any means, except on rare occasions, when he chooses to give full swing to his powers; he does not lay himself out for social successes; but he is a man who seems to know more of every subject than the men about him. I doubt if he will ever succeed at the Bar. He has so little perseverance or steadiness, and indulges in such an erratic, desultory mode of life; but he has made his mark in literature already, and I think he might become a great man if he chose. Whether he ever will choose is a doubtful question."

"I am afraid he must be rather a dissipated, dangerous kind of person," said Marian.

"Well, yes, he is subject to occasional outbreaks of dissipation. They don't last long, and they seem to leave not the faintest impression upon his herculean constitution; but of course that sort of thing does more or less injury to a man's mind, however comparatively harmless the form of his dissipation may be. There are very few men whom John Saltram cannot drink under the table, and rise with a steady brain himself when the wassail is ended; yet I believe, in a general way, few men drink less than he does. At cards he is equally strong; a past-master in all games of skill; and the play is apt to be rather high at one or two of the clubs he belongs to. He has a wonderful power of self-restraint when he cares to exert it; will play six or seven hours every night for three weeks at a stretch, and then not touch a card for six months. Poor old John," said Gilbert Fenton, with a half-regretful sigh; "under happy circumstances, he might be such a good man."

"But I fear he is a dangerous friend for you, Gilbert," exclaimed Marian, horrified by this glimpse of bachelor life.

"No, darling, I have never shared his wilder pleasures. There are a few chosen spirits with whom he consorts at such times. I believe this Sir David Forster is one of them."

"Sir David has the reputation of leading rather a wild life in London," said the Captain, "and of bringing a dissipated set down here every autumn. Things have not gone well with him. His wife, who was a very beautiful girl, and whom he passionately loved, was killed by a fall from her horse a few months after the birth of her first child. The child died too, and the double loss ruined Sir David. He used to spend the greater part of his life at Heatherly, and was a general favourite among the county people; but since that time he has avoided the place, except during the shooting season. He has a hunting-box in the shires, and is a regular daredevil over a big country they tell me."

They had reached the little gate opening from the wood into the park by this time. There was not much difference in the aspect of the sylvan scene upon the other side of the fence. Sir David's domain had been a good deal neglected of late years, and the brushwood and brambles grew thick under the noble old trees. The timber had not yet suffered by its owner's improvidence. The end of all things must have come for Sir David before he would have consented to the spoliation of a place he fondly loved, little as he had cared to inhabit it since the day that shattered all that was brightest and best in his life.

For some time Captain Sedgewick and his companions went along a footpath under the shelter of the trees, and then emerged upon a wide stretch of smooth turf, across which they commanded a perfect view of the principal front of the old house. It was a quadrangular building of the Elizabethan period, very plainly built, and with no special beauty to recommend it to the lover of the picturesque. Whatever charm of form it may have possessed in the past had been ruthlessly extirpated by the modernisation of the windows, which were now all of one size and form—a long gaunt range of unsheltered casements staring blankly out upon the spectator. There were no flower-beds, no terraced walks, or graceful flights of steps before the house; only a bare grassplot, with a stiff line of tall elms on each side, and a wide dry moat dividing it from the turf in the park. Two lodges—ponderous square brick buildings with very small windows, each the exact counterpart of the other, and a marvel of substantial ugliness—kept guard over a pair of tall iron gates, about six hundred yards apart, approached by stone bridges that spanned the moat.

Captain Sedgewick rang a bell hanging by the side of one of these gates, whereat there arose a shrill peal that set the rooks screaming in the tall elms overhead. An elderly female appeared in answer to this summons, and opened the gate in a slow mechanical way, without the faintest show of interest in the people about to enter, and looking as if she would have admitted a gang of obvious burglars with equal indifference.

"Rather a hideous style of place," said Gilbert, as they walked towards the house; "but I think show-places, as a general rule, excel in ugliness. I daresay the owners of them find a dismal kind of satisfaction in considering the depressing influence their dreary piles of bricks-and-mortar must exercise on the minds of strangers; may be a sort of compensation for being obliged to live in such a gaol of a place."

There was a clumsy low stone portico over the door, wide enough to admit a carriage; and lounging upon a bench under this stony shelter they found a sleepy-looking man-servant, who informed Captain Sedgewick that Sir David was at Heatherly, but that he was out shooting with his friends at this present moment. In his absence the man would be very happy to show the house to Captain Sedgewick and his party.

Gilbert Fenton asked about John Saltram.

Yes, Mr. Saltram had arrived at Heatherly on Tuesday evening, two nights ago.

They went over the state-rooms, and looked at the pictures, which were really as good as the Captain had represented them. The inspection occupied a little more than an hour, and they were ready to take their departure, when the sound of masculine voices resounded loudly in the hall, and their conductor announced that Sir David and his friends had come in.

There were only two gentlemen in the hall when they went into that spacious marble-paved chamber, where there were great logs burning on the wide open hearth, in spite of the warmth of the September day. One of these two was Sir David Forster, a big man, with a light-brown beard and a florid complexion. The other was John Saltram, who sat in a lounging attitude on one of the deep window-seats examining his breech-loader. His back was turned towards the window, and the glare of the blazing logs shone full upon his dark face with a strange Rembrandt-like effect.

One glance told Marian Nowell who this man was. That powerful face, with its unfathomable eyes and thoughtful mouth, was not the countenance she had conjured up from the depths of her imagination when Gilbert Fenton had described his friend; yet she felt that this stranger lounging in the window was John Saltram, and no other. He rose, and set down his gun very quietly, and stood by the window waiting while Captain Sedgewick introduced Gilbert to Sir David. Then he came forward, shook hands with his friend, and was thereupon presented to Marian and her uncle by Gilbert, who made these introductions with a kind of happy eagerness.

Sir David was full of friendliness and hospitality, and insisted on keeping them to show Gilbert and Miss Nowell some pictures in the billiard-room and in his own private snuggery, apartments which were not shown to ordinary visitors.

They strolled through these rooms in a leisurely way, Sir David making considerable pains to show Gilbert Fenton the gems of his collection, John Saltram acting as cicerone to Marian. He was curious to discover what this girl was like, whether she had indeed only her beauty to recommend her, or whether she was in sober reality the perfect being Gilbert Fenton believed her to be.

She was very beautiful. The first brief look convinced Mr. Saltram that upon this point at least her lover had indulged in no loverlike exaggeration. There was a singular charm in the face; a higher, more penetrating loveliness than mere perfection of feature; a kind of beauty that would have been at once the delight and desperation of a painter—so fitting a subject for his brush, so utterly beyond the power of perfect reproduction, unless by one of those happy, almost accidental successes which make the triumphs of genius.

John Saltram watched Marian Nowell's face thoughtfully as he talked to her, for the most part, about the pictures which they were looking at together. Before their inspection of these art-treasures was ended, he was fain to confess to himself that she was intelligent as well as beautiful. It was not that she had said anything particularly brilliant, or had shown herself learned in the qualities of the old Dutch masters; but she possessed that charming childlike capacity for receiving information from a superior mind, and that perfect and rapid power of appreciating a clever man's conversation, which are apt to seem so delightful to the sterner sex when exhibited by a pretty woman. At first she had been just a little shy and constrained in her talk with John Saltram. Her lover's account of this man had not inspired her with any exalted opinion of his character. She was rather inclined to look upon him as a person to be dreaded, a friend whose influence was dangerous at best, and who might prove the evil genius of Gilbert Fenton's life. But whatever her opinion on this point might remain, her reserve soon melted before John Saltram's clever talk and kindly conciliating manner. He laid himself out to please on this occasion, and it was very rarely he did that without succeeding.

"I want you to think of me as a kind of brother, Miss Nowell," he said in the course of their talk. "Gilbert and I have been something like brothers for the last twelve years of our lives, and it would be a hard thing, for one of us at least, if our friendship should ever be lessened. You shall find me discretion itself by-and-by, and you shall see that I can respect Gilbert's altered position; but I shouldn't like to lose him, and I don't think you look capable of setting your face against your husband's old friend."

Marian blushed a little at this, remembering that only an hour or two ago she had been thinking that this friendship was a perilous one for Gilbert, and that it would be well if John Saltram's influence over him could be lessened somehow in the future.

"I don't believe I should ever have the power to diminish Gilbert's regard for you, Mr. Saltram, even were I inclined to do so," she said.

"O yes, you would; your power over him will be illimitable, depend upon it. But now I have seen you, I think you will only use it wisely."

Marian shook her head, laughing gaily.

"I am much more fitted to be ruled than to rule, Mr. Saltram," she said. "I am utterly inexperienced in the world, you know, and Mr. Fenton is my superior in every way."

"Your superior in years, I know, but in what else?"

"In everything else. In intellect and judgment, as well as in knowledge of the world. You could never imagine what a quiet changeless life I have led."

"Your intellect is so much the clearer for that, I think. It has not been disturbed by all the narrow petty influences of a life spent in what is called 'society.'"

Before they left the house, Gilbert and the Captain were obliged to promise to dine at Heatherly next day, very much to the secret distaste of the former, who must thus lose an evening with Marian, but who was ashamed to reveal his hopeless condition by a persistent refusal. Captain Sedgewick begged John Saltram to choose an early day for dining at the cottage, and Gilbert gave him a general invitation to Lidford House.

These matters being settled, they departed, accompanied by Mr. Saltram, who proposed to walk as far as the wood with them, and who extended his walk still farther, only leaving them at the gate of the Captain's modest domain. The conversation was general throughout the way back; and they all found plenty to talk about, as they loitered slowly on among the waving shadows of the trees flickering darkly on the winding path by which they went. Gilbert lingered outside the gate after Marian and her uncle had gone into the cottage—he was so eager to hear his friend praise the girl he loved.

"Well, John?" he asked.

"Well, dear old boy, she is all that is beautiful and charming, and I can only congratulate you upon your choice. Miss Nowell's perfection is a subject about which there cannot be two opinions."

"And you think she loves me, Jack?"

"Do I think she loves you? Why, surely, Gil, that is not a question upon which you want another man's judgment?"

"No, of course not, but one is never tired of receiving the assurance of that fact. And you could see by her way of speaking about me——"

"She spoke of you in the prettiest manner possible. She seems to consider you quite a superior being."

"Dear girl, she is so good and simple-hearted. Do you know, Jack, I feel as if I could never be sufficiently grateful to Providence for my happiness in having won such an angel."

"Well, you certainly have reason to consider yourself a very lucky fellow; but I doubt if any man ever deserved good fortune better than you do, Gilbert. And now, good-bye. It's getting unconscionably late, and I shall scarcely get back in time to change my clothes for dinner. We spend all our evenings in pious devotion to billiards, with a rubber or two, or a little lansquenet towards the small hours. Don't forget your engagement to-morrow; good-bye."

They had a very pleasant evening at Heatherly. Sir David's guests at this time consisted of a Major Foljambe, an elderly man who had seen a good deal of service in India; a Mr. Harker, who had been in the church, and had left it in disgust as alike unsuited to his tastes and capacity; Mr. Windus Carr, a prosperous West-end solicitor, who had inherited a first-rate practice from his father, and who devoted his talents to the enjoyment of life, leaving his clients to the care of his partner, a steady-going stout gentleman, with a bald head, and an inexhaustible capacity for business; and last, but by no means least, John Saltram, who possessed more influence over David Forster than any one else in the world.

CHAPTER VI.
SENTENCE OF EXILE.

AFTER the dinner at Heatherly, John Saltram came very often to the cottage. He did not care much for the fellows who were staying with Sir David this year, he told Gilbert. He knew all Major Foljambe's tiger stories by heart, and had convicted him of glaring discrepancies in his description of the havoc he and his brother officers had made among the big game. Windus Carr was a conceited presuming cad, who was always boring them with impossible accounts of his conquests among the fair sex; and that poor Harker was an unmitigated fool, whose brains had run into his billiard-cue. This was the report which John Saltram gave of his fellow-guests; and he left the shooting-party morning after morning to go out boating with Gilbert and Marian, or to idle away the sunny hours on the lawn listening to the talk of the two others, and dropping in a word now and then in a sleepy way as he lay stretched on the grass near them, looking up to the sky, with his arms crossed above his head.

He called at Lidford House one day when Gilbert had told him he should stay at home to write letters, and was duly presented to the Listers, who made a little dinner-party in his honour a few days afterwards, to which Captain Sedgewick and Marian were invited—a party which went off with more brightness and gaiety than was wont to distinguish the Lidford House entertainments. After this there was more boating—long afternoons spent on the winding river, with occasional landings upon picturesque little islands or wooded banks, where there were the wild-flowers Marian Nowell loved and understood so well; more idle mornings in the cottage garden—a happy innocent break in the common course of life, which seemed almost as pleasant to John Saltram as to his friend. He had contrived to make himself popular with every one at Lidford, and was an especial favourite with Captain Sedgewick.

He seemed so thoroughly happy amongst them, and displayed such a perfect sympathy with them in all things, that Gilbert Fenton was taken utterly by surprise by his abrupt departure, which happened one day without a word of warning. He had dined at the cottage on the previous evening, and had been in his wildest, most reckless spirits—that mood to which he was subject at rare intervals, and in which he exercised a potent fascination over his companions. He had beguiled the little party at the cottage into complete forgetfulness of the hour by his unwonted eloquence upon subjects of a deeper, higher kind than it was his habit to speak about; and then at the last moment, when the clock on the mantelpiece had struck twelve, he had suddenly seated himself at the piano, and sung them Moore's "Farewell, but whenever you welcome the hour," in tones that went straight to the hearts of the listeners. He had one of those rare sympathetic voices which move people to tears unawares, and before the song was ended Marian was fairly overcome, and had made a hasty escape from the room ashamed of her emotion.

Late as it was, Gilbert accompanied his friend for a mile of his homeward route. He had secured a latch-key during his last visit to Lidford House, and could let himself in quietly of a night without entrenching upon the regular habits of Mrs. Lister's household.

Once clear of the cottage, John Saltram's gaiety vanished all in a moment, and gave place to a moody silence which Gilbert was powerless to dissipate.

"Is there anything amiss, Jack?" he asked. "I know high spirits are not always a sign of inward contentment with you. Is there anything wrong to-night?"

"No."

"Are you sure of that?"

"Quite sure. I may be a little knocked up perhaps; that's all."

No hint of his intended departure fell from him when they shook hands and wished each other good-night; but early next morning a brief note was delivered to Mr. Fenton at his sister's house to the following effect:—

"MY DEAR GILBERT,—I find myself obliged to leave this place for London at once, and have not time to thank anyone for the kindness I have received during my stay. Will you do the best to repair this omission on my part, and offer my warmest expressions of gratitude to Captain Sedgewick and Miss Nowell for their goodness to me? Pray apologise for me also to Mr. and Mrs. Lister for my inability to make my adieux in a more formal manner than this, a shortcoming which I hope to atone for on some future visit. Tell Lister I shall be very pleased to see him if he will look me up at the Pnyx when he is next in town.

"Ever yours,—JOHN SALTRAM."

This was all. There was no explanation of the reason for this hurried journey,—a strange omission between men who were on terms of such perfect confidence as obtained with these two. Gilbert Fenton was not a little disturbed by this unlooked-for event, fearing that some kind of evil had befallen his friend.

"His money matters may have fallen into a desperate condition," he thought; "or perhaps that woman—that Mrs. Branston, is at the bottom of the business."

He went to the cottage that morning as usual, but not with his accustomed feeling of unalloyed happiness. The serene heaven of his tranquil life was clouded a little by this strange conduct of John Saltram's. It wounded him to think that his old companion was keeping a secret from him.

"I suppose it is because I lectured him a little about Mrs. Branston the other day," he said to himself. "The business is connected with her in some way, I daresay, and poor Jack does not care to arouse my virtuous indignation. That comes of taking a high moral tone with one's friend. He swallows the pill with a decent grace at the time, and shuts one out of his confidence ever afterwards."

Captain Sedgewick expressed himself much surprised and disappointed by Mr. Saltram's departure. Marian said very little upon the subject. There seemed nothing extraordinary to her in the fact that a gentleman should be summoned to London by the claims of business.

Gilbert might have brooded longer upon the mystery involved in his friend's conduct, but that evening's post brought him trouble in the shape of bad news from Melbourne. His confidential clerk—an old man who had been with his father for many years, and who knew every intricacy of the business—wrote him a very long letter, dwelling upon the evil fortune which attended all their Australian transactions of late, and hinting at dishonesty and double-dealing on the part of Gilbert's cousin, Astley Fenton, the local manager.

The letter was a very sensible one, calculated to arouse a careless man from a false sense of security. Gilbert was so much disturbed by it, that he determined upon going back to London by the earliest fast train next morning. It was cutting short his holiday only by a few days. He had meant to return at the beginning of the following week, and he felt that he had already some reason to reproach himself for his neglect of business.

He left Lidford happy in the thought that Captain Sedgewick and Marian were to come to London in October. The period of separation would be something less than a month. And after that? Well, he would of course spend Christmas at Lidford; and he fancied how the holly and mistletoe, the church-decorations and carol-singing, and all the stereotyped genialities of the season,— things that had seemed trite and dreary to him since the days of his boyhood,— would have a new significance and beauty for him when he and Marian kept the sacred festival together. And then how quickly would begin the new year, the year whose spring-tide would see them man and wife! Perhaps there is no period of this mortal life so truly happy as that in which all our thoughts are occupied in looking forward to some great joy to come. Whether the joy, when it does come, is ever so unqualified a delight as it seemed in the distance, or whether it ever comes at all, are questions which we have all solved for ourselves somehow or other. To Gilbert Fenton these day-dreams were bright and new, and he was troubled by no fear of their not being realized.

He went at his business with considerable ardour, and made a careful and detailed investigation of all affairs connected with their Melbourne trading, assisted throughout by Samuel Dwyer, the old clerk. The result of his examination convinced him that his cousin had been playing him false; that the men with whom his pretended losses had been made were men of straw, and the transactions were shadows invented to cover his own embezzlements. It was a complicated business altogether; and it was not until Gilbert Fenton had been engaged upon it for more than a week, and had made searching inquiries as to the status of the firms with which the supposed dealings had taken place, that he was able to arrive at this conclusion. Having at last made himself master of the real state of things, as far as it was in any way possible to do so at that distance from the scene of action, Gilbert saw that there was only one line of conduct open to him as a man of business. That was to go at once to Melbourne, investigate his cousin's transactions on the spot, and take the management of the colonial house into his own hands. To do this would be a sore trial to him, for it would involve the postponement of his marriage. He could scarcely hope to do what he had to do in Melbourne and to get back to England before a later date than that which he had hoped would be his wedding-day. Yet to do anything less than this would be futile and foolish; and it was possible that the future stability of his position was dependent upon his arrangement of these Melbourne difficulties. It was his home, the prosperity of his coming life that he had to fight for; and he told himself that he must put aside all weakness, as he had done once before, when he turned away from the easy-going studies and pleasures of young Oxford life to undertake a hand-to-hand fight with evil fortune.

He had conquered then, as he hoped to conquer now, having an energetic nature, and a strong faith in man's power to master fortune by honest work and patience.

There was no time lost after once his decision was arrived at. He began to put his affairs in order for departure immediately, and wrote to Marian within a few hours of making up his mind as to the necessity of this voyage. He told her frankly all that had happened, that their fortune was at stake, and that it was his bounden duty to take this step hard as it might seem to him. He could not leave England without seeing her once more, he said, recently as they had parted, and brief as his leisure must needs be. There were so many things he would have to say to her on the eve of this cruel separation.

He went down to Lidford one evening when all the arrangements for his voyage were complete, and he had two clear days at his disposal before the vessel he was to go in left Liverpool. The Listers were very much surprised and shocked when he told them what he was going to do; Mrs. Lister bitterly bewailing the insecurity of all commercial positions, and appearing to consider her brother on the verge of bankruptcy.

He found a warm welcome at the cottage from the Captain, who heartily approved of the course he was taking, and was full of hopefulness about the future.

"A few months more or less can make little difference," he said, when Gilbert was lamenting the postponement of his wedding. "Marian will be quite safe in her old uncle's care; and I do not suppose either of you will love each other any the less for the delay. I have such perfect confidence in you, Gilbert, you see; and it is such a happiness to me to know that my darling's future is in the hands of a man I can so thoroughly trust. Were you reduced to absolute poverty, with the battle of life to fight all over again, I would give you my dear girl without fear of the issue. I know you are of the stuff that is not to be beaten; and I believe that neither time nor circumstance could ever change your love for her."

"You may believe that. Every day makes her dearer to me. I should be ashamed to tell you how bitterly I feel this parting, and what a desperate mental struggle I went through before I could make up my mind to go."

Marian came into the room in the midst of this conversation. She was very pale, and her eyes had a dull, heavy look. The bad news in Gilbert's letter had distressed her even more than he had anticipated.

"My darling," he said tenderly, looking down at the changed face, with her cold hand clasped in his own, "how ill you are looking! I fear I made my letter too dismal, and that it frightened you."

"Oh no, no. I am very sorry you should have this bad fortune, Gilbert, that is all."

"There is nothing which I do not hope to repair, dear. The losses are not more than I can stand. All that I take to heart is the separation from you, Marian."

"I am not worth so much regret," she said, with her eyes fixed upon the ground, and her hands clasping and unclasping each other nervously.

"Not worth so much regret, Marian!" he exclaimed. "You are all the world to me; the beginning and end of my universe."

She looked a little brighter by-and-by, when her lover had done his best to cheer her with hopeful talk, which cost him no small effort in the depressed state of his mind. The day went by very slowly, although it was the last which those two were to spend together until Gilbert Fenton's return. It was a hopelessly wet day, with a perpetual drizzling rain and a leaden-gray sky; weather which seemed to harmonise well enough with the pervading gloom of Gilbert's thoughts as he stood by the fire, leaning against an angle of the mantelpiece, and watching Marian's needle moving monotonously in and out of the canvas.

The Captain, who led an easy comfortable kind of life at all times, was apt to dispose of a good deal of his leisure in slumber upon such a day as this. He sat down in his own particular easy-chair, dozing behind the shelter of a newspaper, and lulled agreeably by the low sound of Gilbert and Marian's conversation.

So the quiet hours went by, overshadowed by the gloom of that approaching separation. After dinner, when they had returned to the drawing-room, and Captain Sedgewick had refreshed his intellectual powers with copious draughts of strong tea, he began to talk of Marian's childhood, and the circumstances which had thrown her into his hand.

"I don't suppose my little girl ever showed you her mother's jewel-case, did she, Gilbert?" he asked.

"Never."

"I thought as much. It contains that old-fashioned jewelry I spoke of—family relics, which I have sometimes fancied might be of use to her, if ever her birthright were worth claiming. But I doubt if that will ever happen now that so many years have gone by, and there has been no endeavour to trace her. Run and fetch the case, Marian. There are some of its contents which Gilbert ought to see before he leaves England—papers which I intended to show him when I first told him your mother's story."

Marian left them, and came back in a few minutes carrying an old-fashioned ebony jewel-case, inlaid with brass. She unlocked it with a little key hanging to her watch-chain, and exhibited its contents to Gilbert Fenton. There were some curious old rings, of no great value; a seal-ring with a crest cut on a bloodstone—a crest of that common kind of device which does not imply noble or ancient lineage on the part of the bearer thereof; a necklace and earrings of amethyst; a gold bracelet with a miniature of a young man, whose handsome face had a hard disagreeable expression; a locket containing grey hair, and having a date and the initials "M.G." engraved on the massive plain gold case.

These were all the trinkets. In a secret drawer there was a certificate of marriage between Percival Nowell, bachelor, gentleman, and Lucy Geoffry, spinster, at St. Pancras Church, London. The most interesting contents of the jewel-case consisted of a small packet of letters written by Percival Nowell to Lucy Geoffry before their marriage.

"I have read them carefully ever so many times, with the notion that they might throw some light upon Mr. and Mrs. Nowell's antecedents," said the Captain, as Gilbert held these in his hands, disinclined to look at documents of so private and sacred a character; "but they tell very little. I fancy that Miss Geoffry was a governess in some family in London—the envelopes are missing, you see, so there is no evidence as to where she was living, except that it *was* in London—and that she left her employment to marry this Percival Nowell. You'd like to read the letters yourself, I daresay, Gilbert. Put them in your pocket, and look them over at your leisure when you get home. You can bring them back before you leave Lidford."

Mr. Fenton glanced at Marian to see if she had any objection to his reading the letters. She was quite silent, looking absently at the trinkets lying in the tray before her.

"You don't mind my reading your father's letters, Marian?" he asked.

"Not at all. Only I think you will find them very uninteresting."

"I am interested in everything that concerns you."

He put the papers in his pocket, and sat up for an hour in his room that night reading Percival Nowell's love letters. They revealed very little to him, except the unmitigated selfishness of the writer. That quality exhibited itself in every page. The lovers had met for the first time at the house of some Mr. Crosby, in whose family Miss Geoffry seemed to be living; and there were clandestine meetings spoken of in the Regent's Park, for which reason Gilbert supposed Mr. Crosby's house must have been in that locality. There were broken appointments, for which Miss Geoffry was bitterly reproached by her lover, who abused the whole Crosby household in a venomous manner for having kept her at home at these times.

"If you loved me, as you pretend, Lucy," Mr. Nowell wrote on one occasion, "you would speedily exchange this degrading slavery for liberty and happiness with me, and would be content to leave the future *utterly* in my hands, without question or fear. A really generous woman would do this."

There was a good deal more to the same effect, and it seemed as if the proposal of marriage came at last rather reluctantly; but it did come, and was repeated, and urged in a very pressing manner; while Lucy Geoffry to the last appeared to have hung back, as if dreading the result of that union.

The letters told little of the writer's circumstances or social status. Whenever he alluded to his father, it was with anger and contempt, and in a manner that implied some quarrel between them; but there was nothing to indicate what kind of man the father was.

Gilbert Fenton took the packet back to the cottage next morning. He was to return to London that afternoon, and had only a few hours to spend with Marian. The day was dull and cold, but there was no rain; and they walked together in the garden, where the leaves were beginning to fall, and whence every appearance of summer seemed to have vanished since Gilbert's last visit.

For some time they were both rather silent, pacing thoughtfully up and down the sheltered walk that bounded the lawn. Gilbert found it impossible to put on an appearance of hopefulness on this last day. It was better wholly to give up the attempt, and resign himself to the gloom that brooded over him, shutting out the future. That airy castle of his—the villa on the banks of the Thames—seemed to have faded and vanished altogether. He could not look beyond the Australian journey to the happy time of his return. The hazards of time and distance bewildered him. He felt an unspeakable dread of the distance that was to divide him from Marian Nowell—a dread that grew stronger with every hour. He was destined to suffer a fresh pang before the moment of parting came. Marian turned to him by-and-by with an earnest anxious face, and said,—

"Gilbert, there is something which I think I ought to say to you before you go away."

"What is that, my darling?"

"It is rather hard to say. I fear it will give you pain. I have been thinking about it for a long time. The thought has been a constant reproach to me. Gilbert, it would be better if we were both free; better if you could leave England without any tie to weigh you down with anxieties when you are out yonder, and will have so much occasion for perfect freedom of mind."

"Marian!"

"O, pray, pray don't think me ungrateful or unmindful of your goodness to me. I am only anxious for your happiness. I am not steady enough, or fixed enough, in my mind. I am not worthy of all the thought and care you have given me."

"Marian, have I done anything to forfeit your love?"

"O no, no."

"Then why do you say these things to me? Do you want to break my heart?"

"Would it break your heart if I were to recall my promise, Gilbert?"

"Yes, Marian," he answered gravely, drawing her suddenly to him, and looking into her face with earnest scrutinising eyes; "but if you do not love me, if you cannot love me—and God knows how happy I have been in the belief that I had won your love long ago—let the word be spoken. I will bear it, my dear, I will bear it."

"O no, no," she cried, shocked by the dead whiteness of his face, and bursting into tears. "I will try to be worthy of you. I will try to love you as you deserve to be loved. It was only a fancy of mine that it would be better for you to be free from all thoughts of me. I think it would seem very hard to me to lose your love. I don't think I could bear that, Gilbert."

She looked up at him with an appealing expression through her tears—an innocent, half-childish look that went to his heart—and he clasped her to his breast, believing that this proposal to set him free had been indeed nothing more than a girlish caprice.

"My dearest, my life is bound up with your love," he said. "Nothing can part us except your ceasing to love me."

CHAPTER VII.
"GOOD-BYE."

THE hour for the final parting came at last, and Gilbert Fenton turned his back upon the little gate by which he had watched Marian Nowell standing upon that first summer Sunday evening which sealed his destiny.

He left Lidford weary at heart, weighed down by a depression he had vainly struggled against, and he brooded over his troubles all the way back to town. It seemed as if all the hopes that had made life so sweet to him only a week ago had been swept away. He could not look beyond that dreary Australian exile; he could not bring his thoughts to bear upon the time that was to come afterwards, and which need be no less bright because of this delay.

"She may die while I am away," he thought. "O God, if that were to happen! If I were to come back and find her dead! Such things have been; and men and women have borne them, and gone on living."

He had one more duty to perform before he left England. He had to say good-bye to John Saltram, whom he had not seen since they parted that night at Lidford. He could not leave England without some kind of farewell to his old friend, and he had reserved this last evening for the duty.

He went to the Pnyx on the chance of finding Saltram there, and failing in that, ate his solitary dinner in the coffee-room. The waiters told him that Mr. Saltram had not been at the club for some weeks. Gilbert did not waste much time over his dinner, and went straight from the Pnyx to the Temple, where John Saltram had a second-floor in Figtree-court.

Mr. Saltram was at home. It was his own sonorous voice which answered Gilbert's knock, bidding him enter with a muttered curse upon the interruption by way of addendum. The room into which Mr. Fenton went upon receiving this unpromising invitation was in a state of chaotic confusion. An open portmanteau sprawled upon the floor, and a whole wardrobe of masculine garments seemed to have been shot at random on to the chairs near it; a dozen soda-water bottles, full and empty, were huddled in one corner; a tea-tray tottered on the extreme edge of a table heaped with dusty books and papers; and at a desk in the centre of the room, with a great paraffin lamp flaring upon his face as he wrote, sat John Saltram, surrounded by fallen slips of copy, writing as if to win a wager.

"Who is it? and what do you want?" he asked in a husky voice, without looking up from his paper or suspending the rapid progress of his pen.

"Why, Jack, I don't think I ever caught you so hard at work before."

John Saltram dropped his pen at the sound of his friend's voice and got up. He gave Gilbert his hand in a mechanical kind of way.

"No, I don't generally go at it quite so hard; but you know I have a knack of doing things against time. I have been giving myself a spell of hard work in order to pick up a little cash for the children of Israel."

He dropped back into his chair, and Gilbert took one opposite him. The lamp shone full upon John Saltram's face as he sat at his desk; and after looking at him for a moment by that vivid light, Gilbert Fenton gave a cry of surprise.

"What is the matter, Gil?"

"You are the matter. You are looking as worn and haggard as if you'd had a long illness since I saw you last. I never remember you looking so ill. This kind of thing won't do, John. You'd soon kill yourself at this rate."

"Not to be done, my dear fellow. I am the toughest thing in creation. I have been sitting up all night for the last week or so, and that does rather impair the freshness of one's complexion; but I assure you there's nothing so good for a man as a week or two of unbroken work. I have been doing an exhaustive review of Roman literature for one of the quarterlies, and the subject involved a little more reading than I was quite prepared for."

"And you have really not been ill?"

"Not in the least. I am never ill."

He pushed aside his papers, and sat with his elbow on the desk and his head leaning on his hand, waiting for Gilbert to talk. He was evidently in one of those silent moods which were common to him at times.

Gilbert told him of his Melbourne troubles, and of his immediate departure. The announcement roused him from his absent humour. He dropped his arm from the table suddenly, and sat looking full at Gilbert with a very intent expression.

"This is strange news," he said, "and it will cause the postponement of your marriage, I suppose?"

"Unhappily, yes; that is unavoidable. Hard lines, isn't it, Jack?"

"Well, yes; I daresay the separation seems rather a hardship; but you are young enough to stand a few months' delay. When do you sail?"

"To-morrow."

"So soon?"

"Yes. It is a case in which everything depends upon rapidity of action. I leave Liverpool to-morrow afternoon. I came up from Lidford to-day on purpose to spend a few farewell hours with you. And I have been thinking, Jack, that you might run down to Liverpool with me to-morrow, and see the last of me, eh, old fellow?"

John Saltram hesitated, looking doubtfully at his papers.

"It would be only a kind thing to do, Jack, and a wholesome change for yourself into the bargain. Anything would be better for you than being shut up in these chambers another day."

"Well, Gilbert, I'll go with you," said Mr. Saltram presently with a kind of recklessness. "It is a small thing to do for friendship. Yes, I'll see you off, dear boy. Egad, I wish I could go to Australia with you. I would, if it were not for my engagements with the children and sundry other creditors. I think a new country might do me good. But there's no use in talking about that. I'm bound hand and foot to the old one."

"That reminds me of something I had to say to you, John. There must have been some reason for your leaving Lidford in that sudden way the other day, and your note explained nothing. I thought you and I had no secrets from each other, It's scarcely fair to treat me like that."

"The business was hardly worth explaining," answered the other moodily. "A bill that I had forgotten for the time fell due just then, and I hurried off to set things straight."

"Let me help you somehow or other, Jack."

"No, Gilbert; I will never suffer you to become entangled in the labyrinth of my affairs. You don't know what a hopeless wilderness you would enter if you were desperate enough to attempt my rescue. I have been past redemption for the last ten years, ever since I left Oxford. Nothing but a rich marriage will ever set me straight; and I sometimes doubt if that game is worth the candle, and whether it would not be better to make a clean sweep of my engagements, offer up my name to the execration of mankind and the fiery indignation of solvent journalists,—who would find subject for sensation leaders in my iniquities,— emigrate, and turn bushranger. A wild free life in the wilderness must be a happy exchange for all the petty worries and perplexities of this cursed existence."

"And how about Mrs. Branston, John? By the way, I thought that she might have had something to do with your sudden journey to London."

"No; she had nothing to do with it. I have not seen her since I came back from Lidford."

"Indeed!"

"No. Your lecture had a potent effect, you see," said Mr. Saltram, with something of a sneer. "You have almost cured me of that passion."

"My opinion would have very little influence if you were far gone, John. The fact is, Mrs. Branston, pretty and agreeable as she may be, is not the sort of woman to acquire any strong hold upon you."

"You think not?"

"I am sure of it."

After this John Saltram became more expansive. They sat together until late in the night, talking chiefly of the past, old friends, and half-forgotten days; recalling the scenes through which they had travelled together with a pensive tenderness, and dwelling regretfully upon that careless bygone time when life was fresh for both of them, and the future seemed to lie across the straightest, easiest high-road to reputation and happiness.

Gilbert spoke of that perilous illness of his in Egypt, the fever in which he had been given over by every one, and only saved at last by the exemplary care and devotion of his friend. John Saltram had a profound objection to this thing being talked about, and tried immediately to change the drift of the conversation; but to-night Gilbert was not to be stopped.

"You refuse the help of my purse, Jack," he said, "and forget that I owe you my life. I should never have been to the fore to navigate the good ship Fenton and Co., if it hadn't been for your care. The doctor fellow at Cairo told me as much in very plain terms. Yes, John, I consider myself your debtor to the amount of a life."

"Saving a man's life is sometimes rather a doubtful boon. I think if I had a fever, and some officious fool dragged me through it when I was in a fair way to make a decent end, I should be very savagely disposed towards him."

"Why, John Saltram, you are the last man in the world from whom I should expect that dreary kind of talk. Yet I suppose it's only a natural consequence of shutting yourself up in these rooms for ten days at a stretch."

"What good use have I made of my life in the past, Gilbert?" demanded the other bitterly; "and what have I to look forward to in the future? To marry, and redeem my position by the aid of a woman's money. That's hardly the noblest destiny that can befall a man. And yet I think if Adela Branston were free, and willing to marry me, I might make something of my life. I might go into Parliament, and make something of a name for myself. I could write books instead of anonymous articles. I should scarcely sink down into an idle mindless existence of dinner-giving and dinner-eating. Yes, I think the best thing that could happen to me would be to marry Adela Branston."

They parted at last, John Saltram having faithfully promised his friend to work no more that night, and they met at Euston Square early the next morning for the journey to Liverpool. Gilbert had never found his friend's company more delightful than on this last day. It seemed as if John Saltram put away every thought of self in his perfect sympathy with the thoughts and feelings of the traveller. They dined together, and it was dusk when they wished each other good-bye on the deck of the vessel.

"Good-bye, Gilbert, and God bless you! If—if anything should happen to me—if I should have gone to the bad utterly before you come back, you must try to remember our friendship of the past. Think that I have loved you very dearly—as well as one man ever loved another, perhaps."

"My dear John, you have no need to tell me to think that. Nothing can ever weaken the love between us. And you are not likely to go to the bad. Good bye, dear old friend. I shall remember you every day of my life. You are second only to Marian in my heart. I shall write you an account of my proceedings, and shall expect to hear from you. Once more, good bye."

The bell rang. Gilbert Fenton and his friend shook hands in silence for the last time, and in the next moment John Saltram ran down the steps to the little steamer which had brought them out to the larger vessel. The sails spread wide in the cool evening wind, and the mighty ship glided away into the dusk. John Saltram's last look showed him his friend's face gazing down upon him over the bulwarks full of trust and affection.

He went back to London by the evening express, and reached his chambers at a late hour that night. There had been some attempt at tidying the rooms in his absence; but his books and papers had been undisturbed. Some letters were lying on the desk, amongst them one in a big scrawling hand that was very familiar to Mr. Saltram, the envelope stamped "Lidford." He tore this open eagerly. It was from Sir David Forster.

> "DEAR SALTRAM" (wrote the Baronet),—"What do you mean by this iniquitous conduct? You only obtained my consent to your hurried departure the other day on condition you should come back in a week, yet there are no signs of you.

Foljambe and the lawyer are gone, and I am alone with Harker, whose stupidity is something marvellous. I am dying by inches of this dismal state of things. I can't tell the man to go, you see, for he is really a most worthy creature, although such a consummate fool. For pity's sake come to me. You can do your literary work down here as well as in London, and I promise to respect your laborious hours.—Ever yours,
"DAVID FORSTER."

John Saltram stood with this letter open in his hand, staring blankly at it, like a man lost in a dream.

"Go back!" he muttered at last—"go back, when I thought I did such a great thing in coming away! No, I am not weak enough for that folly."

CHAPTER VIII.
MISSING.

ON the 5th of July in the following year, Gilbert Fenton landed in England, after nearly ten months of exile. He had found hard work to do in the colonial city, and had done it; surmounting every difficulty by a steady resolute course of action.

Astley Fenton had tried to shelter his frauds, heaping falsehood upon falsehood; and had ended by making a full confession, after receiving his cousin's promise not to prosecute. The sums made away with by him amounted to some thousands. Gilbert found that he had been leading a life of reckless extravagance, and was a notorious gambler. So there came an evening when after a prolonged investigation of affairs, Astley Fenton put on his hat, and left his cousin's office for ever. When Gilbert heard of him next, he was clerk to a bookseller in Sydney.

The disentanglement of the Melbourne trading had occupied longer than Gilbert expected; and his exile had been especially dreary to him during the last two months he spent in Australia, from the failure of his English letters. The first two mails after his arrival had brought him letters from Marian and her uncle, and one short note from John Saltram. The mails that followed brought him nothing, and he was inexpressibly alarmed and distressed by this fact. If he could by any possibility have returned to England immediately after the arrival of the first mail which brought him no letter, he would have done so. But his journey would have been wasted had he not remained to complete the work of reorganization he had commenced; so he stayed, sorely against the grain, hoping to get a letter by the next mail.

That came, and with the same dispiriting result to Gilbert Fenton. There was a letter from his sister, it is true; but that was written from Switzerland, where she was travelling with her husband, and brought him no tidings of Marian. He tried to convince himself that if there had been bad news, it must needs have come to him; that the delay was only the result of accident, some mistake of Marian's as to the date of the mail. What more natural than that she should make such a mistake, at a place with such deficient postal arrangements as those which obtained at Lidford? But, argue with himself as he might, this silence of his betrothed was none the less perplexing to him, and he was a prey to perpetual anxiety during the time that elapsed before the sailing of the vessel that was to convey him back to England.

Then came the long monotonous voyage, affording ample leisure for gloomy thoughts, for shapeless fears in the dead watches of the night, when the sea washed drearily against his cabin window, and he lay broad awake counting the hours that must wear themselves out before he could set foot on English ground. As the time of his arrival drew nearer, his mind grew restless and fitful, now full of hope and happy visions of his meeting with Marian, now weighed down by the burden of some unspeakable terror.

The day dawned at last, that sultry summer day, and Gilbert was amongst those eager passengers who quitted the vessel at daybreak.

He went straight from the quay to the railway-station, and the delay of an hour which he had to endure here seemed almost interminable to him. As he paced to and fro the long platform waiting for the London express, he wondered how he had borne all the previous delay, how he had been able to live through that dismal agonizing time. His own patience was a mystery to him now that the ordeal was over.

The express started at last, and he sat quietly in his corner trying to read a newspaper; while his fellow-travellers discussed the state of trade in Liverpool, which seemed from their account to be as desperate and hopeless as the condition of all commerce appears invariably to be whenever commercial matters come under discussion. Gilbert Fenton was not interested in the Liverpool trade at this particular crisis. He knew that he had weathered the storm which had assailed his own fortunes, and that the future lay clear and bright before him.

He did not waste an hour in London, but went straight from one station to another, and was in time to catch a train for Fairleigh, the station nearest to Lidford. It was five o'clock in the afternoon when he arrived at this place, and chartered a fly to take him over to Lidford—a lovely summer afternoon. The sight of the familiar English scenery, looking so exquisite in its summer glory, filled him with a pleasure that was almost akin to pain. He had often walked this road with Marian; and as he drove along he looked eagerly at every distant figure, half hoping to see his darling approach him in the summer sunlight.

Mr. Fenton deposited his carpet-bag at the cosy village inn, where snow-white curtains fluttered gaily at every window in the warm western breeze, and innumerable geraniums made a gaudy blaze of scarlet against the wooden wall. He did not stop here to make any inquiries about those he had come to see. His heart was beating tumultuously in expectation of the meeting that seemed so near. He alighted from the fly, dismissed the driver, and walked rapidly across a field leading by a short cut to the green on which Captain Sedgewick's house stood. This field brought him to the side of the green opposite the Captain's cottage. He stopped for a moment as he came through the little wooden gate, and looked across the grass, where a regiment of geese was marching towards the still pool of willow-shadowed water.

The shutters of the upper rooms were closed, and there was a board above the garden-gate. The cottage was to be let.

Gilbert Fenton's heart gave one great throb, and then seemed to cease beating altogether. He walked across the green slowly, stunned by this unlooked-for blow. Yes, the house was empty. The garden, which he remembered in such exquisite order, had a weedy dilapidated look that seemed like the decay of some considerable time. He rang the bell several times, but there was no answer; and he was turning away from the gate with the stunned confused feeling still upon him, unable to consider what he ought to do next, when he heard himself called by his name, and saw a woman looking at him across the hedge of the neighbouring garden.

"Were you wishing to make any inquiries about the last occupants of Hazel Cottage, sir?" she asked.

"Yes," Gilbert answered huskily, looking at her in an absent unseeing way.

He had seen her often during his visits to the cottage, busy at work in her garden, which was much smaller than the Captain's, but he had never spoken to her before to-day.

She was a maiden lady, who eked out her slender income by letting a part of her miniature abode whenever an opportunity for so doing occurred. The care of this cottage occupied all her days, and formed the delight and glory of her life. It was a little larger than a good-sized doll's house, and furnished with spindle-legged chairs and tables that had been polished to the last extremity of brightness.

"Perhaps you would be so good as to walk into my sitting-room for a few moments, sir," said this lady, opening her garden-gate. "I shall be most happy to afford you any information about your friends."

"You are very good," said Gilbert, following her into the prim little parlour.

He had recovered his self-possession in some degree by this time, telling himself that this desertion of Hazel Cottage involved no more than a change of residence.

"My name is Dodd," said the lady, motioning Mr. Fenton to a chair, "Miss Letitia Dodd. I had the pleasure of seeing you very often during your visits next door. I was not on visiting terms with Captain Sedgewick and Miss Nowell, although we bowed to each other out of doors. I am only a tradesman's daughter—indeed my brother is now carrying on business as a butcher in Fairleigh—and of course I am quite aware of the difference in our positions. I am the last person to intrude myself upon my superiors."

"If you will be so kind as to tell me where they have gone?" Gilbert asked, eager to stop this formal statement of Miss Dodd's social standing.

"Where *they* have gone!" she repeated. "Dear, dear! Then you do not know——"

"I do not know what?"

"Of Captain Sedgewick's death."

"Good God! My dear old friend! When did he die?"

"At the beginning of the year. It was very sudden—a fit of apoplexy. He was seized in the night, poor dear gentleman, and it was only discovered when the servant went to call him in the morning. He only lived two days after the seizure; and never spoke again."

"And Miss Nowell—what made her leave the cottage? She is still at Lidford, I suppose?"

"O dear no, Mr. Fenton. She went away altogether about a month after the Captain's death."

"Where did she go?"

"I cannot tell you that, I did not even know that she intended leaving Hazel Cottage until the day after she left. When I saw the shutters closed and the board up, you might have knocked me down with a feather. Miss Nowell was so much liked in Lidford, and she had more than one invitation from friends to stay with them for the sake of a change after her uncle's death; but she would not visit anywhere. She stayed quite alone in the cottage, with only the old servant."

"But there must surely be some one in the place who knows where she has gone!" exclaimed Gilbert.

"I think not. The landlord of Hazel Cottage does not know. He is my landlord also, and I was asking him about Miss Nowell when I paid my rent the other day. He said he supposed she had gone away to be married. That has been the general impression, in fact, at Lidford. People made sure that Miss Nowell had left to be married to you."

"I have only just returned from Australia. I have come back to fulfil my engagement to Miss Nowell. Can you suggest no one from whom I am likely to obtain information?"

"There is the family at the Rectory; they knew her very well, and were extremely kind to her after her uncle's death. It might be worth your while to call upon Mr. Marchant."

"Yes, I will call," Gilbert answered; "thanks for the suggestion."

He wished Miss Dodd good-afternoon, and left her standing at the gate of her little garden, watching him with profound interest as he walked away towards the village. There was a pleasing mystery in the affair, to the mind of Miss Dodd.

Gilbert Fenton went at once to the Rectory, although it was now past seven o'clock. He had met Mr. and Mrs. Marchant several times, and had visited them with the Listers.

The Rector was at home, sitting over his solitary glass of port by the open window of his snug dining-room, looking lazily out at a group of sons and daughters playing croquet on the lawn. He was surprised to see Mr. Fenton, but welcomed him with much cordiality.

"I have come to you full of care, Mr. Marchant," Gilbert began; "and the pressing nature of my business must excuse the lateness of my visit."

"There is no occasion for any excuse. I am very glad to see you at this time. Pray help yourself to some wine, there are clean glasses near you; and take some of those strawberries, on which my wife prides herself amazingly. People who live in the country all their days are obliged to give their minds to horticulture. And now, what is this care of yours, Mr. Fenton? Nothing very serious, I hope."

"It is very serious to me at present. I think you know that I am engaged to Miss Nowell."

"Perfectly. I had imagined until this moment that you and she were married. When she left Lidford, I concluded that she had gone to stay with friends of yours, and that the marriage would, in all probability, take place at an early period, without any strict observance of etiquette as to her mourning for her uncle. It was natural that we should think this, knowing her solitary position."

"Then you do not know where she went on leaving this place?"

"Not in the faintest degree. Her departure was altogether unexpected by us.

My wife and daughters called upon her two or three times after the Captain's death, and were even anxious that she should come here to stay for a short time; but she would not do that. She seemed grateful, and touched by their anxiety about her, but they could not bring her to talk of her future."

"And she told them nothing of her intention to leave Lidford?"

"Not a word."

This was all that Gilbert Fenton could learn. His interview with the Rector lasted some time longer; but it told him nothing. Whom next could he question? He knew all Marian's friends, and he spent the next day in calling upon them, but with the same result; no one could tell him her reason for leaving Hazel Cottage, or where she had gone.

There remained only one person whom he could question, and that was the old servant who had lived with Captain Sedgewick nearly all the time of his residence at Lidford, and whom Gilbert had conciliated by numerous gifts during his visits to Hazel Cottage. She was a good-humoured honest creature, of about fifty, and had been devoted to the Captain and Marian.

After a good deal of trouble, Gilbert ascertained that this woman had not accompanied her young mistress when she left Lidford, but had taken service in a grocer's family at Fairleigh. Having discovered this, Mr. Fenton set off immediately for the little market-town, on foot this time, and with his mind full of the days when he and Marian had walked this way together.

He found the shop to which he had been directed—a roomy old-fashioned emporium in the High-street, sunk three or four feet below the level of the pavement, and approached by a couple of steps; a shop with a low ceiling, that was made lower by bunches of candles, hams, bacon, and other merchandise hanging from the massive beams that spanned it. Mr. Fenton, having duly stated his business, was shown into the grocer's best parlour—a resplendent apartment, where there were more ornaments in the way of shell-and-feather flowers under glass shades, and Bohemian glass scent-bottles, than were consistent with luxurious occupation, and where every chair and sofa was made a perfect veiled prophet by enshrouding antimacassors. Here Sarah Down, the late Captain's servant, came to Mr. Fenton, wiping her hands and arms upon a spotless canvas apron, and generally apologetic as to her appearance. To this woman Gilbert repeated the question he had asked of others, with the same disheartening result.

"The poor dear young lady felt the Captain's loss dreadfully; as well she might, when they had been so fond of each other," Sarah Down said, in answer to one of Gilbert's inquiries. "I never knew any one grieve so deeply. She wouldn't go anywhere, and she couldn't bear to see any one who came to see her. She used to shut herself up in the Captain's room day after day, kneeling by his bedside, and crying as if her heart would break. I have looked through the keyhole sometimes, and seen her there on her knees, with her face buried in the bedclothes. She didn't care to talk about him even to me, and I had hard work to persuade her to eat or drink enough to keep life in her at this time. When the days were fine, I used to try and get her to walk out a little, for she looked as white as a ghost for want of air; and after a good deal of persuasion, she did go out sometimes of an afternoon, but she wouldn't ask any one to walk with her, though there were plenty she might have asked—the young ladies from the Rectory and others. She preferred being alone, she told me, and I was glad that she should get the air and the change anyhow. She brightened a little after this, but very little. It was all of a sudden one day that she told me she was going away. I wanted to go with her, but she said that couldn't be. I asked her where she was going, and she told me, after hesitating a little, that she was going to friends in London. I knew she had been very fond of two young ladies that she went to school with at Lidford, whose father lived in London; and I thought it was to their house she was going. I asked her if it was, and she said yes. She made arrangements with the landlord about selling the furniture. He is an auctioneer himself, and there was no difficulty about that. The money was to be sent to her at a post-office in London. I wondered at that, but she said it was better so. She paid every sixpence that was owing, and gave me a handsome present over and above my wages; though I didn't want to take anything from her, poor dear young lady, knowing that there was very little left after the Captain's death, except the furniture, which wasn't likely to bring much. And so she went away about two days after she first mentioned that she was going to leave Lidford. It was all very sudden, and I don't think she bade good-bye to any one in the place. She seemed quite broken down with grief in those two last days. I shall never forget her poor pale face when she got into the fly."

"How did she go? From the station here?"

"I don't know anything about that, except that the fly came to the cottage for her and her luggage. I wanted to go to the station with her, to see her off, but she wouldn't let me."

"Did she mention me during the time that followed Captain Sedgewick's death?"

"Only when I spoke about you, sir. I used to try to comfort her, telling her she had you still left to care for her, and to make up for him she'd lost. But she used to look at me in a strange pitiful sort of way, and shake her head. 'I am very miserable, Sarah,' she would say to me; 'I am quite alone in the world now my dear uncle is gone, and I don't know what to do.' I told her she ought to look forward to the time when she would be married, and would have a happy home of her own; but I could never get her to talk of that."

"Can you tell me the name and address of her friends in London—the young ladies with whom she went to school?"

"The name is Bruce, sir; and they live, or they used to live at that time, in St. John's-wood. I have heard Miss Nowell say that, but I don't know the name of the street or number of the house."

"I daresay I shall be able to find them. It is a strange business, Sarah. It is most unaccountable that my dearest girl should have left Lidford without writing me word of her removal and her intentions with regard to the future—that she should have sent me no announcement of her uncle's death, although she must have known how well I loved him, I am going to ask you a question that is very painful to me, but which must be asked sooner or later. Do you know of any one else whom she may have liked better than me—any one whose influence may have governed her at the time she left Lidford?"

"No, indeed, sir," replied the woman, promptly. "Who else was there? Miss Nowell knew so few gentlemen, and saw no one except the Rector's family and two or three ladies after the uncle's death."

"Not at the cottage, perhaps. But she may have seen some one out-of-doors. You say she always went out alone at that time, and preferred to do so."

"Yes, sir, that is true. But it seemed natural enough that she should like to be alone on account of her grief."

"There must have been some reason for her silence towards me, Sarah. She could not have acted so cruelly without some powerful motive. Heaven only knows what it may have been. The business of my life will be to find her—to see her face to face once more, and hear the explanation of her conduct from her own lips."

He thanked the woman for her information, slipped a sovereign into her hand, and departed. He called upon the proprietor of Hazel Cottage, an auctioneer, surveyor, and house-agent in the High-street of Fairleigh, but could obtain no fresh tidings from this gentleman, except the fact that the money realised by the Captain's furniture had been sent to Miss Nowell at a post-office in the City, and had been duly acknowledged by her, after a delay of about a week. The auctioneer showed Gilbert the letter of receipt, which was worded in a very formal business-like manner, and bore no address but "London." The sight of the familiar hand gave him a sharp pang. O God, how he had languished for a letter in that handwriting!

He had nothing more to do after this in the neighbourhood of Lidford, except to pay a pious visit to the Captain's grave, where a handsome slab of granite recorded the virtues of the dead. It lay in the prettiest, most retired part of the churchyard, half-hidden under a wide-spreading yew. Gilbert Fenton sat down upon a low wall near at hand for a long time, brooding over his broken life, and wishing himself at rest beneath that solemn shelter.

"She never loved me," he said to himself bitterly. "I shut my eyes obstinately to the truth, or I might have discovered the secret of her indifference by a hundred signs and tokens. I fancied that a man who loved a woman as I loved her must succeed in winning her heart at last. And I accepted her girlish trust in me, her innocent gratitude for my attentions, as the evidence of her love. Even at the last, when she wanted to release me, I would not understand. I did not expect to be loved as I loved her. I would have given so much, and been content to take so little. What is there I would not have done—what sacrifice of my own pride that I would not have happily made to win her! O my darling, even in your desertion of me you might have trusted me better than this! You would have found me fond and faithful through every trial, your friend in spite of every wrong."

He knelt down by the grave, and pressed his lips to the granite on which George Sedgewick's name was chiselled.

"I owe it to the dead to discover her fate," he said to himself, as he rose from that reverent attitude. "I owe it to the dead to penetrate the secret of her new life, to assure myself that she is happy, and has fallen under no fatal influence."

The Listers were still abroad, and Gilbert was very glad that it was so. It would have excruciated him to hear his sister's comments on Marian's conduct, and to perceive the suppressed exultation with which she would most likely have discussed this unhappy termination to an engagement which had been entered on in utter disregard of her counsel.

CHAPTER IX.
JOHN SALTRAM'S ADVICE.

MR. Fenton discovered the Bruce family in Boundary-road, St. John's-wood, after a good deal of trouble. But they could tell him nothing of their dear friend Miss Nowell, of whom they spoke with the warmest regard. They had never seen her since they had left the school at Lidford, where they had been boarders, and she a daily pupil. They had not even heard of Captain Sedgewick's death.

Gilbert asked these young ladies if they knew of any other acquaintance of Marian's living in or near London. They both answered promptly in the negative. The school was a small one, and they had been the only pupils who came from town; nor had they ever heard Marian speak of any London friends.

Thus ended Mr. Fenton's inquiries in this direction, leaving him no wiser than when he left Lidford. He had now exhausted every possible channel by which he might obtain information. The ground lay open before him, and there was nothing left for him but publicity. He took an advertisement to the *Times* office that afternoon, and paid for six insertions in the second column:—

"Miss MARIAN NOWELL, late of Lidford, Midlandshire, is requested to communicate immediately with G.F., Post-office, Wigmore-street, to whom her silence has caused extreme anxiety. She may rely upon the advertiser's friendship and fidelity under all possible circumstances."

Gilbert felt a little more hopeful after having done this. He fancied this advertisement must needs bring him some tidings of his lost love. The mystery might be happily solved after all, and Marian prove true to him. He tried to persuade himself that this was possible; but it was very difficult to reconcile her line of conduct with the fact of her regard for him.

In the evening he went to the Temple, eager to see John Saltram, from whom he had no intention to keep the secret of his trouble. He found his friend at home, writing, with his desk pushed against the open window, and the dust and shabbiness of his room dismally obvious in the hot July sunshine. He started up as Gilbert entered, and the dark face grew suddenly pale.

"You took me by surprise," he said. "I didn't know you were in England."

"I only landed two days ago," answered Gilbert, as they shook hands. "I daresay I startled you a little, dear old fellow, coming in upon you without a moment's notice, when you fancied I was at the Antipodes. But, you see, I hunted you up directly I was free."

"You have done well out yonder, I hope, Gilbert?"

"Yes; everything has gone well enough with me in business. But my coming home has been a dreary one."

"How is that?"

"Captain Sedgewick is dead, and Marian Nowell is lost."

"Lost! What do you mean by that?"

Mr. Fenton told his friend all that had befallen him since his arrival in England.

"I come to you for counsel and help, John," he said, when he had finished his story.

"I will give you my help, so far as it is possible for one man to help another in such a business, and my counsel in all honesty," answered John Saltram; "but I doubt if you will be inclined to receive it."

"Why should you doubt that?"

"Because it is not likely to agree with your own ideas."

"Speak out, John."

"I think that if Miss Nowell had really loved you, she would never have taken this step. I think that she must have left Lidford in order to escape from her engagement, perhaps expecting your early return. I believe your pursuit of her can only end in failure and disappointment; and although I am ready to assist you in any manner you wish, I warn you against sacrificing your life to a delusion."

"It is not under the delusion that Marian Nowell loves me that I am going to search for her," Gilbert Fenton said slowly, after an interval of silence. "I am not so weak as to believe *that* after what has happened, though I have tried to argue with myself, only this afternoon, that she may still be true to me and that there may have been some hidden reason for her conduct. Granted that she wished to escape from her engagement, she might have trusted to my honour to give her a prompt release the moment I became acquainted with the real state of her feelings. There must have been some stronger influence than this at work when she left Lidford. I want to know the true cause of that hurried departure, John. I want to be sure that Marian Nowell is happy, and in safe hands."

"By what means do you hope to discover this?"

"I rely a good deal upon repeated advertisements in the *Times*. They may bring me tidings of Marian—if not directly, from some person who has seen her since she left Lidford."

"If she really wished to hide herself from you, she would most likely change her name."

"Why should she wish to hide herself from me? She must know that she might trust me. Of her own free will she would never do this cruel thing. There must have been some secret influence at work upon my darling's mind. It shall be my business to discover what that influence was; or, in plainer words still, to discover the man who has robbed me of Marian Nowell's heart."

"It comes to that, then," said John Saltram. "You suspect some unknown rival?"

"Yes; that is the most natural conclusion to arrive at. And yet heaven knows how unwillingly I take that into consideration."

"There is no particular person whom you suspect?"

"No one."

"If there should be no result from your advertisement, what will you do?"

"I cannot tell you just yet. Unless I get some kind of clue, the business will seem a hopeless one. But I cannot imagine that the advertisements will fail completely. If she left Lidford to be married, there must be some record of her marriage. Should my first advertisements fail, my next shall be inserted with a view to discover such a record."

"And if, after infinite trouble, you should find her the wife of another man, what reward would you have for your wasted time and lost labour?"

"The happiness of knowing her to be in a safe and honourable position. I love her too dearly to remain in ignorance of her fate."

"Well, Gilbert, I know that good advice is generally thrown away in such a case as this; but I have a fixed opinion on the subject. To my mind, there is only one wise course open to you, and that is, to let this thing alone, and resign yourself to the inevitable. I acknowledge that Miss Nowell was eminently worthy of your affection; but you know the old song—'If she be not fair to me, what care I how fair she be.' There are plenty of women in the world. The choice is wide enough."

"Not for me, John. Marian Nowell is the only woman I have ever loved, the only woman I ever can love."

"My dear boy, it is so natural for you to believe that just now; and a year hence you will think so differently!"

"No, John. But I am not going to mate any protestations of my constancy. Let the matter rest. I knew that my life is broken—that this blow has left me nothing to hope for or to live for, except the hope of finding the girl who has wronged me. I won't weary you with lamentations. My talk has been entirely of self since I came into this room. Tell me your own affairs, Jack, old friend. How has the world gone with you since we parted at Liverpool last year?"

"Not too smoothly. My financial position becomes a little more obscure and difficult of comprehension every year, as you know; but I rub on somehow. I have been working at literature like a galley-slave; have contributed no end of stuff to the Quarterlies; and am engaged upon a book,—yes Gil, positively a book,—which I hope may do great things for me if ever I can finish it."

"Is it a novel?"

"A novel! no!" cried John Saltram, with a wry face; "it is the romance of reality I deal with. My book is a Life of Jonathan Swift. He was always a favourite study of mine, you know, that brilliant, unprincipled, intolerant, cynical, irresistible, miserable man. Scott's biography seems to me to give but a tame picture, and others are only sketches. Mine will be a pre-Raphaelite study— faithful as a photograph, careful as a miniature on ivory, and life-size."

"I trust it will bring you fame and money when the time comes," answered Gilbert. "And how about Mrs. Branston? Is she as charming as ever?"

"A little more so, if possible. Poor old Michael Branston is dead—went off the hooks rather suddenly about a month ago. The widow looks amazingly pretty in her weeds."

"And you will marry her, I suppose, Jack, as soon as her mourning is over?"

"Well, yes; it is on the cards," John Saltram said, in an indifferent tone.

"Why, how you say that! Is there any doubt as to the lady's fortune?"

"O no; that is all square enough. Michael Branston's will was in the *Illustrated London News*; the personalty sworn under a hundred and twenty thousand,—all left to the widow,—besides real property—a house in Cavendish Square, the villa at Maidenhead, and a place near Leamington."

"It would be a splendid match for you, Jack."

"Splendid, of course. An unprecedented stroke of luck for such a fellow as I. Yet I doubt very much if I am quite the man for that sort of life. I should be apt to fancy it a kind of gilded slavery, I think, Gil, and there would be some danger of my kicking off the chains."

"But you like Mrs. Branston, don't you, Jack?"

"Like her? Yes, I like her too well to deceive her. And she would expect devoted affection from a second husband. She is full of romantic ideas, school-girl theories of life which she was obliged to nip in the bud when she went to the altar with old Branston, but which have burst into flower now that she is free."

"Have you seen her often since her husband's death?"

"Only twice;—once immediately after the funeral, and again yesterday. She is living in Cavendish Square just now."

"I hope you will marry her. I should like to see you safe in smooth water, and with some purpose in life. I should like to see you turn your back upon the loneliness of these dreary chambers."

"They are not very brilliant, are they? I don't know how many generations of briefless barristers these chairs and tables have served. The rooms have an atmosphere of failure; but they suit me very well. I am not always here, you know. I spend a good deal of my time in the country."

"Whereabouts?"

"Sometimes in one direction, sometimes in another; wherever my truant fancy leads me. I prefer such spots as are most remote from the haunts of men, unknown to cockneys; and so long as there is a river within reach of my lodging, I can make myself tolerably happy with a punt and a fishing-rod, and contrive to forget my cares."

"You have not been to Lidford since I left England, I suppose?"

"Yes; I was at Heatherly a week or two in the winter. Poor old David Forster would not let me alone until I went down to him. He was ill, and in a very dismal condition altogether, abandoned by the rest of his cronies, and a close prisoner in the house which has so many painful associations for him. It was a work of charity to bear him company."

"Did you see Captain Sedgewick, or Marian, while you were down there?"

"No. I should have liked to have called upon the kind old Captain; but Forster was unconscionably exacting,—there was no getting away from him."

Gilbert stepped with his friend until late that night, smoking and drinking a mild mixture of brandy and soda-water, and talking of the things that had been doing on this side of the globe while he had been on the other. No more was said about Marian, or Gilbert's plans for the future. In his own mind that one subject reigned supreme, shutting out every other thought; but h did not want to make himself a nuisance to John Saltram, and he knew that there are bounds to the endurance of which friendship is capable.

The two friends seemed cheerful enough as they smoked their cigars in the summer dusk, the quiet of the flagged court below rarely broken by a passing footfall. It was the pleasantest evening which Gilbert Fenton had spent for a long time, in spite of the heavy burden on his mind, in spite of the depressing view which Mr. Saltram took of his position.

"Dear old John," he said, as they shook hands at parting, "I cannot tell you what a happiness it has been to me to see you again. We were never separated so long before since the day when I ate my first dinner at Balliol."

The other seemed touched by this expression of regard, but disinclined to betray his emotion, after the manner of Englishmen on such occasions.

"My dear Gilbert, it ought to be very pleasant to me to hear that. But I doubt if I am worthy of so much. As far as my own liking for you goes, there is no inequality between us; but you are a better fellow than I am by a long way, and are not likely to profit much in the long-run by your friendship for a reprobate like me."

"That's all nonsense, John. That kind of vague self-accusation means nothing. I have no doubt I shall live to see you a great man, and to be proud enough of being able to claim you as the chosen friend of my youth. Mr. Branston's death has cleared the way for you. The chances of a distinguished future are within your grasp."

"The chances within my grasp! Yes. My dear Gilbert, I tell you there are some men for whom everything in this world comes too late."

"What do you mean by that?"

"Only that I doubt if you will ever see me Adela Branston's husband."

"I can't understand you, John."

"My dear fellow, there is nothing strange in that. There are times when I cannot understand myself."

CHAPTER X.
JACOB NOWELL.

THE days went by, and brought Gilbert Fenton no reply to his advertisement. He called at the post-office morning and evening, only to find the same result; and a dull blank feeling, a kind of deadness of heart and mind, began to steal over him with the progress of the days. He went through the routine of his business-life steadily enough, working as hard as he had ever worked; but it was only by a supreme effort that he could bring his mind to bear upon the details of business—all interest in his office-work was gone.

The advertisement had appeared for the sixth time, and Gilbert had framed a second, offering a reward of twenty pounds for any direct evidence of the marriage of Marian Nowell; when a letter was handed to him one evening at the post-office—a letter in a common blue envelope, directed in a curious crabbed hand, and bearing the London post-mark.

His heart beat loud and fast as he tore open this envelope It contained only a half-sheet of paper, with these words written upon it in the cramped half-illegible hand which figured on the outside:

"The person advertising for Marian Nowell is requested to call at No. 5, Queen Anne's Court, Wardour Street, any evening after seven."

This was all. Little as this brief note implied, however, Gilbert made sure that the writer must be in a position to give him some kind of information about the object of his search. It was six o'clock when he received the communication. He went from the post-office to his lodgings with his mind in a tumult of excitement, made a mere pretence of taking a hasty dinner, and set off immediately afterwards for Wardour Street.

There was more than time for him to walk, and he hoped that the walk might have some effect in reducing the fever of his mind. He did not want to present himself before strangers—who, no doubt, only wanted to make a barter of any knowledge they possessed as to Marian's whereabouts—in a state of mental excitement. The address to which he was going mystified him beyond measure. What could people living in such a place as this know of her whom he sought?

He was in Wardour Street at a quarter before seven, but he had considerable trouble in finding Queen Anne's Court, and the clocks of the neighbourhood were striking the hour as he turned into a narrow alley with dingy-looking shops on one side and a high dead wall on the other. The gas was glimmering faintly in the window of No. 5, and a good deal of old silver, tarnished and blackened, huddled together behind the wire-guarded glass, was dimly visible in the uncertain light. There was some old jewellery too, and a little wooden bowl of sovereigns or gold coins of some kind or other.

On a brass plate upon the door of this establishment there appeared the name of Jacob Nowell, silversmith and money-changer.

Gilbert Fenton stared in amazement at this inscription. It must needs be some relative of Marian's he was about to see.

He opened the door, bewildered a little by this discovery, and a shrill bell gave notice of his entrance to those within. A tall lanky young man, with a sallow face and sleek black hair, emerged quickly from some door in the obscure background, and asked in a sharp voice what the visitor pleased to want.

"I wish to see Mr. Nowell, the writer of a letter addressed to the post-office in Wigmore Street."

The sallow-faced young man disappeared without a word, leaving Gilbert standing in the dimly lighted shop, where he saw more old silver crowded upon shelves behind glass doors, carved ebony cabinets looming out of the dusk, and here and there an old picture in a tarnished frame. On the counter there was a glass case containing foreign bank-notes and gold, some curious old watches, and other trinkets, a baby's coral, a battered silver cup, and a gold snuff-box.

While Gilbert waited thus he heard voices in a room at the back—the shrill tones of the sallow young man and a feeble old voice raised querulously—and then, after a delay which seemed long to his impatience, the young man reappeared and told him Mr. Nowell was ready to see him.

Gilbert went into the room at the end of the shop—a small dark parlour, more crowded with a heterogeneous collection of plate, pictures, and bric-a-brac of all kinds than the shop itself. Sultry as the July evening was, there was a fire burning in the pinched rusty grate, and over this fire the owner of the room bent affectionately, with his slippered feet on the fender, and his bony hands clasping his bony knees.

He was an old man, with long yellowish-white hair streaming from beneath a velvet skull-cap, and bright black eyes deep set in a pale thin face. His nose was a sharp aquiline, and gave something of a bird-like aspect to a countenance that must once have been very handsome. He was wrapped in a long dressing-gown of some thick grey woollen stuff.

The sallow-faced young man lingered by the half-glass door between the parlour and the shop, as if he would fain have remained a witness to the interview about to take place between his master and the stranger; but the old man looked round at him sharply, and said,—

"That will do, Tulliver; you can go back to the shop. If Abrahams brings that little lot again to-night, tell him I'll give five-and-nine an ounce, not a fraction more."

Mr. Tulliver retired, leaving the door ajar ever so little; but the penetrating black eyes of the master were quick to perceive this manoeuvre.

"Will you be so good as to shut that door, sir, quite securely?" he said to Gilbert. "That young man is very inquisitive; I'm afraid I've kept him too long. People talk of old servants; but half the robberies in the world are committed by old servants. Be seated, if you please, sir. You find this room rather close, perhaps. Some people do; but I'm old and chilly, and I can't live without a fire."

"I have come to you in great anxiety of mind," said Gilbert, as he seated himself upon the only disengaged chair in the room, "and with some hope that you may be able to set my mind at ease by affording me information about Miss Marian Nowell."

"I can give you no information about her."

"Indeed!" cried Gilbert, with a bitter pang of disappointment; "and yet you answered my advertisement."

"I did, because I have some reason to suppose this Marian Nowell may be my granddaughter."

"That is quite possible."

"Can you tell me her father's name?"

"Percival Nowell. Her mother was a Miss Lucy Geoffry."

"Right," said the old man. "Percival Nowell was my only son—my only child of late years. There was a girl, but she died early. He was my only son, and his mother and I were foolish enough to be proud of his good looks and his clever ways; and we brought him up a gentleman, sent him to an expensive school, and after that to the University, and pinched ourselves in every way for his sake. My father was a gentleman; and it was only after I had failed as a professional man, through circumstances which I need not explain to you now, that I took to this business. I would have made any sacrifice in reason for that boy of mine. I wanted him to be a gentleman, and to make his way in one of the learned professions. After a great deal of chopping and changing, he fixed upon the Bar, took chambers in the Temple, made me pay all the fees, and pretended to study. But I soon found that he was leading a wild dissipated life, and was never likely to be good for anything. He got into debt, drew bills upon me, and behaved altogether in a most shameful manner. When I sent for him, and remonstrated with him upon his disgraceful conduct, he told me that I was a miser, that I spent my life in a dog-kennel for the sake of hoarding money, and that I deserved nothing better than his treatment of me. I may have been better off at this time than I had cared to let him know, for I had soon found out what a reckless scoundrel I had to deal with; but if he had behaved decently, he would have found me generous and indulgent enough. As it was, I told him to go about his business, and never to expect another sixpence from me as long as he lived. How he managed to exist after this, I hardly know. He was very much mixed up with a disreputable lot of turf-men, and I believe he made money by betting. His mother robbed me for him, I found out afterwards, and contrived to send him a good deal of money at odd times. My business as a dealer in second-hand silver was better then than it is now, and I had had so much money passing through my hands that it was pretty easy for my wife to cheat me. Poor soul! she has been dead and gone these fifteen years, and I have freely forgiven her. She loved that young man to distraction. If he had wanted a step to reach the object of his wishes, she would have laid herself down in the dust and let him walk over her body. I suppose it is in the nature of mothers to love their sons like that. Well, sir, I never saw my gentleman after that day. I had plenty of letters from him, all asking for money; threatening letters, pitiful letters, letters in which he swore he would destroy himself if he didn't receive a remittance by return of post; but I never sent him a shilling. About a year after our last meeting, I received the announcement of his marriage with Miss Geoffry. He wrote to tell me that, if I would allow him a decent income, he would reform and lead a steady life. That letter I did answer: to the effect that, if he chose to come here and act as my shopman, I would give him board and lodging for himself and his wife, and such wages as he should deserve. I told him that I had given him his chance as a gentleman, and he had thrown it away. I would give him the opportunity now of succeeding in a humbler career by sheer industry and perseverance as I had succeeded myself. If he thought that I had made a fortune, there was so much the more reason for him to try his luck. This was the last letter I ever wrote to him. It was unanswered; but about a year and a half afterwards there came a few lines to his mother, telling her of the birth of a daughter, which was to be called Marian, after her. This last letter came from Brussels."

"And did you hear no more of your son after this?" Gilbert asked.

"Nothing. I think his mother used to get letters from him in secret for some time; that these failed suddenly at last; and that anxiety about her worthless son—anxiety which she tried to hide from me—shortened her life. She never complained, poor soul! never mentioned Percy's name until the last, when she begged me to be kind to him if he should ever come to throw himself upon my kindness. I gave her my promise that, if that came to pass, he should find me a better friend to him than he deserved. It is hard to refuse the last prayer of a faithful wife who has done her duty patiently for nearly thirty years."

"Have you any reason to suppose your son still living?"

"I have no evidence of his death. Often and often, after my poor wife was gone, I have sat alone here of a night thinking of him; thinking that he might come in upon me at any moment; almost listening for his footstep in the quiet of the place. But he never came. He would have found me very soft-hearted at such times. My mind changed to him a good deal after his mother's death. I used to think of him as he was in his boyhood, when Marian and I had such great hopes of him, and would sit and talk of him for hours together by this fireside. An old man left quite alone as I was had plenty of time for such thoughts. Night after night I have fancied I heard his step, and have looked up at that door expecting to see him open it and come in; but he never came. He may be dead. I suppose he is dead; or he would have come to make another attempt at getting money out of me."

"You have never taken any measures for finding him?" inquired Gilbert.

"No. If he wanted me, he knew where I was to be found. *I* was a fixture. It was his business to come to me. When I saw the name of Marian Nowell in your advertisement a week ago, I felt curious to know whether it could be my grandchild you were looking for. I held off till this morning, thinking it wasn't worth my while to make any inquiries about the matter; but I couldn't get it out of my head somehow; and it ended by my answering your advertisement. I am an old man, you see, without a creature belonging to me; and it might be a comfort to me to meet with some one of my own flesh and blood. The bit of money I may leave behind me when I die won't be much; but it might as well go to my son's child as to a stranger."

"If your son's child can be found, you will discover her to be well worthy of your love. Yes, though she has done me a cruel wrong, I believe her to be all that is good and pure and true."

"What is the wrong that she has done you?"

Gilbert told Jacob Nowell the story of his engagement, and the bitter disappointment which had befallen him on his return from Australia. The old man listened with every appearance of interest. He approved of Gilbert's notion of advertising for the particulars of a possible marriage, and offered to bear his part in the expenses of the search for his granddaughter.

Gilbert smiled at this offer.

"You do not know what a worthless thing money is to me now," he said, "or now lightly I hold my own trouble or loss in this matter."

He left Queen Anne's Court soon after this, after having promised Jacob Nowell to return and report progress so soon as there should be anything worth telling. He went back to Wigmore Street heavy-hearted, depressed by the reaction that followed the vain hope which the silversmith's letter had inspired. It mattered little to him to know the antecedents of Marian's father, while Marian's destiny remained still hidden from him.

CHAPTER XI.
THE MARRIAGE AT WYGROVE.

ON the following day Gilbert Fenton took his second advertisement to the office in Printing House Square; an advertisement offering a reward of twenty pounds for any reliable information as to the marriage of Marian Nowell. A week went by, during which the advertisement appeared on alternate days; and at the end of that time there came a letter from the parish-clerk of Wygrove, a small town about forty miles farther from London than Lidford, stating that, on the 14th of March, John Holbrook and Marian Nowell had been married at the church in that place. Gilbert Fenton left London by an early train upon the morning after his receipt of this letter; and at about three o'clock in the afternoon found himself on the outskirts of Wygrove, rather a difficult place to reach, involving a good deal of delay at out-of-the-way junctions, and a six-mile journey by stage-coach from the nearest station.

It was about the dullest dreariest little town to which his destiny had ever brought Gilbert Fenton, consisting of a melancholy high-street, with a blank market-place, and a town hall that looked as if it had not been opened within the memory of man; a grand old gothic church, much too large for the requirements of the place; a grim square brick box inscribed "Ebenezer;" and a few prim villas straggling off into the country.

On one side of the church there was a curious little old-fashioned court, wonderfully neat and clean, with houses the parlours whereof were sunk below the level of the pavement, after the manner of these old places. There was a great show of geraniums in the casements, and a general aspect of brightness and order distinguished all these modest dwellings. It was to this court that Mr. Fenton had been directed on inquiring for Thomas Stoneham, the parish-clerk, at the inn where the coach deposited him. He was fortunate enough to find Mr. Stoneham sunning himself on the threshold of his domicile, smoking an after-dinner pipe. A pleasant clattering of tea-things sounded from the neat little parlour within, showing that, early as it was, there were already preparations for the cup which cheers without inebriating in the Stoneham household.

Thomas Stoneham, supported by a freshly-painted door of a vivid green and an extensive brass plate engraved with his name and functions, was a personage of some dignity. He was a middle-aged man, ponderous and slow of motion, with a latent pomposity, which he rendered as agreeable as possible by the urbanity of his manners. He was a man of a lofty spirit, who believed in his office as something exalted above all other dignities of this earth—less lucrative, of course, than a bishopric or the woolsack, and of a narrower range, but quite as important on a small scale. "The world might get on pretty well without bishops," thought Mr. Stoneham, when he pondered upon these things as he smoked his churchwarden pipe; "but what would become of a parish in which there was no clerk?"

This gentleman, seeing Gilbert Fenton approach, was quick to surmise that the stranger came in answer to the letter he had written the day before. The advent of a stranger in Wygrove was so rare an occurrence, that it was natural enough for him to jump at this conclusion.

"I believe you are Mr. Stoneham," said Gilbert, "and the writer of a letter in answer to an advertisement in the *Times*."

"My name is Stoneham, sir; I am the clerk of this parish, and have been for twenty years and more, as I think I may have stated in the letter to which you refer. Will you be so kind as to step inside?"

Mr. Stoneham waved his hand towards the parlour, to which apartment Gilbert descended. Here he found Mrs. Stoneham, a meek little sandy-haired woman, who seemed to be borne down by the weight of her lord's dignity; and Miss Stoneham, also meek and sandy, with a great many stiff little corkscrew ringlets budding out all over her head and a sharp little inquiring nose.

These ladies would have retired on Gilbert's entrance, but he begged them to remain; and after a good deal of polite hesitation they consented to do so, Mrs. Stoneham resuming her seat before the tea-tray, and Miss Stoneham retiring to a little table by the window, where she was engaged in trimming a bonnet.

"I want to know all about this marriage, Mr. Stoneham," Gilbert began, when he had seated himself in a shining mahogany arm-chair by the empty fire-place. "First and foremost, I want you to tell me where Mr. and Mrs. Holbrook are now living."

The parish-clerk shook his head with a stately slowness.

"Not to be done, sir," he said: "when Mr. and Mrs. Holbrook left here they went the Lord knows where. They went away the very day they were married. There was a fly waiting for them at the church-door, with their luggage upon it, when the ceremony was over, ready to drive them to Grangewick station. I saw them get into it and drive away; and that's every mortal thing that I know as to what became of them after they were married in yonder church."

"You don't know who this Mr. Holbrook is?"

"No more than the babe unborn, sir. He was a stranger in this place, was only here long enough to get the license for his marriage. I should take him to be a gentleman; but he wasn't a pleasant person to speak to—rather stand-off-ish in his manners. He wasn't the sort of man I should have chosen if I'd been a pretty young woman like Miss Nowell; but there's no accounting for taste, and she seemed uncommonly fond of him. I never saw any one more agitated than she was when they were married. She was crying in a quiet way all through the service, and when it was over she fainted dead-off. I daresay it did seem hard to her to be married like that, without so much as a friend to give her away. She was in mourning, too, deep mourning."

"Can you give me any description of this man—this Mr. Holbrook?"

"Well, no, sir: he was an ordinary kind of person to look at; might be any age between thirty and forty; not a gentleman that I should have taken a fancy to myself, as I said before; but young women are that wayward and uncertain like, there's no knowing where to have them."

"Was Miss Nowell long at Wygrove before her marriage?"

"About three weeks. She lodged with Miss Long, up the town, a friend of my daughter's. If you'd like to ask any questions of Miss Long, our Jemima might step round there with you presently."

"I should be very glad to do so," Gilbert answered quickly. He asked several more questions; but Mr. Stoneham could give him no information, except as to the bare fact of the marriage. Gilbert knew now that the girl he had so fondly loved and so entirely trusted was utterly lost to him; that he had been jilted cruelly and heartlessly, as he could but own to himself. Yes, she had jilted him— had in all probability never loved him. He blamed himself for having urged his suit too ardently, with little reference to Marian's own feelings, with a rooted obstinate conviction that he needed only to win her in order to insure the happiness of both.

Having fully proved Mr. Stoneham's inability to afford him any further help in this business, Gilbert availed himself of the fair Jemima's willingness to "step round" to Miss Long's domicile with him, in the hope of obtaining fuller information from that lady. While Miss Stoneham was engaged in putting on her bonnet for this expedition, the clerk proposed to take Gilbert across to the church and show him the entry of the marriage in the register. "With a view to the satisfactory settlement of the reward," Mr. Stoneham added in a fat voice, and with the air of a man to whom twenty pounds more or less was an affair of very little moment.

Gilbert assented to this, and accompanied Mr. Stoneham to a little side-door which admitted them into the old church, where the light shone dimly through painted windows, in which there seemed more leaden framework than glass. The atmosphere of the place was cold even on this sultry July afternoon, and the vestry to which Mr. Stoneham conducted his companion had a damp mouldy smell.

He opened a cupboard, with a good deal of jingling of a great bunch of keys, and produced the register; a grim-looking volume bound in dingy leather, and calculated to inspire gloomy feelings in the minds of the bridegrooms and brides who had occasion to inscribe their names therein; a volume upon which the loves and the graces who hover around the entrance to the matrimonial state had shed no ray of glamour.

Thomas Stoneham laid this book before Gilbert, open at the page on which Marian's marriage was recorded. Yes, there was the familiar signature in the fair flowing hand he had loved so well. It was his Marian, and no other, whom John Holbrook had married in that gloomy old church.

The signature of the bridegroom was in a stiff straight hand, all the letters formed with unusual precision, as if the name had been written in a slow laboured way.

Who could this John Holbrook be? Gilbert was quite certain that he had never heard the name at Lidford, nor could he believe that if any attachment between this man and Marian Nowell had existed before his own acquaintance with her, Captain Sedgewick would have been so dishonourable as to keep the fact a secret from him. This John Holbrook must needs, therefore, be some one who had come to Lidford during Gilbert's absence from England; yet Sarah Down had been able to tell him of no new visitor at Hazel Cottage.

He copied the record of the marriage on a leaf in his pocket-book, paid Mr. Stoneham a couple of ten-pound notes, and left the church. The clerk's daughter was waiting for him in the little court outside, and they went at once to the house where Miss Nowell had lodged during her residence at Wygrove.

It was a house in a neat little terrace on the outskirts of the town; a house approached by a flight of steep stone steps of spotless purity, and a half-glass door, which opened at once into a bright airy-looking parlour, faintly perfumed with rose-leaves and lavender mouldering in the china vases on the mantelpiece. Here Gilbert was introduced to Miss Long, a maiden lady of uncertain age, who wore stiff bands of suspiciously black hair under an imposing structure of lace and artificial flowers, and a rusty black-silk dress, the body of which fitted so tightly as to seem like a kind of armour. This lady received Mr. Fenton very graciously, and declared herself quite ready to give him any information in her power about Miss Nowell.

It happened unfortunately, however, that her power was of a most limited extent.

"A sweeter young lady never lived than Miss Nowell," she said. "I've had a great many people occupying these apartments since my father's death left me thrown upon my own resources. I've had lodgers that I might call permanent, in a manner of speaking; but I never had any one that I took to as I took to Miss Nowell, though she was hardly with me three weeks from first to last."

"Did she seem happy in her mind during that time?" Gilbert asked.

"Well, no; I cannot say that she did. I should have expected to see a young lady that was going to be married to the man she loved much more cheerful and hopeful about the future than Miss Nowell was. She told me that her uncle had not been dead many weeks, and I thought at first that this was the only grief she had on her mind; but after some time, when I found her very low and downhearted, and had won upon her to trust me almost as if I had been an old friend, she owned to me that she had behaved very badly to a gentleman she had been engaged to, and that the thought of her wickedness to him preyed upon her mind. 'I don't think any good can ever come of my marriage, Miss Long,' she said to me; 'I think I must surely be punished for my falsehood to the good man who loved me so truly. But there are some things in life that seem like fate. They come upon us in a moment, and we have no strength to fight against them. I believe it was my fate to love John Holbrook. There is nothing in this world I could refuse to do for his sake. If he had asked me for my life, I must have given it to him as freely as I gave him my love. From the first hour in which I saw him he was my master.'"

"This Mr. Holbrook was very fond of her, I suppose?"

"I daresay he was, sir; but he was not a man that showed his feelings very much. They used to go for long walks together, though it was March and cold windy weather, and she always seemed happier when he brought her home. He came every evening to drink tea with her, and I used to hear them talking as I sat at work in the next room. She was happy enough when he was with her. It was only when she was alone that she would give way to low spirits and gloomy thoughts about the future."

"Did she ever tell you anything about Mr. Holbrook—his position or profession? how long she had known him? how and where they had first met?"

"No, sir. She told me once that he was not rich; I think that is about all she ever said of him, except when she spoke of his influence over her, and her trust in him."

"Have you any idea where they were going to live after their marriage?"

"I cannot tell you the name of the place. Miss Nowell said that a friend of Mr. Holbrook's was going to lend him an old farm-house in a very pretty part of the country. It would be very lonely, she said, and her husband would have sometimes to leave her to attend to his business in London; but she would not mind that. 'Some day, I daresay, he will let me live in London with him,' she said; 'but I don't like to ask him that yet.'"

"Did she drop no hint as to the whereabouts of this place to which they were going?"

"It was somewhere in Hampshire; that is all I can remember."

"I would give a great deal to know more," Gilbert said with a sigh. "In what manner did this Mr. Holbrook impress you? You were interested in the young lady, and would therefore naturally be interested in her lover. Did he strike you as worthy of her?"

"*I* cannot say that he did, sir," Miss Long answered doubtfully. "I could see that he had great power over her, though his manner to her was always very gentle; but I cannot say that I took to him myself. I daresay he is a very clever man; but he had a cold proud way that kept one at a distance from him, and I seemed to know no more of him at the last than I had known on the first day I saw him. I believe he loved Miss Nowell, and that's about all the good I do believe of him."

After this, there was no more to be asked of Miss Long; so Gilbert thanked her for her civility, and bade good evening at once to her and to Miss Stoneham. There was time for him to catch the last coach to Grangewick station. He determined upon going from Grangewick to Lidford, instead of returning to London. He wanted, if possible, to find out something more about this man Holbrook, who must surely have been known to some one at Lidford during his secret courtship of Marian Nowell.

He wasted two days at Lidford, making inquiries on this subject, in as quiet a manner as possible and in every imaginable quarter; but without the slightest result. No one either at Lidford or Fairleigh had ever heard of Mr. Holbrook.

Gilbert's last inquiries were made in a singular direction. After exhausting every likely channel of information, he had a few hours left before the departure of the fast train by which he had determined to return to London; and this leisure he devoted to a visit to Heatherly Park, in the chance of finding Sir David Forster at home. It was just possible that Mr. Holbrook might be one of Sir David's innumerable bachelor acquaintances.

Gilbert walked from Lidford to Heatherly by that romantic woodland path by which he had gone with Marian and her uncle on the bright September afternoon when he first saw Sir David's house. The solitary walk awakened very bitter thoughts; the memory of those hopes which had then made the sunshine of his life, and without which existence seemed a weary purposeless journey across a desert land.

Sir David was at home, the woman at the lodge told him; and he went on to the house, and rang a great clanging bell, which made an alarming clamour in the utter stillness of the place.

A gray-haired old servant answered the summons, and ushered Gilbert into the state drawing-room, an apartment with a lofty arched roof, eight long windows, and a generally ecclesiastical aspect, which was more suggestive of solemn grandeur than of domestic comfort.

Here Gilbert waited for about ten minutes, at the end of which time the man returned, to request that he would be so kind as to go to Sir David's study. His master was something of an invalid, the man told Gilbert.

They went through the billiard-room to a very snug little apartment, with dark-panelled walls and one large window opening upon a rose-garden on the southern side of the house. There was a ponderous carved-oak bookcase on one side of the room; on all the others the paraphernalia of sporting—gunnery and fishing-tackle, small-swords, whips, and boxing-gloves—artistically arranged against the panelling; and over the mantelpiece an elaborate collection of meerschaum pipes. Through a half-open door Gilbert caught a glimpse of a comfortable bedchamber leading out of this room.

Sir David was sitting on a low easy-chair near the window, with one leg supported on a luxuriously-cushioned rest, invented for the relief of gouty subjects. Although not yet forty, the baronet was a chronic sufferer from this complaint.

"My dear Mr. Fenton, how good of you to come to me!" he exclaimed, shaking hands very cordially with Gilbert. "Here I am, laid by the heels in this dreary old place, and quite alone. You can't imagine what a treat it is to see a friendly intelligent face from the outer world."

"The purpose of my visit is such a purely selfish one, that I am really ashamed to receive such a kindly greeting, Sir David. If I had known you were here and an invalid, I should have gladly come to see you; but I didn't know it. I have been at Lidford on a matter of business for the last two days; and I came here on the hazard of finding you, and with a faint hope that you might be able to give me some help in an affair which is supremely important to me."

Sir David Forster looked at Gilbert Fenton curiously for a moment, and then took up an empty meerschaum that lay upon a little table near him, and began to fill it with a thoughtful air. Gilbert had dropped into an arm-chair on the opposite side of the open window, and was watching the baronet's face, puzzled a little by that curious transient expression which had just flitted across it.

"What is the business?" Sir David asked presently; "and how can I be of use to you?"

"I think you knew all about my engagement to Miss Nowell, when I was here last September, Sir David," Gilbert began presently.

"Yes, Saltram told me you were engaged; not but what it was easy enough to see how the land lay, without any telling."

"Miss Nowell has jilted me. I love her too dearly to be able to entertain any vindictive feeling against her; but I do feel vindictively disposed towards the man who has robbed me of her, for I know that only a very powerful influence would have induced her to break faith with me; and this man must needs have known the dishonourable thing he was doing when he tempted her away from me. I want to know who he is, Sir David, and how he came to acquire such an influence over my plighted wife."

"My dear Fenton, you are going on so fast! You say Miss Nowell has jilted you. She is married to some one else, then, I suppose?"

"She is married to a Mr. Holbrook. I came to Lidford the night before last, with the hope of finding out something about him; but all my endeavours have resulted in failure. It struck me at last, as a kind of forlorn hope, that this Mr. Holbrook might possibly be one of your autumnal visitors; and I came here to ask you that question."

"No," answered the baronet; "I have had no visitor called Holbrook. Is the name quite strange to yourself?"

"Entirely strange."

"And this Mr. Holbrook is now Miss Nowell's husband? and you want to know who he is? With what end?"

"I want to find the man who has done me the deadliest wrong one man can do another."

"My dear fellow, don't you see that it is fate, and not Mr. Holbrook, that has done you this wrong? If Miss Nowell had really loved you as she ought to have loved you, it would have been quite impossible for her to be tempted away from you. It was her destiny to marry this Holbrook, rely upon it; and had you been on the spot to protect your own interests, the result would have been just the same. Believe me, I am very sorry for you, and can fully sympathise with your feelings in this business; but I cannot see what good could possibly arise out of a meeting between you and your fortunate rival. The days of duelling are past; and even if it were not so, I think you are too generous to seek to deprive Miss Nowell of her husband."

"I do not know about that. There are some wrongs which all a man's Christianity is not wide enough to cover. I think if that man and I were to meet, there would be very little question of mercy on my side. I hold a man who could act as he has acted unworthy of all consideration—utterly unworthy of the woman he has won from me."

"My dear fellow, you know the old saying. A man who is in love thinks everything fair. There is no such thing as honour in such a case as this. Of course, I don't want to defend this Holbrook; I only want to awaken your senses to the absurdity of any vindictive pursuit of the man. If the lady did not love you, believe me you are well out of the business."

"Yes, that is what every one would tell me, I daresay," Gilbert answered impatiently. "But is there to be no atonement for my broken life, rendered barren to me by this man's act? I tell you, Sir David, there is no such thing as pardon for a wrong like this. But I know how foolish this talk must seem to you: there is always something ridiculous in the sufferings of a jilted lover."

"Not at all, my dear Fenton. I heartily wish that I could be of use to you in this matter; but there is very little chance of that; and, believe me, there is only one rational course open to you, which is, to forget Miss Nowell, or Mrs. Holbrook, with all possible assiduity."

Gilbert smiled, a melancholy incredulous smile. Sir David's advice was only the echo of John Saltram's counsel—the counsel which he would receive from every man of the world, no doubt—the counsel which he himself would most likely have given to a friend under the same circumstances.

Sir David was very cordial, and wanted his visitor to dine and sleep at Heatherly; but this Gilbert declined. He was eager to get back to London now that his business was finished.

He arrived in town late that night; and went back to his office-work next day with a dreary feeling that he must needs go through the same dull routine day after day in all the time to come, without purpose or hope in his life, only because a man must go on living somehow to the end of his earthly pilgrimage, whether the sun shine upon him or not.

He went to Queen Anne's Court one evening soon after his return, and told Mr. Nowell all he had discovered at Wygrove. The old man showed himself keenly interested in his grand-daughter's fate.

"I would give a great deal to see her before I die," he said. "Whatever I have to leave will be hers. It may be little or much—I won't speak about that; but I've lived a hard life, and saved where other men would have spent. I should like to see my son's child; I should like to have some one of my own flesh and blood about me in my last days."

"Would it not be a good plan to put an advertisement into the *Times*, addressed to Mrs. Holbrook, from a relation? She would be likely to answer that, when she would not reply to any appeal coming directly from me."

"Yes," answered Jacob Nowell; "and her husband would let her come to me for the sake of what I may have to leave her. But that can't be helped, I suppose; it is the fate of a man who lives as I have lived, to be cared for at last only for what he has to give. I'll put in such an advertisement as you speak of; and we'll see what comes of it."

CHAPTER XII.
A FRIENDLY COUNSELLOR.

GILBERT Fenton called several times in the Temple without being able to see John Saltram; a slip of paper pasted on the outer door of that gentleman's chamber informed the public that he was "out of town," and that was all. Gilbert took the trouble to penetrate the domicile of the laundress who officiated in Mr. Saltram's chambers, in order to obtain some more particular information as to her employer's movements, and after infinite difficulty succeeded in finding that industrious matron in the remote obscurity of a narrow court near the river. But the laundress could tell Mr. Fenton very little. She did not know whither Mr. Saltram had gone, or when he was likely to return. He was one of the most uncertingest gentlemen she had to do for; and he had been out of town a great deal lately; which was not to be wondered at, considering the trying hot weather, when it was not to be supposed that gentlefolks as was free to do what they pleased would stay in London. It was hard enough upon working people with five children to wash and mend and cook for, and over in the court besides, and provisions dearer than they had been these ten years. Gilbert asked if Mr. Saltram had left any orders about his letters; but the woman told him, no; there never was such a careless gentleman about letters. He never cared about having them sent after him, and would let them lie in the box till the dust got thick upon them.

Gilbert left a brief note for John Saltram with the woman—a note begging his friend to come to him when he was next in London; and having done this, he paid no more visits to the Temple, but waited patiently for Mr. Saltram's coming, feeling very sure that his request would not be neglected. If anything could have intensified the gloom of his mind at this time it would have been the absence of that one friend, whom he loved better than he had ever loved any one in this world, except Marian Nowell. He stayed in town all through the blank August and September season, working harder than he had worked since the early days of his commercial life, taking neither pleasure nor interest in anything, and keeping as much as possible out of the way of all his old acquaintance.

No answer came to Jacob Nowell's advertisement, although it appeared several times; and the old man began to despair of ever seeing his granddaughter. Gilbert used to drop in upon him sometimes of an evening during this period, at his urgent request. He was interested in the solitary silversmith for Marian's sake, and very willingly sacrificed an occasional evening for his gratification. He fancied that these visits of his inspired some kind of jealousy in the breast of the sallow-faced, sleek-haired shopman; who regarded him always on these occasions with a look of suppressed malevolence, and by every stratagem in his power tried to find out the nature of the conversation between the visitor and his employer, making all kinds of excuses to come into the parlour, and showing himself proof against the most humiliating treatment from his master.

"Does that young man expect you to leave him money? and does he look upon me as a possible rival?" Gilbert asked one night, provoked by the shopman's conduct.

"Very likely," Mr. Nowell answered, with a malicious grin.

"One gets good service from a man who expects his reward in the future. Luke Tulliver serves me very well indeed, and of course I am not responsible for his delusions."

"Do you know, Mr. Nowell, that is a man I should scarcely care to trust. To my mind there is a warning of danger in his countenance."

"My dear sir, I have never trusted any one in my life," answered the silversmith promptly. "I don't for a moment suppose that Luke Tulliver would be honest if I gave him an opportunity to cheat me. As to the badness of his countenance, that is so much the better. I like to deal with an obvious rogue. The really dangerous subject is your honest fool, who goes on straight enough till he has lulled one into a false security, and then turns thief all at once at the instigation of some clever tempter."

"That young man lives in the house with you, I suppose?"

"Yes; my household consists of Luke Tulliver, and an old woman who does the cooking and other work. There are a couple of garrets at the top of the house where the two sleep; my own bedroom is over this; and the room over the shop is full of pictures and other unsaleable stuff, which I have seldom occasion to show anybody. My business is not what it once was, Mr. Fenton. I have made some rather lucky hits in the way of picture-dealing in the course of my business career, but I haven't done a big line lately."

Gilbert was inclined to believe that Jacob Nowell was a much richer man than he cared to confess, and that the fortune which Marian Nowell might inherit in the future was a considerable one. The old man had all the attributes of a miser. The house in which he lived had the aspect of a place in which money has been made and hoarded day by day through long dull years.

* * * * *

It was not until the end of October that John Saltram made his appearance at his old friend's lodgings. He had just come up from the country, and was looking his best—brighter and younger than Gilbert had seen him look for a long time.

"My dear Jack, I began to think I should never see you again. What have you been doing all this time, and where have you been?"

"I have been hard at work, as usual, for the reviews, down Oxford way, at a little place on the river. And how has the world been going with you, Gilbert? I saw your advertisement offering a reward for evidence of Miss Nowell's marriage. Was there any result?"

"Yes; I know all about the marriage now, but I don't know who or what the man is," Gilbert answered; and then went on to give his friend a detailed account of his experience at Wygrove, and his visit to Sir David Forster.

"My dear foolish Gilbert," said John Saltram, "how much useless trouble you have given yourself! Was it not enough to know that this girl had broken faith with you? I think, were I in your place, that would be the end of the story for me. And now you know more than that—you know that she is another man's wife. If you find her, nothing can come of it."

"It is the man I want to find, John; the man whom I shall make it the business of my life to discover."

"For what good?"

"For the deadliest harm to him," Gilbert answered moodily. "If ever he and I meet, I will have some payment for my broken life; some compensation for my ruined hopes. We two should not meet and part lightly, rely upon it."

"You can make no excuse for his love, that fatal irresistible passion, which outweighs truth and honour when they are set in the opposite scale. I did not think you could be so hard, Gilbert; I thought you would have more mercy on the man who wronged you."

"I could pardon any injury but this. I will never forgive this."

John Saltram shrugged his shoulders with a deprecating air.

"It is a mistake, my dear fellow," he said. "Life is not long enough for these strong passions. There is nothing in the world worth the price these bitter hatreds and stormy angers cost us. You have thrown away a great deal of deep feeling on a lady, whose misfortune it was not to be able to return your affection as she might have done—as you most fully deserved at her hands. Why waste any further emotion in regrets that we as useless as they are foolish?"

"You may as well ask me why I exist," Gilbert answered quietly. "Regret for all I have lost is a part of my life."

After this there was no more to be said, and Mr. Saltram went on to speak of pleasanter topics. The two men dined together, and sat by the fire afterwards with a bottle of claret between them, smoking their cigars, and talking till late into the night.

It was not to be supposed that Adela Branston's name could be omitted entirely from this confidential talk.

"I have seen nothing and heard very little of her while I have been away," John Saltram said, in answer to a question of Gilbert's; "but I called in Cavendish-square this afternoon, and was fortunate enough to find her at home. She wants me to dine with her next Sunday, and I half promised to do so. Will you come too? I know that she would be glad to see you."

"I cannot see that I am wanted, John."

"But I tell you that you are wanted. I wish you to go with me. Mrs. Branston likes you amazingly, if you care to know the opinion of so frivolous a person."

"I am very much flattered by Mrs. Branston's kindly estimate of me, but I do not think I have any claim to it, except the fact that I am your friend. I shall be happy to go with you on Sunday, if you really wish it."

"I do really wish it. I shall drop Mrs. Branston a line to say you will come. She asked me to bring you whenever I had an opportunity. The dinner-hour is seven. I'll call for you here a few minutes before. I don't promise you a very lively evening, remember. There will only be Adela, and a lady she has taken as her companion."

"I don't care about lively evenings. I have been nowhere in society since I returned from Melbourne. I have done with all that kind of thing."

"My dear Gilbert, that sort of renunciation will never do," John Saltram said earnestly. "A man cannot turn his back upon society at your age. Life lies all before you, and it rests with yourself to create a happy future. Let the dead bury their dead."

"Yes, John; and what is left for the living when that burial is over? I don't want to make myself obnoxious by whining over my troubles, but they are not to be lessened by philosophy, and I can do nothing but bear them as best I may. I had long been growing tired of society, in the conventional acceptation of the word, and all the stereotyped pleasures of a commercial man's life. Those things are less than nothing when a man has nothing brighter and fairer beyond them—no inner life by which the common things of this world are made precious. It is only dropping out of the arena a little earlier than I might have done otherwise. I have a notion that I shall wind up my affairs next year, sell my business, and go abroad. I could manage to retire upon a very decent income, in spite of my losses the other day."

"Don't dream of that, Gilbert; for heaven's sake, don't dream of anything so mad as that. What would a man of your age be without some kind of career? A mere purposeless wanderer on the face of the earth. Stick to business, dear old fellow. Believe me, there is nothing like work to make a man forget any foolish trouble of this kind. And you will forget it, Gilbert, be assured of that. If I were not certain it would be so, I should——"

He stopped suddenly, staring absently at the fire with a darkening brow.

"You would do what, John?"

"Hate this man Holbrook almost as savagely as you hate him, for having come between you and your happiness. Yet, if Marian Nowell did not love you—as a wife should love her husband, with all her heart and soul—it was ten thousand times better that the knot should be cut in time, however roughly. Think what your misery would have been if you had discovered after your marriage that her heart had never been really yours."

"I cannot imagine that possible. I have no shadow of doubt that I should have succeeded in winning her heart if this man had not robbed me of her. My absence gave him his opportunity. Had I been at hand to protect my own interests, I do not think his influence could have prevailed against me."

"It is quite natural that you should think that," John Saltram said gravely. "Yet you may be mistaken. A woman's love is such a capricious thing, and so often bestowed upon the least deserving amongst those who seek it."

After this they were silent for some time, and then Gilbert told his friend about his acquaintance with Jacob Nowell, and the old man's futile endeavours to find his grandchild; to all of which Mr. Saltram listened attentively.

"Then you fancy there is a good bit of money in question?" he said, when Gilbert told him everything.

"I fancy so. But I have no actual ground for the belief. The place in which the old man lives is poor enough, and he has carefully abstained from any hint as to what he might leave his granddaughter. Whatever it is, Marian ought to have it; and there is very little chance of that, unless she comes forward in response to Mr. Nowell's advertisements."

"It is a pity she should lose the chance of this inheritance, certainly," said Mr. Saltram.

And then the conversation changed, and they talked of other subjects until it was time for them to part.

John Saltram walked back to the Temple in a very sombre mood, meditating upon his friend's trouble.

"Poor old Gilbert," he said to himself, "this business has touched him more deeply than I could have thought possible. I wish things had happened otherwise. What is it Lady Macbeth says? 'Naught's had, all's spent, when our desire is got without content.' I wonder whether the fulfilment of one's heart's desire ever does bring perfect contentment? I think not. There is always something wanting. And if a man comes by his wish basely, there is a taint of poison in the wine of life that neutralizes all its sweetness."

CHAPTER XIII.
MRS. PALLINSON HAS VIEWS.

AT seven o'clock on Sunday evening, as the neighbouring church bells were just sounding their last peal, Mr. Fenton found himself on the threshold of Mrs. Branston's house in Cavendish-square. It was rather a gloomy mansion, pervaded throughout with evidences of its late owner's oriental career; old Indian cabinets; ponderous chairs of elaborately-carved ebony, clumsy in form and barbaric in design; curious old china and lacquered ware of every kind, from gigantic vases to the tiniest cups and saucers; ivory temples, and gods in silver and clay, crowded the drawing-rooms and the broad landings on the staircase. The curtains and chair-covers were of Indian embroidery; the carpets of oriental manufacture. Everything had a gaudy semi-barbarous aspect.

Mrs. Branston received her guests in the back drawing-room, a smaller and somewhat snugger apartment than the spacious chamber in front, which was dimly visible in the light of a single moderator lamp and the red glow of a fire through the wide-open archway between the two rooms. In the inner room the lamps were brighter, and the fire burned cheerily; and here Mrs. Branston had established for herself a comfortable nook in a deep velvet-cushioned arm-chair, very low and capacious, sheltered luxuriously from possible draughts by a high seven-leaved Japanese screen. The fair Adela was a chilly personage, and liked to bask in her easy-chair before the fire. She looked very pretty this evening, in her dense black dress, with the airiest pretence of a widow's cap perched on her rich auburn hair, and a voluminous Indian shawl of vivid scarlet making a drapery about her shoulders. She was evidently very pleased to see John Saltram, and gave a cordial welcome to his friend. On the opposite side of the fire-place there was a tall, rather grim-looking lady, also in mourning, and with an elaborate headdress of bugles and ornaments of a feathery and beady nature, which were supposed to be flowers. About her neck this lady wore numerous rows of jet beads, from which depended crosses and lockets of the same material: she had jet earrings and jet bracelets; and had altogether a beaded and bugled appearance, which would have been eminently fascinating to the untutored taste of a North American Indian.

This lady was Mrs. Pallinson, a widow of limited means, and a distant relation of Adela Branston's. Left quite alone after her husband's death, and feeling herself thoroughly helpless, Adela had summoned this experienced matron to her aid; whereupon Mrs. Pallinson had given up a small establishment in the far north of London, which she was in the habit of speaking about on occasions as her humble dwelling, and had taken up her quarters in Cavendish-square, where she was a power of dread to the servants.

Gilbert fancied that Mrs. Pallinson was by no means too favourably disposed towards John Saltram. She had sharp black eyes, very much like the jet beads with which her person was decorated, and with these she kept a close watch upon Mrs. Branston and Mr. Saltram when the two were talking together. Gilbert saw how great an effort it cost her at these times to keep up the commonplace conversation which he had commenced with her, and how intently she was trying to listen to the talk upon the other side of the fire-place.

The dinner was an admirable one, the wines perfection, Mr. Branston having been a past-master of the art of good living, and having stocked his cellars with a view to a much longer life than had been granted to him; the attendance was careful and complete; the dining-room, with its rather old-fashioned furniture and heavy crimson hangings, a picture of comfort; and Mrs. Branston a most charming hostess. Even Gilbert was fain to forget his own troubles and enjoy life a little in that agreeable society.

The two gentlemen accompanied the ladies back to the drawing-room. There was a grand piano in the front room, and to this Adela Branston went at Mr. Saltram's request, and began to play some of Handel's oratorio music, while he stood beside the piano, talking to her as she played. Mrs. Pallinson and Gilbert were thus left alone in the back room, and the lady did her best to improve the occasion by extorting what information she could from Mr. Fenton about his friend.

"Adela tells me that you and Mr. Saltram are friends of very long standing, Mr. Fenton," she began, fanning herself slowly with a shining black fan as she sat opposite Gilbert, awful of aspect in the sombre splendour of her beads and bugles.

"Yes; we were at Oxford together, and have been fast friends ever since."

"Indeed!—how really delightful! The young men of the present day appear to me generally so incapable of a sincere friendship. And you and Mr. Saltram have been friends all that time? He is a literary man, I understand. I have not had the pleasure of reading any of his works; but Adela tells me he is extremely clever."

"He is very clever."

"And steady, I hope. Literary men are so apt to be wild and dissipated; and Adela has such a high opinion of your friend. I hope he is steady."

"I scarcely know what a lady's notion of steadiness may involve," Gilbert answered, smiling; "but I daresay when my friend marries he will be steady enough. I cannot see that literary tastes and dissipated habits have any natural affinity. I should rather imagine that a man with resources of that kind would be likely to lead a quieter life than a man without such resources."

"Do you really think so? I fancied that artists and poets and people of that kind were altogether a dangerous class. And you think that Mr. Saltram will be steady when he is married? He is engaged to be married, I conclude by your manner of saying that."

"I had no idea my words implied anything of the kind. No, *I* do not think John Saltram is engaged."

Mrs. Pallinson glanced towards the piano, where the two figures seemed very close to each other in the dim light of the room. Adela's playing had been going on in a desultory kind of manner, broken every now and then by her conversation with John Saltram, and had evidently been intended to give pleasure only to that one listener.

While she was still playing in this careless fitful way, a servant announced Mr. Pallinson; and a gentleman entered whom Gilbert had no difficulty in recognizing as the son of the lady he had been conversing with. This new-comer was a tall pale-faced young man, with intensely penetrating black eyes exactly like his mother's, sharp well-cut features, and an extreme precision of dress and manner. His hands, which were small and thin, were remarkable for their whiteness, and were set-off by spotless wristbands, which it was his habit to smooth fondly with his slim fingers in the intervals of his discourse. Mrs. Pallinson rose and embraced this gentleman with stately affection.

"My son Theobald—Mr. Fenton," she said. "My son is a medical practitioner, residing at Maida-hill; and it is a pleasure to him to spend an occasional evening with his cousin Adela and myself."

"Whenever the exigencies of professional life leave me free to enjoy that happiness," Mr. Pallinson added in a brisk semi-professional manner. "Adela has been giving you some music, I see. I heard one of Handel's choruses as I came upstairs."

He went into the front drawing-room, shook hands with Mrs. Branston, and established himself with a permanent air beside the piano. Adela did not seem particularly glad to see him; and John Saltram, who had met him before in Cavendish-square, received him with supreme indifference.

"I am blessed, as I daresay you perceive, Mr. Fenton, in my only son," Mrs. Pallinson said, when the young man had withdrawn to the adjoining apartment. "It was my misfortune to lose an admirable husband very early in life; and I have been ever since that loss wholly devoted to my son Theobald. My care has been amply rewarded by his goodness. He is a most estimable and talented young man, and has already attained an excellent position in the medical profession."

"You have reason to be proud of him," Gilbert answered kindly.

"I *am* proud of him, Mr. Fenton. He is the sole delight and chief object of my life. His career up to this hour has been all that the fondest mother could desire. If I can only see him happily and advantageously married, I shall have nothing left to wish for."

"Indeed!" thought Gilbert. "Then I begin to perceive the reason of Mrs. Pallinson's anxiety about John Saltram. She wants to secure Mrs. Branston's handsome fortune for this son of hers. Not much chance of that, I think, fascinating as the doctor may be. Plain John Saltram stands to win that prize."

They went into the front drawing-room presently, and heard Mr. Pallinson play the "Hallelujah Chorus," arranged as a duet, with his cousin. He was a young man who possessed several accomplishments in a small way—could sing a little, and play the piano and guitar a little, sketch a little, and was guilty of occasional effusions in the poetical line which were the palest, most invertebrate reflections of Owen Meredith. In the Maida-hill and St. John's-wood districts he was accounted an acquisition for an evening party; and his dulcet accents and engaging manners had rendered him a favourite with the young mothers of the neighbourhood, who believed implicitly in Mr. Pallinson's gray powders when their little ones' digestive organs had been impaired by injudicious diet, and confided in Mr. Pallinson's carefully-expressed opinion as the fiat of an inscrutable power.

Mr. Theobald Pallinson himself cherished a very agreeable opinion of his own merits. Life seemed to him made on purpose that Theobald Pallinson should flourish and succeed therein. He could hardly have formed any idea of the world except as an arena for himself. He was not especially given to metaphysics; but it would not have been very difficult for him to believe that the entire universe was an emanation from the brain of Theobald Pallinson—a phenomenal world existing only in his sense of sight and touch. Happy in this opinion of himself, it is not to be supposed that the surgeon had any serious doubt of ultimate success with his cousin. He regarded John Saltram as an interloper, who had gained ground in Mrs. Branston's favour only by the accident of his own absence from the stage. The Pallinsons had not been on visiting terms with Adela during the life of the East Indian merchant, who had not shown himself favourably disposed to his wife's relations; and by this means Mr. Saltram had enjoyed advantages which Theobald Pallinson told himself could not have been his, had he, Theobald, been at hand to engage his cousin's attention by those superior qualities of mind and person which must needs have utterly outshone the other. All that Mr. Pallinson wanted was opportunity; and that being now afforded him, he looked upon the happy issue of events as a certainty, and already contemplated the house in Cavendish-square, the Indian jars and cabinets, the ivory chessmen and filigree-silver rosewater-bottles, the inlaid desks and Japanese screens, the ponderous plate and rare old wines, with a sense of prospective proprietorship.

It seemed as if John Saltram had favoured this gentleman's views by his prolonged absence from the scene, holding himself completely aloof from Adela Branston at a time when, had he been inclined to press his suit, he might have followed her up closely. Mrs. Branston had been not a little wounded by this apparent neglect on the part of one whom she loved better than anything else in the world; but she was inclined to believe any thing rather than that John Saltram did not care for her; and she had contrived to console herself with the idea that his avoidance of her had been prompted by a delicate consideration for her reputation, and a respect for the early period of her mourning. To-night, in his society, she had an air of happiness which became her wonderfully; and Gilbert Fenton fancied that a man must needs be hard and cold whose heart could not be won by so bright and gracious a creature.

She spoke more than once, in a half-playful way, of Mr. Saltram's absence from London; but the deeper feeling underneath the lightness of her manner was very evident to Gilbert.

"I suppose you will be running away from town again directly," she said, "without giving any one the faintest notice of your intention. I can't think what charm it is that you find in country life. I have so often heard you profess your indifference to shooting, and the ordinary routine of rustic existence. Perhaps the secret is, that you fear your reputation as a man of fashion would suffer were you to be seen in London at such a barbarous season as this."

"I have never rejoiced in a reputation for fashion," Mr. Saltram answered, with his quiet smile—a smile that gave a wonderful brightness to his face; "and I think I like London in the autumn better than at any other time. One has room to move about. I have been in the country of late because I really do appreciate rural surroundings, and have found myself able to write better in the perfect quiet of rural life."

"It is rather hard upon your friends that you should devote all your days to literature."

"And still harder upon the reading public, perhaps. But, my dear Mrs. Branston, remember, I must write to live."

Adela gave a little impatient sigh. She was thinking how gladly she would have made this man master of her ample fortune; wondering whether he would ever claim from her the allegiance she was so ready to give.

Mr. Pallinson did his best to engage his cousin's attention during the rest of the evening. He brought her her tea-cup, and hovered about her while she sipped the beverage with that graceful air of suppressed tenderness which constant practice in the drawing-rooms of Maida-hill had rendered almost natural to him; but, do what he would, he could not distract Mrs. Branston's thoughts and looks from John Saltram. It was on him that her eyes were fixed while the accomplished Theobald was giving her a lively account of a concert at the Eyre Arms; and it was the fascination of his presence which made her answer at random to her cousin's questions about the last volume of the Laureate's, which she had been lately reading. Even Mr. Pallinson, obtuse as he was apt to be when called upon to comprehend any fact derogatory to his own self-esteem, was fain to confess to himself that this evening's efforts were futile, and that this dark-faced stranger was the favourite for those matrimonial stakes he had entered himself to run for. He looked at Mr. Saltram with a critical eye many times in the course of the evening, wondering what possible merit any sensible woman could perceive in such a man. But then, as Theobald Pallinson reflected, the misfortune is that so few women are sensible; and it was gradually becoming evident to him that Michael Branston's widow was amongst the most foolish of her sex.

Mrs. Pallinson kept a sharp watch upon Adela throughout the evening, plunging into the conversation every now and then with a somewhat dictatorial and infallible air, and generally contriving to drag some praise of Theobald into her talk: now dilating rapturously upon that fever case which he had managed so wonderfully the other day, proving his judgment superior to that of an eminent consulting physician; anon launching out into laudation of his last poem, which had been set to music by a young lady in St. John's-wood; and by-and-by informing the company of her son's artistic talents, and his extraordinary capacity as a judge of pictures. To these things the surgeon himself listened with a deprecating air, smoothing his wristbands, and caressing his slim white hands, while he playfully reproved his parent for her maternal weakness.

Mr. Pallinson held his ground near his cousin's chair till the last moment, while John Saltram sat apart by one of the tables, listlessly turning over a volume of engravings, and only looking up at long intervals to join in the conversation. He had an absent weary look, which puzzled Gilbert Fenton, who, being only a secondary personage in this narrow circle, had ample leisure to observe his friend.

The three gentlemen left at the same time, Mr. Pallinson driving away in a neat miniature brougham, after politely offering to convey his cousin's guests to their destination. It was a bright starlight night, and Gilbert walked to the Temple with John Saltram, through the quietest of the streets leading east-wards. They lit their cigars as they left the square, and walked for some time in a friendly companionable silence. When they did speak, their talk was naturally of Adela Branston.

"I thought she was really charming to-night," Gilbert said, "in spite of that fellow's efforts to absorb her attention. It is pretty easy to see how the land lies in that direction; and it such a rival were likely to injure you, you have a very determined one in Mr. Pallinson."

"Yes; the surgeon has evidently fixed his hopes upon poor old Michael Branston's money. But I don't think he will succeed."

"You will not allow him to do so, I hope?"

"I don't know about that. Then you really admire the little woman, Gilbert?"

"Very much; as much as I have ever admired any woman except Marian Nowell."

"Ah, your Marian is a star, single and alone in her brightness, like that planet up yonder! But Adela Branston is a good little soul, and will make a charming wife. Gilbert, I wish to heaven you would fall in love with her!"

Gilbert Fenton stared aghast at his companion, as he tossed the end of his cigar into the gutter.

"Why, John, you must be mad to say such a thing."

"No, it is by no means a mad notion. I want to see you cured, Gilbert. I do like you, dear boy, you know, as much as it is possible for a selfish worthless fellow like me to like any man. I would give a great deal to see you happy; and I am sure that you might be so as Adela Branston's husband. I grant you that I am the favourite at present; but she is just the sort of woman to be won by any man who would really prove himself worthy of her. Her liking for me is a mere idle fancy, which would soon die out for want of fuel. You are my superior in every way—younger, handsomer, better. Why should you not go in for this thing, Gil?"

"Because I have no heart to give any woman, John. And even if I were free, I would not give my heart to a woman whose affection had to be diverted from another channel before it could be bestowed upon me. I can't imagine what has put such a preposterous idea into your head, or why it is that you shrink from improving your own chances with Mrs. Branston."

"You must not wonder at anything that I do or say, Gilbert. It is my nature to do strange things—my destiny to take the wrong turning in life!"

"When shall I see you again?" Gilbert asked, when they were parting at the Temple gates.

"I can scarcely tell you that. I must go back to Oxford to-morrow."

"So soon?"

"Yes, my work gets on better down there. I will let you know directly I return to London."

On this they parted, Gilbert considerably mystified by his friend's conduct, but not caring to push his questions farther. He had his own affairs to think of, that one business which absorbed almost the whole of his thoughts—the business of his search for the man who had robbed him of his promised wife, this interval, in which he remained inactive, devoting himself to the duties of his commercial life, was only a pause in his labours. He was not the less bent upon bringing about a face-to-face meeting between himself and Marian's husband because of this brief suspension of his efforts.

CHAPTER XIV.
FATHER AND SON.

WHILE Gilbert Fenton was deliberating what steps to take next in his quest of his unknown enemy, a gentleman arrived at a small hotel near Charing Cross—a gentleman who was evidently a stranger to England, and whose portmanteaus and other travelling paraphernalia bore the names of New York manufacturers. He was a portly individual of middle age, and was still eminently handsome. He dressed well, lived expensively, and had altogether a prosperous appearance. He took care to inform the landlord of the hotel that he was not an American, but had returned to the land of his birth after an absence of something like fifteen years, and after realizing a handsome fortune upon the other side of the Atlantic. He was a very gracious and communicative person, and seemed to take life in an easy agreeable manner, like a man whose habit it was to look on the brighter side of all things, provided his own comfort was secured. Norton Percival was the name on this gentleman's luggage, and on the card which he gave to the waiter whom he desired to look after his letters. After dining sumptuously on the evening of his arrival in London, this Mr. Percival strolled out in the autumn darkness, and made his way through the more obscure streets between Charing Cross and Wardour-street. The way seemed familiar enough to him, and he only paused now and then to take note of some alteration in the buildings which he had to pass. The last twenty years have not made much change in this neighbourhood, and the traveller from New York found little to surprise him.

"The place looks just as dull and dingy as it used to look when I was a lad," he said to himself. "I daresay I shall find the old court unchanged in all these years. But shall I find the old man alive? I doubt that. Dead more likely, and his money gone to strangers. I wonder whether he had much money, or whether he was really as poor as he made himself out. It's difficult to say. I know I made him bleed pretty freely, at one time and another, before he turned rusty; and it's just possible I may have had pretty nearly all he had to give."

He was in Wardour-street by this time, looking at the dimly-lighted shops where brokers' ware of more or less value, old oak carvings, doubtful pictures, and rusted armour loomed duskily upon the passer-by. At the corner of Queen Anne's Court he paused, and peered curiously into the narrow alley.

"The court is still here, at any rate," he muttered to himself, "and I shall soon settle the other question."

His heart beat faster than it was wont to beat as he drew near his destination. Was it any touch of real feeling, or only selfish apprehension, that quickened its throbbing? The man's life had been so utterly reckless of others, that it would be dangerous to give him credit for any affectionate yearning—any natural remorseful pang in such a moment as this. He had lived for self, and self alone; and his own interests were involved in the issue of to-night.

A few steps brought him before Jacob Nowell's window. Yes, it was just as he remembered it twenty years before—the same dingy old silver, the same little heap of gold, the same tray of tarnished jewelry glimmered in the faint light of a solitary gas-burner behind the murky glass. On the door-plate there was still Jacob Nowell's name. Yet all this might mean nothing. The grave might have closed over the old silversmith, and the interest of trade necessitate the preservation of the familiar name.

The gentleman calling himself Percival went into the shop. How well he remembered the sharp jangling sound of the bell! and how intensely he had hated it and all the surroundings of his father's sordid life in the days when he was pursuing his headlong career as a fine gentleman, and only coming to Queen Anne's Court for money! He remembered what an incubus the shop had been upon him; what a pursuing phantom and perpetual image of his degradation in the days of his University life, when he was incessantly haunted by the dread that his father's social status would be discovered. The atmosphere of the place brought back all the old feelings, and he was young again, a nervous supplicant for money, which was likely to be refused to him.

The sharp peal of the bell produced Mr. Luke Tulliver, who emerged from a little den in a corner at the back of the shop, where he had been engaged copying items into a stock-book by the light of a solitary tallow-candle. The stranger looked like a customer, and Mr. Tulliver received him graciously, turning up the gas over the counter, which had been burning at a diminished and economical rate hitherto.

"Did you wish to look at anything in antique silver, sir?" he asked briskly. "We have some very handsome specimens of the Queen Anne period."

"No, I don't want to look at anything. I want to know whether Jacob Nowell is still living?"

"Yes, sir. Mr. Nowell is my master. You might, have noticed his name upon the door-plate if you had looked! Do you wish to see him?"

"I do. Tell him that I am an old friend, just come from America."

Luke Tulliver went into the parlour behind the half-glass door, Norton Percival following upon him closely. He heard the old man's voice saying,

"I have no friend in America; but you may tell the person to come in; I will see him."

The voice trembled a little; and the silversmith had raised himself from his chair, and was looking eagerly towards the door as Norton Percival entered, not caring to wait for any more formal invitation. The two men faced each other silently in the dim light from one candle on the mantelpiece, Jacob Nowell looking intently at the bearded face of his visitor.

"You can go, Tulliver," he said sharply to the shopman. "I wish to be alone with this gentleman."

Luke Tulliver departed with his usual reluctant air, closing the door as slowly as it was possible for him to close it, and staring at the stranger till the last moment that it was possible for him to stare.

When he was gone the old man took the candle from the mantelpiece, and held it up before the bearded face of the traveller.

"Yes, yes, yes," he said slowly; "at last! It is you, Percival, my only son. I thought you were dead long ago. I had a right to consider you dead."

"If I had thought my existence could be a matter of interest to you, I should hardly have so long refrained from all communication with you. But your letters led me to suppose you utterly indifferent to my fate."

"I offered you and your wife a home."

"Yes, but on conditions that were impossible to me. I had some pride in those days. My education had not fitted me to stand behind a counter and drive hard bargains with dealers of doubtful honesty. Nor could I bring my wife to such a home as this."

"The time came when you left that poor creature without any home," said the old man sternly.

"Necessity has no law, my dear father. You may imagine that my life, without a profession and without any reliable resources, has been rather precarious. When I seemed to have acted worst, I have been only the slave of circumstances."

"Indeed! and have you no pity for the fate of your wife, no interest in the life of your only child?"

"My wife was a poor helpless creature, who contrived to make my life wretched," Mr. Nowell, alias Percival, answered coolly. "I gave her every sixpence I possessed when I sent her home to England; but luck went dead against me for a long time after that, and I could neither send her money nor go to her. When I heard of her death, I heard in an indirect way that my child had been adopted by some old fool of a half-pay officer; and I was naturally glad of an accident which relieved me of a heavy incubus. An opportunity occurred about the same time of my entering on a tolerably remunerative career as agent for some Belgian ironworks in America; and I had no option but to close with the offer at once or lose the chance altogether. I sailed for New York within a fortnight after poor Lucy's death, and have lived in America for the last fifteen years. I have contrived to establish a tolerably flourishing trade there on my own account; a trade that only needs capital to become one of the first in New York."

"Capital!" echoed Jacob Nowell; "I thought there was something wanted. It would have been a foolish fancy to suppose that affection could have had anything to do with your coming to me."

"My dear father, it is surely possible that affection and interest may sometimes go together. Were I a pauper, I would not venture to present myself before you at all; but as a tolerably prosperous trader, with the ability to propose an alliance that should be to our mutual advantage, I considered I might fairly approach you."

"I have no money to invest in your trade," the old man answered sternly. "I am a very poor man, impoverished for life by the wicked extravagance of your youth. If you have come to me with any hope of obtaining money from me, you have wasted time and trouble."

"Let that subject drop, then," Percival Nowell said lightly. "I suppose you have some remnant of regard for me, in spite of our old misunderstanding, and that my coming is not quite indifferent to you."

"No," the other answered, with a touch of melancholy; "it is not indifferent to me. I have waited for your return these many years. You might have found me more tenderly disposed towards you, had you come earlier; but there are some feelings which seem to wear out as a man grows older,—affections that grow paler day by day, like colours fading in the sun. Still, I am glad to see you once more before I die. You are my only son, and you must needs be something nearer to me than the rest of the world, in spite of all that I have suffered at your hands."

"I could not come back to England sooner than this," the young man said presently. "I had a hard battle to fight out yonder."

There had been very little appearance of emotion upon either side so far. Percival Nowell took things as coolly as it was his habit to take everything, while his father carefully concealed whatever deeper feeling might be stirred in the depths of his heart by this unexpected return.

"You do not ask any questions about the fate of your only child," the old man said, by-and-by.

"My dear father, that is of course a subject of lively interest to me; but I did not suppose that you could be in a position to give me any information upon that point."

"I do happen to know something about your daughter, but not much."

Jacob Nowell went on to tell his son all that he had heard from Gilbert Fenton respecting Marian's marriage. Of his own advertisements, and wasted endeavours to find her, he said nothing.

"And this fellow whom she has jilted is pretty well off, I suppose?" Percival said thoughtfully.

"He is an Australian merchant, and, I should imagine, in prosperous circumstances."

"Foolish girl! And this Holbrook is no doubt an adventurer, or he would scarcely have married her in such a secret way. Have you any wish that she should be found?"

"Yes, I have a fancy for seeing her before I die. She is my own flesh and blood, like you, and has not injured me as you have. I should like to see her."

"And if she happened to take your fancy, you would leave her all your money, I suppose?"

"Who told you that I have money to leave?" cried the old man sharply. "Have I not said that I am a poor man, hopelessly impoverished by your extravagance?"

"Bah, my dear father, that is all nonsense. My extravagance is a question of nearly twenty years ago. If I had swamped all you possessed in those days—which I don't for a moment believe—you have had ample time to make a fresh fortune since then. You would never have lived all those years in Queen Anne's Court, except for the sake of money-making. Why, the place stinks of money. I know your tricks: buying silver from men who are in too great a hurry to sell it to be particular about the price; lending money at sixty per cent, a sixty which comes to eighty before the transaction is finished. A man does not lead such a life as yours for nothing. You are rolling in money, and you mean to punish me by leaving it all to Marian."

The silversmith grew pale with anger during this speech of his son's.

"You are a consummate scoundrel," he said, "and are at liberty to think what you please. I tell you, once for all, I am as poor as Job. But if I had a million, I would not give you a sixpence of it."

"So be it," the other answered gaily. "I have not performed the duties of a parent very punctually hitherto; but I don't mind taking some trouble to find this girl while I am in England, in order that she may not lose her chances with you."

"You need give yourself no trouble on that score. Mr. Fenton has promised to find her for me."

"Indeed! I should like to see this Mr. Fenton."

"You can see him if you please; but you are scarcely likely to get a warm reception in that quarter. Mr. Fenton knows what you have been to your daughter and to me."

"I am not going to fling myself into his arms. I only want to hear all he can tell me about Marian."

"How long do you mean to stay in England?"

"That is entirely dependent upon the result of my visit. I had hoped that if I found you living, which I most earnestly desired might be the case, I should find in you a friend and coadjutor. I am employed in starting a great iron company, which is likely—I may say certain—to result in large gains to all concerned in it; and I fancied I should experience no difficulty in securing your co-operation. There are the prospectuses of the scheme" (he flung a heap of printed papers on the table before his father), "and there is not a line in them that I cannot guarantee on my credit as a man of business. You can look over them at your leisure, or not, as you please. I think you must know that I always had an independent spirit, and would be the last of mankind to degrade myself by any servile attempt to alter your line of conduct towards me."

"Independent spirit! Yes!" cried the old man in a mocking tone; "a son extorts every sixpence he can from his father and mother—ay, Percy, from his weak loving mother; I know who robbed me to send you money—and then, when he can extort no more, boasts of his independence. But that will do. There is no need that we should quarrel. After twenty years' severance, we can afford to let bygones be bygones. I have told you that I am glad to see you. If you come to me with disinterested feelings, that is enough. You may take back your prospectuses. I have nothing to embark in Yankee speculations. If your scheme is a good one, you will find plenty of enterprising spirits willing to join you; if it is a bad one, I daresay you will contrive to find dupes. You can come and see me again when you please. And now good-night. I find this kind of talk rather tiring at my age."

"One word before I leave you," said Percival. "On reflection, I think it will be as well to say nothing about my presence in England to this Mr. Fenton. I shall be more free to hunt for Marian without his co-operation, even supposing he were inclined to give it. You have told me all that he could tell me, I daresay."

"I believe I have."

"Precisely. Therefore no possible good could come of an encounter between him and me, and I shall be glad if you will keep my name dark."

"As you please, though I can see no reason for secrecy in the matter."

"It is not a question of secrecy, but only of prudential reserve."

"It may be as you wish," answered the old man, carelessly. "Good-night."

He shook hands with his son, who departed without having broken bread in his father's house, a little dashed by the coldness of his reception, but not entirely without hope that some profit might arise to him out of this connection in the future.

"The girl must be found," he said to himself. "I am convinced there has been a great fortune made in that dingy hole. Better that it should go to her than to a stranger. I'm very sorry she's married; but if this Holbrook is the adventurer I suppose him, the marriage may come to nothing. Yes; I must find her. A father returned from foreign lands is rather a romantic notion—the sort of notion a girl is pretty sure to take kindly to."

CHAPTER XV.
ON THE TRACK.

GILBERT Fenton saw no more of his friend John Saltram after that Sunday evening which they had spent together in Cavendish-square. He called upon Mrs. Branston before the week was ended, and was so fortunate as to find that lady alone; Mrs. Pallinson having gone on a shopping expedition in her kinswoman's dashing brougham.

The pretty little widow received Gilbert very graciously; but there was a slight shade of melancholy in her manner, a pensiveness which softened and refined her, Gilbert thought. Nor was it long before she allowed him to discover the cause of her sadness. After a little conventional talk upon indifferent subjects, she began to speak of John Saltram.

"Have you seen much of your friend Mr. Saltram since Sunday?" she asked, with that vain endeavour to speak carelessly with which a woman generally betrays her real feeling.

"I have not seen him at all since Sunday. He told me he was going back to Oxford—or the neighbourhood of Oxford, I believe—almost immediately; and I have not troubled myself to hunt him up at his chambers."

"Gone back already!" Mrs. Branston exclaimed, with a disappointed petulant look that was half-childish, half-womanly. "I cannot imagine what charm he finds in a dull village on the banks of the river. He has confessed that the place is the dreariest and most obscure in the world, and that he has neither shooting nor any other kind of amusement. There must be some mysterious attraction, Mr. Fenton. I think your friend is a good deal changed of late. Haven't you found him so?"

"No, Mrs. Branston, I cannot say that I have discovered any marked alteration in him since my return from Australia. John Saltram was always wayward and fitful. He may have been a little more so lately, perhaps, but that is all."

"You have a very high opinion of him, I suppose?"

"He is very dear to me. We were something more than friends in the ordinary acceptation of the word. Do you remember the story of those two noble young Venetians who inscribed upon their shield *Fraires, non amici?* Saltram and I have been brothers rather than friends."

"And you think him a good man?" Adela asked anxiously.

"Most decidedly; I have reason to think so. I believe him to be a noble-hearted and honourable man; a little neglectful or disdainful of conventionalities, wearing his faith in God and his more sacred feelings anywhere than upon his sleeve; but a man who cannot fail to come right in the long-run."

"I am so glad to hear you say that. I have known Mr. Saltram some time, as you may have heard and like him very much. But my cousin Mrs. Pallinson has quite an aversion to him, and speaks against him with such a positive air at times, that I have been almost inclined to think she must be right. I am very inexperienced in the ways of the world, and am naturally disposed to lean a little upon the opinions of others."

"But don't you think there may be a reason for Mrs. Pallinson's dislike of my friend?"

Adela Branston blushed at this question, and then laughed a little.

"I think I know what you mean," she said. "Yes, it is just possible that Mrs. Pallinson may be jealously disposed towards any acquaintance of mine, on account of that paragon of perfection, her son Theobald. I have not been so blind as not to see her views in that quarter. But be assured, Mr. Fenton, that whatever may happen to me, I shall never become Mrs. Theobald Pallinson."

"I hope not. I am quite ready to acknowledge Mr. Pallinson's merits and accomplishments, but I do not think him worthy of you."

"It is rather awful, isn't it, for me to speak of marriage at all within a few months of my husband's death? But when a woman has money, people will not allow her to forget that she is a widow for ever so short a time. But it is quite a question if I shall ever marry again. I have very little doubt that real happiness is most likely to be found in a wise avoidance of all the perils and perplexities of that foolish passion which we read of in novels, if one could only be wise; don't you think so, Mr. Fenton?"

"My own experience inclines me to agree with you, Mrs. Branston," Gilbert answered, smiling at the little woman's naïveté.

"Your own experience has been unfortunate, then? I wish I were worthy of your confidence. Mr. Saltram told me some time ago that you were engaged to a very charming young lady."

"The young lady in question has jilted me."

"Indeed! And you are very angry with her, of course?"

"I loved her too well to be angry with her. I reserve my indignation for the scoundrel who stole her from me."

"It is very generous of you to make excuses for the lady," Mrs. Branston said; and would fain have talked longer of this subject, but Gilbert concluded his visit at this juncture, not caring to discuss his troubles with the sympathetic widow.

He left the great gloomy gorgeous house in Cavendish square more than ever convinced of Adela Branston's affection for his friend, more than ever puzzled by John Saltram's indifference to so advantageous an alliance.

Within a few days of this visit Gilbert Fenton left London. He had devoted himself unflinchingly to his business since his return to England, and had so planned and organized his affairs as to be able now to absent himself for some little time from the City. He was going upon what most men would have called a fool's errand—his quest of Marian's husband; but he was going with a steady purpose in his breast—a determination never to abandon the search till it should result in success. He might have to suspend it from time to time, should he determine to continue his commercial career; but the purpose would be nevertheless the ruling influence of his life.

He had but one clue for his guidance in setting out upon this voyage of discovery. Miss Long had told him that the newly-married couple were to go to some farm-house in Hampshire which had been lent to Mr. Holbrook by a friend. It was in Hampshire, therefore, that Gilbert resolved to make his first inquiries. He told himself that success was merely a question of time and patience. The business of tracing these people, who were not to be found by any public inquiry, would be slow and wearisome no doubt. He was prepared for that. He was prepared for a thousand failures and disappointments before he alighted on the one place in which Mr. Holbrook's name must needs be known, the town or village nearest to the farm-house that had been lent to him. And even if, after unheard-of trouble and perseverance on his part, he should find the place he wanted, it was quite possible that Marian and her husband would have gone elsewhere, and his quest would have to begin afresh. But he fancied that he could hardly fail to obtain some information as to their plan of life, if he could find the place where they had stayed after their marriage.

His own scheme of action was simple enough. He had only to travel from place to place, making careful inquiries at post-offices and in all likely quarters at every stage of his journey. He went straight to Winchester, having a fancy for the quiet old city and the fair pastoral scenery surrounding it, and thinking that Mr. Holbrook's borrowed retreat might possibly be in this neighbourhood. The business proved even slower and more tedious than he had supposed; there were so many farms round about Winchester, so many places which seemed likely enough, and to which he went, only to find that no person of the name of Holbrook had ever been heard of by the inhabitants.

He made his head-quarters in the cathedral city for nearly a week, and explored the country round, in a radius of thirty miles, without the faintest success. It was fine autumn weather, calm and clear, the foliage still upon the trees, in all its glory of gold and brown, with patches of green lingering here and there in sheltered places. The country was very beautiful, and Gilbert Fenton's work would have been pleasant enough if the elements of peace had been in his breast. But they were not. Bitter regrets for all he had lost, uneasy fears and wild imaginings about the fate of her whom he still loved with a fond useless passion,—these and other gloomy thoughts haunted him day by flay, clouding the calm loveliness of the scenes on which he looked, until all outer things seemed to take their colour from his own mind. He had loved Marian Nowell as it is not given to many men to love; and with the loss of her, it seemed to him as if the very springs of his life were broken. All the machinery of his existence was loosened and out of gear, and he could scarcely have borne the dreary burden of his days, had it not been for that one feverish hope of finding the man who had wronged him.

The week ended without bringing him in the smallest degree nearer the chance of success. Happily for himself, he had not expected to succeed in a week. On leaving Winchester, he started on a kind of vagabond tour through the county, on a horse which he hired in the cathedral city, and which carried him from twenty to thirty miles a day. This mode of travelling enabled him to explore obscure villages and out-of-the-way places that lay off the line of railway. Everywhere he made the same inquiries, everywhere with the same result.

Another week came to an end. He had made his voyage of discovery through more than half of the county, as his pocket-map told him, and was still no nearer success than when he left London.

He spent his Sunday at a comfortable inn in a quiet little town, where there was a curious old church, and a fine peal of bells that seemed to him to be ringing all day long. It was a dull rainy day. He went to church in the morning, and in the afternoon stood at the coffee-room window watching the townspeople going by to their devotions in an absent unseeing way, and thinking of his own troubles; pausing, just a little, now and then, from that egotistical brooding to wonder how these people endured the dull monotonous round of their lives, and what crosses and disappointments they had to suffer in their small obscure way.

The inn was very empty, and the landlord waited upon Mr. Fenton in person at his dinner. Gilbert had the coffee-room all to himself, and it looked comfortable enough when the curtains were drawn, the lamps lighted, and the small dinner-table wheeled in front of a blazing fire.

"I have been thinking over what you were asking me last night, sir," the host of the White Swan began, while Gilbert was eating his fish; "and though I can't say that I ever heard the name of Holbrook, I fancy I may have seen the lady and gentleman you are looking for."

"Indeed!" exclaimed Gilbert eagerly, pushing away his plate, and turning full on the landlord.

"I hope you won't let me spoil your dinner, sir; I know that sole's fresh. I'm a pretty good judge of those things, and choose every bit of fish that's cooked in this house. But as I was saying, sir, with regard to this lady and gentleman, I think you said that the people you are looking for were strangers to this part of the country, and were occupying a farm-house that had been lent to them."

"Precisely."

"Well, sir, I remember some time in the early part of the year, I think it must have been about March———"

"Yes, the people I am looking for would have arrived in March."

"Indeed, sir! That makes it seem likely. I remember a lady and gentleman coming here from the railway station—we've got a station close by our town, as you know, sir, I daresay. They wanted a fly to take them and their luggage on somewhere—I can't for the life of me remember the name of the place—but it was a ten-mile drive, and it was a farm—*that* I could swear to—Something Farm. If it had been a place I'd known, I think I should have remembered the name."

"Can I see the man who drove them?" Gilbert asked quickly.

"The young man that drove them, sir, has left me, and has left these parts a month come next Tuesday. Where he has gone is more than I can tell you. He was very good with horses; but he turned out badly, cheated me up hill and down dale, as you may say—though what hills and dales have got to do with it is more than I can tell—and I was obliged to get rid of him."

"That's provoking. But if the people I want are anywhere within ten miles of this place, I don't suppose I should be long finding them. Yet the mere fact of two strangers coming here, and going on to some place called a farm, seems very slight ground to go upon. The month certainly corresponds with the time at which Mr. and Mrs. Holbrook came to Hampshire. Did you take any particular notice of them?"

"I took particular notice of the lady. She was as pretty a woman as ever I set eyes upon—quite a girl. I noticed that the gentleman was very careful and tender with her when he put her into the carriage, wrapping her up, and so on. He looked a good deal older than her, and I didn't much like his looks altogether."

"Could you describe him?"

"Well—no, sir. The time was short, and he was wrapped up a good deal; the collar of his overcoat turned up, and a scarf round his neck. He had dark eyes, I remember, and rather a stern look in them."

This was rather too vague a description to make any impression upon Gilbert. It was something certainly to know that his rival had dark eyes, if indeed this man of whom the landlord spoke really were his rival. He had never been able to make any mental picture of the stranger who had come between him and his betrothed. He had been inclined to fancy that the man must needs be much handsomer than himself, possessed of every outward attribute calculated to subjugate the mind of an inexperienced girl like Marian; but the parish-clerk at Wygrove and Miss Long had both spoken in a disparaging tone of Mr. Holbrook's personal appearance; and, remembering this, he was fain to believe that Marian had been won by some charm more subtle than that of a handsome face.

He went on eating his dinner in silence for some little time, meditating upon what the landlord had told him. Then, as the man cleared the table, lingering over his work, as if eager to impart any stray scraps of information he might possess, Gilbert spoke to him again.

"I should have fancied that, as a settled inhabitant of the place, you would be likely to know every farm and farm-house within ten miles—or within twenty miles," he said.

"Well, sir, I daresay I do know the neighbourhood pretty well, in a general way. But I think, if I'd known the name of the place this lady and gentleman were going to, it would have struck me more than it did, and I should have remembered it. I was uncommonly busy through that afternoon, for it was market-day, and there were a mort of people going in and out. I never did interfere much with the fly business; it was only by taking the gentleman out some soda-and-brandy that I came to take the notice I did of the lady's looks and his care of her. I know it was a ten-mile drive, and that I told the gentleman the fare, so as there might be no bother between him and William Tyler, my man, at the end; and he agreed to it in a liberal off-hand kind of way, like a man who doesn't care much for money. As to farms within ten miles of here, there are a dozen at least, one way and another—some small, and some large."

"Do you know of any place in the ownership of a gentleman who would be likely to lend his house to a friend?"

"I can't say I do, sir. They're tenant-farmers about here mostly, and rather a roughish lot, as you may say. There's a place over beyond Crosber, ten miles off and more; I don't know the name of it, or the person it belongs to; but I've noticed it many a time as I've driven by; a curious old-fashioned house, standing back off one of the lanes out of Crosber, with a large garden before it. A queer lonesome place altogether. I should take it to be two or three hundred years old; and I shouldn't think the house had had money spent upon it within the memory of man. It's a dilapidated tumbledown old gazabo of a place, and yet there's a kind of prettiness about it in summer-time, when the garden is full of flowers. There's a river runs through some of the land about half a mile from the house."

"What kind of a place is Crosber?"

"A bit of a village on the road from here to Portsmouth. The house I'm telling you about is a mile from Crosber at the least, away from the main road. There's two or three lanes or by-roads about there, and it lies in one of them that turns sharp off by the Blue Boar, which is about the only inn where you can bait a horse thereabouts."

"I'll ride over there to-morrow morning, and have a look at this queer old house. You might give me the names of any other farms you know about this neighbourhood, and their occupants."

This the landlord was very ready to do. He ran over the names of from ten to fifteen places, which Gilbert jotted down upon a leaf of his pocket-book, afterwards planning his route upon the map of the county which he carried for his guidance. He set put early the next morning under a low gray sky, with clouds in the distance that threatened rain. The road from the little market-town to Crosber possessed no especial beauty. The country was flat and uninteresting about here, and needed the glory of its summer verdure to brighten and embellish it. But Mr. Fenton did not give much thought to the scenes through which he went at this time; the world around and about him was all of one colour—the sunless gray which pervaded his own life. To-day the low dull sky and the threatening clouds far away upon the level horizon harmonised well with his own thoughts—with the utter hopelessness of his mind. Hopelessness!—yes, that was the word. He had hazarded all upon this one chance, and its failure was the shipwreck of his life. The ruin was complete. He could not build up a new scheme of happiness. In the full maturity of his manhood, his fate had come to him. He was not the kind of man who can survive the ruin of his plans, and begin afresh with other hopes and still fairer dreams. It was his nature to be constant. In all his life he had chosen for himself only one friend—in all his life he had loved but one woman.

He came to the little village, with its low sloping-roofed cottages, whose upper stories abutted upon the road and overshadowed the casements below; and where here and there a few pennyworths of gingerbread, that seemed mouldy with the mould of ages, a glass pickle-bottle of bull's-eyes or sugar-sticks, and half a dozen penny bottles of ink, indicated the commercial tendencies of Crosber. A little farther on, he came to a rickety-looking corner-house, with a steep thatched roof overgrown by stonecrop and other parasites, which was evidently the shop of the village, inasmuch as one side of the window exhibited a show of homely drapery, while the other side was devoted to groceries, and a shelf above laden with great sprawling loaves of bread. This establishment was also the post-office, and here Gilbert resolved to make his customary inquiries, when he had put up his horse.

Almost immediately opposite this general emporium, the sign of the Blue Boar swung proudly across the street in front of a low rather dilapidated-looking hostelry, with a wide frontage, and an archway leading into a spacious desolate yard, where one gloomy cock of Spanish descent was crowing hoarsely on the broken roof of a shed, surrounded by four or five shabby-looking hens, all in the most wobegone stage of moulting, and appearing as if eggs were utterly remote from their intentions. This Blue Boar was popularly supposed to have been a most distinguished and prosperous place in the coaching days, when twenty coaches passed daily through the village of Crosber; and was even now much affected as a place of resort by the villagers, to the sore vexation of the rector and such good people as believed in the perfectibility of the human race and the ultimate suppression of public-houses.

Here Mr. Fenton dismounted, and surrendered his horse to the keeping of an unkempt bareheaded youth who emerged from one of the dreary-looking buildings in the yard, announced himself as the hostler, and led off the steed in triumph to a wilderness of a stable, where the landlord's pony and a fine colony of rats were luxuriating in the space designed for some twelve or fifteen horses.

Having done this, Gilbert crossed the road to the post-office, where he found the proprietor, a deaf old man, weighing half-pounds of sugar in the background, while a brisk sharp-looking girl stood behind the counter sorting a little packet of letters.

It was to the damsel, as the more intelligent of these two, that Gilbert addressed himself, beginning of course with the usual question. Did she know any one, a stranger, sojourning in that neighbourhood called Holbrook?

The girl shook her head without a moment's hesitation. No, she knew no one of that name.

"And I suppose all the letters for people in this neighbourhood pass through your hands?"

"Yes, sir, all of them; I couldn't have failed to notice if there had been any one of that name."

Gilbert gave a little weary sigh. The information given him by the landlord of the White Swan had seemed to bring him so very near the object of his search, and here he was thrown back all at once upon the wide field of conjecture, not a whit nearer any certain knowledge. It was true that Crosber was only one among several places within ten miles of the market-town, and the strangers who had been driven from the White Swan in March last might have gone to any one of those other localities. His inquiries were not finished yet, however.

"There is an old house about a mile from here," he said to the girl; "a house belonging to a farm, in the lane yonder that turns off by the Blue Boar. Have you any notion to whom it belongs, or who lives there?"

"An old house in that lane across the way?" the girl said, reflecting. "That's Golder's lane, and leads to Golder's-green. There's not many houses there; it's rather a lonesome kind of place. Do you mean a big old-fashioned house standing far back in a garden?"

"Yes; that must be the place I want to know about."

"It must be the Grange, surely. It was a gentleman's house once; but there's only a bailiff lives there now. The farm belongs to some gentleman down in Midlandshire, a baronet; I can't call to mind his name at this moment, though I have heard it often enough. Mr. Carley's daughter—Carley is the name of the bailiff at the Grange—comes here for all they want."

Gilbert gave a little start at the name of Midlandshire. Lidford was in Midlandshire. Was it not likely to be a Midlandshire man who had lent Marian's husband his house?

"Do you know if these people at the Grange have had any one staying with them lately—any lodgers?" he asked the girl.

"Yes; they have lodgers pretty well every summer. There were some people this year, a lady and gentleman; but they never seemed to have any letters, and I can't tell you their names."

"Are they living there still?"

"I can't tell you that. I used to see them at church now and then in the summer-time; but I haven't seen them lately. There's a church at Golder's-green almost as near, and they may have been there."

"Will you tell me what they were like?" Gilbert asked eagerly.

His heart was beating loud and fast, making a painful tumult in his breast. He felt assured that he was on the track of the people whom the innkeeper had described to him; the people who were, in all probability, Mr. and Mrs. Holbrook.

"The lady is very pretty and very young—quite a girl. The gentleman older, dark, and not handsome."

"Yes. Has the lady gray eyes, and dark-brown hair, and a very bright expressive face?"

"Yes, sir."

"Pray try to remember the name of the gentleman to whom the Grange belongs. It is of great importance to me to know that."

"I'll ask my father, sir," the girl answered good-naturedly; "he's pretty sure to know."

She went across the shop to the old man who was weighing sugar, and bawled her question into his ear. He scratched his head in a meditative way for some moments.

"I've heard the name times and often," he said, "though I never set eyes upon the gentleman. William Carley has been bailiff at the Grange these twenty years, and I don't believe as the owner has ever come nigh the place in all that time. Let me see,—it's a common name enough, though the gentleman is a baronight. Forster—that's it—Sir something Forster."

"Sir David?" cried Gilbert.

"You've hit it, sir. Sir David Forster—that's the gentleman."

Sir David Forster! He had little doubt after this that the strangers at the Grange had been Marian and her husband. Treachery, blackest treachery somewhere. He had questioned Sir David, and had received his positive assurance that this man Holbrook was unknown to him; and now, against that there was the fact that the baronet was the owner of a place in Hampshire, to be taken in conjunction with that other fact that a place in Hampshire had been lent to Mr. Holbrook by a friend. At the very first he had been inclined to believe that Marian's lover must needs be one of the worthless bachelor crew with which the baronet was accustomed to surround himself. He had only abandoned that notion after his interview with Sir David Forster; and now it seemed that the baronet had deliberately lied to him. It was, of course, just possible that he was on a false scent after all, and that it was to some other part of the country Mr. Holbrook had brought his bride; but such a coincidence seemed, at the least, highly improbable. There was no occasion for him to remain in doubt very long, however. At the Grange he must needs be able to obtain more definite information.

CHAPTER XVI.
FACE TO FACE.

GILBERT Fenton left the homely little post-office and turned into the lane leading to Golder's-green—a way which may have been pleasant enough in summer, but had no especial charm at this time. The level expanse of bare ploughed fields on each side of the narrow road had a dreary look; the hedges were low and thin; a tall elm, with all its lower limbs mercilessly shorn, uplifted its topmost branches to the dull gray sky, here and there, like some transformed prophetess raising her gaunt arms in appeal or malediction; an occasional five-barred gate marked the entrance to some by-road to the farm; on one side of the way a deep black-looking ditch lay under the scanty shelter of the low hedge, and hinted at possible water rats to the traveller from cities who might happen to entertain a fastidious aversion to such small deer.

The mile seemed a very long one to Gilbert Fenton. Since his knowledge of Sir David Forster's ownership of the house to which he was going, his impatience was redoubled. He had a feverish eagerness to come at the bottom of this mystery. That Sir David had lied to him, he had very little doubt. Whoever this Mr. Holbrook was, it was more likely that he should have escaped the notice of Lidford people as a guest at Heatherly than under any other circumstances. At Heatherly it was such a common thing for strangers to come and go, that even the rustic gossips had left off taking much interest in the movements of the Baronet or his guests. There was one thought that flashed suddenly into Gilbert's mind during that gloomy walk under the lowering gray sky.

If this man Holbrook were indeed a friend of Sir David Forster's, how did it happen that John Saltram had failed to recognize his name? The intimacy between Forster and Saltram was of such old standing, that it seemed scarcely likely that any acquaintance of Sir David's could be completely unknown to the other. Were they all united in treachery against him? Had his chosen friend—the man he loved so well—been able to enlighten him, and had he coldly withheld his knowledge? No, he told himself, that was not possible. Sir David Forster might be the falsest, most unprincipled of mankind; but he could not believe John Saltram capable of baseness, or even coldness, towards him.

He was at the end of his journey by this time. The Grange stood in front of him—a great rambling building, with many gables, gray lichen-grown walls, and quaint old diamond-paned casements in the upper stories. Below, the windows were larger, and had an Elizabethan look, with patches of stained glass here and there. The house stood back from the road, with a spacious old-fashioned garden before it; a garden with flower-beds of a Dutch design, sheltered from adverse winds by dense hedges of yew and holly; a pleasant old garden enough, one could fancy, in summer weather. The flower-beds were for the most part empty now, and the only flowers to be seen were pale faded-looking chrysanthemums and Michaelmas daises. The garden was surrounded by a high wall, and Gilbert contemplated it first through the rusty scroll-work of a tall iron gate, surmounted by the arms and monogram of the original owner. On one side of the house there was a vast pile of building, comprising stables and coach-houses, barns and granaries, arranged in a quadrangle. The gate leading into this quadrangle was open, and Gilbert saw the cattle standing knee-deep in a straw-yard.

He rang a bell, which had a hoarse rusty sound, as if it had not been rung very often of late; and after he had waited for some minutes, and rung a second time, a countrified-looking woman emerged from the house, and came slowly along the wide moss-grown gravel-walk towards him. She stared at him with the broad open stare of rusticity, and did not make any attempt to open the gate, but stood with a great key in her hand, waiting for Gilbert to speak.

"This is Sir David Forster's house, I believe," he said.

"Yes, sir, it be; but Sir David doesn't live here."

"I know that. You have some lodgers here—a lady and gentleman called Holbrook."

He plunged at once at this assertion, as the easiest way of arriving at the truth. He had a conviction that this solitary farm-house was the place to which his unknown rival had brought Marian.

"Yes, sir," the woman answered, still staring at him in her Blow stupid way. "Mrs. Holbrook is here, but Mr. Holbrook is away up in London. Did you wish to see the lady?"

Gilbert's heart gave a great throb. She was here, close to him! In the next minute he would be face to face with her, with that one woman whom he loved, and must continue to love, until the end of his life.

"Yes," he said eagerly, "I wish to see her. You can take me to her at once. I am an old friend. There is no occasion to carry in my name."

He had scarcely thought of seeing Marian until this moment. It was her husband he had come to seek; it was with him that his reckoning was to be made; and any meeting between Marian and himself was more likely to prove a hindrance to this reckoning than otherwise. But the temptation to seize the chance of seeing her again was too much for him. Whatever hazard there might be to his scheme of vengeance in such an encounter slipped out of his mind before the thought of looking once more at that idolised face, of hearing the loved voice once again. The woman hesitated for a few moments, telling Gilbert that Mrs. Holbrook never had visitors, and she did not know whether she would like to see him; but on his administering half-a-crown through the scroll-work of the gate, she put the key in the lock and admitted him. He followed her along the moss-grown path to a wide wooden porch, over which the ivy hung like a voluminous curtain, and through a half-glass door into a low roomy hall, with massive dark oak-beams across the ceiling, and a broad staircase of ecclesiastical aspect leading to a gallery above. The house had evidently been a place of considerable grandeur and importance in days gone by; but everything in it bore traces of neglect and decay. The hall was dark and cold, the wide fire-place empty, the iron dogs red with rust. Some sacks of grain were stored in one corner, a rough carpenter's bench stood under one of the mullioned windows, and some garden-seeds were spread out to dry in another.

The woman opened a low door at the end of this hall, and ushered Gilbert into a sitting-room with three windows looking out upon a Dutch bowling-green, a quadrangle of smooth turf shut in by tall hedges of holly. The room was empty, and the visitor had ample leisure to examine it while the woman went to seek Mrs. Holbrook.

It was a large room with a low ceiling, and a capacious old-fashioned fire-place, where a rather scanty fire was burning in a dull slow way. The furniture was old and worm-eaten,—furniture that had once been handsome,—and was of a ponderous fashion that defied time. There was a massive oaken cabinet on one side of the room, a walnut-wood bureau with brass handles on the other. A comfortable looking sofa, of an antiquated design, with chintz-covered cushions, had been wheeled near the fire-place; and close beside it there was a small table with an open desk upon it, and some papers scattered loosely about. There were a few autumn flowers in a homely vase upon the centre table, and a work-basket with some slippers, in Berlin wool work, unfinished.

Gilbert Fenton contemplated all these things with supreme tenderness. It was here that Marian had lived for so many months—alone most likely for the greater part of the time. He had a fixed idea that the man who had stolen his treasure was some dissipated worldling, altogether unworthy so sacred a trust. The room had a look of loneliness to him. He could fancy the long solitary hours in this remote seclusion.

He had to wait for some little time, walking slowly up and down; very eager for the interview that was to come, yet with a consciousness that his fate would seem only so much the darker to him afterwards, when he had to turn his back upon this place, with perhaps no hope of ever seeing Marian again. At last there came a light footfall; the door was opened, and his lost love came into the room.

Gilbert Fenton was standing near the fire-place, with his back to the light. For the first few moments it was evident that Marian did not recognize him. She came towards him slowly, with a wondering look in her face, and then stopped suddenly with a faint cry of surprise.

"You here!" she exclaimed. "O, how did you find this place? Why did you come?"

She clasped her hands, looking at him in a half-piteous way that went straight to his heart. What he had told Mrs. Branston was quite true. It was not in him to be angry with this girl. Whatever bitterness there might have been in his mind until this moment fled away at sight of her. His heart had no room for any feeling but tenderness and pity.

"Did you imagine that I should rest until I had seen you once more, Marian? Did you suppose I should submit to lose you without hearing from your own lips why I have been so unfortunate?"

"I did not think you would waste time or thought upon any one so wicked as I have been towards you," she answered slowly, standing before him with a pale sad face and downcast eyes. "I fancied that whatever love you had ever felt for me—and I know how well you did love me—would perish in a moment when you found how basely I had acted. I hoped that it would be so."

"No, Marian; love like mine does not perish so easily as that. O, my love, my love, why did you forsake me so cruelly? What had I done to merit your desertion of me?"

"What had you done! You had only been too good to me. I know that there is no excuse for my sin. I have prayed that you and I might never meet again. What can I say? From first to last I have been wrong. From first to last I have acted weakly and wickedly. I was flattered and gratified by your affection for me; and when I found that my dear uncle had set his heart upon our marriage, I yielded against my own better reason, which warned me that I did not love you as you deserved to be loved. Then for a long time I was blind to the truth. I did not examine my own heart. I was quite able to estimate all your noble qualities, and I fancied that I should be very happy as your wife. But you must remember that at the last, when you were leaving England, I asked you to release me, and told you that it would be happier for both of us to be free."

"Why was that, Marian?"

"Because at that last moment I began to doubt my own heart."

"Had there been any other influence at work, Marian? Had you seen your husband, Mr. Holbrook, at that time?" She blushed crimson, and the slender hands nervously clasped and unclasped themselves before she spoke.

"I cannot answer that question," she said at last.

"That is quite as good as saying 'yes.' You had seen this man; he had come between us already. O, Marian, Marian, why were you not more candid?"

"Because I was weak and foolish. I could not bear to make you unhappy. O, believe me, Gilbert, I had no thought of falsehood at that time. I fully meant to be true to my promise, come what might."

"I am quite willing to believe that," he answered gently. "I believe that you acted from first to last under the influence of a stronger will than your own. You can see that I feel no resentment against you. I come to you in sorrow, not in anger. But I want to understand how this thing came to pass. Why was it that you never wrote to me to tell me the complete change in your feelings?"

"It was thought better not," Marian faltered, after a pause.

"By you?"

"No; by my husband."

"And you suffered him to dictate to you in that matter. Against your own sense of right?"

"I loved him," she answered simply. "I have never refused to obey him in anything. I will own that I thought it would be better to write and tell you the truth; but my husband thought otherwise. He wished our marriage to remain a secret from you, and from all the world for some time to come. He had his own reasons for that—reasons I was bound to respect. I cannot think how you came to discover this out-of-the-world place."

"I have taken some trouble to find you, Marian, and it is a hard thing to find you the wife of another; but the bitterness of it must be borne. I do not want to reproach you when I tell you that my life has been broken utterly by this blow. I want you to believe in my truth and honour, to trust me now as you might have trusted me when you first discovered that you could not love me. Since I am not to be your husband, let me be the next best thing—your friend. The day may come in which, you will have need of an honest man's friendship."

She shook her head sadly.

"You are very good," she said; "but there is no possibility at friendship between you and me. If you will only say that you can forgive me for the great wrong I have done you, there will be a heavy burden lifted from my heart; and whatever you may think now, I cannot doubt that in the future you will find some one far better worthy of your love than ever I could have been."

"That is the stereotyped form of consolation, Marian, a man is always referred to—that shadowy and perfect creature who is to appear in the future, and heal all his wounds. There will be no such after-love for me. I staked all when I played the great game; and have lost all. But why cannot I be your friend, Marian?"

"Can you forgive my husband for his part in the wrong that has been done you? Can you be his friend, knowing what he has done?"

"No!" Gilbert answered fiercely between his set teeth. "I can forgive your weakness, but not the man's treachery."

"Then you can never be mine," Marian said firmly.

"Remember, I am not talking of a common friendship, a friendship of daily association. I offer myself to you as refuge in the hour of trouble, a counsellor in perplexity, a brother always waiting in the background of your life to protect or serve you. Of course, it is quite possible you may never have need of protection or service—God knows, I wish you all happiness—but there are not many lives quite free from trouble, and the day may come in which you will want a friend."

"If it ever does, I will remember your goodness."

Gilbert looked scrutinisingly at Marian Holbrook as she stood before him with the cold gray light of the sunless day full upon her face. He wanted to read the story of her life in that beautiful face, if it were possible. He wanted to know whether she was happy with the man who had stolen her from him.

She was very pale, but that might be fairly attributed to the agitation caused by his presence. Gilbert fancied that there was a careworn look in her face, and that her beauty had faded a little since those peaceful days at Lidford, when these two had wasted the summer hours in idle talk under the walnut trees in the Captain's garden. She was dressed very plainly in black. There was no coquettish knot of ribbon at her throat; no girlish trinkets dangled at her waist—all those little graces and embellishments of costume which seem natural to a woman whose life is happy, were wanting in her toilet to-day; and slight as these indications were, Gilbert did not overlook them.

Did he really wish her to be happy—happy with the rival he so fiercely hated? He had said as much; and in saying so, he had believed that he was speaking the truth. But he was only human; and it is just possible that, tenderly as he still loved this girl, he may have been hardly capable of taking pleasure in the thought of her happiness.

"I want you to tell me about your husband, Marian," he said after a pause; "who and what he is."

"Why should I do that?" she asked, looking at him with a steady, almost defiant, expression. "You have said that you will never forgive him. What interest can you possibly feel in his affairs?"

"I am interested in him upon your account."

"I cannot tell you anything about him. I do not know how you could have discovered even his name."

"I learned that at Wygrove, where I first heard of your marriage."

"Did you go to Wygrove, then?"

"Yes; I have told you that I spared no pains to find you. Nor shall I spare any pains to discover the history of the man who has wronged me. It would be wiser for you to be frank with me, Marian. Rely upon it that I shall sooner or later learn the secret underlying this treacherous business."

"You profess to be my friend, and yet are avowedly say husband's enemy. Why cannot you be truly generous, Gilbert, and pardon him? Believe me, he was not willingly treacherous; it was his fate to do you this wrong."

"A poor excuse for a man, Marian. No, my charity will not stretch far enough for that. But I do not come to you quite on a selfish errand, to speak solely of my own wrongs. I have something to tell you of real importance to yourself."

"What is that?"

Gilbert Fenton described the result of his first advertisement, and his acquaintance with Jacob Nowell.

"It is my impression that this old man is rich, Marian; and there is little doubt that he would leave all he possesses to you, if you went to him at once."

"I do not care very much about money for my own sake," she answered with rather a mournful smile; "but we are not rich, and I should be glad of anything that would improve my husband's position. I should like to see my grandfather: I stand so much alone in the world that it would be very sweet to me to find a near relation."

"Your husband must surely have seen Mr. Nowell's advertisement," Gilbert said after a pause. "It was odd that he did not tell you about it—that he did not wish you to reply to it."

"The advertisement may have escaped him, or he may have looked upon it as a trap to discover our retreat," Marian answered frankly.

"I cannot understand the motive for such secrecy."

"There is no occasion that you should understand it. Every life has its own mystery—its peculiar perplexities. When I married my husband, I was prepared to share all his troubles. I have been obedient to him in everything."

"And has your marriage brought you happiness, Marian?"

"I love my husband," she answered with a plaintive reproachful look, as if there had been a kind of cruelty in his straight question. "I do not suppose that there is such a thing as perfect happiness in the world."

The answer was enough for Gilbert Fenton. It told him that this girl's life was not all sunshine.

He had not the heart to push his inquiries farther. He felt that he had no right to remain any longer, when in all probability his presence was a torture to the girl who had injured him.

"I will not prolong my visit, Marian," he said regretfully.

"It was altogether a foolish one, perhaps; but I wanted so much to see you once more, to hear some explanation of your conduct from your own lips."

"My conduct can admit of neither explanation nor justification," she replied humbly. "I know how wickedly I have acted. Believe me, Gilbert, I am quite conscious of my unworthiness, and how little right I have to expect your forgiveness."

"It is my weakness, rather than my merit, not to be able to cherish any angry feeling against you, Marian. Mine has been a slavish kind of love. I suppose that sort of thing never is successful. Women have an instinctive contempt for men who love them with such blind unreasonable idolatry."

"I do not know how that may be; but I know that I have always respected and esteemed you," she answered in her gentle pleading way.

"I am grateful to you even for so much as that. And now I suppose I must say good-bye—rather a hard word to say under the circumstances. Heaven knows when you and I may meet again."

"Won't you stop and take some luncheon? I dine early when my husband is away; it saves trouble to the people of the house. The bailiff's daughter always dines with me when I am alone; but I don't suppose you will mind sitting down with her. She is a good girl, and very fond of me."

"I would sit down to dinner with a chimney-sweep, if he were a favourite of yours, Marian—or Mrs. Holbrook; I suppose I must call you that now."

After this they talked of Captain Sedgewick for a little, and the tears came to Marian's eyes as she spoke of that generous and faithful protector. While they were talking thus, the door was opened, and a bright-faced countrified-looking girl appeared carrying a tray. She was dressed in a simple pretty fashion, a little above her station as a bailiff's daughter, and had altogether rather a superior look, in spite of her rusticity, Gilbert thought.

She was quite at her ease in his presence, laying the cloth briskly and cleverly, and chattering all the time.

"I am sure I'm very glad any visitor should come to see Mrs. Holbrook," she said; "for she has had a sad lonely time of it ever since she has been here, poor dear. There are not many young married women would put up with such a life."

"Nelly," Marian exclaimed reproachfully, "you know that I have had nothing to put up with—that I have been quite happy here."

"Ah, it's all very well to say that, Mrs. Holbrook; but I know better. I know how many lonely days you've spent, so downhearted that you could scarcely speak or look up from your book, and that only an excuse for fretting.—If you're a friend of Mr. Holbrook's, you might tell him as much, sir; that he's killing his pretty young wife by inches, by leaving her so often alone in this dreary place. Goodness knows, it isn't that I want to get rid of her. I like her so much that I sha'n't know what to do with myself when she's gone. But I love her too well not to speak the truth when I see a chance of its getting to the right ears."

"I am no friend of Mr. Holbrook's," Gilbert answered; "but I think you are a good generous-hearted girl."

"You are a very foolish girl," Marian exclaimed; "and I am extremely angry with you for talking such utter nonsense about me. I may have been a little out of spirits sometimes in my husband's absence; but that is all. I shall begin to think that you really do want to get rid of me, Nell, say what you will."

"That's a pretty thing, when you know that I love you as dearly as if you were my sister; to say nothing of father, who makes a profit by your being here, and would be fine and angry with me for interfering. No, Mrs. Holbrook; it's your own happiness I'm thinking of, and nothing else. And I do say that it's a shame for a pretty young woman like you to be shut up in a lonely old farmhouse while your husband is away, enjoying himself goodness knows where; and when he is here, I can't see that he's very good company, considering that he spends the best part of his time—"

The girl stopped abruptly, warned by a look from Marian. Gilbert saw this look, and wondered what revelation of Mr. Holbrook's habits the bailiff's daughter had been upon the point of making; he was so eager to learn something of this man, and had been so completely baffled in all his endeavours hitherto.

"I will not have my affairs talked about in this foolish way, Ellen Carley," Marian said resolutely.

And then they all three sat down to the dinner-table. The dishes were brought in by the woman who had admitted Gilbert. The dinner was excellent after a simple fashion, and very nicely served; but for Mr. Fenton the barn-door fowl and home-cured ham might as well have been the grass which the philosopher believed the French people might learn to eat. He was conscious of nothing but the one fact that he was in Marian's society for perhaps the last time in his life. He wondered at himself not a little for the weakness which made it so sweet to him to be with her.

The moment came at last in which he must needs take his leave, having no possible excuse for remaining any longer.

"Good-bye, Marian," he said. "I suppose we are never likely to meet again."

"One never knows what may happen; but I think it is far better we should not meet, for many reasons."

"What am I to tell your grandfather when I see him?"

"That I will come to him as soon as I can get my husband's permission to do so."

"I should not think there would be any difficulty about that, when he knows that this relationship is likely to bring you fortune."

"I daresay not."

"And if you come to London to see Mr. Nowell, there will be some chance of our meeting again."

"What good can come of that?"

"Not much to me, I daresay. It would be a desperate, melancholy kind of pleasure. Anything is better than the idea of losing sight of you for ever—of leaving this room to-day never to look upon your face again."

He wrote Jacob Nowell's address upon one of his own cards, and gave it to Marian; and then prepared to take his departure. He had an idea that the bailiff's daughter would conduct him to the gate, and that he would be able to make some inquiries about Mr. Holbrook on his way. It is possible that Marian guessed his intentions in this respect; for she offered to go with him to the gate herself; and he could not with any decency refuse to be so honoured.

They went through the hall together, where all was as still and lifeless as it had been when he arrived, and walked slowly side by side along the broad garden-path in utter silence. At the gate Gilbert stopped suddenly, and gave Marian his hand.

"My darling," he said, "I forgive you with all my heart; and I will pray for your happiness."

"Will you try to forgive my husband also?" she asked in her plaintive beseeching way.

"I do not know what I am capable of in that direction. I promise that, for your sake, I will not attempt to do him any injury."

"God bless you for that promise! I have so dreaded the chance of a meeting between you two. It has often been the thought of that which has made me unhappy when that faithful girl, Nelly, has noticed my low spirits. You have removed a great weight from my mind."

"And you will trust me better after that promise?"

"Yes; I will trust you as you deserve to be trusted, with all my heart."

"And now, good-bye. It is a hard word for me to say; but I must not detain you here in the cold."

He bent his head, and pressed his lips upon the slender little hand which held the key of the gate. In the next moment he was outside that tall iron barrier; and it seemed to him as if he were leaving Marian in a prison. The garden, with its poor pale scentless autumn flowers, had a dreary look under the dull gray sky. He thought of the big empty house, with its faded traces of vanished splendour, and of Marian's lonely life in it, with unspeakable pain. How different from the sunny home which he had dreamed of in the days gone by—the happy domestic life which he had fancied they two might lead!

"And she loves this man well enough to endure the dullest existence for his sake," he said to himself as he turned his back at last upon the tall iron gate, having lingered there for some minutes after Marian had re-entered the house. "She could forget all our plans for the future at his bidding."

He thought of this with a jealous pang, and with all his old anger against his unknown rival. Moved by an impulse of love and pity for Marian, he had promised that this man should suffer no injury at his hands; and, having so pledged himself, he must needs keep his word. But there were certain savage feelings and primitive instincts in his breast not easily to be vanquished; and he felt that now he had bound himself to keep the peace in relation to Mr. Holbrook, it would be well that those two should not meet.

"But I will have some explanation from Sir David Forster as to that lie he told me," he said to himself; "and I will question John Saltram about this man Holbrook."

John Saltram—John Holbrook. An idea flashed into his brain that seemed to set it on fire. What if John Saltram and John Holbrook were one! What if the bosom friend whom he had introduced to his betrothed had played the traitor, and stolen her from him! In the next moment he put the supposition away from him, indignant with himself for being capable of thinking such a thing, even for an instant. Of all the men upon earth who could have done him this wrong, John Saltram was the last he could have believed guilty. Yet the thought recurred to him many times after this with a foolish tiresome persistence; and he found himself going over the circumstances of his friend's acquaintance with Marian, his hasty departure from Lidford, his return there later during Sir David Forster's illness. Let him consider these facts as closely as he might, there was no especial element of suspicion in them. There might have been a hundred reasons for that hurried journey to London—nay, the very fact itself argued against the supposition that Mr. Saltram had fallen in love with his friend's plighted wife.

And now, the purpose of his life being so far achieved, Gilbert Fenton rode back to Winchester next day, restored his horse to its proprietor, and went on to London by an evening train.

CHAPTER XVII.
MISS CARLEY'S ADMIRERS.

THERE were times in which Marian Holbrook's life would have been utterly lonely but for the companionship of Ellen Carley. This warm-hearted outspoken country girl had taken a fancy to Mr. Holbrook's beautiful wife from the hour of her arrival at the Grange, one cheerless March evening, and had attached herself to Marian from that moment with unalterable affection and fidelity. The girl's own life at the Grange had been lonely enough, except during the brief summer months, when the roomy old house was now and then enlivened a little by the advent of a lodger,—some stray angler in search of a secluded trout stream, or an invalid who wanted quiet and fresh air. But in none of these strangers had Ellen ever taken much interest. They had come and gone, and made very little impression upon her mind, though she had helped to make their sojourn pleasant in her own brisk cheery way.

She was twenty-one years of age, very bright-looking, if not absolutely pretty, with dark expressive eyes, a rosy brunette complexion, and very white teeth. The nose belonged to the inferior order of pug or snub; the forehead was low and broad, with dark-brown hair rippling over it—hair which seemed always wanting to escape from its neat arrangement into a multitude of mutinous curls. She was altogether a young person whom the admirers of the soubrette style of beauty might have found very charming; and, secluded as her life at the Grange had been, she had already more than one admirer.

She used to relate her love affairs to Marian Holbrook in the quiet summer evenings, as the two sat under an old cedar in the meadow nearest the house—a meadow which had been a lawn in the days when the Grange was in the occupation of great folks; and was divided from a broad terrace-walk at the back of the house by a dry grass-grown moat, with steep sloping banks, upon which there was a wealth of primroses and violets in the early spring. Ellen Carley told Mrs. Holbrook of her admirers, and received sage advice from that experienced young matron, who by-and-by confessed to her humble companion the error of her own girlhood, and how she had jilted the most devoted and generous lover that ever a woman could boast of.

For some months—for the bright honeymoon period of her wedded life—Marian had been completely happy in that out-of-the-world region. It is not to be supposed that she had done so great a wrong to Gilbert Fenton except under the influence of a great love, or the dominion of a nature powerful enough to subjugate her own. Both these influences had been at work. Too late she had discovered that she had never really loved Gilbert Fenton; that the calm grateful liking which she had told herself must needs be the sole version of the grand passion whereof her nature was capable, had been only the tamest, most ordinary kind of friendship after all, and that in the depths of her soul there was a capacity for an utterly different attachment—a love which was founded on neither respect nor gratitude, but which sprang into life in a moment, fatal and all-absorbing from its birth.

Heaven knows she had struggled bravely against this luckless passion, had resisted long and steadily the assiduous pursuit, the passionate half-despairing pleading, of her lover, who would not be driven away, and who invented all kinds of expedients for seeing her, however difficult the business might be, or however resolutely she might endeavour to avoid him. It was only after her uncle's death, when her mind was weakened by excessive grief, that her strong determination to remain faithful to her absent betrothed had at last given way before the force of those tender passionate prayers, and she had consented to the hasty secret marriage which her lover had proposed. Her consent once given, not a moment had been lost. The business had been hurried on with the utmost eagerness by the impetuous lover, who would give her as little opportunity as possible of changing her mind, and who had obtained complete mastery of her will from the moment in which she promised to be his wife.

She loved him with all the unselfish devotion of which her nature was capable; and no thought of the years to come, or of what her future life might be with this man, of whose character and circumstances she knew so very little, ever troubled her. Having sacrificed her fidelity to Gilbert Fenton, she held all other sacrifices light as air—never considered them at all, in fact. When did a generous romantic girl of nineteen ever stop to calculate the chances of the future, or fear to encounter poverty and trouble with the man she loved? To Marian this man was henceforth all the world. It was not that he was handsomer, or better, or in any obvious way superior to Gilbert Fenton. It was only that he was just the one man able to win her heart. That mysterious attraction which reason can never reduce to rule, which knows no law of precedent or experience, reigned here in full force. It is just possible that the desperate circumstances of the attachment, the passionate pursuit of the lover, not to be checked by any obstacle, may have had an influence upon the girl's mind. There was a romance in such love as this that had not existed in Mr. Fenton's straightforward wooing; and Marian was too young to be quite proof against the subtle charm of a secret, romantic, despairing passion.

For some time she was very happy; and the remote farm-house, with its old-fashioned gardens and fair stretch of meadow-land beyond them, where all shade and beauty had not yet been sacrificed to the interests of agriculture, seemed to her in those halcyon days a kind of earthly paradise. She endured her husband's occasional absence from this rural home with perfect patience. These absences were rare and brief at first, but afterwards grew longer and more frequent. Nor did she ever sigh for any brighter or gayer life than this which they led together at the Grange. In him were the beginning and end of her hopes and dreams; and so long as he was pleased and contented, she was completely happy. It was only when a change came in him—very slight at first, but still obvious to his wife's tender watchful eyes—that her own happiness was clouded. That change told her that whatever he might be to her, she was no longer all the world to him. He loved her still, no doubt; but the bright holiday-time of his love was over, and his wife's presence had no longer the power to charm away every dreary thought. He was a man in whose disposition there was a lurking vein of melancholy—a kind of chronic discontent very common to men of whom it has been said that they might do great things in the world, and who have succeeded in doing nothing.

It is not to be supposed that Mr. Holbrook intended to keep his wife shut away from the world in a lonely farm-house all her life. The place suited him very well for the present; the apartments at the Grange, and the services of Mr. Carley and his dependents, had been put at his disposal by the owner of the estate, together with all farm and garden produce. Existence here therefore cost him very little; his chief expenses were in gifts to the bailiff and his underlings, which he bestowed with a liberal hand. His plans for the future were as yet altogether vague and unsettled. He had thoughts of emigration, of beginning life afresh in a new country—anything to escape from the perplexities that surrounded him here; and he had his reasons for keeping his wife secluded. Nor did his conscience disturb him much—he was a man who had his conscience in very good training—as to the unfairness of this proceeding. Marian was happy, he told himself; and when time came for some change in the manner of her existence, he doubted if the change would be for the better.

So the days and weeks and months had passed away, bringing little variety with them, and none of what the world calls pleasure. Marian read and worked and rambled in the country lanes and meadows with Ellen Carley, and visited the poor people now and then, as she had been in the habit of doing at Lidford. She had not very much to give them, but gave all she could; and she had a gentle sympathetic manner, which made her welcome amongst them, most of all where there were children, for whom she had always a special attraction. The little ones clung to her and trusted her, looking up at her lovely face with spontaneous affection.

William Carley, the bailiff, was a big broad-shouldered man, with a heavy forbidding countenance, and a taciturn habit by no means calculated to secure him a large circle of friends. His daughter and only child was afraid of him; his wife had been afraid of him in her time, and had faded slowly out of a life that had been very joyless, unawares, hiding her illness from him to the last, as if it had been a sort of offence against him to be ill. It was only when she was dying that the bailiff knew he was going to lose her; and it must be confessed that he took the loss very calmly.

Whatever natural grief he may have felt was carefully locked in his own breast. His underlings, the farm-labourers, found him a little more "grumpy" than usual, and his daughter scarcely dared open her lips to him for a month after the funeral. But from that time forward Miss Carley, who was rather a spirited damsel, took a very different tone with her father. She was not to be crushed and subdued into a mere submissive shadow, as her mother had been. She had a way of speaking her mind on all occasions which was by no means agreeable to the bailiff. If he drank too much overnight, she took care to tell him of it early next morning. If he went about slovenly and unshaven, her sharp tongue took notice of the fact. Yet with all this, she waited upon him, and provided for his comfort in a most dutiful manner. She saved his money by her dexterous management of the household, and was in all practical matters a very treasure among daughters. William Carley liked comfort, and liked money still better, and he was quite aware that his daughter was valuable to him, though he was careful not to commit himself by any expression of that opinion.

He knew her value so well that he was jealously averse to the idea of her marrying and leaving him alone at the Grange. When young Frank Randall, the lawyer's son, took to calling at the old house very often upon summer evenings, and by various signs and tokens showed himself smitten with Ellen Carley, the bailiff treated the young man so rudely that he was fain to cease from coming altogether, and to content himself with an occasional chance meeting in the lane, when Ellen had business at Crosber, and walked there alone after tea. He would not have been a particularly good match for any one, being only an articled clerk to his father, whose business in the little market-town of Malsham was by no means extensive; and William Carley spoke of him scornfully as a pauper. He was a tall good-looking young fellow, however, with a candid pleasant face and an agreeable manner; so Ellen was not a little angry with her father for his rudeness, still more angry with him for his encouragement of her other admirer, a man called Stephen Whitelaw, who lived about a mile from the Grange, and farmed his own land, an estate of some extent for that part of the country.

"If you must marry," said the bailiff, "and it's what girls like you seem to be always thinking about, you can't do better than take up with Steph Whitelaw. He's a warm man, Nell, and a wife of his will never want a meal of victuals or a good gown to her back. You'd better not waste your smiles and your civil words on a beggar like young Randall, who won't have a home to take you to for these ten years to come—not then, perhaps—for there's not much to be made by law in Malsham now-a-days. And when his father dies—supposing he's accommodating enough to die in a reasonable time, which it's ten to one he won't be—the young man will have his mother and sisters to keep upon the business very likely, and there'd be a nice look-out for you. Now, if you marry my old friend Steph, he can make you a lady."

This was a very long speech for Mr. Carley. It was grumbled out in short spasmodic sentences between the slow whiffs of his pipe, as he sat by the fire in a little parlour off the hall, with his indefatigable daughter at work at a table near him.

"Stephen Whitelaw had need be a gentleman himself before he could make me a lady," Nelly answered, laughing. "I don't think fine clothes can make gentlefolks; no, nor farming one's own land, either, though that sounds well enough. I am not in any hurry to leave you, father, and I'm not one of those girls who are always thinking of getting married; but come what may, depend upon it, I shall never marry Mr. Whitelaw."

"Why not, pray?" the bailiff asked savagely.

Nelly shook out the shirt she had been repairing for her father, and then began to fold it, shaking her head resolutely at the same time.

"Because I detest him," she said; "a mean, close, discontented creature, who can see no pleasure in life except money-making. I hate the very sight of his pale pinched face, father, and the sound of his hard shrill voice. If I had to choose between the workhouse and marrying Stephen Whitelaw, I'd choose the workhouse; yes, and scrub, and wash, and drudge, and toil there all my days, rather than be mistress of Wyncomb Farm."

"Well, upon my word," exclaimed the father, taking the pipe from his mouth, and staring aghast at his daughter in a stupor of indignant surprise, "you're a pretty article; you're a nice piece of goods for a man to bring up and waste his substance upon—a piece of goods that will turn round upon one and refuse a man who farms his own land. Mind, he hasn't asked you yet, my lady; and never may, for aught I know."

"I hope he never will, father," Nelly answered quietly, unsubdued by this outburst of the bailiff's.

"If he does, and you don't snap at such a chance, you need never look for a sixpence from me; and you'd best make yourself scarce pretty soon into the bargain. I'll have no such trumpery about my house."

"Very well, father; I daresay I can get my living somewhere else, without working much harder than I do here."

This open opposition on the girl's part made William Carley only the more obstinately bent upon that marriage, which seemed to him such a brilliant alliance, which opened up to him the prospect of a comfortable home for his old age, where he might repose after his labours, and live upon the fat of the land without toil or care. He had a considerable contempt for the owner of Wyncomb Farm, whom he thought a poor creature both as a man and a farmer; and he fancied that if his daughter married Stephen Whitelaw, he might become the actual master of that profitable estate. He could twist such a fellow as Stephen round his fingers, he told himself, when invested with the authority of a father-in-law.

Mr. Whitelaw was a pale-faced little man of about five-and-forty years of age; a man who had remained a bachelor to the surprise of his neighbours, who fancied, perhaps, that the owner of a good house and a comfortable income was in a manner bound by his obligation to society to take to himself a partner with whom to share these advantages. He had remained unmarried, giving no damsel ground for complaint by any delusive attentions, and was supposed to have saved a good deal of money, and to be about the richest man in those parts, with the exception of the landed gentry.

He was by no means an attractive person in this the prime of his manhood. He had a narrow mean-looking face, with sharp features, and a pale sickly complexion, which looked as if he had spent his life in some close London office rather than in the free sweet air of his native fields. His hair was of a reddish tint, very sleek and straight, and always combed with extreme precision upon each side of his narrow forehead; and he had scanty whiskers of the same unpopular hue, which he was in the habit of smoothing with a meditative air upon his sallow cheeks with the knobby fingers of his bony hand. He was of a rather nervous temperament, inclined to silence, like his big burly friend, William Carley, and had a deprecating doubtful way of expressing his opinion at all times. In spite of this humility of manner, however, he cherished a secret pride in his superior wealth, and was apt to remind his associates, upon occasion, that he could buy up any one of them without feeling the investment.

After having attained the discreet age of forty-five without being a victim to the tender passion, Mr. Whitelaw might reasonably have supposed himself exempt from the weakness so common to mankind. But such self-gratulation, had he indulged in it, would have been premature; for after having been a visitor at the Grange, and boon-companion of the bailiff's for some ten years, it slowly dawned upon him that Ellen Carley was a very pretty girl, and that he would have her for his wife, and no other. Her brisk off-hand manner had a kind of charm for his slow apathetic nature; her rosy brunette face, with its bright black eyes and flashing teeth, seemed to him the perfection of beauty. But he was not an impetuous lover. He took his time about the business, coming two or three times a week to smoke his pipe with William Carley, and paying Nelly some awkward blundering compliment now and then in his deliberate hesitating way. He had supreme confidence in his own position and his money, and was troubled by no doubt as to the ultimate success of his suit. It was true that Nelly treated him in by no means an encouraging manner—was, indeed, positively uncivil to him at times; but this he supposed to be mere feminine coquetry; and it enhanced the attractions of the girl he designed to make his wife. As to her refusing him when the time came for his proposal, he could not for a moment imagine such a thing possible. It was not in the nature of any woman to refuse to be mistress of Wyncomb, and to drive her own whitechapel cart—a comfortable hooded vehicle of the wagonette species, which was popular in those parts.

So Stephen Whitelaw took his time, contented to behold the object of his affection two or three evenings a week, and to gaze admiringly upon her beauty as he smoked his pipe in the snug little oak-wainscoted parlour at the Grange, while his passion grew day by day, until it did really become a very absorbing feeling, second only to his love of money and Wyncomb Farm. These dull sluggish natures are capable of deeper passions than the world gives them credit for; and are as slow to abandon an idea as they are to entertain it.

It was Ellen Carley's delight to tell Marian of her trouble, and to protest to this kind confidante again and again that no persuasion or threats of her father's should ever induce her to marry Stephen Whitelaw—which resolution Mrs. Holbrook fully approved. There was a little gate opening from a broad green lane into one of the fields at the back of the Grange; and here sometimes of a summer evening they used to find Frank Randall, who had ridden his father's white pony all the way from Malsham for the sake of smoking his evening cigar on that particular spot. They used to find him seated there, smoking lazily, while the pony cropped the grass in the lane close at hand. He was always eager to do any little service for Mrs. Holbrook; to bring her books or anything else she wanted from Malsham—anything that might make an excuse for his coming again by appointment, and with the certainty of seeing Ellen Carley. It was only natural that Marian should be inclined to protect this simple love-affair, which offered her favourite a way of escape from the odious marriage that her father pressed upon her. The girl might have to endure poverty as Frank Randall's wife; but that seemed a small thing in the eyes of Marian, compared with the horror of marrying that pale-faced mean-looking little man, whom she had seen once or twice sitting by the fire in the oak parlour, with his small light-grey eyes fixed in a dull stare upon the bailiff's daughter.

CHAPTER XVIII.
JACOB NOWELL'S WILL.

AT his usual hour, upon the evening after his arrival in London, Gilbert Fenton called at the silversmith's shop in Queen Anne's Court. He found Jacob Nowell weaker than when, he had seen him last, and with a strange old look, as if extreme age had come upon him suddenly. He had been compelled to call in a medical man, very much against his will; and this gentleman had told him that his condition was a critical one, and that it would be well for him to arrange his affairs quickly, and to hold himself prepared for the worst.

He seemed to be slightly agitated when Gilbert told him that his granddaughter had been found.

"Will she come to me, do you think?" he asked.

"I have no doubt that she will do so, directly she hears how ill you have been. She was very much pleased at the idea of seeing you, and only waited for her husband's permission to come. But I don't suppose she will wait for that when she knows of your illness. I shall write to her immediately."

"Do," Jacob Nowell said eagerly; "I want to see her before I die. You did not meet the husband, then, I suppose?"

"No; Mr. Holbrook was not there."

He told Jacob Nowell all that it was possible for him to tell about his interview with Marian; and the old man seemed warmly interested in the subject. Death was very near him, and the savings of the long dreary years during which his joyless life had been devoted to money-making must soon pass into other hands. He wanted to know something of the person who was to profit by his death; he wanted to be sure that when he was gone some creature of his own flesh and blood would remember him kindly; not for the sake of his money alone, but for something more than that.

"I shall make my will to-morrow," he said, before Gilbert left him. "I don't mind owning to you that I have something considerable to bequeath; for I think I can trust you. And if I should die before my grandchild comes to me, you will see that she has her rights, won't you? You will take care that she is not cheated by her husband, or by any one else?"

"I shall hold it a sacred charge to protect her interests, so far as it is possible for me to do so."

"That's well. I shall make you one of the executors to my will, if you've no objection."

"No. The executorship will bring me into collision with Mr. Holbrook, no doubt; but I have resolved upon my line of conduct with regard to him, and I am prepared for whatever may happen. My chief desire now is to be a real friend to your granddaughter; for I believe she has need of friends."

The will was drawn up next day by an attorney of by no means spotless reputation, who had often done business for Mr. Nowell in the past, and who may have known a good deal about the origin of some of the silver which found its way to the old silversmith's stores. He was a gentleman frequently employed in the defence of those injured innocents who appear at the bar of the Old Bailey; and was not at all particular as to the merits of the cases he conducted. This gentleman embodied Mr. Nowell's desires with reference to the disposal of his worldly goods in a very simple and straightforward manner. All that Jacob Nowell had to leave was left to his granddaughter, Marian Holbrook, for her own separate use and maintenance, independent of any husband whatsoever.

This was clear enough. It was only when there came the question, which a lawyer puts with such deadly calmness, as to what was to be done with the money in the event of Marian Holbrook's dying intestate, that any perplexity arose.

"Of course, if she has children, you'd like the money to go to them," said Mr. Medler, the attorney; "that's clear enough, and had better be set out in your will. But suppose she should have no children, you'd scarcely like all you leave to go to her husband, who is quite a stranger to you, and who may be a scoundrel for aught you know."

"No; I certainly shouldn't much care about enriching this Holbrook."

"Of course not; to say nothing of the danger there would be in giving him so strong an interest in his wife's death. Not but what I daresay he'll contrive to squander the greater part of the money during her lifetime. Is it all in hard cash?"

"No; there is some house-property at Islington, which pays a high interest; and there are other freeholds."

"Then we might tie those up, giving Mrs. Holbrook only the income. It is essential to provide against possible villany or extravagance on the part of the husband. Women are so weak and helpless in these matters. And in the event of your granddaughter dying without children, wouldn't you rather let the estate go to your son?"

"To him!" exclaimed Jacob Nowell. "I have sworn that I would not leave him sixpence."

"That's a kind of oath which no man ever considers himself bound to keep," said the lawyer in his most insinuating tone. "Remember, it's only a remote contingency. The chances are that your granddaughter will have a family to inherit this property, and that she will survive her father. And then, if we give her power to make a will, of course it's pretty certain that she'll leave everything to this husband of hers. But I don't think we ought to do that, Mr. Nowell. I think it would be a far wiser arrangement to give this young lady only a life interest in the real estate. That makes the husband a loser by her death, instead of a possible gainer to a large amount. And I consider that your son's name has a right to come in here."

"I cannot acknowledge that he has any such right. His extravagance almost ruined me when he was a young man; and his ingratitude would have broken my heart, if I had been weak enough to suffer myself to be crushed by it."

"Time works changes amongst the worst of us, Mr. Nowell, I daresay your son has improved his habits in all these years and is heartily sorry for the errors of his youth."

"Have you seen him, Medler?" the old man asked quickly.

"Seen your son lately? No; indeed, my dear sir, I had no notion that he was in England."

The fact is, that Percival Nowell had called upon Mr. Medler more than once since his arrival in London; and had discussed with that gentleman the chances of his father's having made, or not made, a will, and the possibility of the old man's being so far reconciled to him as to make a will in his favour. Percival Nowell had gone farther than this, and had promised the attorney a handsome percentage upon anything that his father might be induced to leave him by Mr. Medler's influence.

The discussion lasted for a long time; Mr. Medler pushing on, stage by stage, in the favour of his secret client, anxious to see whether Jacob Nowell might not be persuaded to allow his son's name to take the place of his granddaughter, whom he had never seen, and who was really no more than a stranger to him, the attorney took care to remind him. But on this point the old man was immovable. He would leave his money to Marian, and to no one else. He had no desire that his son should ever profit by the labours and deprivations of all those joyless years in which his fortune had been scraped together. It was only as the choice of the lesser evil that he would consent to Percival's inheriting the property from his daughter, rather than it should fall into the hands of Mr. Holbrook. The lawyer had hard work before he could bring his client to this point; but he did at last succeed in doing so, and Percival Nowell's name was written in the will.

"I don't suppose Nowell will thank me much for what I've done, though I've had difficulty enough in doing it," Mr. Medler said to himself, as he walked slowly homewards after this prolonged conference in Queen Anne's Court. "For of course the chances are ten to one against his surviving his daughter. Still these young women sometimes go off the hooks in an unexpected way, and he *may* come into the reversion."

There was only one satisfaction for the attorney, and that lay in the fact that this long, laborious interview had been all in the way of business, and could be charged for accordingly: "To attending at your own house with relation to drawing up the rough draft of your will, and consultation of two hours and a half thereupon;" and so on. The will was to be executed next day; and Mr. Medler was to take his clerk with him to Queen Anne's Court, to act as one of the witnesses. He had obtained one other triumph in the course of the discussion, which was the insertion of his own name as executor in place of Gilbert Fenton, against whom he raised so many specious arguments as to shake the old man's faith in Marian's jilted lover.

Percival Nowell dropped in upon his father that night, and smoked his cigar in the dingy little parlour, which was so crowded with divers kinds of merchandise as to be scarcely habitable. The old man's son came here almost every evening, and behaved altogether in a very dutiful way. Jacob Nowell seemed to tolerate rather than to invite his visits, and the adventurer tried in vain to get at the real feelings underlying that emotionless manner.

"I think I might work round the governor if I had time," this dutiful son said to himself, as he reflected upon the aspect of affairs in Queen Anne's Court; "but I fancy the old chap has taken his ticket for the next world—booked through—per express train, and the chances are that he'll keep his word and not leave me sixpence. Rather hard lines that, after my taking the trouble to come over here and hunt him up."

There was one fact that Mr. Nowell the younger seemed inclined to ignore in the course of these reflections; and that was the fact that he had not left America until he had completely used up that country as a field for commercial enterprise, and had indeed made his name so far notorious in connection with numerous shady transactions as to leave no course open to him except a speedy departure. Since his coming to England he had lived entirely on credit; and, beyond the fine clothes he wore and the contents of his two portmanteaus, he possessed nothing in the world. It was quite true that he had done very well in New York; but his well-being had been secured at the cost of other people; and after having started some half-dozen speculations, and living extravagantly upon the funds of his victims, he was now as poor as he had been when he left Belgium for America, the commission-agent of a house in the iron trade. In this position he might have prospered in a moderate way, and might have profited by the expensive education which had given him nothing but showy agreeable manners, had he been capable of steadiness and industry. But of these virtues he was utterly deficient, possessing instead a genius for that kind of swindling which keeps just upon the safe side of felony. He had lived pleasantly enough, for many years, by the exercise of this agreeable talent; so pleasantly indeed that he had troubled himself very little about his chances of inheriting his father's savings. It was only when he had exhausted all expedients for making money on "the other side" that he turned his thoughts in the direction of Queen Anne's Court, and began to speculate upon the probability of Jacob Nowell's good graces being worth the trouble of cultivation. The prospectuses which he had shown his father were mere waste paper, the useless surplus stationery remaining from a scheme that had failed to enlist the sympathies of a Transatlantic public. But he fancied that his only chance with the old man lay in an assumption of prosperity; so he carried matters with a high hand throughout the business, and swaggered in the little dusky parlour behind the shop just as he had swaggered on New-York Broadway or at Delmonico's in the heyday of his commercial success.

He called at Mr. Medler's office the day after Jacob Nowell's will had been executed, having had no hint of the fact from his father. The solicitor told him what had been done, and how the most strenuous efforts on his part had only resulted in the insertion of Percival's name after that of his daughter.

Whatever indignation Mr. Nowell may have felt at the fact that his daughter had been preferred before him, he contrived to keep hidden in his own mind. The lawyer was surprised at the quiet gravity with which he received the intelligence. He listened to Mr. Medler's statement of the case with the calmest air of deliberation, seemed indeed to be thinking so deeply that it was as if his thoughts had wandered away from the subject in hand to some theme which allowed of more profound speculation.

"And if she should die childless, I should get all the free-hold property?" he said at last, waking up suddenly from that state of abstraction, and turning his thoughtful face upon the lawyer.

"Yes; all the real estate would be yours."

"Have you any notion what the property is worth?"

"Not an exact notion. Your father gave me a list of investments. Altogether, I should fancy, the income will be something handsome—between two and three thousand a year, perhaps. Strange, isn't it, for a man with all that money to have lived such a life as your father's?"

"Strange indeed," Percival Nowell cried with a sneer. "And my daughter will step into two or three thousand a year," he went on: "very pleasant for her, and for her husband into the bargain. Of course I'm not going to say that I wouldn't rather have had the income myself. You'd scarcely swallow that, as a man of the world, you see, Medler. But the girl is my only child, and though circumstances have divided us for the greater part of our lives, blood is thicker than water; and in short, since there was no getting the governor to do the right thing, and leave this money to me, it's the next best thing that he should leave it to Marian."

"To say nothing of the possibility of her dying without children, and your coming into the property after all," said Mr. Medler, wondering a little at Mr. Nowell's philosophical manner of looking at the question.

"Sir," exclaimed Percival indignantly, "do you imagine me capable of speculating upon the untimely death of my only child?"

The lawyer shrugged his shoulders doubtfully. In the course of his varied experience he had found men and women capable of very queer things when their pecuniary interests were at stake; and he had not a most exalted opinion of Mr. Nowell's virtue—he knew too many secrets connected with his early career.

"Remember, if ever by any strange chance you should come into this property, you have me to thank for getting your name into the will, and for giving your daughter only a life interest. She would have had every penny left to her without reserve, if I hadn't fought for your interests as hard as ever I fought for anything in the whole course of my professional career."

"You're a good fellow, Medler; and if ever fortune should favour me, which hardly seems on the cards, I sha'n't forget what I promised you the other day. I daresay you did the best you could for me, though it doesn't amount to much when it's done."

Long after Percival Nowell had left him, Mr. Medler sat idle at his desk meditating upon his interview with that gentleman.

"I can't half understand his coolness," he said to himself; "I expected him to be as savage as a bear when he found that the old man had left him nothing. I thought I should hear nothing but execrations and blasphemies; for I think I know my gentleman pretty well of old, and that he's not a person to take a disappointment of this kind very sweetly. There must be something under that quiet manner of his. Perhaps he knows more about his daughter than he cares to let out; knows that she is sickly, and that he stands a good chance of surviving her."

There was indeed a lurking desperation under Percival Nowell's airy manner, of which the people amongst whom he lived had no suspicion. Unless some sudden turn in the wheel of fortune should change the aspect of affairs for him very soon, ruin, most complete and utter, was inevitable. A man cannot go on very long without money; and in order to pay his hotel-bill Mr. Nowell had been obliged to raise the funds from an accommodating gentleman with whom he had done business in years gone by, and who was very familiar with his own and his father's autograph. The bill upon which this gentleman advanced the money in question bore the name of Jacob Nowell, and was drawn at three months. Percival had persuaded himself that before the three months were out his father would be in his grave, and his executors would scarcely be in a position to dispute the genuineness of the signature. In the meantime the money thus obtained enabled him to float on. He paid his hotel-bill, and removed to lodgings in one of the narrow streets to the north-east of Tottenham Court Road; an obscure lodging enough, where he had a couple of comfortable rooms on the first floor, and where his going out and coming in attracted little notice. Here, as at the hotel, he chose to assume the name of Norton instead of his legitimate cognomen.

CHAPTER XIX.
GILBERT ASKS A QUESTION.

GILBERT Fenton called at John Saltram's chambers within a day or two of his return from Hampshire. He had a strange, almost feverish eagerness to see his old friend again; a sense of having wronged him for that one brief moment of thought in which the possibility of his guilt had flashed across his mind; and with this feeling there was mingled a suspicion that John Saltram had not acted quite fairly to him; that he had kept back knowledge which must have come to him as an intimate ally of Sir David Forster.

He found Mr. Saltram at home in the familiar untidy room, with the old chaos of books and papers about him. He looked tired and ill, and rose to greet his visitor with a weary air, as if nothing in the world possessed much interest for him now-a-days.

"Why, John, you are as pallid as a ghost!" Gilbert exclaimed, grasping the hand extended to him, and thinking of that one moment in which he had fancied he was never to touch that hand again. "You have been at the old work, I suppose—overdoing it, as usual!"

"No, I have been working very little for these last few days. The truth is, I have not been able to work. The divine afflatus wouldn't come down upon me. There are times when a man's brain seems to be made of melted butter. Mine has been like that for the last week or so."

"I thought you were going back to your fishing village near Oxford."

"No, I was not in spirits for that. I have dined two or three times in Cavendish Square, and have been made much of, and have contrived to forget my troubles for a few hours."

"You talk of your troubles as if you were very heavily burdened; and yet, for the life of me, I cannot see what you have to complain of," Gilbert said wonderingly.

"Of course not. That is always the case with one's friends—even the best of them. It's only the man who wears the shoe that knows why it pinches and galls him. But what have you been doing since I saw you last?"

"I have been in Hampshire."

"Indeed!" said John Saltram, looking him full in the face. "And what took you into that quarter of the world?"

"I thought you took more interest in my affairs than to have to ask that question. I went to look for Marian Holbrook,—and I found her."

"Poor old fellow!" Mr. Saltram said gently. "And was there any satisfaction for you in the meeting?"

"Yes, and no. There was a kind of mournful pleasure in seeing the dear face once more."

"She must have been surprised to see you."

"She was, no doubt, surprised—unpleasantly, perhaps; but she received me very kindly, and was perfectly frank upon every subject except her husband. She would tell me nothing about him—neither his position in the world, nor his profession, if he has one, as I suppose he has. She owned he was not rich, and that is about all she said of him. Poor girl, I do not think she is happy!"

"What ground have you for such an idea?"

"Her face, which told me a great deal more than her words. Her beauty is very much faded since the summer evening when I first saw her in Lidford Church. She seems to lead a lonely life in the old farm-house to which her husband brought her immediately after their marriage—a life which few women would care to lead. And now, John, I want to know how it is you have kept back the truth from me in this matter; that you have treated me with a reserve which I had no right to expect from a friend."

"What have I kept from you"

"Your knowledge of this man Holbrook."

"What makes you suppose that I have any knowledge of him?"

"The fact that he is a friend of Sir David Forster's. The house in which I found Marian belongs to Sir David, and was lent by him to Mr. Holbrook."

"I do not know every friend of Forster's. He is a man who picks up his acquaintance in the highways and byways, and drops them when he is tired of them."

"Will you tell me, on your honour, that you know nothing of this Mr. Holbrook?"

"Certainly."

Gilbert Fenton gave a weary sigh, and then seated himself silently opposite Mr. Saltram. He could not afford to doubt this friend of his. The whole fabric of his life must have dropped to pieces if John Saltram had played him false. His single venture as a lover having ended in shipwreck, he seemed to have nothing left him but friendship; and that kind of hero-worship which had made his friend always appear to him something better than he really was, had grown stronger with him since Marian's desertion.

"O Jack," he said presently, "I could bear anything in this world better than the notion that you could betray me—that you could break faith with me for the sake of another man."

"I am not likely to do that. There is no man upon, this earth I care for very much except you. I am not a man prone to friendship. In fact, I am a selfish worthless fellow at the best, Gilbert, and hardly merit your serious consideration. It would be wiser of you to think of me as I really am, and to think very little of me."

"You did not show yourself remarkably selfish when you nursed me through that fever, at the hazard of your own life."

"Pshaw! that was nothing. I could not have done less in the position in which we two were. Such sacrifices as those count for very little. It is when a man's own happiness is in the scale that the black spot shows itself. I tell you, Gilbert, I am not worth your friendship. It would be better for you to go your own way, and have nothing more to do with me."

Mr. Saltram had said this kind of thing very often in the past, so that the words had no especial significance to Gilbert. He only thought that his friend was in one of those gloomy moods which were common to him at times.

"I could not do without your friendship, Jack," he said. "Remember how barren the world is to me now. I have nothing left but that."

"A poor substitute for better things, Gilbert. I am never likely to be much good to you or to myself. By the way, have you seen anything lately of that old man you told me about—Miss Nowell's grandfather?"

"I saw him the other night. He is very ill—dying, I believe. I have written to Marian to tell her that if she does not come very quickly to see him, there is a chance of her not finding him alive."

"And she will come of course."

"I suppose so. She talked of waiting for her husband's consent; but she will scarcely do that when she knows her grandfather's precarious state. I shall go to Queen Anne's Court after I leave you, to ascertain if there has been any letter from her to announce her coming. She is a complete stranger in London, and may be embarrassed if she arrives at the station alone. But I should imagine her husband would meet her there supposing him to be in town."

Mr. Fenton stayed with his friend about an hour after this; but John Saltram was not in a communicative mood to-night, and the talk lagged wearily. It was almost a relief to Gilbert when they had bidden each other good-night, and he was out in the noisy streets once more, making his way towards Queen Anne's Court.

CHAPTER XX.
DRIFTING AWAY.

GILBERT Fenton found Jacob Nowell worse; so much worse, that he had been obliged to take to his bed, and was lying in a dull shabby room upstairs, faintly lighted by one tallow candle on the mantelpiece. Marian was there when Gilbert went in. She had arrived a couple of hours before, and had taken her place at once by the sick-bed. Her bonnet and shawl were thrown carelessly upon a dilapidated couch by the window. Gilbert fancied she looked like a ministering angel as she sat by the bed, her soft brown hair falling loosely round the lovely face, her countenance almost divine in its expression of tenderness and pity.

"You came to town alone, Marian?" he asked in a low voice.

The old man was in a doze at this moment, lying with his pinched withered face turned towards his granddaughter, his feeble hand in hers.

"Yes, I came alone. My husband had not come back, and I would not delay any longer after receiving your letter. I am very glad I came. My poor grandfather seemed so pleased to see me. He was wandering a little when I first came in, but brightened wonderfully afterwards, and quite understood who I was."

The old man awoke presently. He was in a semi-delirious state, but seemed to know his granddaughter, and clung to her, calling her by name with senile fondness. His mind wandered back to the past, and he talked to his son as if he had been in the room, reproaching him for his extravagance, his college debts, which had been the ruin of his careful hard-working father. At another moment he fancied that his wife was still alive, and spoke to her, telling her that their grandchild had been christened after her, and that she was to love the girl. And then the delirium left him for a time, his mind grew clearer, and he talked quite rationally in his low feeble way.

"Is that Mr. Fenton?" he asked; "the room's so dark, I can't see very well. She has come to me, you see. She's a good girl. Her eyes are like my wife's. Yes, she's a good girl. It seems a hard thing that I should have lived all these years without knowing her; lived alone, with no one about me but those that were on the watch for my money, and eager to cheat me at every turn. My life might have been happier if I'd had a grandchild to keep me company, and I might have left this place and lived like a gentleman for her sake. But that's all past and gone. You'll be rich when I'm dead, Marian; yes, what most people would count rich. You won't squander the money, will you, my dear, as your father would, if it were left to him?"

"No, grandfather. But tell me about my father. Is he still living?" the girl asked eagerly.

"Never mind him, child," answered Jacob Nowell. "He hasn't troubled himself about you, and you can't do better than keep clear of him. No good ever came of anything he did yet, and no good ever will come. Don't you have anything to do with him, Marian. He'll try to get all your money away from you, if you give him a chance—depend upon that."

"He is living, then? O, my dear grandfather, do tell me something more about him. Remember that whatever his errors may have been, he is my father—the only relation I have in the world except yourself."

"His whole life has been one long error," answered Jacob Nowell. "I tell you, child, the less you know of him the better."

He was not to be moved from this, and would say no more about his son, in spite of Marian's earnest pleading. The doctor came in presently, for the second time that evening, and forbade his patient's talking any more. He told Gilbert, as he left the house, that the old man's life was now only a question of so many days or so many hours.

The old woman who did all the work of Jacob Nowell's establishment—a dilapidated-looking widow, whom nobody in that quarter ever remembered in any other condition than that of widowhood—had prepared a small bedroom at the back of the house for Marian; a room in which Percival had slept in his early boyhood, and where the daughter found faint traces of her father's life. Mr. Macready as Othello, in a spangled tunic, with vest of actual satin let into the picture, after the pre-Raphaelite or realistic tendency commonly found in such juvenile works of art, hung over the narrow painted mantelpiece. The fond mother had had this masterpiece framed and glazed in the days when her son was still a little lad, unspoiled by University life and those splendid aspirations which afterwards made his home hateful to him. There were some tattered books upon a shelf by the bed—school prizes, an old Virgil, a "Robinson Crusoe" shorn of its binding. The boy's name was written in them in a scrawling schoolboy hand; not once, but many times, after the fashion of juvenile bibliopoles, with primitive rhymes in Latin and English setting forth his proprietorship in the volumes. Caricatures were scribbled upon the fly-leaves and margins of the books, the date whereof looked very old to Marian, long before her own birth.

It was not till very late that she consented to leave the old man's side and go to the room which had been got ready for her, to lie down for an hour. She would not hear of any longer rest though the humble widow was quite pathetic in her entreaties that the dear young lady would try to get a good night's sleep, and would leave the care of Mr. Nowell to her, who knew his ways, poor dear gentleman, and would watch over him as carefully as if he had been her own poor husband, who kept his bed for a twelvemonth before he died, and had to be waited on hand and foot. Marian told this woman that she did not want rest. She had come to town on purpose to be with her grandfather, and would stay with him as long as he needed her care.

She did, however, consent to go to her room for a little in the early November dawn, when Jacob Nowell had fallen into a profound sleep; but when she did lie down, sleep would not come to her. She could not help listening to every sound in the opposite room—the falling of a cinder, the stealthy footfall of the watcher moving cautiously about now and then; listening still more intently when all was silent, expecting every moment to hear herself summoned suddenly. The sick-room and the dark shadow of coming death brought back the thought of that bitter time when her uncle was lying unconscious and speechless in the pretty room at Lidford, with the wintry light shining coldly upon his stony face; while she sat by his pillow, watching him in hopeless silent agony, waiting for that dread change which they had told her was the only change that could come to him on earth. The scene re-acted itself in her mind to-night, with all the old anguish. She shut it out at last with a great effort, and began to think of what her grandfather had said to her.

She was to be rich. She who had been a dependant upon others all her life was to know the security and liberty that must needs go along with wealth. She was glad of this, much more for her husband's sake than her own. She knew that the cares which had clouded their life of late, which had made him seem to love her less than he had loved her at first, had their chief origin in want of money. What happiness it would be for her to lift this burden from his life, to give him peace and security for the years to come! Her thoughts wandered away into the bright region of day-dreams after this, and she fancied what their lives might be without that dull sordid trouble of pecuniary embarrassments. She fancied her husband, with all the fetters removed that had hampered his footsteps hitherto, winning a name and a place in the world. It is so natural for a romantic inexperienced girl to believe that the man she loves was born to achieve greatness; and that if he misses distinction, it is from the perversity of his surroundings or from his own carelessness, never from the fact of his being only a very small creature after all.

It was broad daylight when Marian rose after an hour of sleeplessness and thought, and refreshed herself with the contents of the cracked water-jug upon the rickety little wash-stand. The old man was still asleep when she went back to his room; but his breathing was more troubled than it had been the night before, and the widow, who was experienced in sickness and death, told Marian that he would not last very long. The shopman, Luke Tulliver, had come upstairs to see his master, and was hovering over the bed with a ghoulish aspect. This young man looked very sharply at Marian as she came into the room—seemed indeed hardly able to take his eyes from her face—and there was not much favour in his look. He knew who she was, and had been told how kindly the old man had taken to her in those last moments of his life; and he hated her with all his heart and soul, having devoted all the force of his mind for the last ten years to the cultivation of his employer's good graces, hoping that Mr. Nowell, having no one else to whom to leave his money, would end by leaving it all to him. And here was a granddaughter, sprung from goodness knows where, to cheat him out of all his chances. He had always suspected Gilbert Fenton of being a dangerous sort of person, and it was no doubt he who had brought about this introduction, to the annihilation of Mr. Tulliver's hopes. This young man took his place in a vacant chair by the fire, as if determined to stop; while Marian seated herself quietly by the sleeper's pillow, thinking only of that one occupant of the room, and supposing that Mr. Tulliver's presence was a mark of fidelity.

The old man woke with a start presently, and looked about him in a slow bewildered way for some moments.

"Who's that?" he asked presently, pointing to the figure by the hearth.

"It's only Mr. Tulliver, sir," the widow answered. "He's so anxious about you, poor young man."

"I don't want him," said Jacob Nowell impatiently. "I don't want his anxiety; I want to be alone with my granddaughter."

"Don't send me away, sir," Mr. Tulliver pleaded in a piteous tone. "I don't deserve to be sent away like a stranger, after serving you faithfully for the last ten years———"

"And being well paid for your services," gasped the old man. "I tell you I don't want you. Go downstairs and mind the shop."

"It's not open yet, sir," remonstrated Mr. Tulliver.

"Then it ought to be. I'll have no idling and shirking because I'm ill. Go down and take down the shutters directly. Let the business go on just as if I was there to watch it."

"I'm going, sir," whimpered the young man; "but it does seem rather a poor return after having served you as I have, and loved you as if you'd been my own father."

"Very much men love their fathers now-a-days! I didn't ask you to love me, did I? or hire you for that, or pay you for it? Pshaw, man, I know you. You wanted my money like the rest of them, and I didn't mind your thinking there was a chance of your getting it. I've rather encouraged the notion at odd times. It made you a better servant, and kept you honest. But now that I'm dying, I can afford to tell the truth. This young lady will have all my money, every sixpence of it, except five-and-twenty pounds to Mrs. Mitchin yonder. And now you can go. You'd have got something perhaps in a small way, if you'd been less of a sneak and a listener; but you've played your cards a trifle too well."

The old man had raised himself up in his bed, and rallied considerably while he made this speech. He seemed to take a malicious pleasure in his shopman's disappointment. But when Luke Tulliver had slowly withdrawn from the room, with a last venomous look at Marian, Jacob Nowell sank back upon his pillow exhausted by his unwonted animation.

"You don't know what a deep schemer that young man has been, Marian," he said, "and how I have laughed in my sleeve at his manoeuvres."

The dull November day dragged itself slowly through, Marian never leaving her post by the sick-bed. Jacob Nowell spent those slow hours in fitful sleep and frequent intervals of wakefulness, in which he would talk to Marian, however she might urge him to remember the doctor's injunctions that he should be kept perfectly quiet. It seemed indeed to matter very little whether he obeyed the doctor or not, since the end was inevitable.

One of the curates of the parish came in the course of the day, and read and prayed beside the old man's bed, Jacob Nowell joining in the prayers in a half-mechanical way. For many years of his life he had neglected all religious duties. It was years since he had been inside a church; perhaps he had not been once since the death of his wife, who had persuaded him to go with her sometimes to the evening service, when he had generally scandalised her by falling asleep during the delivery of the sermon. All that the curate told him now about the necessity that he should make his peace with his God, and prepare himself for a world to come, had a far-off sound to him. He thought more about the silver downstairs, and what it was likely to realize in the auction-room. Even in this supreme hour his conscience did not trouble him much about the doubtful modes by which some of the plate he had dealt in had reached his hands. If he had not bought the things, some other dealer would have bought them. That is the easy-going way in which he would have argued the question, had he been called upon to argue it at all.

Mr. Fenton came in the evening to see the old man, and stood for a little time by the bedside watching him as he slept, and talking in a low voice to Marian. He asked her how long she was going to remain in Queen Anne's Court, and found her ideas very vague upon that subject.

"If the end is so near as the doctor says, it would be cruel to leave my grandfather till all is over," she said.

"I wonder that your husband has not come to you, if he is in London," Gilbert remarked to her presently. He found himself very often wondering about her husband's proceedings, in no indulgent mood.

"He may not be in London," she answered, seeming a little vexed by the observation. "I am quite sure that he will do whatever is best."

"But if he should not come to you, and if your grandfather should die while you are alone here, I trust you will send for me and let me give you any help you may require. You can scarcely stay in this house after the poor old man's death."

"I shall go back to Hampshire immediately; if I am not wanted here for anything—to make arrangements for the funeral. O, how hard it seems to speak of that while he is still living!"

"You need give yourself no trouble on that account. I will see to all that, if there is no more proper person to do so."

"You are very good. I am anxious to go back to the Grange as quickly as possible."

Gilbert left soon after this. He felt that his presence was of no use in the sick-room, and that he had no right to intrude upon Marian at such a time.

CHAPTER XXI.
FATHER AND DAUGHTER.

ALMOST immediately after Gilbert's departure, another visitor appeared in the dimly lighted shop, where Luke Tulliver was poring over a newspaper at one end of the counter under a solitary gas-burner.

The new-comer was Percival Nowell, who had not been to the house since his daughter's arrival.

"Well," said this gentleman, in his usual off-hand manner, "how's the governor?"

"Very ill; going fast, the doctor says."

"Eh? As bad as that? Then there's been a change since I was here last."

"Yes; Mr. Nowell was taken much worse yesterday morning. He had a kind of fit, I fancy, and couldn't get his speech for some time afterwards. But he got over that, and has talked well enough since then," Mr. Tulliver concluded ruefully, remembering his master's candid remarks that morning.

"I'll step upstairs and have a look at the old gentleman," said Percival.

"There's a young lady with him," Mr. Tulliver remarked, in a somewhat mysterious tone.

"A young lady!" the other cried. "What young lady?"

"His granddaughter."

"Indeed!"

"Yes; she came up from the country yesterday evening, and she's been sitting with him ever since. He seems to have taken to her very much. You'd think she'd been about him all her life; and she's to have all his money, he says. I wonder what his only son will say to that," added Mr. Tulliver, looking very curiously at Percival Nowell, "supposing him to be alive? Rather hard upon him, isn't it?"

"Uncommonly," the other answered coolly. He saw that the shopman suspected his identity, though he had carefully avoided all reference to the relationship between himself and the old man in Luke Tulliver's presence, and had begged his father to say nothing about him.

"I should like to see this young lady before I go up to Mr. Nowell's room," he said presently. "Will you step upstairs and ask her to come down to me?"

"I can go if you wish, but I don't suppose she'll leave the old gentleman."

"Never mind what you suppose. Tell her that I wish to say a few words to her upon particular business."

Luke Tulliver departed upon his errand, while Percival Nowell went into the parlour, and seated himself before the dull neglected fire in the lumbering old arm-chair in which his father had sat through the long lonely evenings for so many years. Mr. Nowell the younger was not disturbed by any sentimental reflections upon this subject, however; he was thinking of his father's will, and the wrong which was inflicted upon him thereby.

"To be cheated out of every sixpence by my own flesh and blood!" he muttered to himself. "That seems too much for any man to bear."

The door was opened by a gentle hand presently, and Marian came into the room. Percival Nowell rose from his seat hastily and stood facing her, surprised by her beauty and an indefinable likeness which she bore to her mother—a likeness which brought his dead wife's face back to his mind with a sudden pang. He had loved her after his own fashion once upon a time, and had grown weary of her and neglected her after the death of that short-lived selfish passion; but something, some faint touch of the old feeling, stirred his heart as he looked at his daughter to-night. The emotion was as brief as the breath of a passing wind. In the next moment he was thinking of his father's money, and how this girl had emerged from obscurity to rob him of it.

"You wish to speak to me on business, I am told," she said, in her clear low voice, wondering at the stranger's silence and deliberate scrutiny of her face.

"Yes, I have to speak to you on very serious business, Marian," he answered gravely.

"You are an utter stranger to me, and yet call me by my Christian name."

"I am not an utter stranger to you. Look at me, Mrs. Holbrook. Have you never seen my face before?"

"Never."

"Are you quite sure of that? Look a little longer before you answer again."

"Yes!" she cried suddenly, after a long pause. "You are my father!"

There had come back upon her, in a rapid flash of memory, the picture of a room in Brussels—a room lighted dimly by two wax-candles on the chimney-piece, where there was a tall dark man who snatched her up in his arms and kissed her before he went out. She remembered caring very little for his kisses, and having a childish consciousness of the fact that it was he who made her mamma cry so often in the quiet lonely evenings, when the mother and child were together in that desolate continental lodging.

Yet at this moment she was scarcely disposed to think much about her father's ill-conduct. She considered only that he was her father, and that they had found each other after long years of separation. She stretched out her arms, and would have fallen upon his breast; but something in his manner repelled her, something downcast and nervous, which had a chilling effect upon her, and gave her time to remember how little cause she had to love him. He did not seem aware of the affectionate impulse which had moved her towards him at first. He gave her his hand presently. It was deadly cold, and lay loosely in her own.

"I was asking my grandfather about you this morning," she said, wondering at his strange manner, "but he would not tell me where you were."

"Indeed! I am surprised to find you felt so much interest in me; I'm aware that I don't deserve as much. Yet I could plead plenty of excuses for my life, if I cared to trouble you with them; but I don't. It would be a long story; and when it was told, you might not believe it. Most men are, more or less, the slave of circumstances. I have suffered that kind of bondage all my life. I have known, too, that you were in good hands—better off in every way than you could have been in my care—or I should have acted differently in relation to you."

"There is no occasion to speak of the past," Marian replied gravely. "Providence was very good to me; but I know my poor mother's last days were full of sorrow. I cannot tell how far it might have been in your power to prevent that. It is not my place to blame, or even to question your conduct."

"You are an uncommonly dutiful daughter," Mr. Nowell exclaimed with rather a bitter laugh; "I thought that you would have repudiated me altogether perhaps; would have taken your tone from my father, who has grown pig-headed with old age, and cannot forgive me for having had the aspirations of a gentleman."

"It is a pity there should not be union between my grandfather and you at such a moment as this," Marian said.

"O, we are civil enough to each other. I bear no malice against the old man, though many sons in my position might consider themselves hardly used. And now I may as well go upstairs and pay my respects. Why is not your husband with you, by the bye?"

"He is not wanted here; and I do not even know that he is in London."

"Humph! He seems rather a mysterious sort of person, this husband of yours."

Marian took no notice of this remark, and the father and daughter went upstairs to the sick-room together. The old silversmith received his son with obvious coolness, and was evidently displeased at seeing Marian and her father together.

Percival Nowell, however, on his part, appeared to be in an unusually affectionate and dutiful mood this evening. He held his place by the bedside resolutely, and insisted on sharing Marian's watch that night. So all through the long night those two sat together, while the old man passed from uneasy slumber to more uneasy wakefulness, and back to troubled sleep again, his breathing growing heavier and more laboured with every hour. They were very quiet, and could have found but little to say to each other, had there been no reason for their silence. That first brief impulsive feeling of affection past, Marian could only think of this newly-found father as the man who had made her mother's life lonely and wretched while he pursued his own selfish pleasures; and who had allowed her to grow to womanhood without having been the object of one thought or care upon his part. She could not forget these things, as she sat opposite to him in the awful silence of the sick-room, stealing a glance at his face now and then, and wondering at the strange turn of fortune which had brought them thus together.

It was not a pleasant face by any means—not a countenance to inspire love or confidence. Handsome still, but with a faded look, like a face that had grown pallid and wrinkled in the feverish atmosphere of vicious haunts—under the flaring gas that glares down upon the green cloth of a rouge-et-noir table, in the tumult of crowded race-courses, the press and confusion of the betting-ring—it was the face of a battered *roué*, who had lived his life, and outlived the smiles of fortune; the face of a man to whom honest thoughts and hopes had long been unknown. There was a disappointed peevish look about the drooping corners of the mouth, an angry glitter in the eyes.

He did not look at his daughter very often as they sat together through that weary vigil, but kept his eyes for the greater part of the time upon the wasted face on the pillow, which looked like a parchment mask in the dim light. He seemed to be deep in thought, and several times in the night Marian heard him breathe an impatient sigh, as if his thoughts were not pleasant to him. More than once he rose from his chair and paced the room softly for a little time, as if the restlessness of his mind had made that forced quiet unendurable. The early morning light came at last, faint and wan and gray, across a forest of blackened chimney-pots, and by that light the watchers could see that Jacob Nowell had changed for the worse.

He lingered till late that afternoon. It was growing dusk when he died, making a very peaceful end of life at the last, with his head resting upon Marian's shoulder, and his cold hand clasped in hers. His son stood by the bed, looking down upon him at that final moment with a fixed inscrutable face. Gilbert Fenton called that evening, and heard of the old man's death from Luke Tulliver. He heard also that Mrs. Holbrook intended to sleep in Queen Anne's Court that night, and did not therefore intrude upon her, relying upon being able to see her next morning. He left his card, with a few words of condolence written upon it in pencil.

Mr. Nowell was with his daughter in the little parlour behind the shop when Luke Tulliver gave her this card. He asked who the visitor was.

"Mr. Fenton, a gentleman I knew at Lidford in my dear uncle's lifetime. My grandfather liked him very much."

"Mr. Fenton! Yes, my father told me all about him. You were engaged to him, and jilted him for this man you have married—very foolishly, as it seems to me; for he could certainly have given you a better position than that which you appear to occupy now."

"I chose for my own happiness," Marian answered quietly, "and I have only one subject for regret; that is, that I was compelled to act with ingratitude towards a good man. But Mr. Fenton has forgiven me; has promised to be my friend, if ever I should have need of his friendship. He has very kindly offered to take all trouble off my hands with respect to—to the arrangements for the funeral."

"He is remarkably obliging," said Percival Nowell with a sneer; "but as the only son of the deceased, I consider myself the proper person to perform that final duty."

"I do not wish to interfere with your doing so. Of course I did not know how near at hand you were when Mr. Fenton made that offer, or I should have told him."

"You mean to remain until the funeral is over, I suppose?"

"I think not; I want to go back to Hampshire as soon as possible—by an early train to-morrow morning, if I can. I do not see that there is any reason for my remaining. I could not prove my respect or affection for my grandfather any more by staying."

"Certainly not," her father answered promptly. "I think you will be quite right in getting away from this dingy hole as quick as you can."

"It is not for that. But I have promised to return directly I was free to do so."

"And you go back to Hampshire? To what part of Hampshire?"

Marian told him the name of the place where she was living. He wrote the address in his pocket-book, and was especially careful that it should be correctly written, as to the name of the nearest town, and in all other particulars.

"I may have to write to you, or to come to you, perhaps," he said. "It's as well to be prepared for the contingency."

After this Mr. Nowell sent out for a "Railway Guide," in order to give his daughter all necessary information about the trains for Malsham. There was a tolerably fast train that left Waterloo at seven in the morning, and Marian decided upon going by that. She had to spend the evening alone with her father while Mrs. Mitchin kept watch in the dismal chamber upstairs. Mr. Nowell asked his daughter's permission to light his cigar, and having obtained it, sat smoking moodily all the evening, staring into the fire, and very rarely addressing his companion, who had taken a Bible out of her travelling-bag, and was reading those solemn, chapters which best harmonised with her feelings at this moment; thinking as she read of the time when her guardian and benefactor lay in his last calm rest, and she had vainly tried to find comfort in the same words, and had found herself staring blankly at the sacred page, with eyes that were dry and burning, and to which there came no merciful relief from tears.

Her father glanced at her askance now and then from his arm-chair by the fire, as she sat by the little round table looking down at her book, the light of the candles shining full upon her pensive face. He looked at her with no friendliness in his eyes, but with that angry sparkle which had grown almost habitual to them of late, since the world had gone ill with him. After one of those brief stolen looks, a strange smile crept over his face. He was thinking of a little speech of Shakespeare's Richard about his nephew, the youthful Prince of Wales:

So young, so wise, they say do ne'er live long.

"How pious she is!" he said to himself with a diabolical sneer. "Did the half-pay Captain teach her that, I wonder? or does church-going, and psalm-singing, and Bible-reading come natural to all women? I know my mother was good at it, and my wife too. She used to fly to her Bible as a man flies to dram-drinking, or his pipe, when things go wrong."

He got tired of his cigar at last, and went out into the shop, where he began to question Mr. Tulliver as to the extent and value of the stock-in-trade, and upon other details of the business; to all of which inquiries the shopman replied in a suspicious and grudging spirit, giving his questioner the smallest possible amount of information.

"You're an uncommonly cautious young man," Mr. Nowell exclaimed at last. "You'll never stand in your own light by being too anxious to oblige other people. I daresay, though, you could speak fast enough, if it was made worth your while."

"I don't see what is to make it worth my while," Luke Tulliver answered coolly. "My duty is to my dead master, and those that are to come after him. I don't want strangers coming sniffing and prying into the stock. Mr. Nowell's books were kept so that I couldn't cheat him out of a sixpence, or the value of a sixpence; and I mean to hand 'em over to the lawyer in a manner that will do me credit. My master has not been a generous master to me, considering how I've served him, and I've got nothing but my character to look to; but that I have got, and I don't want it tampered with."

"Who is going to tamper with it?" said Mr. Nowell. "So you'll hand over the stock-books to the lawyer, will you, without a leaf missing, or an erasure, or an item marked off as sold that never was sold, or any little dodges of that kind, eh, Mr. Tulliver?"

"Of course," answered the shopman, looking defiantly at the questioner, who was leaning across the counter with folded arms, staring at Luke Tulliver with an ironical grin upon his countenance.

"Then you are a very remarkable man. I should have thought such a chance as a death as unexpected as my—as old Mr. Nowell's would have made the fortune of a confidential clerk like you."

"I'm not a thief," answered Mr. Tulliver with an air of virtuous indignation; "and you can't know much about old Jacob Nowell if you think that anybody could cheat him, living or dead. There's not an entry in the book that isn't signed with his initials, in his own hand. When a thing was sold and crossed off the book, he put his initials to the entry of the sale. He went through the books every night till a week ago, and he'd as soon have cut his own head off as omit to do it, so long as he could see the figures in the book or hold his pen."

Mr. Medler the lawyer came in while Percival Nowell and the shopman were talking. He had been away from his office upon business that evening, and had only just received the tidings of the silversmith's death.

Luke Tulliver handed him the books and keys of the cases in which the tarnished plate was exhibited. He went into all the details of the business carefully, setting his seal upon books and papers, and doing all that he could to make matters secure without hindrance to the carrying on of the trade.

He was surprised to hear that Mrs. Holbrook was in the house, and proposed paying his respects to her that evening; but this Mr. Nowell prevented. She was tired and out of spirits, he told the attorney; it would be better for him to see her next day. It was convenient to Mr. Nowell to forget Marian's intention of returning to Hampshire by an early train on the following morning at this juncture.

When he went back to the parlour by-and-by, after Mr. Medler had finished his business in the shop, and was trudging briskly towards his own residence, Mr. Nowell told his daughter that the lawyer had been there, but did not inform her of his desire to see her.

"I suppose you know all about your grandfather's will?" he said by-and-by, when he had half-finished another cigar.

Marian had put away her book by this time, and was looking dreamily at the fire, thinking of her husband, who need never know those weary sordid cares about money again, now that she was to be rich.

Her father's question startled her out of that agreeable day-dream.

"Yes," she said; "my grandfather told me that he had left all his money to me. I know that must seem unjust to you, papa; but I hope my husband will allow me to do something towards repairing that injustice in some measure."

"In some measure!" Mr. Nowell thought savagely. "That means a pittance that would serve to keep life in a pauper, I suppose; and that is to be contingent upon her husband's permission." He made no audible reply to his daughter's speech, and seemed, indeed, so much absorbed in his own thoughts, that Marian doubted if he had heard her; and so the rest of the long evening wore itself out in dismal silence, whilst stealthy footsteps sounded now and then upon the stairs. Later Mr. Nowell was summoned to a conference with some mysterious person in the shop, whom Marian supposed to be the undertaker; and returning from this interview with a gloomy face, he resumed his seat by the fire.

It seemed very strange to Marian that they two, father and daughter, should be together thus, so near and yet so wide apart; united by the closest tie of kindred, brought together thus after years of severance, yet with no bond of sympathy between them; no evidence of remorseful tenderness on the side of him whose life had been one long neglect of a father's duty.

"How could I expect that he would care for me in the smallest degree, after his desertion of my mother?" Marian thought to herself, as she meditated upon her father's coldness, which at first had seemed so strange to her. She had fancied that, what ever his sins in the past had been, his heart would have melted at the sight of his only child. She had thought of him and dreamed of him so often in her girlhood, elevating him in her romantic fancy into something much better and brighter than he really was—a sinner at best, it is true, but a sinner of a lofty type, a noble nature gone astray. She had imagined a reunion with him in the days to come, when it should be her delight to minister to his declining years—to be the consolation of his repentant soul. And now she had found him she knew these things could never be—that there was not one feeling of sympathy possible between her and that broken-down, dissipated-looking man of the world.

The dismal evening came to an end at last, and Marian bade her father goodnight, and went upstairs to the little room where the traces of his boyhood had interested her so keenly when first she looked upon them. Mr. Nowell promised to come to Queen Anne's Court at a quarter past six next morning, to escort his daughter to the station, an act of parental solicitude she had not expected from him. He took his departure immediately afterwards, being let out of the shop-door by Luke Tulliver, who was in a very cantankerous humour, and took no pains to disguise the state of his feelings. The lawyer Mr. Medler had pried into everything, the shopman told Percival Nowell; had declared himself empowered to do this, as the legal adviser of the deceased; and had seemed as suspicious as if he, Luke Tulliver, meant to rob his dead master. Mr. Tulliver's sensitive nature had been outraged by such a line of conduct.

"And what has he done with the books?" Mr. Nowell asked.

"They're all in the desk yonder, and that fellow Medler has taken away the keys."

"Sharp practice," said Mr. Nowell; "but to a man with your purity of intention it can't matter what precautions are taken to insure the safety of the property."

"Of course it don't matter," the other answered peevishly; "but I like to be treated as a gentleman."

"Humph! And you expect to retain your place here, I suppose, if the business is carried on?"

"It's too good a business to be let drop," replied Mr. Tulliver; "but I shouldn't think that young lady upstairs would be much of a hand at trade. I wouldn't mind offering a fair price for the business,—I've got a tidy little bit of money put away, though my salary has been small enough, goodness knows; but I've lived with the old gentleman, and never wasted a penny upon pleasure; none of your music-halls, or dancing-saloons, or anything of that kind, for me,—or I wouldn't mind paying an annual sum out of the profits of the trade for a reasonable term. If you've any influence with the young lady, perhaps you could put it to her, and get her to look at things in that light," Mr. Tulliver added, becoming quite obsequious as it dawned upon him that this interloping stranger might be able to do him a service.

"I'll do my best for you, Tulliver," Mr. Nowell replied, in a patronising tone. "I daresay the young lady will be quite willing to entertain any reasonable proposition you may make."

Faithful to his promise Mr. Nowell appeared at a quarter past six next morning, at which hour he found his daughter quite ready for her journey. She was very glad to get away from that dreary house, made a hundredfold more dismal by the sense of what lay in the closed chamber, where the candles were still burning in the yellow fog of the November morning, and to which Marian had gone with hushed footsteps to kneel for the last time beside the old man who was so near her by the ties of relationship, and whom she had known for so brief a space. She was glad to leave that dingy quarter of the town, which to one who had never lived in an English city seemed unspeakably close and wretched; still more glad to think that she was going back to the quiet home, where her husband would most likely join her very soon. She might find him there when she arrived, perhaps; for he knew nothing of this journey to London, or could only hear of it at the Grange, where she had left a letter for him, enclosing that brief note of Gilbert Fenton's which had informed her of her grandfather's fatal illness. There were special reasons why she should not ask him to meet her in Queen Anne's Court, however long she might have been compelled to stay there.

Mr. Nowell was much more affectionate in his manner to his daughter this morning, as they sat in the cab driving to the station, and walked side by side upon the platform in the quarter of an hour's interval before the departure of the train. He questioned her closely upon her life in the present, and her plans for the future, expressing himself in a remarkably generous manner upon the subject of her grandfather's will, and declaring himself very well pleased that his own involuntary neglect was to be so amply atoned for by the old man's liberality. He found his daughter completely ignorant of the world, as gentle and confiding as he had found her mother in the past. He sounded the depths of her innocent mind during that brief promenade; and when the train bore her away at last, and the platform was clear, he remained for some time walking up and down in profound meditation, scarcely knowing where he was. He looked round him in an absent way by-and-by, and then hurriedly left the station, and drove straight to Mr. Medler's office, which was upon the ground floor of a gloomy old house in one of the dingier streets in the Soho district, and in the upper chambers whereof the attorney's wife and numerous offspring had their abode. He came down to his client from his unpretending breakfast-table in a faded dressing-gown, with smears of egg and greasy traces of buttered toast about the region of his mouth, and seemed not particularly pleased to see Mr. Nowell. But the conference that followed was a long one; and it is to be presumed that it involved some chance of future profit, since the lawyer forgot to return to his unfinished breakfast, much to the vexation of Mrs. Medler, a faded lady with everything about her in the extremest stage of limpness, who washed the breakfast-things with her own fair hands, in consideration of the multitudinous duties to be performed by that hapless solitary damsel who in such modest households is usually denominated "the girl."

CHAPTER XXII.
AT LIDFORD AGAIN.

GILBERT Fenton called in Queen Anne's Court within a few hours of Marian's departure, and was not a little disappointed when he was told that she had gone back to Hampshire. He had relied upon seeing her again—not once only, but several times—before her return. He had promised Jacob Nowell that he would watch over and protect her interests; and it was a sincere unqualified wish to do this that influenced him now. More than a dear friend, the sweetest and dearest of all womankind, she could never be to him. He accepted the position with resignation. The first sharp bitterness of her loss was over. That he should ever cease to love her was impossible; but it seemed to him that a chivalrous friendship for her, a disinterested brotherly affection, was in no manner incompatible with that hapless silent love. No word of his, in all their intercourse to come, should ever remind her of that hidden devotion; no shadow of the past should ever cloud the calm brightness of the present. It was a romantic fancy, perhaps, for a man of business, whose days were spent in the very press and tumult of commercial life; but it had lifted Gilbert Fenton out of that slough of despond into which he had fallen when Marian seemed utterly lost to him—vanished altogether out of his existence.

He had a sense of bitter disappointment, therefore, when he found that she had gone, leaving neither letter nor message for him. How little value his friendship must needs possess for her, when she could abandon him thus without a word! He had felt sure that she would consult him upon her affairs; but no, she had her husband to whom to appeal, and had no need of any other counsellor.

"I was a fool to think that I could ever be anything to her, even a friend," he said to himself bitterly; "women are incapable of friendship. It is all or nothing with them; a blind self-abnegation or the coldest indifference. Devotion cannot touch them, unless the man who gives it happen to be that one man out of a thousand who has the power to bewitch their senses. Truth and affection, of themselves, have no value with them. How many people spoke to me of this Holbrook as an unattractive man; and yet he won my love away from me, and holds her with an influence so complete, that my friendship seems worthless to her. She cannot give me a word or a thought."

Mr. Fenton made some inquiries about the funeral arrangements and found that these had been duly attended to by the lawyer, and a gentleman who had been with Jacob Nowell a good deal of late, who seemed to be some relation to the old man, Mr. Tulliver said, and took a great deal upon himself. This being done, there was, of course, no occasion for Gilbert to interfere, and he was glad to be released from all responsibility. Having ascertained this, he asked for the address of the late Mr. Nowell's lawyer; and being told it, went at once to Mr. Medler's office. He did not consider himself absolved from the promise he had made the old man by Marian's indifference, and was none the less anxious to watch over her interests because she seemed to set so little value on his friendship.

He told Mr. Medler who he was, and the promise he had given to Jacob Nowell, abstaining, of course, from any reference to the position he had once occupied towards Marian. He described himself as her friend only—a friend of long standing, who had been intimate with her adopted guardian.

"I know how ignorant Mrs. Holbrook is of the world and of all business matters," he went on to say, "and I am naturally anxious that her interests should be protected."

"I should think there was very little doubt that her husband will see after those," the lawyer answered, with something of a sneer; "husbands are generally supposed to do that, especially where there is money at stake."

"I do not know Mr. Holbrook; and he has kept himself in the background so persistently up to this point, and has been altogether so underhanded in his proceedings, that I have by no means a good opinion of him. Mr. Nowell told me that he intended to leave his money to his granddaughter in such a manner, that it would be hers and hers only—free from the control of any husband. He has done so, I presume?"

"Yes," Mr. Medler replied, with the air of a man who would fain have withheld the information; "he has left it for her own separate use and maintenance."

"And it is a property of some importance, I conclude?"

"Of some importance—yes," the lawyer answered, in the same tone.

"Ought not Mrs. Holbrook to have remained to hear the reading of the will?"

"Well, yes, decidedly; it would have been more in the usual way of things; but her absence can have no ill effect upon her interests. Of course it will be my duty to make her acquainted with the contents of the will."

Gilbert Fenton was not prepossessed by Mr. Medler's countenance, which was not an open candid index to a spotless soul, nor by his surroundings, which were of the shabbiest; but the business being in this man's hands, it might be rather difficult to withdraw it—dangerous even. The man held the will, and in holding that had a certain amount of power.

"There is no one except Mrs. Holbrook interested in Mr. Nowell's will, I suppose?" Gilbert said presently.

"No one directly and immediately, except an old charwoman, who has a legacy of five-and-twenty pounds."

"But there is some one else interested in an indirect manner I infer from your words?"

"Yes. Mrs. Holbrook takes the whole of the personalty, but she has only a life-interest in the real estate. If she should have children, it will go to them on her death; if she should die childless, it will go to her father, supposing him to survive her."

"To her father? That is rather strange, isn't it?"

"I don't know that. It was the old man's wish that the will should be to that effect."

"I understood from him that he did not know whether his son was alive or dead."

"Indeed! I believe he had news of his son very lately."

"Curious that he should not have told me, knowing as he did my interest in everything relating to Mrs. Holbrook."

"Old people are apt to be close; and Jacob Nowell was about one of the closest customers I ever met with," answered the lawyer.

Gilbert left him soon after this, and chartered a hansom in the next street, which carried him back to the City. He was very uncertain as to what he ought to do for Marian, doubtful of Mr. Medler's integrity, and yet anxious to abstain from any act that might seem uncalled for or officious. She had her husband to look after her interests, as the lawyer had reminded him, and it was scarcely probable that Mr. Holbrook would neglect any steps necessary to secure his wife's succession to whatever property Jacob Nowell had left. It seemed to Gilbert that he could do nothing at present, except write to Marian, telling her of his interview with the lawyer, and advising her to lose no time in placing the conduct of her affairs in more respectable hands than those of Mr. Medler. He mentioned his own solicitors, a City firm of high standing, as gentlemen whom she might wisely trust at this crisis of her life.

This done, he could only wait the issue of events, and he tried to occupy himself as much as possible with his business at St. Helens—that business which he seriously intended getting rid of as soon as he could meet with a favourable opportunity for so doing. He worked with that object in view. In spite of his losses in Australia, he was in a position to retire from commerce with a very fair income. He had lost all motive for sustained exertion, all desire to become rich. A man who has no taste for expensive bachelor pleasures and no home has very little opportunity for getting rid of large sums of money. Mr. Fenton had taken life pleasantly enough, and yet had never spent five hundred a year. He could retire with an income of eight hundred and having abandoned all idea of ever marrying this seemed to him more than sufficient.

The Listers had come back to England, and Mrs. Lister had written to her brother more than once, begging him to run down to Lidford. Of course she had expressed herself freely upon the subject of Marian's conduct in these letters, reprobating the girl's treachery and ingratitude, and congratulating Gilbert upon his escape from so ineligible a connection. Mr. Fenton had put his sister off with excuses hitherto, and had subjected himself thereby to sundry feminine reproaches upon his coldness and want of affection for Mrs. Lister and her children. "It was very different when Marian Nowell was here," she wrote; "you thought it no trouble to come to us then."

No answer came to his letter to Mrs. Holbrook—which scarcely called for a reply, unless it had been a few lines of thanks, in acknowledgment of his interest in her behalf. He had looked for such a letter, and was a little disappointed by its non-appearance. The omission, slight as it was, served to strengthen his bitter feeling that his friendship in this quarter was unneeded and unvalued.

Business in the City happened to be rather slack at this time; and it struck Mr. Fenton all at once that he could scarcely have a better opportunity for wasting two or three days in a visit of duty to the Listers, and putting an end to his sister's reproachful letters. He had a second motive for going to Lidford; a motive which had far greater weight with him than his brotherly affection just at this time. He wanted to see Sir David Forster, to call that gentleman to some account for the deliberate falsehood he had uttered at their last meeting. He had no bloodthirsty or ferocious feelings upon the subject, he could even understand that the Baronet might have been bound by his own ideas of honour to tell a lie in the service of his friend; but he wanted to extort some explanation of the line of conduct Sir David had taken, and he wanted to ascertain from him the character of Marian's husband. He had made inquiries about Sir David at the club, and had been told that he was still at Heatherly.

He went down to Lidford by an afternoon train, without having troubled himself to give Mrs. Lister any notice of his coming. The November evening had closed in upon the quiet rural landscape when he drove from the station to Lidford. A cold white mist enfolded all things here, instead of the stifling yellow fog that had filled the London streets when he walked westwards from the City at the same hour on the previous evening. Above his head the sky was clear and bright, the mist-wreaths melting away as they mounted towards the stars. The lighted windows in the village street had a pleasant homely look; the snug villas, lying back from the high road with a middle distance of dark lawn and glistening shrubbery, shone brightly upon the traveller as he drove by, the curtains not yet drawn before some of the windows, the rooms ruddy in the firelight. In one of them he caught a brief glimpse of a young matron seated by the fire with her children clustered at her knee, and the transient picture struck him with a sudden pang. He had dreamed so fondly of a home like this; pleasant rooms shining in the sacred light of the hearth, his wife and children waiting to bid him welcome when the day's work was done. All other objects which men live and toil for seemed to him poor and worthless in the absence of this one dear incentive to exertion, this one sweet recompense for every care. Even Lidford House, which had never before seemed to him the perfection of a home, had a new aspect for him to-night, and reminded him sharply of his own loss. He envied Martin Lister the quiet jog-trot happiness of his domestic life; his love for and pride in his children; the calm haven of that comfortable hearth by which he sat to-night, with his slippered feet stretched luxuriously upon a fender-stool of his wife's manufacture, and his daughter sitting on a hassock close to his easy-chair, reading in a book of fairy tales.

Of course they were all delighted to see him, at once pleased and surprised by the unexpected visit. He had brought a great parcel of toys for the two children; and Selwyn Lister, a fine boisterous boy in a Highland costume, was summoned downstairs to assist at the unpacking of these treasures. It was half-past seven, and the Listers had dined at six: but in an incredibly short space of time the Sutherland table had been drawn out to a cosy position near the fire and spread with a substantial repast, while Mrs. Lister took her place behind the ponderous old silver urn which had been an heirloom in her husband's family for the last two centuries. The Listers were full of talk about their own travels— a long-delayed continental tour which had been talked of ever since their return from the honeymoon trip to Geneva and Chamouni; and were also very eager to hear Gilbert's adventures in Australia, of which he had given them only very brief accounts in his letters. There was nothing said that night about Marian, and Gilbert was grateful for his sister's forbearance.

CHAPTER XXIII.
CALLED TO ACCOUNT.

GILBERT walked over to Heatherly after luncheon next day, taking of preference the way which led him past Captain Sedgewick's cottage and through the leafless wood where he and Marian had walked together when the foliage was in its summer glory. The leaves lay thick upon the mossy ground now; and the gaunt bare branches of the trees had a weird awful look in the utter silence of the place. His footsteps trampling upon the fallen leaves had an echo; and he turned to look behind him more than once, fancying he was followed.

The old house, with its long lines of windows, had a prison-like aspect under the dull November day. Gilbert wondered how such a man as Sir David Forster could endure his existence there, embittered as it was by the memory of that calamity which had taken all the sunlight out of his life, and left him a weary and purposeless hunter after pleasure. But Sir David had been prostrate under the heavy hand of his hereditary foe, the gout, for a long time past; and was fain to content himself with such company as came to him at Heatherly, and such amusement as was to be found in the society of men who were boon companions rather than friends. Gilbert Fenton heard the familiar clash of the billiard-balls as he went into the hall, where a couple of liver-coloured setters were dozing before a great fire that roared half-way up the wide chimney. There was no other life in the hall; and Mr. Fenton was conducted to the other end of the house, and ushered into that tobacco-tainted snuggery in which he had last seen the Baronet. His suspicions were on the alert this time; and he fancied he could detect a look of something more than surprise in Sir David's face when the servant announced him—an uneasy look, as of a man taken at a disadvantage.

The Baronet was very gracious, however, and gave him a hearty welcome.

"I'm uncommonly glad to see you, my dear Fenton," he said, "Indeed, I have been pleased to see worse fellows than you lately, since this infernal gout has laid me up in this dreary old place. The house is pretty full now, I am happy to say. I have friends who will come to shoot my partridges, though they won't remember my solitude in a charitable spirit before the first of September. You'll stop and dine, I hope; or perhaps you can put up here altogether for a week or so. My housekeeper shall find you a good room; and I can promise you pleasant company. Say yes, now, like a good fellow, and I'll send a man to Lidford for your traps."

"Thanks—no. You are very kind; but I am staying with my sister for a few days, and must return to town before the end of the week. The fact of the matter is, Sir David, I have come here to-day to ask you for some explanation of your conduct at our last interview. I don't want to say anything rude or disagreeable; for I am quite willing to believe that you felt kindly towards me, even at the time when you deceived me. I suppose there are some positions in which a man can hardly expect fair play, and that mine was such a position. But you certainly did deceive me, Sir David, and grossly."

"That last is rather an unpleasant word, Mr. Fenton. In what respect did I deceive you?"

"I came here on purpose to ask you if Mr. Holbrook, the man who robbed me of my promised wife, were a friend of yours, and you denied all knowledge of him."

"Granted. And what then, my dear sir?"

"When I came to ask you that question, I had no special reason for supposing this Mr. Holbrook was known to you. It only struck me that, being a stranger in the village, as the result of my inquiries had proved to me, he might be one of your many visitors. I knew at that time that Mr. Holbrook had taken his wife to a farm-house in Hampshire immediately after their marriage—a house lent to him by a friend; but I did not know that you had any estate in that county. I have been to Hampshire since then, and have found Mrs. Holbrook at the Grange, near Crosber—in your house."

"You have found her! Well, Mr. Fenton, the circumstantial evidence is too strong for me, so I must plead guilty. Yes; I did deceive you when I told you that Holbrook was unknown to me; but I pledged my word to keep his secret—to give you no clue, should you ever happen to question me, that could lead to your discovery of your lost love's whereabouts. It was considered, I conclude, that any meeting between you two must needs result unpleasantly. At any rate, there was a strong desire to avoid you; and in common duty to my friend I was compelled to respect that desire."

"Not a very manly wish on the part of my successful rival," said Gilbert.

"It may have been the lady's wish rather than Mr. Holbrook's."

"I have reason to know that it was otherwise. I have heard from Marian's own lips that she would have written a candid confession of the truth had she been free to do so. It was her husband who prevented her giving me notice of my desertion."

"I cannot pretend to explain his conduct," Sir David answered gravely. "I only know that I pledged myself to keep his secret; and felt bound to do so, even at the cost of a lie."

"And this man is your friend. You must know whether he is worthy to be Marian Nowell's husband. The circumstances of her life do not seem to me favourable to happiness, so far as I have been able to discover them; nor did I think her looking happy when we met. But I should be glad to know that she has not fallen into bad hands."

"And I suppose by this time your feelings have cooled down a little. You have abandoned those revengeful intentions you appeared to entertain, when you were last in this house?"

"In a great measure, yes. I have promised Marian that, should I and her husband meet, as we must do, I believe, sooner or later, she need apprehend no violence on my part. He has won the prize; any open resentment would seem mere schoolboy folly. But you cannot suppose that I feel very kindly towards him, or ever shall."

"Upon my soul, I think men are hardly responsible for their actions where a woman is concerned," Sir David exclaimed after a pause. "We are the veriest slaves of destiny in these matters. A man sees the only woman in the world he can love too late to win her with honour. If he is strong enough to act nobly, he turns his back upon the scene of his temptation, all the more easily should the lady happen to be staunch to her affianced, or her husband, as the case may be. But if *she* waver—if he sees that his love is returned—heaven help him! Honour, generosity, friendship, all go by the board; and for the light in those fatal eyes, for the dangerous music of that one dear voice, he sacrifices all that he has held highest in life until that luckless time. I *know* that Holbrook held it no light thing to do you this wrong; I know that he fought manfully against temptation. But, you see, fate was the stronger; and he had to give way at the last."

"I cannot agree with that way of looking at things, Sir David. The world is made up of people who take their own pleasure at any cost to others, and then throw the onus of their misdoings upon Providence. I have long ago forgiven the girl who jilted me, and have sworn to be her faithful and watchful friend in all the days to come. I want to be sure that her future is a bright one—much brighter than it seemed when I saw her in your lonely old house near Crosber. She has had money left her since then; so poverty can no longer be a reason for her being hidden from the world."

"I am very glad to hear that; my friend is not a rich man."

"So Marian told me. But I want to learn something more than that about him. Up to this moment he has been the most intangible being I ever heard of. Will you tell me who and what he is—his position in the world, and so on?"

"Humph!" muttered Sir David meditatively; "I don't know that I can tell you much about him. His position is like that of a good many others of my acquaintance—rather vague and intangible, to use the word you employed just now. He is not well off; he is a gentleman by birth, with some small means of his own, and he 'lives, sir, lives.' That is about all I can say of him—from a worldly point of view. With regard to his affection for Miss Nowell, I know that he loved her passionately, devotedly, desperately—the strongest expression you can supply to describe a man's folly. I never saw any fellow so far gone. Heaven knows, I did my best to argue him out of his fancy—urged your claim, the girl's poverty, every reason against the marriage; but friendly argumentation of that kind goes very little way in such a case. He took his own course. It was only when I found the business was decided upon, that I offered him my house in Hampshire; a place to which I never go myself, but which brings me in a decent income in the hands of a clever bailiff. I knew that Holbrook had no home ready for his wife, and I thought it would give them a pleasant retreat enough for a few months, while the honey and rose-leaves still sweetened the wine-cup of their wedded life. They have stayed there ever since, as you seem to know; so I conclude they have found the place agreeable. Confoundedly dreary, I should fancy it myself; but then I'm not a newly married man."

The Baronet gave a brief sigh, and his thoughts went back for a moment to the time when he too was in Arcadia; when a fair young wife was by his side, and when no hour of his existence seemed ever dull or weary to him. It was all changed now! He had billiards and whist, and horses and hounds, and a vast collection of gunnery, and great stores of wine in the gloomy arched vaults beneath the house, where a hundred prisoners had been kept under lock and key when Heatherly had fallen into the hands of the Cromwellian soldiery, and the faithful retainers of the household were fain to lay down their arms. He had all things that make up the common pleasures and delights of a man's existence; but he had lost the love which had given these things a new charm, and without which all life seemed to him flat, stale, and unprofitable. He could sympathise with Gilbert Fenton much more keenly than that gentleman would have supposed possible; for a man suffering from this kind of affliction is apt to imagine that he has a copyright in that species of grief, and that no other man ever did or ever can experience a like calamity. The same manner of trouble may come to others, of course, but not with a similar intensity. Others will suffer and recover, and find a balm elsewhere. He alone is constant until death!

"And you can tell me nothing more about Mr. Holbrook?" he asked after a pause.

"Upon my honour, nothing. I think you will do wisely to leave these two people to take their own way in the future without any interference on your part. You speak of watchful friendship and all that kind of thing, and I can quite appreciate your disinterested desire to befriend the woman whom you once hoped to make your wife. But, believe me, my dear Fenton, no manner of good can possibly come of your intervention. Those two have chosen their road in life, and must travel along it, side by side, through good or evil fortune. Holbrook would naturally be jealous of any friendship between his wife and you; while such a friendship could not fail to keep alive bitter thoughts in your mind—could not fail to sharpen the regret which you fancy just now is to be life-long. I have no doubt I seem to speak in a hard worldly spirit."

"You speak like a man of the world, Sir David," the other answered quietly; "and I cannot deny that there is a certain amount of wisdom in your advice. No, my friendship is not wanted by either of those two, supposing even that I were generous enough to be able to give it to both. I have learnt that lesson already from Marian herself. But you must remember that I promised her poor old grandfather—the man who died a few days ago—that I would watch over her interests with patient fidelity, that I would be her friend and protector, if ever the hour should come in which she would need friendship and protection. I am not going to forget this promise, or to neglect its performance; and in order to be true to my word, I am bound to make myself acquainted with the circumstances of her married life, and the character of her husband."

"Cannot you be satisfied with knowing that she is happy?"

"I have seen her, Sir David, and am by no means assured of her happiness."

"And yet it was a love-match on both sides. Holbrook, as I have told you, loved her passionately."

"That passionate kind of love is apt to wear itself out very quickly with some men. Your bailiff's daughter complained bitterly of Mr. Holbrook's frequent absence from the Grange, of the dulness and loneliness of my poor girl's life."

"Women are apt to be exacting," Sir David answered with a deprecating shrug of the shoulders. "My friend Holbrook has the battle of life to fight, and could not spend all his days playing the lover. If his wife has had money left her, that will make some difference in their position. A man is never at his best when he is worried by debts and financial difficulties."

"And Mr. Holbrook was in debt when he married, I suppose?"

"He was. I must confess that I find that complaint a very common one among my acquaintance," the Baronet added with a laugh.

"Will you tell me what this Holbrook is like in person, Sir David? I have questioned several people about him, and have never obtained anything beyond the vaguest kind of description."

Sir David Forster laughed aloud at this request.

"What! you want to know whether your rival is handsome, I suppose? like a woman, who always commences her inquiries about another woman by asking whether she is pretty. My dear Fenton, all personal descriptions are vague. It is almost impossible to furnish a correct catalogue of any man's features. Holbrook is just one of those men whom it is most difficult to describe—not particularly good-looking, nor especially ill-looking; very clever, and with plenty of expression and character in his face. Older than you by some years, and looking older than he really is."

"Thanks; but there is not one precise statement in your description. Is the man dark or fair—short or tall?"

"Rather dark than fair; rather tall than short."

"That will do, Sir David," Gilbert said, starting suddenly to his feet, and looking the Baronet in the face intently. "The man who robbed me of my promised wife is the man whom I introduced to her; the man who has come between me and all my hopes, who hides himself from my just anger, and skulks in the background under a feigned name, is the one friend whom I have loved above all other men—John Saltram!"

Sir David faced him without flinching. If it was acted surprise which appeared upon his countenance at the sound of John Saltram's name, the acting was perfect. Gilbert could discover nothing from that broad stare of blank amazement.

"In heaven's name, what can have put such a preposterous notion into your head?" Sir David asked coolly.

"I cannot tell you. The conviction has grown upon me, against my own will. Yes, I have hated myself for being able to suspect my friend. You do not know how I have loved that man, or how our friendship began at Oxford long ago with something like hero-worship on my side. I thought that he was born to be great and noble; and heaven knows I have felt the disappointments and shortcomings of his career more keenly than he has felt them himself. No, Sir David, I don't think it is possible for any man to comprehend how I have loved John Saltram."

"And yet, without a shred of evidence, you believe him guilty of betraying you."

"Will you give me your word of honour that Marian's husband and John Saltram are not one and the same person?"

"No," answered Sir David impatiently; "I am tired of the whole business. You have questioned and cross-questioned me quite long enough, Mr. Fenton, and I have answered you to the best of my ability, and have given you rational advice, which you will of course decline to take. If you think your friend has wronged you, go to him, and tax him with that wrong. I wash my hands of the affair altogether, from this moment; but, without wishing to be offensive, I cannot help telling you, that to my mind you are acting very foolishly in this business."

"I daresay it may seem so to you. You would think better of me if I could play the stoic, and say, 'She has jilted me, and is dead to me henceforward.' But I cannot do that. I have the memory of her peaceful girlhood—the happy days in which I knew her first—the generous protector who sheltered her life. I am pledged to the dead, Sir David."

He left Heatherly soon after this, though the Baronet pressed him to stay to dinner.

CHAPTER XXIV.
TORMENTED BY DOUBT.

THE long homeward walk gave Gilbert ample leisure for reflection upon his interview with Sir David; a very unsatisfactory interview at the best. Yes, the conviction that the man who had wronged him was no other than his own familiar friend, had flashed upon him with a new force as the Baronet answered his questions about John Holbrook. The suspicion which had entered his mind after he left the lonely farm-house near Crosber, and which he had done his uttermost to banish, as if it had been a suggestion of the evil one, came back to him to-day with a form and reality which it had lacked before. It seemed no longer a vague fancy, a dark unwelcome thought that bordered on folly. It had taken a new shape altogether, and appeared to him almost a certainty.

Sir David's refusal to make any direct denial of the fact seemed to confirm his suspicion. Yet it was, on the other hand, just possible that Sir David, finding him on a false scent, should have been willing to let him follow it, and that the real offender should be screened by this suspicion of John Saltram. But then there arose in his mind a doubt that had perplexed him sorely for a long time. If his successful rival had been indeed a stranger to him, what reason could there be for so much mystery in the circumstances of the marriage? and why should Marian have so carefully avoided telling him anything about her husband? That his friend, having betrayed him, should shrink from the revelation of his falsehood, should adopt any underhand course to avoid discovery, seemed natural enough. Yet to believe this was to think meanly of the man whom he had loved so well, whom he had confided in so implicitly until the arising of this cruel doubt.

He had known long ago, when the first freshness of his boyish delusions faded away before the penetrating clear daylight of reality, he had known long ago that his friend was not faultless; that except in that one faithful alliance with himself, John Saltram had been fickle, wayward, vacillating, unstable, and inconstant, true to no dream of his youth, no ambition of his early manhood content to drop one purpose after another, until his life was left without any exalted aim. But Gilbert had fancied his friend's nature was still a noble one in spite of the comparative failure of his life. It was very difficult for him to imagine it possible that this friend could act falsely and ungenerously, could steal his betrothed from him, and keep the secret of his guilt, pretending to sympathise with the jilted lover all the while.

But though Mr. Fenton told himself at one moment that this was impossible, his thoughts travelled back to the same point immediately afterwards, and the image of John Saltram arose before him as that of his hidden foe. He remembered the long autumn days which he and his friend had spent with Marian—those unclouded utterly happy days, which he looked back upon now with a kind of wonder. They had been so much together, Marian so bright and fascinating in her innocent enjoyment of the present, brighter and happier just then than she had ever seemed to him before, Gilbert remembered with a bitter pang. He had been completely unsuspicious at the time, untroubled by one doubtful thought; but it appeared to him now that there had been a change in Marian from the time of his friend's coming—a new joyousness and vivacity, a keener delight in the simple pleasures of their daily life, and withal a fitfulness, a tendency to change from gaiety to thoughtful silence, that he had not remarked in her before.

Was it strange if John Saltram had fallen in love with her? was it possible to see her daily in all the glory of her girlish loveliness, made doubly bewitching by the sweetness of her nature, the indescribable charm of her manner—was it possible to be with her often, as John Saltram had been, and not love her? Gilbert Fenton had thought of his friend as utterly impregnable to any such danger; as a man who had spent all his stock of tender emotion long ago, and who looked upon matrimony as a transaction by which he might mend his broken fortunes. That this man should fall a victim to the same subtle charm which had subjugated himself, was a possibility that never occurred to Gilbert's mind, in this happy period of his existence. He wanted his friend's approval of his choice; he wished to see his passion justified in the eyes of the man whom it was his habit to regard in somewise as a superior creature; and it had been a real delight to him to hear Mr. Saltram's warm praises of Marian.

Looking back at the past to-day from a new point of view, he wondered at his own folly. What was more natural than that John Saltram should have found his doom, as he had found it, unthought of, undreamed of, swift, and fatal? Nor was it difficult for him to believe that Marian—who had perhaps never really loved him, who had been induced to accept him by his own pertinacity and her uncle's eager desire for the match—should find a charm and a power in John Saltram that had been wanting in himself. He had seen too many instances of his friend's influence over men and women, to doubt his ability to win this innocent inexperienced girl, had he set himself to win her. He recalled with a bitter smile how his informants had all described his rival in a disparaging tone, as unworthy of so fair a bride; and he knew that it was precisely those qualities which these common people were unable to appreciate that constituted the subtle charm by which John Saltram influenced others. The rugged power and grandeur of that dark face, which vulgar critics denounced as plain and unattractive, the rare fascination of a manner that varied from an extreme reserve to a wild reckless vivacity, the magic of the deep full voice, with its capacity for the expression of every shade of emotion—these were attributes to be passed over and ignored by the vulgar, yet to exercise a potent influence upon sensitive sympathetic natures.

"How that poor little Anglo-Indian widow loves him, without any effort to win or hold her affection on his side!" Gilbert said to himself, as he walked back to Lidford in the darkening November afternoon, brooding always on the one subject which occupied all his thoughts; "and can I doubt his power to supersede me if he cared to do so—if he really loved Marian, as he never has loved Mrs. Branston? What shall I do? Go to him at once, and tell him my suspicion, tax him broadly with treachery, and force him to a direct confession or denial? Shall I do this? Or shall I bide my time, wait and watch with dull dogged patience, till I can collect some evidence of his guilt? Yes, let it be so. If he has been base enough to do me this great wrong—mean enough to steal my betrothed under a false name, and to keep the secret of his wrong-doing at any cost of lies and deceit—let him go on to the end, let him act out the play to the last; and when I bring his falsehood home to him, as I must surely do, sooner or later,—yes, if he is capable of deceiving me, he shall continue the lie to the last, he shall endure all the infamy of his false position."

And then, after a pause, he said to himself,—

"And at the end, if my suspicions are confirmed, I shall have lost all I have ever valued in life since my mother died—my plighted wife, and the one chosen friend whose companionship could make existence pleasant to me. God grant that this fancy of mine is as baseless as Sir David Forster declared it to be! God grant that I may never find a secret enemy in John Saltram!"

Tossed about thus upon a sea of doubts, Mr. Fenton returned to Lidford House, where he was expected to be bright and cheerful, and entertain his host and hostess with the freshest gossip of the London world. He did make a great effort to keep up a show of cheerfulness at the dinner-table; but he felt that his sister's eyes were watching him with a pitiless scrutiny, and he knew that the attempt was an ignominious failure.

When honest Martin was snoring in his easy-chair before the drawing-room fire, with the red light shining full upon his round healthy countenance, Mrs. Lister beckoned her brother over to her side of the hearth, where she had an embroidery-frame, whereon was stretched some grand design in Berlin wool-work, to which she devoted herself every now and then with a great show of industry. She had been absorbed in a profound calculation of the stitches upon the canvas and on the coloured pattern before her until this moment; but she laid aside her work with a solemn air when Gilbert went over to her, and he knew at once what was coming.

"Sit down, Gilbert," she said; and her brother dropped into a chair by her side with a faint sigh of resignation. "I want to talk to you seriously, as a sister ought to talk to a brother, without any fear of offending. I'm very sorry to see you have not yet forgotten that wicked ungrateful girl Marian Nowell."

"Who told you that I have not forgotten her?"

"Your own face, Gilbert. It's no use for you to put on a pretence of being cheerful and light-hearted with me. I know you too well to be deceived by that kind of thing—I could see how absent-minded you were all dinner-time, in spite of your talk. You can't hoodwink an affectionate sister."

"I don't wish to hoodwink you, my dear," Mr. Fenton answered quietly, "or to affect a happiness which I do not feel, any more than I wish to make a parade of my grief. It is natural for an Englishman to be reticent on such matters; but I do not mind owning to you that Marian Nowell is unforgotten by me, and that the loss of her will have an enduring influence upon my life; and having said as much as that, Belle, I must request that you will not expatiate any more upon this poor girl's breach of faith. I have forgiven her long ago, and I shall always regard her as the purest and dearest of women."

"What! you can hold her up as a paragon of perfection after she has thrown you over in the most heartless manner? Upon my word, Gilbert, I have no common patience with such folly. Your weakness in this affair from first to last has been positively deplorable."

"I am sorry you disapprove of my conduct, Belle; but as it is not a very pleasant subject, don't you think we may as well avoid it now and henceforward?"

"O, very well, Gilbert," the lady exclaimed, with an offended air; "of course, if you choose to exclude me from your confidence, I must submit; but I do think it rather hard that your only sister should not he allowed to speak of a business that concerns you so nearly."

"What good can arise out of any discussion of this subject, Belle? You think me weak and foolish; granted that I am both, you cannot cure me of my weakness or my folly."

"And am I never to hope that you will find some one else, better worthy of your regard than Marian Nowell?"

"I fear not, Belle. For me there is no one else."

Mrs. Lister breathed a profound sigh, and resumed the counting of her stitches. Yet perhaps, after all, it was better that her brother should cherish the memory of this unlucky attachment. It would preserve him from the hazard of any imprudent alliance in the future, and leave his fortune free, to descend by-and-by to the juvenile Listers. Isabella was not a particularly mercenary person, but she was a woman of the world, and had an eye to the future aggrandisement of her children.

She was very kind and considerate to Gilbert after this, carefully avoiding any farther allusions to his lost love, and taking all possible pains to make his visit pleasant to him. She was so affectionate and cordial, and seemed so really anxious for him to stay, that he could not in common decency hurry back to town quite so soon as he had intended. He prolonged his visit to the end of that week, and then to the beginning of the next; and when he did at last find himself free to return to London, the second week was nearly ended.

CHAPTER XXV.
MISSING AGAIN.

GILBERT Fenton was very glad to have made his escape from Lidford at last, for his mind was full of anxiety about Marian. Again and again he had argued with himself upon the folly and uselessness of this anxiety. She, for whose interests he was so troubled, was safe enough no doubt, protected by a husband, who was most likely a man of the world, and quite as able to protect her as Gilbert himself could be. He told himself this; but still the restless uneasy sense that he was neglecting his duty, that he was false to the promise made to old Jacob Nowell, tormented and perplexed him. He felt that he ought to be doing something—that he had no right to remain in ignorance of the progress of Marian's affairs—that he should be at hand to frustrate any attempt at knavery on the part of the lawyer—to be sure that the old man's wealth suffered no diminution before it reached the hands of his heiress.

Gilbert Fenton felt that his promise to the dead bound him to do these things, and felt at the same time the weakness of his own position with relation to Marian. By what right could he interfere in the conduct of her affairs? what claim could he assert to defend her interests? who would listen to any romantic notion about a promise made to the dead?

He went to Queen Anne's Court upon the night of his return to London. The silversmith's shop looked exactly the same as when he had first seen it: the gas burning dimly, the tarnished old salvers and tankards gleaming duskily in the faint light, with all manner of purple and greenish hues. Mr. Tulliver was in his little den at the back of the shop, and emerged with his usual rapidity at the ringing of the door-bell.

"O, it's you, is it, sir?" he asked in an indifferent, half-insolent tone. "What can I do for you this evening?"

"Is your late master's granddaughter, Mrs. Holbrook, here?" Gilbert asked.

"No; Mrs. Holbrook went away on the morning after my master's death. I told you that when you called here last."

"I am quite aware of that; but I thought it likely Mrs. Holbrook might return here with her husband, to take possession of the property, which I suppose you know now belongs to her."

"Yes, I know all about that; but she hasn't come yet to take possession; she doesn't seem in such a desperate hurry about it. I daresay she knows that things are safe enough. Medler the lawyer is not the kind of party to be cheated out of sixpence. He has taken an inventory of every article in the place, and the weight and value of every article. Your friend Mrs. Holbrook needn't be afraid. I suppose she's some relation of yours, by-the-bye, sir, judging by the interest you seem to take in her affairs?"

"Yes," Gilbert said, not caring to answer this question directly, "I do take a warm interest in Mrs. Holbrook's affairs, and I am very anxious to see her placed in undisputed possession of her late grandfather's property."

"I should think her husband would see after that," Mr. Tulliver remarked with a sneer.

Gilbert left the court after having asked a few questions about Jacob Nowell's funeral. The old man had been buried at Kensalgreen, followed to the grave only by the devoted Tulliver, Mr. Medler, and the local surgeon who had attended him in his last illness. He had lived a lonely friendless life, holding himself aloof from his fellow-creatures; and there were neither neighbours nor friends to lament his ending. The vagabond boys of the neighbourhood had clustered round the door to witness the last dismal ceremony of Mr. Nowell's existence, and had hung about the shop-front for some time after the funeral *cortège* had departed, peering curiously down into the darksome area, and speculating upon the hoards of wealth which the old miser had hidden away in coal-cellars and dust-bins, under the stone flags of the scullery, or in the crannies of the dilapidated walls. There were no bounds to the imagination of these street Arabs, who had been in the habit of yelping and whooping at the old man's heels when he took his infrequent walks abroad, assailing him with derisive epithets alluding to his miserly propensities. Amongst the elders of the court there was some little talk about the dead man, and the probable disposal of his property, with a good deal of argument and laying down of the law on the part of the graver and wiser members of that community; some people affecting to know to a sixpence the amount of Jacob Nowell's savings, others accrediting him with the possession of fabulous riches, and all being unanimous in the idea that the old man's heir or heirs, as the case might be, would speedily scatter his long-hoarded treasures. Many of these people could remember the silversmith's prodigal son; but none among them were aware of that gentleman's return. They wondered a good deal as to whether he was still living, and whether the money had been left to him or to that pretty young woman who had appeared in the last days of the old man's life, no one knowing whence she had come. There was nothing to be gained from questioning Luke Tulliver, the court knew of old experience. The most mysterious dungeons of the Spanish Inquisition, the secret chambers under the leads in Venice, were not closer or deeper than the mind of that young man. The court had been inclined to think that Luke Tulliver would come into all his master's money; and opinion inclined that way even yet, seeing that Mr. Tulliver still held his ground in the shop, and that no strangers had been seen to enter the place since the funeral.

From Queen Anne's Court Gilbert Fenton went on to the gloomy street where Mr. Medler had his office and abode. It was not an hour for a professional visit; but Gilbert found the lawyer still hard at work at his desk, under the lurid light of a dirty-looking battered old oil-lamp, which left the corners of the dingy wainscoted room in profound obscurity. He looked up from his papers with some show of surprise on hearing Mr. Fenton's name announced by the slipshod maid-of-all-work who had admitted the late visitor, Mr. Medler's solitary clerk having departed to his own dwelling some hours before.

"I must ask you to excuse this untimely call, Mr. Medler," Gilbert said politely; "but the fact of the matter is, I am a little anxious about my friend Mrs.

Holbrook and her affairs, and I thought you the most likely person to give me some information about them. I should have called in business hours; but I have only just returned from the country, and did not care to delay my inquiries until to-morrow. I have just come from Queen Anne's Court, and am rather surprised to find that neither Mrs. Holbrook nor her husband has been there. You have seen or heard from them since the funeral, I suppose?"

"No, Mr. Fenton, I have neither seen nor heard of them. I wrote a formal letter to Mrs. Holbrook, setting out the contents of the will; but there has been no answer as yet."

"Strange, is it not?" Gilbert exclaimed, with an anxious look.

"Well, yes, it is certainly not the usual course of proceeding. However, there is time enough yet. The funeral has not been over much more than a week. The property is perfectly safe, you know."

"Of course; but it is not the less extraordinary that Mr. Holbrook should hang back in this manner. I will go down to Hampshire the first thing to-morrow and see Mrs. Holbrook."

"Humph!" muttered the lawyer; "I can't say that I see any necessity for that. But of course you know best."

Gilbert Fenton did start for Hampshire early the next morning by the same train in which Marian had travelled after her grandfather's death. It was still quite early in the day when he found himself at Malsham, that quiet comfortable little market-town where he had first discovered a clue to the abode of his lost love. He went to the hotel, and hired a fly to take him to Crosber, where he left the vehicle at the old inn, preferring to walk on to the Grange. It was a bright November day, with a pale yellow sunlight shining on the level fields, and distant hills that rose beyond them crowned with a scanty fringe of firs, that stood out black and sharp against the clear autumn sky. It was a cheerful day, and a solitary bird was singing here and there, as if beguiled by that pleasant warmth and sunshine into the fond belief that winter was still far off and the glory of fields and woods not yet departed. Gilbert's spirits rose in some degree under the influence of that late brightness and sweet rustic calm. He fancied that there might be still some kind of happiness for him in the long years to come; pale and faint like the sunlight of to-day—an autumnal calm. If he might be Marian's friend and brother, her devoted counsellor, her untiring servant, it seemed to him that he could be content, that he could live on from year to year moderately happy in the occasional delight of her society; rewarded for his devotion by a few kind words now and then,—a letter, a friendly smile,—rewarded still more richly by her perfect trust in him.

These thoughts were in his mind to-day as he went along the lonely country lane leading to the Grange; thoughts which seemed inspired by the tranquil landscape and peaceful autumn day; thoughts which were full of the purest love and charity,—yes, even for his unknown rival, even if that rival should prove to be the one man in all this world from whom a deep wrong would seem most bitter.

"What am I, that I should measure the force of his temptation," he said to himself, "or the strength of his resistance? Let me be sure that he loves my darling as truly as I love her, that the chief object of his life has been and will be her happiness, and then let me put away all selfish vindictive thoughts, and fall quietly into the background of my dear one's life, content to be her brother and her friend."

The Grange looked unchanged in its sombre lonely aspect. The chrysanthemums were all withered by this time, and there were now no flowers in the old-fashioned garden. The bell was answered by the same woman who had admitted him before, and who made no parley about letting him in this time.

"My young missus said I was to be sure and let her know if you came, sir," she said; "she's very anxious to see you."

"Your young mistress; do you mean Mrs. Holbrook?"

"No, sir; Miss Carley, master's daughter."

"Indeed! I remember the young lady; I shall be very happy to see her if she has anything to say to me; but it is Mrs. Holbrook I have come to see. She is at home, I suppose?"

"O dear no, sir; Mrs. Holbrook has left, without a word of notice, gone nobody knows where. That is what has made our young missus fret about it so."

"Mrs. Holbrook has left!" Gilbert exclaimed in blank amazement; "when?"

"It's more than a week ago now, sir."

"And do none of you know why she went away, or where she has gone?"

"No more than the dead, sir. But you'd better see Miss Carley; she'll be able to tell you all about it."

The woman led him into the house, and to the room in which he had seen Marian. There was no fire here to-day, and the room had a desolate unoccupied look, though the sun was shining cheerfully on the old-fashioned many-paned windows. There were a few books, which Gilbert remembered as Marian's literary treasures, neatly arranged on a rickety old chiffonier by the fire-place, and the desk and work-basket which he had seen on his previous visit.

He was half bewildered by what the woman had told him, and his heart beat tumultuously as he stood by the empty hearth, waiting for Ellen Carley's coming. It seemed to him as if the girl never would come. The ticking of an old eight-day clock in the hall had a ghastly sound in the dead silence of the house, and an industrious mouse made itself distinctly heard behind the wainscot.

At last a light rapid footstep came tripping across the hall, and Ellen Carley entered the room. She was looking paler than when Gilbert had seen her last, and the bright face was very grave.

"For heaven's sake tell me what this means, Miss Carley," Gilbert began eagerly. "Your servant tells me that Mrs. Holbrook has left you—in some mysterious way, I imagine, from what the woman said."

"O, sir, I am so glad you have come here; I should have written to you if I had known where to address a letter. Yes, sir, she has gone—that dear sweet young creature—and I fear some harm has come to her."

The girl burst into tears, and for some minutes could say no more.

"Pray, pray be calm," Gilbert said gently, "and tell me all you can about this business. How did Mrs. Holbrook leave this place? and why do you suspect that any harm has befallen her?"

"There is every reason to think so, sir. Is it like her to leave us without a word of notice, knowing, as she must have known, the unhappiness she would cause to me, who love her so well, by such a step? She knew how I loved her. I think she had scarcely a secret from me."

"If you will only tell me the manner of her departure," Gilbert said rather impatiently.

"Yes, yes, sir; I am coming to that directly. She seemed happier after she came back from London, poor dear; and she told me that her grandfather had left her money, and that she was likely to become quite a rich woman. The thought of this gave her so much pleasure—not for her own sake, but for her husband's, whose cares and difficulties would all come to an end now, she told me. She had been back only a few days, when I left home for a day and a night, to see my aunt—an old woman and a constant invalid, who lives at Malsham. I had put off going to her for a long time, for I didn't care about leaving Mrs. Holbrook; but I had to go at last, my aunt thinking it hard that I couldn't spare time to spend a day with her, and tidy up her house a bit, and see to the girl that waits upon her, poor helpless thing. So I started off before noon one day, after telling Mrs. Holbrook where I was going, and when I hoped to be back. She was in very good spirits that morning, for she expected her husband next day. 'I have told him nothing about the good fortune that has come to me, Nelly,' she said; 'I have only written to him, begging him to return as quickly as possible, and he will be here to-morrow by the afternoon express.' Mr. Holbrook is a great walker, and generally walks from Malsham here, by a shorter way than the high-road, across some fields and by the river-bank. His wife used always to go part of the way to meet him when she knew he was coming. I know she meant to go and meet him this time. The way is very lonely, and I have often felt fidgety about her going alone, but she hadn't a bit of fear; and I didn't like to offer to go with her, feeling sure that Mr. Holbrook would be vexed by seeing me at such a time. Well, sir, I had arranged everything comfortably, so that she should miss nothing by my being away, and I bade her good-bye, and started off to walk to Malsham. I can't tell you how hard it seemed to me to leave her, for it was the first time we had been parted for so much as a day since she came to the Grange. I thought of her all the while I was at my aunt's; who has very fidgety ways, poor old lady, and isn't a pleasant person to be with. I felt quite in a fever of impatience to get home again; and was very glad when a neighbour's spring-cart dropped me at the end of the lane, and I saw the gray old chimneys above the tops of the trees. It was four o'clock in the afternoon when I got home; father was at tea in the oak-parlour where we take our meals, and the house was as quiet as a grave. I came straight to this room, but it was empty; and when I called Martha, she told me Mrs. Holbrook had gone out at one o'clock in the day, and had not been home since, though she was expected back to dinner at three. She had been away three hours then, and at a time when I knew she could not expect Mr. Holbrook, unless she had received a fresh letter from him to say that he was coming by an earlier train than usual. I asked Martha if there had been any letters for Mrs. Holbrook that day; and she told me yes, there had been one by the morning post. It was no use asking Martha what kind of letter it looked, and whether it was from Mr. Holbrook, for the poor ignorant creature can neither read nor write, and one handwriting is the same as another to her. Mrs. Holbrook had told her nothing as to where she was going, only saying that she would be back in an hour or two. Martha let her out at the gate, and watched her take the way towards the river-bank, and, seeing this, made sure she was going to meet her husband. Well, sir, five o'clock struck, and Mrs. Holbrook had not come home. I began to feel seriously uneasy about her. I told my father so; but he took the matter lightly enough at first, saying it was no business of ours, and that Mrs. Holbrook was just as well able to take care of herself as any one else. But after five o'clock I couldn't rest a minute longer; so I put on my bonnet and shawl and went down by the river-bank, after sending one of the farm-labourers to look for my poor dear in the opposite direction. It's a very lonely walk at the best of times, though a few of the country folks do go that way between Malsham and Crosber on market-days. There's scarcely a house to be seen for miles, except Wyncomb Farmhouse, Stephen Whitelaw's place, which lies a little way back from the river-bank, about a mile from here; besides that and a solitary cottage here and there, you won't see a sign of human life for four or five miles. Anybody might be pushed into the river and made away with in broad daylight, and no one need be the wiser. The loneliness of the place struck me with an awful fear that afternoon, and from that moment I began to think that I should never see Mrs. Holbrook again."

"What of her husband? He was expected on this particular afternoon, you say?"

"He was, sir; but he did not come till the next day. It was almost dark when I went to the river-bank. I walked for about three miles and a half, to a gate that opened into the fields by which Mr. Holbrook came across from Malsham. I knew his wife never went farther than this gate, but used to wait for him here, if she happened to be the first to reach it. I hurried along, half running all the way, and calling aloud to Mrs. Holbrook every now and then with all my might. But there was no answer. Some men in a boat loaded with hay stopped to ask me what was the matter, but they could tell me nothing. They were coming from Malsham, and had seen no one along the bank. I called at Mr. Whitelaw's as I came back, not with much hope that I should hear anything; but what could I do but make inquiries anywhere and everywhere? I was almost wild with fright by this time. They could tell me nothing at Wyncomb Farm. Stephen Whitelaw was alone in the kitchen smoking his pipe by a great fire. He hadn't been out all day, he told me, and none of his people had seen or heard anything out of the common. As to any harm having come to Mrs. Holbrook by the river-bank, he said he didn't think that was possible, for his men had been at work in the fields near the river all the afternoon, and must have seen or heard if there had been anything wrong. There was some kind of comfort in this, and I left the farm with my mind a little lighter than it had been when I went in there. I knew that

Stephen Whitelaw was no friend to Mrs. Holbrook; that he had a kind of grudge against her because she had been on some one else's side—in—in something." Ellen Carley blushed as she came to this part of her story, and then went on rather hurriedly to hide her confusion. "He didn't like her, sir, you see. I knew this, but I didn't think it possible he could deceive me in a matter of life and death. So I came home, hoping to find Mrs. Holbrook there before me. But there were no signs of her, nor of her husband either, though I had fully expected to see him. Even father owned that things looked bad now, and he let me send every man about the place—some one way, and some another—to hunt for my poor darling. I went into Crosber myself, though it was getting late by this time, and made inquiries of every creature I knew in the village; but it was all no good: no one had seen anything of the lady I was looking for."

"And the husband?" Gilbert asked again; "what of him?"

"He came next day at the usual hour, after we had been astir all night, and the farm-labourers had been far and wide looking for Mrs. Holbrook. I never saw any one seem so shocked and horrified as he did when we told him how his wife had been missing for more than four-and-twenty hours. He is not a gentleman to show his feelings much at ordinary times, and he was quiet enough in the midst of his alarm; but he turned as white as death, and I never saw the natural colour come back to his face all the time he was down here."

"How long did he stay?"

"He only left yesterday. He was travelling about the country all the time, coming back here of a night to sleep, and with the hope that we might have heard something in his absence. The river was dragged for three days; but, thank God, nothing came of that. Mr. Holbrook set the Malsham police to work—not that they're much good, I think; but he wouldn't leave a stone unturned. And now I believe he has gone to London to get help from the police there. But O, sir, I can't make it out, and I have lain awake, night after night thinking of it, and puzzling myself about it, until all sorts of dreadful fancies come into my mind."

"What fancies?"

"O, sir, I scarcely dare tell you; but I loved that sweet young lady so well, that I have been as watchful and jealous in all things, that concerned her as if she had been my own sister. I have thought sometimes that her husband had grown tired of her; that, however dearly he might have loved her at first, as I suppose he did, his love had worn out little by little, and he felt her a burden to him. What other reason could there be for him to keep her hidden away in this dull place, month after month, when he must have seen that her youth and beauty and gaiety of heart were slowly vanishing away, if he had eyes to see anything?"

"But, good Heavens!" Gilbert exclaimed, startled by the sudden horror of the idea which Ellen Carley's words suggested, "you surely do not imagine that Marian's husband had any part in her disappearance? that he could be capable of——"

"I don't know what to think, sir," the girl answered, interrupting him. "I know that I have never liked Mr. Holbrook—never liked or trusted him from the first, though he has been civil enough and kind enough in his own distant way to me. That dear young lady could not disappear off the face of the earth, as it seems she has done, without the evil work of some one. As to her leaving this place of her own free will, without a word of warning to her husband or to me, that I am sure she would never dream of doing. No, sir, there has been foul play of some kind, and I'm afraid I shall never see that dear face again."

The girl said this with an air of conviction that sent a deadly chill to Gilbert Fenton's heart. It seemed to him in this moment of supreme anguish as if all his trouble of the past, all his vague fears and anxieties about the woman he loved, had been the foreshadowing of this evil to come. He had a blank helpless feeling, a dismal sense of his own weakness, which for the moment mastered him. Against any ordinary calamity he would have held himself bravely enough, with the natural strength of an ardent hopeful character; but against this mysterious catastrophe courage and manhood could avail nothing. She was gone, the fragile helpless creature he had pledged himself to protect; gone from all who knew her, leaving not the faintest clue to her fate. Could he doubt that this energetic warm-hearted girl was right, and that some foul deed had been done, of which Marian Holbrook was the victim?

"If she lives, I will find her," he said at last, after a long pause, in which he had sat in gloomy silence, with his eyes fixed upon the ground, meditating the circumstances of Marian's disappearance. "Living or dead, I will find her. It shall be the business of my life from this hour. All my serious thoughts have been of her from the moment in which I first knew her. They will be doubly hers henceforward."

"How good and true you are!" Ellen Carley exclaimed admiringly; "and how you must have loved her! I guessed when you were here last that it was you to whom she was engaged before her marriage, and told her as much; but she would not acknowledge that I was right. O, how I wish she had kept faith with you! how much happier she might have been as your wife!"

"People have different notions of happiness, you see, Miss Carley," Gilbert answered with a bitter smile. "Yes, you were right; it was I who was to have been Marian Nowell's husband, whose every hope of the future was bound up in her. But all that is past; whatever bitterness I felt against her at first—and I do not think I was ever very bitter—has passed away. I am nothing now but her friend, her steadfast and constant friend."

"Thank heaven that she has such a friend," Ellen said earnestly. "And you will make it your business to look for her, sir?"

"The chief object of my life, from this hour."

"And you will try to discover whether her husband is really true, or whether the search that he has made for her has been a blind to hide his own guilt?"

"What grounds have you for supposing his guilt possible?" asked Gilbert. "There are crimes too detestable for credibility; and this would be such a one. You may imagine that I have no friendly feeling towards this man, yet I cannot for an instant conceive him capable of harming a hair of his wife's head."

"Because you have not brooded upon this business as I have, sir, for hours and hours together, until the smallest things seem to have an awful meaning. I have thought of every word and every look of Mr. Holbrook's in the past, and all my thoughts have pointed one way. I believe that he was tired of his sweet young wife; that his marriage was a burden and a trouble to him somehow; that it had arisen out of an impulse that had passed away."

"All this might be, and yet the man be innocent."

"He might be—yes, sir. It is a hard thing, perhaps, even to think him guilty for a moment. But it is so difficult to account in any common way for Mrs. Holbrook's disappearance. If there had been murder done" (the girl shuddered as she said the words)—"a common murder, such as one hears of in lonely country places—surely it must have come to light before this, after the search that has been made all round about. But it would have been easy enough for Mr. Holbrook to decoy his wife away to London or anywhere else. She would have gone anywhere with him, at a moment's notice. She obeyed him implicitly in everything."

"But why should he have taken her away from this place in a secret manner?" asked Gilbert; "he was free to remove her openly. And then you describe him as taking an amount of trouble in his search for her, which might have been so easily avoided, had he acted with ordinary prudence and caution. Say that he wanted to keep the secret of his marriage from the world in which he lives, and to place his wife in even a more secluded spot than this—which scarcely seems possible—what could have been easier for him than to take her away when and where he pleased? No one here would have had any right to question his actions."

Ellen Carley shook her head doubtfully.

"I don't know, sir," she answered slowly; "I daresay my fancies are very foolish; they may have come, perhaps, out of thinking about this so much, till my brain has got addled, as one may say. But it flashed upon me all of a sudden one night, as Mr. Holbrook was standing in our parlour talking about his wife—it flashed upon me that he was in the secret of her disappearance, and that he was only acting with us in his pretence of anxiety and all that; I fancied there was a guilty look in his face, somehow."

"Did you tell him about his wife's good fortune—the money left her by her grandfather?"

"I did, sir; I thought it right to tell him everything I could about my poor dear young lady's journey to London. She had told him of that in her letters, it seemed, but not about the money. She had been keeping that back for the pleasure of telling him with her own lips, and seeing his face light up, she said to me, when he heard the good news. I asked him about the letter which had come in the morning of the day she disappeared, and whether it was from him; but he said no, he had not written, counting upon being with his wife that evening. It was only at the last moment he was prevented coming."

"You have looked for that letter, I suppose?"

"O yes, sir; I searched, and Mr. Holbrook too, in every direction, but the letter wasn't to be found. He seemed very vexed about it, very anxious to find it. We could not but think that Mrs. Holbrook had gone to meet some one that day, and that the letter had something to do with her going out. I am sure she would not have gone beyond the garden and the meadow for pleasure alone. She never had been outside the gate without me, except when she went to meet her husband."

"Strange!" muttered Gilbert.

He was wondering about that letter: what could have been the lure which had beguiled Marian away from the house that day; what except a letter from her husband? It seemed hardly probable that she would have gone to meet any one but him, or that any one else would have appointed a meeting on the river-bank. The fact that she had gone out at an earlier hour than the time at which she had been in the habit of meeting her husband when he came from the Malsham station, went some way to prove that the letter had influenced her movements. Gilbert thought of the fortune which had been left to Marian, and which gave her existence a new value, perhaps exposed her to new dangers. Her husband's interests were involved in her life; her death, should she die childless, must needs deprive him of all advantage from Jacob Nowell's wealth. The only person to profit from such an event would be Percival Nowell; but he was far away, Gilbert believed, and completely ignorant of his reversionary interest in his father's property. There was Medler the attorney, a man whom Gilbert had distrusted from the first. It was just possible that the letter had been from him; yet most improbable that he should have asked Mrs. Holbrook to meet him out of doors, instead of coming to her at the Grange, or that she should have acceded to such a request, had he made it.

The whole affair was encompassed with mystery, and Gilbert Fenton's heart sank as he contemplated the task that lay before him.

"I shall spend a day or two in this neighbourhood before I return to town," he said to Ellen Carley presently; "there are inquiries that I should like to make with my own lips. I shall be only going over old ground, I daresay, but it will be some satisfaction to me to do it for myself. Can you give me house-room here for a night or two, or shall I put up at Crosber?"

"I'm sure father would be very happy to accommodate you here, sir. We've plenty of room now; too much for my taste. The house seems like a wilderness now Mrs. Holbrook is gone."

"Thanks. I shall be very glad to sleep here. There is just the chance that you may have some news for me, or I for you."

"Ah, sir, it's only a very poor chance, I'm afraid," the girl answered hopelessly.

She went with Gilbert to the gate, and watched him as he walked away towards the river. His first impulse was to follow the path which Marian had taken that day, and to see for himself what manner of place it was from which she had so mysteriously vanished.

CHAPTER XXVI.
IN BONDAGE.

ADELA Branston found life very dreary in the splendid gloom of her town house. She would have infinitely preferred the villa near Maidenhead for the place of her occupation, had it not been for the fact that in London she was nearer John Saltram, and that any moment of any day might bring him to her side.

The days passed, however—empty useless days, frittered away in frivolous occupations, or wasted in melancholy idleness; and John Saltram did not come, or came so rarely that the only effect of his visits was to keep up the fever and restlessness of the widow's mind.

She had fancied that life would be so bright for her when the day of her freedom came; that she would reap so rich a harvest of happiness as a reward for the sacrifice which she had made in marrying old Michael Branston, and enduring his peevishness and ill-health with tolerable good-humour during the half-dozen years of their wedded life. She had fancied this; and now her release had come to her, and was worthless in her sight, because the one man she cared for had proved himself cold and indifferent.

In spite of his coldness, however, she told herself that he loved her, that he had loved her from the earliest period of their acquaintance.

She was a poor weak little woman, the veriest spoilt child of fortune, and she clung to this belief with a fond foolish persistence, a blind devoted obstinacy, against which the arguments of Mrs. Pallinson were utterly vain, although that lady devoted a great deal of time and energy to the agreeable duty which she called "opening dear Adela's eyes about that dissipated good-for-nothing Mr. Saltram."

To a correct view of this subject Adela Branston's eyes were not to be opened in any wise. She was wilfully, resolutely blind, clinging to the hope that this cruel neglect on John Saltram's part arose only from his delicacy of feeling, and tender care for her reputation.

"But O, how I wish that he would come to me!" she said to herself again and again, as those slow dreary days went by, burdened and weighed down by the oppressive society of Mrs. Pallinson, as well as by her own sad thoughts. "My husband has been dead ever so long now, and what need have we to study the opinion of the world so much? Of course I wouldn't marry him till a year, or more, after poor Michael's death; but I should like to see him often, to be sure that he still cares for me as he used to care—yes, I am sure he used—in the dear old days at Maidenhead. Why doesn't he come to me? He knows that I love him. He must know that I have no brighter hope than to make him the master of my fortune; and yet he goes on in those dismal Temple chambers, toiling at his literary work as if he had not a thought in the world beyond earning so many pounds a week."

This was the perpetual drift of Mrs. Branston's meditations; and in the absence of any sign or token of regard from John Saltram, all Mrs. Pallinson's attempts to amuse her, all the fascinations and accomplishments of the elegant Theobald, were thrown away upon an unreceptive soil.

There were not many amusements open to a London public at that dull season of the year, except the theatres, and for those places of entertainment Mrs. Pallinson cherished a shuddering aversion. But there were occasional morning and evening "recitals," or concerts, where the music for the most part was of a classical and recondite character—feasts of melody, at which long-buried and forgotten sonatas of Gluck, or Bach, or Chembini were introduced to a discriminating public for the first time; and to these Mrs. Pallinson and Theobald conducted poor Adela Branston, whose musical proclivities had never yet soared into higher regions than those occupied by the sparkling joyous genius of Rossini, and to whom the revived sonatas, or the familiar old-established gems of classical art, were as unintelligible as so much Hebrew or Syriac. Perhaps they were not much more delightful to Mrs. Pallinson; but that worthy matron had a profound veneration for the conventionalities of life, and these classical matinées and recitals seemed to her exactly the correct sort of thing for the amusement of a young widow whose husband had not very long ago been consigned to the tomb.

So poor Adela was dragged hither and thither to gloomy concert-rooms, where the cold winter's light made the performers look pale and wan, or to aristocratic drawing-rooms, graciously lent to some favoured pianiste by their distinguished owners; and so, harassed and weary, but lacking spirit to oppose her own feeble inclinations to the overpowering force of Mrs. Pallinson's will, the helpless little widow went submissively wherever they chose to take her, tormented all the while by the thought of John Saltram's coldness, and wondering when this cruel time of probation would be at an end, and he would show himself her devoted slave once more. It was very weak and foolish to think of him like this, no doubt; undignified and unwomanly, perhaps; but Adela Branston was little more than a child in knowledge of the world, and John Saltram was the only man who had ever touched her heart. She stood quite alone in the world too, lonely with all her wealth, and there was no one to share her affection with this man, who had acquired so complete an influence over her.

She endured the dreary course of her days patiently enough for a considerable time, not knowing any means whereby she might release herself from the society of her kinswoman, or put an end to the indefatigable attentions of the popular Maida Hill doctor. She would have gladly offered Mrs. Pallinson a liberal allowance out of her fortune to buy that lady off, and be her own mistress once more, free to act and think for herself, had she dared to make such a degrading proposition to a person of Mrs. Pallinson's dignity. But she could not venture to do this; and she felt that no one but John Saltram, in the character of her future husband, could release her from the state of bondage into which she had weakly suffered herself to fall. In the meantime she defended the man she loved with an unflinching spirit, resolutely refusing to have her eyes opened to the worthlessness of his character, and boldly declaring her disbelief of those sad accounts which Theobald affected to have heard from well-informed acquaintance of his own, respecting the follies and dissipations of Mr. Saltram's career, his debts, his love of gambling, his dealings with money-lenders, and other foibles common to the rake's progress.

It was rather a hard battle for the lonely little woman to fight, but she had fortune on her side; and at the worst, her kinsfolk treated her with a certain deference, even while they were doing their utmost to worry her into an untimely grave. If little flatteries, and a perpetual indulgence in all small matters, such as a foolish nurse might give to a spoilt child, could have made Adela happy, she had certainly no reason to complain, for in this manner Mrs. Pallinson was the most devoted and affectionate of companions. If her darling Adela looked a little paler than usual, or confessed to suffering from a headache, or owned to being nervous or out of spirits, Mrs. Pallinson's anxiety knew no bounds, and Theobald was summoned from Maida Hill without a minute's delay, much to poor Adela's annoyance. Indeed, she grew in time to deny the headaches, and the low spirits, or the nervousness resolutely, rather than bring upon herself a visitation from Mr. Theobald Pallinson; and in spite of all this care and indulgence she felt herself a prisoner in her own house, somehow; more dependent than the humblest servant in that spacious mansion; and she looked out helplessly and hopelessly for some friend through whose courageous help she might recover her freedom. Perhaps she only thought of one champion as at all likely to come to her rescue; indeed, her mind had scarcely room for more than that one image, which occupied her thoughts at all times.

Her captivity had lasted for a period which seemed a very long time, though it was short enough when computed by the ordinary standard of weeks and months, when a circumstance occurred which gave her a brief interval of liberty. Mr. Pallinson fell a victim to some slight attack of low fever; and his mother, who was really most devoted to this paragon of a son, retired from the citadel in Cavendish Square for a few days in order to nurse him. It was not that the surgeon's illness was in any way dangerous, but the mother could not trust her darling to the care of strangers and hirelings.

Adela Branston seemed to breathe more freely in that brief holiday. Relieved from Mrs. Pallinson's dismal presence, life appeared brighter and pleasanter all at once; a faint colour came back to the pale cheeks, and the widow was even beguiled into laughter by some uncomplimentary observations which her confidential maid ventured upon with reference to the absent lady.

"I'm sure the house itself seems lighter and more cheerful-like without her, ma'am," said this young person, who was of a vivacious temperament, and upon whom the dowager's habitual dreariness had been a heavy affliction; "and you're looking all the better already for not being worried by her."

"Berners, you really must not say such things," Mrs. Branston exclaimed reproachfully. "You ought to know that my cousin is most kind and thoughtful, and does everything for the best."

"O, of course, ma'am; but some people's best is quite as bad as other people's worst," the maid answered sharply; "and as to kindness and thoughtfulness, Mrs. Pallinson is a great deal too kind and thoughtful, I think; for her kindness and thoughtfulness won't allow you a moment's rest. And then, as if anybody couldn't see through her schemes about that precious son of hers—with his finicking affected ways!"

And at this point the vivacious Berners gave a little imitation of Theobald Pallinson, with which liberty Adela pretended to be very much offended, laughing at the performance nevertheless.

Mrs. Branston passed the first day of her freedom in luxurious idleness. It was such an inexpressible relief not to hear the perpetual click of Mrs. Pallinson's needle travelling in and out of the canvas, as that irreproachable matron sat at her embroidery-frame, on which a group of spaniels, after Sir Edwin Landseer, were slowly growing into the fluffy life of Berlin wool; a still greater relief, not to be called upon to respond appropriately to the dull platitudes which formed the lady's usual conversation, when she was not abusing John Saltram, or sounding the praises of her beloved son.

The day was a long one for Adela, in spite of the pleasant sense of freedom; for she had begun the morning with the thought of what a delightful thing it would be if some happy accident should bring Mr. Saltram to Cavendish-square on this particular day; and having once started with this idea, she found herself counting the hours and half-hours with impatient watchfulness until the orthodox time for visiting was quite over, and she could no longer beguile herself with the hope that he would come. She wanted so much to see him alone. Since her husband's death, they had met only in the presence of Mrs. Pallinson, beneath the all-pervading eye and within perpetual ear-shot of that oppressive matron. Adela fancied that if they could only meet for one brief half-hour face to face, without the restraint of that foreign presence, all misunderstanding would be at an end between them, and John Saltram's affection for her, in which she believed with a fond credulity, would reveal itself in all its truth and fulness.

"I daresay it is my cousin Pallinson who has kept him away from me all this time," Adela said to herself with a very impatient feeling about her cousin Pallinson. "I know how intolerant he is of any one he dislikes; and no doubt he has taken a dislike to her; she has done everything to provoke it, indeed by her coldness and rudeness to him."

That day went by, and the second and third day of the dowager's absence; but there was no sign of John Saltram. Adela thought of writing to ask him to come to her; but that seemed such a desperate step, she could not think how she should word the letter, or how she could give it to one of the servants to post. No, she would contrive to post it herself, if she did bring herself to write. And then she thought of a still more desperate step. What if she were to call upon Mr. Saltram at his Temple chambers? It would be a most unwarrantable thing for her to do, of course; an act which would cause Mrs. Pallinson's hair to stand on end in virtuous horror, could it by any means come to her knowledge; but Adela did not intend that it ever should be known to Mrs. Pallinson; and about the opinion of the world in the abstract, Mrs. Branston told herself that she cared very little. What was the use of being a rich widow, if she was to be hedged-in by the restrictions which encompass the steps of an unwedded damsel just beginning life? Emboldened by the absence of her dowager kinswoman, Mrs. Branston felt herself independent, free to do a foolish thing, and ready to abide the hazard of her folly.

So, upon the fourth day of her freedom, despairing of any visit from John Saltram, Adela Branston ordered the solemn-looking butler to send for a cab, much to the surprise of that portly individual.

"Josephs has just been round asking about the carriage, mum," he said, in a kind of suggestive way; "whether you'd please to want the b'rouche or the broom, and whether you'd drive before or after luncheon."

"I shall not want the carriage this morning; send for a cab, if you please, Parker. I am going into the City, and don't care about taking the horses there."

The solemn Parker bowed and retired, not a little mystified by this order. His mistress was a kind little woman enough, but such extreme consideration for equine comfort is hardly a feminine attribute, and Mr. Parker was puzzled. He told Josephs the coachman as much when he had dispatched an underling to fetch the cleanest four-wheeler procurable at an adjacent stand.

"She's a-going to her banker's I suppose," he said meditatively; "going to make some new investments perhaps. Women are always a-fidgeting and chopping and changing with their money."

Mrs. Branston kept the cab waiting half an hour, according to the fairest reckoning. She was very particular about her toilette that morning, and inclined to be discontented with the sombre plainness of her widow's garb, and to fancy that the delicate border of white crape round her girlish face made her look pale, not to say sallow. She came downstairs at last, however, looking very graceful and pretty in her trailing mourning robes and fashionable crape bonnet, in which the profoundest depth of woe was made to express itself with a due regard to elegance. She came down to the homely hackney vehicle attended by the obsequious Berners, whose curiosity was naturally excited by this solitary expedition.

"Where shall I tell the man to drive, mum?" the butler asked with the cab-door in his hand.

Mrs. Branston felt herself blushing, and hesitated a little before she replied.

"The Union Bank, Chancery-lane. Tell him to go by the Strand and Temple-bar."

"I can't think what's come to my mistress," Miss Berners remarked as the cab drove off. "Catch *me* driving in one of those nasty vulgar four-wheel cabs, if I had a couple of carriages and a couple of pairs of horses at my disposal. There's some style about a hansom; but I never could abide those creepy-crawley four-wheelers."

"I admire your taste, Miss Berners; and a dashing young woman like you's a credit to a hansom," replied Mr. Parker gallantly. "But there's no accounting for the vagaries of the female sex; and I fancy somehow Mrs. B. didn't want any of us to know where she was going; she coloured-up so when I asked her for the direction. You may depend there's something up, Jane Berners. She's going to see some poor relation perhaps—Mile-end or Kentish-town way—and was ashamed to give the address."

"I don't believe she has any relations, except old Mother Pallinson and her son," Miss Berners answered.

And thereupon the handmaiden withdrew to her own regions with a discontented air, as one who had been that day cheated out of her legitimate rights.

CHAPTER XXVII.
ONLY A WOMAN.

THE cabman did not hurry his tall raw-boned steed, and the drive to Temple-bar seemed a very long one to Adela Branston, whose mind was disturbed by the consciousness that she was doing a foolish thing. Many times during the journey, she was on the point of stopping the man and telling him to drive back to Cavendish-square; but in spite of these moments of doubt and vacillation she suffered the vehicle to proceed, and only stopped the man when they were close to Temple-bar.

Here she told him where she wanted to go; upon which he plunged down an obscure side street, and stopped at one of the entrances to the Temple. Here Mrs. Branston alighted, and had to inquire her way to Mr. Saltram's chambers. She was so unaccustomed to be out alone, that this expedition seemed something almost awful to her when she found herself helpless and solitary in that strange locality. She had fancied that the cab would drive straight to Mr. Saltram's door.

The busy lawyers flitting across those grave courts and passages turned to glance curiously at the pretty little widow. She had the air of a person not used to be on foot and unattended—a kind of aerial butterfly air, as of one who belonged to the useless and ornamental class of society; utterly different from the appearance of such humble female pedestrians as were wont to make the courts and alleys of the Temple a short-cut in their toilsome journeys to and fro. Happily a porter appeared, who was able to direct her to Mr. Saltram's chambers, and civilly offered to escort her there; for which service she rewarded him with half-a-crown, instead of the sixpence which he expected as his maximum recompense; she was so glad to have reached the shelter of the dark staircase in safety. The men whom she had met had frightened her by their bold admiring stares; and yet she was pleased to think that she was looking pretty.

The porter did not leave her until she had been admitted by Mr. Saltram's boy, and then retired, promising to be in the way to see her back to her carriage. How the poor little thing trembled when she found herself on the threshold of that unfamiliar door! What a horrible dingy lobby it was! and how she pitied John Saltram for having to live in such place! He was at home and alone, the boy told her; would she please to send in her card?

No, Mrs. Branston declined to send in her card. The boy could say that a lady wished to see Mr. Saltram.

The truth was, she wanted to surprise this man; to see how her unlooked-for presence would affect him. She fancied herself beloved by him, poor soul! and that she would be able to read some evidence of his joy at seeing her in this unexpected manner.

The boy went in to his master and announced the advent of a lady, the first he had ever seen in those dismal premises.

John Saltram started up from his desk and came with a hurried step to the door, very pale and almost breathless.

"A lady!" he gasped, and then fell back a pace or two on seeing Adela, with a look which was very much like disappointment.

"You here, Mrs. Branston!" he exclaimed; "I—you are the last person in the world I should have expected to see."

Perhaps he felt that there was a kind of rudeness in this speech, for he added hastily, and with a faint smile,—

"Of course I am not the less honoured by your visit."

He moved a chair forward, the least dilapidated of the three or four which formed his scanty stock, and placed it near the neglected fire, which he tried to revive a little by a judicious use of the poker.

"You expected to see some one else, I think," Adela said; quite unable to hide her wounded feelings.

She had seen the eagerness in his pale face when he came to the door, and the disappointed look with which he had recognised her.

"Scarcely; but I expected to receive news of some one else."

"Some one you are very anxious to hear about, I should imagine, from your manner just now," said Adela, who could not forbear pressing the question a little.

"Yes, Mrs. Branston, some one about whom I am anxious; a relation, in short."

She looked at him with a puzzled air. She had never heard him talk of his relations, had indeed supposed that he stood almost alone in the world; but there was no reason that it should be so, except his silence on the subject. She watched him for some moments in silence, as he stood leaning against the opposite angle of the chimney-piece waiting for her to speak. He was looking very ill, much changed since she had seen him last, haggard and worn, with the air of a man who had not slept properly for many nights. There was an absent far-away look in his eyes: and Adela Branston felt all at once that her presence was nothing to him; that this desperate step which she had taken had no more effect upon him than the commonest event of every-day life; in a word, that he did not love her. A cold deathlike feeling came over her as she thought this. She had set her heart upon this man's love, and had indeed some justification for supposing that it was hers. It seemed to her that life was useless—worse than useless, odious and unendurable—without it.

But even while she was thinking this, with a cold blank misery in her heart, she had to invent some excuse for this unseemly visit.

"I have waited so anxiously for you to call," she said at last, in a nervous hesitating way, "and I began to fear that you must be ill, and I wished to consult you about the management of my affairs. My lawyers worry me so with questions which I don't know how to answer, and I have so few friends in the world whom I can trust except you; so at last I screwed up my courage to call upon you."

"I am deeply honoured by your confidence, Mrs. Branston," John Saltram answered, looking at her gravely with those weary haggard eyes, with the air of a man who brings his thoughts back to common life from some far-away region with an effort. "If my advice or assistance can be of any use to you, they are completely at your service. What is this business about which your solicitor bothers you?"

"I'll explain that to you directly," Adela answered, taking some letters from her pocket-book. "How good you are! I knew that you would help me; but tell me first why you have never been to Cavendish-square in all this long time. I fear I was right; you have been ill, have you not?"

"Not exactly ill, but very much worried and overworked."

A light dawned on Adela Branston's troubled mind. She began to think that Mr. Saltram's strange absent manner, his apparent indifference to her presence, might arise from preoccupation, caused by those pecuniary difficulties from which the Pallinsons declared him so constant a sufferer. Yes, she told herself, it was trouble of this kind that oppressed him, that had banished him from her all this time. He was too generous to repair his shattered fortunes by means of her money; he was too proud to confess his fallen state.

A tender pity took possession of her. All that was most sentimental in her nature was awakened by the idea of John Saltram's generosity. What was the use of her fortune, if she could not employ it for the relief of the man she loved?

"You are so kind to me, Mr. Saltram," she faltered, after a troubled pause; "so ready to help me in my perplexities, I only wish you would allow me to be of some use to you in yours, if you have any perplexities; and I suppose everybody has, of some kind or other. I should be so proud if you would give me your confidence—so proud and happy!" Her voice trembled a little as she said this, looking up at him all the while with soft confiding blue eyes, the fair delicate face looking its prettiest in the coquettish widow's head-gear.

A man must have been harder of heart than John Saltram who could remain unmoved by a tenderness so evident. This man was touched, and deeply. The pale careworn face grew more troubled, the firmly-moulded lips quivered ever so little, as he looked down at the widow's pleading countenance; and then he turned his head aside with a sudden half-impatient movement.

"My dear Mrs. Branston, you are too good to me; I am unworthy, I am in every way unworthy of your kindness."

"You are not unworthy, and that is no answer to my question; only an excuse to put me off. We are such old friends, Mr. Saltram, you might trust me. You own that you have been worried—overworked—worried about money matters, perhaps. I know that gentlemen are generally subject to that kind of annoyance; and you know how rich I am, how little employment I have for my money, though you can never imagine how worthless and useless it seems to me. Why won't you trust me? why won't you let me be your banker?"

She blushed crimson as she made this offer, dreading that the man she loved would turn upon her fiercely in a passion of offended pride. She sat before him trembling, dreading the might of his indignation.

But there was no anger in John Saltram's face when he looked round at her; only grief and an expression that was like pity.

"The offer is like you," he said with suppressed feeling; "but the worries of which I spoke just now are not money troubles. I do not pretend to deny that my affairs are embarrassed, and have been for so long that entanglement has become their normal state; but if they were ever so much more desperate, I could not afford to trade upon your generosity. No, Mrs. Branston, that is just the very last thing in this world that I could consent to do."

"It is very cruel of you to say that," Adela answered, with the tears gathering in her clear blue eyes, and with a little childish look of vexation, which would have seemed infinitely charming in the eyes of a man who loved her. "There can be no reason for your saying this, except that you do not think me worthy of your confidence—that you despise me too much to treat me like a friend. If I were that Mr. Fenton now, whom you care for so much, you would not treat me like this."

"I never borrowed a sixpence from Gilbert Fenton in my life, though I know that his purse is always open to me. But friendship is apt to end when money transactions begin. Believe me, I feel your goodness, Mrs. Branston, your womanly generosity; but it is my own unworthiness that comes between me and your kindness. I can accept nothing from you but the sympathy which it is your nature to give to all who need it."

"I do indeed sympathise with you; but it seems so hard that you will not consent to make some use of all that money which is lying idle. It would make me so happy if I could think it were useful to you; but I dare not say any more. I have said too much already, perhaps; only I hope you will not think very badly of me for having acted on impulse in this way."

"Think badly of you, my dear kind soul! What can I think, except that you are one of the most generous of women?"

"And about these other troubles, Mr. Saltram, which have no relation to money matters; you will not give me your confidence?"

"There is nothing that I can confide in you, Mrs. Branston. Others are involved in the matter of which I spoke, I am not free to talk about it."

Poor Adela felt herself repulsed at every point. It seemed very hard. Had she been mistaken about this man all the time? mistaken and deluded in those old happy days during her husband's lifetime, when he had been so constant a visitor at the river-side villa, and had seemed exactly what a man might seem who cherished a tenderness which he dared not reveal in the present, but which in a brighter future might blossom into the full-blown flower of love?

"And now about your own affairs, my dear Mrs. Branston?" John Saltram said with a forced cheerfulness, drawing his chain up to the table and assuming a business-like manner. "These tiresome letters of your lawyers'; let me see what use I can be in the matter."

Adela Branston produced the letters with rather an absent air. They were letters about very insignificant affairs; the renewal of a lease or two; the reinvestment of a sum of money that had been lent on mortgage, and had fallen in lately; transactions that scarcely called for the employment of Mr. Saltram's intellectual powers. But he gave them very serious attention nevertheless, well aware, all the time that this business consultation was only the widow's excuse for her visit; and while she seemed to be listening to his advice, her eyes were wandering round the room all the time, noting the dust and confusion, the soda-water bottles huddled in one corner, the pile of books heaped in a careless mass in another, the half-empty brandy-bottle between a couple of stone ink-jars on the mantelpiece. She was thinking what a dreary place it was, and that there was the stamp of decay and ruin somehow upon the man who occupied it. And she loved him so well, and would have given all the world to have redeemed his life.

It is doubtful whether Adela Branston heard one syllable of that counsel which Mr. Saltram administered so gravely. Her mind was full of the failure of this desperate step which she had taken. He seemed farther from her now than before they had met, obstinately adverse to profit by her friendship, cold and cruel.

"You will come and dine with us very soon, I hope," she said as she rose to go, "My cousin, Mrs. Pallinson, will be home in a day or two. She has been nursing her son for the last few days; but he is much better, and I expect her back immediately. We shall be so pleased to see you; you will name an early day, won't you? Monday shall we say, or Sunday? You can't plead business on Sunday."

"My dear Mrs. Branston, I really am not well enough for visiting."

"But dining with us does not come under the head of visiting. We will be quite alone, if you wish it. I shall be hurt if you refuse to come."

"If you put it in that way, I cannot refuse; but I fear you will find me wretched company."

"I am not afraid of that. And now I must ask you to forgive me for having wasted so much of your time, before I say good-morning."

"There has been no time of mine wasted. I have learned to know your generous heart even better than I knew it before, and I think I always knew that it was a noble one. Believe me, I am not ungrateful or indifferent to so much goodness."

He accompanied her downstairs, and through the courts and passages to the place where she had left her cab, in spite of the ticket-porter, who was hanging about ready to act as escort. He saw her safely seated in the hackney vehicle, and then walked slowly back to his chambers, thinking over the interview which had just concluded.

"Poor little soul," he said softly to himself; "dear little soul! There are men who would go to the end of the world for a woman like that; yes, if she had not a sixpence. And to think that I, who thought myself so strong in the wisdom of the world, should have let such a prize slip through my fingers? For what? For a fancy, for a caprice that has brought confusion and shame upon me—disappointment and regret."

He breathed a profound sigh. From first to last life had been more or less a disappointment to this man. He had lived alone; lived for himself, despising the ambitious aims and lofty hopes of other men, thinking the best prizes this world can give scarcely worth that long struggle which is so apt to end in failure; perfect success was so rare a result, it seemed to him. He made a rough calculation of his chances in any given line when he was still fresh from college, and finding the figures against him, gave up all thoughts of doing great things. By-and-by, when his creditors grew pressing and it was necessary for him to earn money in some way, he found that it was no trouble to him to write; so he wrote with a spasmodic kind of industry, but a forty-horse power when he chose to exercise it. For a long time he had no thought of winning name or fame in literature. It was only of late it had dawned upon him that he had wasted labour and talent, out of which a wiser man would have created for himself a reputation; and that reputation is worth something, if only as a means of making money.

This conviction once arrived at, he had worked hard at a book which he thought must needs make some impression upon the world whenever he could afford time to complete it. In the meanwhile his current work occupied so much of his life, that he was fain to lay the *magnum opus* aside every now and then, and it still needed a month or two of quiet labour.

CHAPTER XXVIII.
AT FAULT.

GILBERT Fenton took up his abode at the dilapidated old inn at Crosber, thinking that he might be freer there than at the Grange; a dismal place of sojourn under the brightest circumstances, but unspeakably dreary for him who had only the saddest thoughts for his companions. He wanted to be on the spot, to be close at hand to hear tidings of the missing girl, and he wanted also to be here in the event of John Holbrook's return—to come face to face with this man, if possible, and to solve that question which had sorely perplexed him of late—the mystery that hung about the man who had wronged him.

He consulted Ellen Carley as to the probability of Mr. Holbrook's return. The girl seemed to think it very unlikely that Marian's husband would ever again appear at the Grange. His last departure had appeared like a final one. He had paid every sixpence he owed in the neighbourhood, and had been liberal in his donations to the servants and hangers-on of the place. Marian's belongings he had left to Ellen Carley's care, telling her to pack them, and keep them in readiness for being forwarded to any address he might send. But his own books and papers he had carefully removed.

"Had he many books here?" Gilbert asked.

"Not many," the girl answered; "but he was a very studious gentleman. He spent almost all his time shut up in his own room reading and writing."

"Indeed!"

In this respect the habits of the unknown corresponded exactly with those of John Saltram. Gilbert Fenton's heart beat a little quicker at the thought that he was coming nearer by a step to the solution of that question which was always uppermost in his mind now.

"Do you know if he wrote books—if he was what is called a literary man—living by his pen?" he asked presently.

"I don't know; I never heard his wife say so. But Mrs. Holbrook was always reserved about him and his history. I think he had forbidden her to talk about his affairs. I know I used to fancy it was a dull life for her, poor soul, sitting in his room hour after hour, working while he wrote. He used not to allow her to be with him at all at first, but little by little she persuaded him to let her sit with him, promising not to disturb him by so much as a word; and she never did. She seemed quite happy when she was with him, contented, and proud to think that her presence was no hindrance to him."

"And you think he loved her, don't you?"

"At first, yes; but I think a kind of weariness came over him afterwards, and that she saw it, and almost broke her heart about it. She was so simple and innocent, poor darling, it wasn't easy for her to hide anything she felt."

Gilbert asked the bailiff's daughter to describe Mr. Holbrook to him, as she had done more than once before. But this time he questioned her closely, and contrived that her description of this man's outward semblance should be especially minute and careful.

Yes, the picture which arose before him as Ellen Carley spoke was the picture of John Saltram. The description seemed in every particular to apply to the face and figure of his one chosen friend. But then all such verbal pictures are at best vague and shadowy, and Gilbert knew that he carried that one image in his mind, and would be apt unconsciously to twist the girl's words into that one shape. He asked if any picture or photograph of Mr. Holbrook had been left at the Grange, and Ellen Carley told him no, she had never even seen a portrait of Marian's husband.

He was therefore fain to be content with the description which seemed so exactly to fit the friend he loved, the friend to whom he had clung with a deeper, stronger feeling since this miserable suspicion had taken root in his mind.

"I think I could have forgiven him if he had come between us in a bold and open way," he said to himself, brooding over this harassing doubt of his friend; "yes, I think I could have forgiven him, in spite of the bitterness of losing her. But to steal her from me with cowardly treacherous secrecy, to hide my treasure in an obscure corner, and then grow weary of her, and blight her fair young life with his coldness,—can I forgive him these things? can all the memory of the past plead with me for him when I think of these things? O God, grant that I am mistaken; that it is some other man who has done this, and not John Saltram; not the man I have loved and honoured for fifteen years of my life!"

But his suspicions were not to be put away, not to be driven out of his mind, let him argue against them as he might. He resolved, therefore, that as soon as he should have made every effort and taken every possible means towards the recovery of the missing girl, he would make it his business next to bring this thing home to John Saltram, or acquit him for ever.

It is needless to dwell upon that weary work, which seemed destined to result in nothing but disappointment. The local constabulary and the London police alike exerted all their powers to obtain some trace of Marian Holbrook's lost footsteps; but no clue to the painful mystery was to be found. From the moment when she vanished from the eyes of the servant-woman watching her departure from the Grange gate, she seemed to have disappeared altogether from the sight of mankind. If by some witchcraft she had melted into the dim autumnal mist that hung about the river-bank, she could not have left less trace, or vanished more mysteriously than she had done. The local constabulary gave in very soon, in spite of Gilbert Fenton's handsome payment in the present, and noble promises of reward in the future. The local constabulary were honest and uninventive. They shook their heads gloomily, and said "Drownded."

"But the river has been dragged," Gilbert cried eagerly, "and there has been nothing found."

He shuddered at the thought of that which might have been hauled to shore in the foul weedy net. The face he loved, changed, disfigured, awful—the damp clinging hair.

"Holes," replied the chief of the local constabulary, sententiously; "there's holes in that there river where you might hide half a dozen drownded men, and never hope to find 'em, no more than if they was at the bottom of the Atlantic

Ocean. Lord bless your heart, sir, you Londoners don't know what a river is, in a manner of speaking," added the man, who was most likely unacquainted with the existence of the Thames, compared with which noble stream this sluggish Hampshire river was the veriest ditch. "I've known a many poor creatures drownded in that river, and never one of 'em to come to light—not that the river was dragged for *them*. Their friends weren't of the dragging class, they weren't."

The London police were more hopeful and more delusive. They were always hearing of some young lady newly arrived at some neighbouring town or village who seemed to answer exactly to the description of Mrs. Holbrook. And, behold, when Gilbert Fenton hurried off post-haste to the village or town, and presented himself before the lady in question, he found for the most part that she was ten years older than Marian, and as utterly unlike her as it was possible for one Englishwoman to be unlike another.

He possessed a portrait of the missing girl—a carefully finished photograph, which had been given to him in the brief happy time when she was his promised wife; and he caused this image to be multiplied and distributed wherever the search for Marian was being made. He neglected no possible means by which he might hope to obtain tidings; advertising continually, in town and country, and varying his advertisements in such a manner as to insure attention either from the object of his inquiries, or any one acquainted with her.

But all his trouble was in vain. No reply, or, what was worse, worthless and delusive replies, came to his advertisements. The London police, who had pretended to be so hopeful at first, began to despair in a visible manner, having put all their machinery into play, and failed to obtain even the most insignificant result. They were fain to confess at last that they could only come to pretty much the same conclusion as that arrived at by their inferiors, the rustic officials; and agreed that in all probability the river hid the secret of Marian Holbrook's fate. She had been the victim of either crime or accident. Who should say which? The former seemed the more likely, as she had vanished in broad daylight, when, it was scarcely possible that her footsteps could go astray; while in that lonely neighbourhood a crime was never impossible.

"She had a watch and chain, I suppose?" the officer inquired. "Ladies will wear 'em."

Gilbert ascertained from Ellen Carley that Marian had always worn her watch and chain, had worn them when she left the Grange for the last time. She had a few other trinkets too, which she wore habitually, quaint old-fashioned things, of some value.

How well Gilbert remembered those little family treasures, which she had exhibited to him at Captain Sedgewick's bidding!

"Ah," muttered the officer when he heard this, "quite enough to cost her her life, if she met with one of your ugly customers. I've known a murder committed for the sake of three-and-sixpence in my time; and pushing a young woman into the river don't count for murder among that sort of people. You see, some one may come by and fish her out again; so it can't well be more than manslaughter."

A dull horror came over Gilbert Fenton as he heard these professional speculations, but at the worst he could not bring himself to believe that these men were right, and that the woman he loved had been the victim of some obscure wretch's greed, slain in broad daylight for the sake of a few pounds' worth of jewelry.

When everything had been done that was possible to be done in that part of the country, Mr. Fenton went back to London. But not before he had become very familiar with the household at the Grange. From the first he had liked and trusted Ellen Carley, deeply touched by her fidelity to Marian. He made a point of dropping in at the Grange every evening, when not away from Crosber following up some delusive track started by his metropolitan counsellors. He always went there with a faint hope that Ellen Carley might have something to tell him, and with a vague notion that John Holbrook might return unexpectedly, and that they two might meet in the old farm-house. But Mr. Holbrook did not reappear, nor had Ellen any tidings for her evening visitor; though she thought of little else than Marian, and never let a day pass without making some small effort to obtain a clue to that mystery which now seemed so hopeless. Gilbert grew to be quite at home in the little wainscoted parlour at the Grange, smoking his cigar there nightly in a tranquil contemplative mood, while Mr. Carley puffed vigorously at his long clay pipe. There was a special charm for him in the place that had so long being Marian's home. He felt nearer to her, somehow, under that roof, and as if he must needs be on the right road to some discovery. The bailiff, although prone to silence, seemed to derive considerable gratification from Mr. Fenton's visits, and talked to that gentleman with greater freedom than he was wont to display in his intercourse with mankind. Ellen was not always present during the whole of the evening, and in her absence the bailiff would unbosom himself to Gilbert on the subject of his daughter's undutiful conduct; telling him what a prosperous marriage the girl might make if she had only common sense enough to see her own interests in the right light, and wasn't the most obstinate self-willed hussy that ever set her own foolish whims and fancies against a father's wishes.

"But a woman's fancies sometimes mean a very deep feeling, Mr. Carley," pleaded Gilbert; "and what worldly-wise people call a good home, is not always a happy one. It's a hard thing for a young woman to marry against her inclination."

"Humph!" muttered the bailiff in a surly tone. "It's a harder thing for her to marry a pauper, I should think, and to bring a regiment of children into the world, always wanting shoes and stockings. But you're a bachelor, you see, Mr. Fenton, and can't be expected to know what shoes and stockings are. Now there happens to be a friend of mine—a steady, respectable, middle-aged man—who worships the ground my girl walks on, and could make her mistress of as good a house as any within twenty miles of this, and give a home to her father in his old age, into the bargain; for I'm only a servant here, and it can't be expected that I am to go on toiling and slaving about this place for ever. I don't say but what

I've saved a few pounds, but I haven't saved enough to keep me out of the workhouse."

This seemed to Gilbert rather a selfish manner of looking at a daughter's matrimonial prospects, and he ventured to hint as much in a polite way. But the bailiff was immovable.

"What a young woman wants is a good home," he said decisively; "whether she has the sense to know it herself, or whether she hasn't, that's what she's got to look for in life."

Gilbert had not spent many evenings at the Grange before he had the honour of being introduced to the estimable middle-aged suitor, whose claims Mr. Carley was always setting forth to his daughter. He saw Stephen Whitelaw, and that individual's colourless expressionless countenance, redeemed from total blankness only by the cunning visible in the small grey eyes, impressed him with instant distrust and dislike.

"God forbid that frank warm-hearted girl should ever be sacrificed to such a fellow as this," he said to himself, as he sat on the opposite side of the hearth, smoking his cigar, and meditatively contemplating Mr. Whitelaw conversing in his slow solemn fashion with the man who was so eager to be his father-in-law.

In the course of that first evening of their acquaintance, Gilbert was surprised to see how often Stephen Whitelaw looked at him, with a strangely-attentive expression, that had something furtive in it, some hidden meaning, as it seemed to him. Whenever Gilbert spoke, the farmer looked up at him, always with the same sharp inquisitive glance, the same cunning twinkle in his small eyes. And every time he happened to look at Mr. Whitelaw during that evening, he found the watchful eyes turned towards him in the same unpleasant manner. The sensation caused by this kind of surveillance on the part of the farmer was so obnoxious to him, that at parting he took occasion to speak of it in a friendly way.

"I fancy you and I must have met before to-night, Mr. Whitelaw," he said; "or that you must have some notion to that effect. You've looked at me with an amount of interest my personal merits could scarcely call for."

"No, no, sir," the farmer answered in his usual slow deliberate way; "it isn't that; I never set eyes on you before I came into this room to-night. But you see, Ellen, she's interested in you, and I take an interest in any one she takes to. And we've all of us thought so much about your searching for that poor young lady that's missing, and taking such pains, and being so patient-like where another would have given in at the first set-off—so, altogether, you're a general object of interest, you see."

Gilbert did not appear particularly flattered by this compliment. He received it at first with rather an angry look, and then, after a pause, was vexed with himself for having been annoyed by the man's clumsy expression of sympathy—for it was sympathy, no doubt, which Mr. Whitelaw wished to express.

"It has been sad work, so far," he said. "I suppose you can give me no hint, no kind of advice as to any step to be taken in the future."

"Lord bless you, no sir. Everything that could be done was done before you came here. Mr. Holbrook didn't leave a stone unturned. He did his duty as a man and a husband, sir. The poor young lady was drowned—there's no doubt about that."

"I don't believe it," Gilbert said, with a quiet resolute air, which seemed quite to startle Mr. Whitelaw.

"You don't believe she was drowned! You mean to say you think she's alive, then?" he asked, with unusual sharpness and quickness of speech.

"I have a firm conviction that she still lives; that, with God's blessing, I shall see her again."

"Well, sir," Mr. Whitelaw replied, relapsing into his accustomed slowness, and rubbing his clumsy chin with his still clumsier hand, in a thoughtful manner, "of course it ain't my place to go against any gentleman's convictions—far from it; but if you see Mrs. Holbrook before the dead rise out of their graves, my name isn't Stephen Whitelaw. You may waste your time and your trouble, and you may spend your money as it was so much water, but set eyes upon that missing lady you never will; take my word for it, or don't take my word for it, as you please."

Gilbert wondered at the man's earnestness. Did he really feel some kind of benevolent interest in the fate of a helpless woman, or was it only a vulgar love of the marvellous and horrible that moved him? Gilbert leaned to the latter opinion, and was by no means inclined to give Stephen Whitelaw credit for any surplus stock of benevolence. He saw a good deal more of Ellen Carley's suitor in the course of his evening visits to the Grange, and had ample opportunity for observing Mr. Whitelaw's mode of courtship, which was by no means of the demonstrative order, consisting in a polite silence towards the object of his affections, broken only by one or two clumsy but florid compliments, delivered in a deliberate but semi-jocose manner. The owner of Wyncomb Farm had no idea of making hard work of his courtship. He had been angled for by so many damsels, and courted by so many fathers and mothers, that he fancied he had but to say the word when the time came, and the thing would be done. Any evidence of avoidance, indifference, or even dislike upon Ellen Carley's part, troubled him in the smallest degree. He had heard people talk of young Randall's fancy for her, and of her liking for him, but he knew that her father meant to set his heel upon any nonsense of this kind; and he did not for a moment imagine it possible that any girl would resolutely oppose her father's will, and throw away such good fortune as he could offer her—to ride in her own chaise-cart, and wear a silk gown always on Sundays, to say nothing of a gold watch and chain; and Mr. Whitelaw meant to endow his bride with a ponderous old-fashioned timepiece and heavy brassy-looking cable which had belonged to his mother.

CHAPTER XXIX.
BAFFLED, NOT BEATEN.

THE time came when Gilbert Fenton was fain to own to himself that there was no more to be done down in Hampshire: professional science and his own efforts had been alike futile. If she whom he sought still lived—and he had never for a moment suffered himself to doubt this—it was more than likely that she was far away from Crosber Grange, that there had been some motive for her sudden flight, unaccountable as that flight might seem in the absence of any clue to the mystery.

Every means of inquiry being exhausted in Hampshire, there was nothing left to Gilbert but to return to London—that marvellous city, where there always seems the most hope of finding the lost, wide as the wilderness is.

"In London I shall have clever detectives always at my service," Gilbert thought; "in London I may be able to solve the question of John Holbrook's identity."

So, apart from the fact that his own affairs necessitated his prompt return to the great city, Gilbert had another motive for leaving the dull rural neighbourhood where he had wasted so many anxious hours, so much thought and care.

For the rest, he knew that Ellen Carley would be faithful—always on the watch for any clue to the mystery of Marian Holbrook's fate, always ready to receive the wanderer with open arms, should any happy chance bring her back to the Grange. Assured of this, he felt less compunction in turning his back upon the spot where his lost love had vanished from the eyes of men.

Before leaving, he gave Ellen a letter for Marian's husband, in the improbable event of that gentleman's reappearance at the Grange—a few simple earnest lines, entreating Mr. Holbrook to believe in the writer's faithful and brotherly affection for his wife, and to meet him in London on an early occasion, in order that they might together concert fresh means for bringing about her restoration to her husband and home. He reminded Mr. Holbrook of his friendship for Captain Sedgewick, and that good man's confidence in him, and declared himself bound by his respect for the dead to be faithful to the living—faithful in all forgiveness of any wrong done him in the past.

He went back to London cruelly depressed by the failure of his efforts, and with a blank dreary feeling that there was little more for him to do, except to wait the working of Providence, with the faint hope that one of those happy accidents which sometimes bring about a desired result when all human endeavour has been in vain, might throw a sudden light on Marian Holbrook's fate.

During the whole of that homeward journey he brooded an those dark suspicions of Mr. Holbrook which Ellen Carley had let fall in their earlier interviews. He had checked the girl on these occasions, and had prevented the full utterance of her thoughts, generously indignant that any suspicion of foul play should attach to Marian's husband, and utterly incredulous of such a depth of guilt as that at which the girl's hints pointed; but now that he was leaving Hampshire, he felt vexed with himself for not having urged her to speak freely—not having considered her suspicions, however preposterous those suspicions might have appeared to him.

Marian's disappearance had taken a darker colour in his mind since that time. Granted that she had left the Grange of her own accord, having some special reason for leaving secretly, at whose bidding would she have so acted except her husband's—she who stood so utterly alone, without a friend in the world? But what possible motive could Mr. Holbrook have had for such an underhand course—for making a conspiracy and a mystery out of so simple a fact as the removal of his wife from a place whence he was free to remove her at any moment? Fair and honest motive for such a course there could be none. Was it possible, looking at the business from a darker point of view, to imagine any guilty reason for the carrying out of such a plot? If this man had wanted to bring about a life-long severance between himself and his wife, to put her away somewhere, to keep her hidden from the eyes of the world—in plainer words, to get rid of her—might not this pretence of losing her, this affectation of distress at her loss, be a safe way of accomplishing his purpose? Who else was interested in doing her any wrong? Who else could have had sufficient power over her to beguile her away from her home?

Pondering on these questions throughout all that weary journey across a wintry landscape of bare brown fields and leafless trees, Gilbert Fenton travelled London-wards, to the city which was so little of a home for him, but in which his life had seemed pleasant enough in its own commonplace fashion until that fatal summer evening when he first saw Marian Nowell's radiant face in the quiet church at Lidford.

He scarcely stopped to eat or drink at the end of his journey, regaling himself only with a bottle of soda-water, imperceptibly flavoured with cognac by the hands of a ministering angel at the refreshment-counter of the Waterloo Station, and then hurrying on at once in a hansom to that dingy street in Soho where Mr. Medler sat in his parlour, like the proverbial spider waiting for the advent of some too-confiding fly.

The lawyer was at home, and seemed in no way surprised to see Mr. Fenton.

"I have come to you about a bad business, Mr. Medler," Gilbert began, seating himself opposite the shabby-looking office-table, with its covering of dusty faded baize, upon which there seemed to be always precisely the same array of papers in little bundles tied with red tape; "but first let me ask you a question: Have you heard from Mrs. Holbrook?"

"Not a line."

"And have you taken no further steps, no other means of communicating with her?" Gilbert asked.

"Not yet. I think of sending my clerk down to Hampshire, or of going down myself perhaps, in a day or two, if my business engagements will permit me."

"Do you not consider the case rather an urgent one, Mr. Medler? I should have supposed that your curiosity would have been aroused by the absence of any reply to your letters—that you would have looked at the business in a more serious light than you appear to have done—that you would have taken alarm, in short."

"Why should I do so?" the lawyer demanded carelessly.

"It is Mrs. Holbrook's business to look after her affairs. The property is safe enough. She can administer to the will as soon as she pleases. I certainly wonder that the husband has not been a little sharper and more active in the business."

"You have heard nothing of him, then, I presume?"

"Nothing."

Gilbert remembered what Ellen Carley had told him about Marian's keeping the secret of her newly-acquired fortune from her husband, until she should be able to tell it to him with her own lips; waiting for that happy moment with innocent girlish delight in the thought that he was to owe prosperity to her.

It seemed evident, therefore, that Mr. Holbrook could know nothing of his wife's inheritance, nor of Mr. Medler's existence, supposing the lawyer's letter to have reached the Grange before Marian's disappearance, and to have been destroyed or carried away by her.

He inquired the date of this letter; whereupon Mr. Medler referred to a letter-book in which there was a facsimile of the document. It had been posted three days before Marian left the Grange.

Gilbert now proceeded to inform Mr. Medler of his client's mysterious disappearance, and all the useless efforts that had been made to solve the mystery. The lawyer listened with an appearance of profound interest and astonishment, but made no remark till the story was quite finished.

"You are right, Mr. Fenton," he said at last. "It is a bad business, a very bad business. May I ask you what is the common opinion among people in that part of the world—in the immediate neighbourhood of the event, as to this poor lady's fate?"

"An opinion with which I cannot bring myself to agree—an opinion which I pray God may prove as unfounded as I believe it to be. It is generally thought that Mrs. Holbrook has fallen a victim to some common crime—that she was robbed, and then thrown into the river."

"The river has been dragged, I suppose?"

"It has; but the people about there seem to consider that no conclusive test."

"Had Mrs. Holbrook anything valuable about her at the time of her disappearance?"

"Her watch and chain and a few other trinkets."

"Humph! There are scoundrels about the country who will commit the darkest crime for the smallest inducement. I confess the business has rather a black look, Mr. Fenton, and that I am inclined to concur with the country people."

"An easy way of settling the question for those not vitally interested in the lady's fate," Gilbert answered bitterly.

"The lady is my client, sir, and I am bound to feel a warm interest in her affairs," the lawyer said, with the lofty tone of a man whose finer feelings have been outraged.

"The lady was once my promised wife, Mr. Medler," returned Gilbert, "and now stands to me in the place of a beloved and only sister. For me the mystery of her fate is an all-absorbing question, an enigma to the solution of which I mean to devote the rest of my life, if need be."

"A wasted life, Mr. Fenton; and in the meantime that river down yonder may hide the only secret."

"O God!" cried Gilbert passionately, "how eager every one is to make an end of this business! Even the men whom I paid and bribed to help me grew tired of their work, and abandoned all hope after the feeblest, most miserable attempts to earn their reward."

"What can be done in such a case, Mr. Fenton?" demanded the lawyer, shrugging his shoulders with a deprecating air. "What can the police do more than you or I? They have only a little more experience, that's all; they have no recondite means of solving these social mysteries. You have advertised, of course?"

"Yes, in many channels, with a certain amount of caution, but in such a manner as to insure Mrs. Holbrook's identification, if she had fallen into the hands of any one willing to communicate with me, and to insure her own attention, were she free to act for herself."

"Humph! Then it seems to me that everything has been done that can be done."

"Not yet. The men whom I employed in Hampshire—they were recommended to me by the Scotland-yard authorities, certainly—may not have been up to the mark. In any case, I shall try some one else. Do you know anything of the detective force?"

Mr. Medler assumed an air of consideration, and then said, "No, he did not know the name of a single detective; his business did not bring him in contact with that class of people." He said this with the tone of a man whose practice was of the loftiest and choicest kind—conveyancing, perhaps, and the management of estates for the landed gentry, marriage-settlements involving the disposition of large fortunes, and so on; whereas Mr. Medler's business lying chiefly among the criminal population, his path in life might have been supposed to be not very remote from the footsteps of eminent police-officers.

"I can get the information elsewhere," Gilbert said carelessly. "Believe me, I do not mean to let this matter drop."

"My dear sir, if I might venture upon a word of friendly advice—not in a professional spirit, but as between man and man—I should warn you against wasting your time and fortune upon a useless pursuit. If Mrs. Holbrook has vanished from the world of her own free will—a thing that often happens, eccentric as it may be—she will reappear in good time of her own free will. If she has been the victim of a crime, that crime will no doubt come to light in due course, without any efforts of yours."

"That is the common kind of advice, Mr. Medler," answered Gilbert.

"Prudent counsel, no doubt, if a man could be content to take it, and well meant; but, you see, I have loved this lady, love her still, and shall continue so to love her till the end of my life. It is not possible for me to rest in ignorance of her fate."

"Although she jilted you in favour of Mr. Holbrook?" suggested the lawyer with something of a sneer.

"That wrong has been forgiven. Fate did not permit me to be her husband, but I can be her friend and brother. She has need of some one to stand in that position, poor girl! for her lot is very lonely. And now I want you to explain the conditions of her grandfather's will. It is her father who would profit, I think I gathered from our last conversation, in the event of Marian's death."

"In the event of her dying childless—yes, the father would take all."

"Then he is really the only person who could profit by her death?"

"Well, yes," replied the lawyer with some slight hesitation; "under her grandfather's will, yes, her father would take all. Of course, in the event of her father having died previously, the husband would come in as heir-at-law. You see it was not easy to exclude the husband altogether."

"And do you believe that Mr. Nowell is still living to claim his inheritance?"

"I believe so. I fancy the old man had some tidings of his son before the will was executed; that he, in short, heard of his having been met with not long ago, over in America."

"No doubt he will speedily put in an appearance now," said Gilbert bitterly—"now that there is a fortune to be gained by the assertion of his identity."

"Humph!" muttered the lawyer. "It would not be very easy for him to put his hand on sixpence of Jacob Nowell's money, in the absence of any proof of Mrs. Holbrook's death. There would be no end of appeals to the Court of Chancery; and after all manner of formulas he might obtain a decree that would lock up the property for twenty-four years. I doubt, if the executor chose to stick to technicals, and the business got into chancery, whether Percival Nowell would live long enough to profit by his father's will."

"I am glad of that," said Gilbert. "I know the man to be a scoundrel, and I am very glad that he is unlikely to be a gainer by any misfortune that has befallen his daughter. Had it been otherwise, I should have been inclined to think that he had had some hand in this disappearance."

The lawyer looked at Mr. Fenton with a sharp inquisitive glance.

"In other words, you would imply that Percival Nowell may have made away with his daughter. You must have a very bad opinion of human nature, Mr. Fenton, to conceive anything so horrible."

"My suspicions do not go quite so far as that," said Gilbert. "God forbid that it should be so. I have a firm belief that Marian Holbrook lives. But it is possible to get a person out of the way without the last worst crime of which mankind is capable."

"It would seem more natural to suspect the husband than the father, I should imagine," Mr. Medler answered, after a thoughtful pause.

"I cannot see that. The husband had nothing to gain by his wife's disappearance, and everything to lose."

"He might have supposed the father to be dead, and that he would step into the fortune. He might not know enough of the law of property to be aware of the difficulties attending a succession of that kind. There is a most extraordinary ignorance of the law of the land prevailing among well-educated Englishmen. Or he may have been tired of his wife, and have seen his way to a more advantageous alliance. Men are not always satisfied with one wife in these days, and a man who married in such a strange underhand manner would be likely to have some hidden motive for secrecy."

The suggestion was not without force for Gilbert Fenton. His face grew darker, and he was some time before he replied to Mr. Medler's remarks. That suspicion which of late had been perpetually floating dimly in his brain—that vague distrust of his one chosen friend, John Saltram, flashed upon him in this moment with a new distinctness. If this man, whom he had so loved and trusted, had betrayed him, had so utterly falsified his friend's estimate of his character, was it not easy enough to believe him capable of still deeper baseness, capable of growing weary of his stolen wife, and casting her off by some foul secret means, in order to marry a richer woman? The marriage between John Holbrook and Marian Nowell had taken place several months before Michael Branston's death, at a time when perhaps Adela Branston's admirer had begun to despair of her release. And then fate had gone against him, and Mrs. Branston's fortune lay at his feet when it was too late.

Thus, and thus only, could Gilbert Fenton account in any easy manner for John Saltram's avoidance of the Anglo-Indian's widow. A little more than a year ago it had seemed as if the whole plan of his life was built upon a marriage with this woman; and now that she was free, and obviously willing to make him the master of her fortune, he recoiled from the position, unreasonably and unaccountably blind or indifferent to its advantages.

"There shall be an end of these shapeless unspoken doubts," Gilbert said to himself. "I will see John Saltram to-day, and there shall be an explanation between us. I will be his dupe and fool no longer. I will get at the truth somehow."

Gilbert Fenton said very little more to the lawyer, who seemed by no means sorry to get rid of him. But at the door of the office he paused.

"You did not tell me the names of the executors to Jacob Nowell's will," he said.

"You didn't ask me the question," answered Mr. Medler curtly. "There is only one executor—myself."

"Indeed! Mr. Nowell must have had a very high opinion of you to leave you so much power."

"I don't know about power. Jacob Nowell knew me, and he didn't know many people. I don't say that he put any especial confidence in me—for it was his habit to trust no one, his boast that he trusted no one. But he was obliged to name some one for his executor, and he named me."

"Shall you consider it your duty to seek out or advertise for Percival Nowell?" asked Gilbert.

"I shall be in no hurry to do that, in the absence of any proof of his daughter's death. My first duty would be to look for her."

"God grant you may be more fortunate than I have been! There is my card, Mr. Medler. You will be so good as to let me have a line immediately, at that address, if you obtain any tidings of Mrs. Holbrook."

"I will do so."

CHAPTER XXX.
STRICKEN DOWN.

A hansom carried Gilbert Fenton to the Temple, without loss of time. There was a fierce hurry in his breast, a heat and fever which he had scarcely felt since the beginning of his troubles; for his lurking suspicion of his friend had gathered shape and strength all at once, and possessed his mind now to the exclusion of every other thought.

He ran quickly up the stairs. The outer and inner doors of John Saltram's chambers were both ajar. Gilbert pushed them open and went in. The familiar sitting-room looked just a little more dreary than usual. The litter of books and papers, ink-stand and portfolio, was transferred to one of the side-tables, and in its place, on the table where his friend had been accustomed to write, Gilbert saw a cluster of medicine-bottles, a jug of toast-and-water, and a tray with a basin of lukewarm greasy-looking beef-tea.

The door between the two rooms stood half open, and from the bedchamber within Gilbert heard the heavy painful breathing of a sleeper. He went to the door and looked into the room. John Saltram was lying asleep, in an uneasy attitude, with both arms thrown over his head. His face had a haggard look that was made all the more ghastly by two vivid crimson spots upon his sunken cheeks; there were dark purple rings round his eyes, and his beard was of more than a week's growth.

"Ill," Gilbert muttered, looking aghast at this dreary picture, with strangely conflicting feelings of pity and anger in his breast; "struck down at the very moment when I had determined to know the truth."

The sick man tossed himself restlessly from side to side in his feverish sleep, changed his position two or three times with evident weariness and pain, and then opened his eyes and stared with a blank unseeing gaze at his friend. That look, without one ray of recognition, went to Gilbert's heart somehow.

"O God, how fond I was of him!" he said to himself. "And if he has been a traitor! If he were to die like this, before I have wrung the truth from him—to die, and I not dare to cherish his memory—to be obliged to live out my life with this doubt of him!"

This doubt! Had he much reason to doubt two minutes afterwards, when John Saltram raised himself on his gaunt arm, and looked piteously round the room?

"Marian!" he called. "Marian!"

"Yes," muttered Gilbert, "it is all true. He is calling his wife."

The revelation scarcely seemed a surprise to him. Little by little that suspicion, so vague and dim at first, had gathered strength, and now that all his doubts received confirmation from those unconscious lips, it seemed to him as if he had known his friend's falsehood for a long time.

"Marian, come here. Come, child, come," the sick man cried in feeble imploring tones. "What, are you afraid of me? Is this death? Am I dead, and parted from her? Would anything else keep her from me when I call for her, the poor child that loved me so well? And I have wished myself free of her—God forgive me!—wished myself free."

The words were muttered in broken gasping fragments of sentences; but Gilbert heard them and understood them very easily. Then, after looking about the room, and looking full at Gilbert without seeing him, John Saltram fell back upon his tumbled pillows and closed his eyes. Gilbert heard a slipshod step in the outer room, and turning round, found himself face to face with the laundress—that mature and somewhat depressing matron whom he had sought out a little time before, when he wanted to discover Mr. Saltram's whereabouts.

This woman, upon seeing him, burst forth immediately into jubilation.

"O, sir, what a providence it is that you've come!" she cried. "Poor dear gentleman, he has been that ill, and me not knowing what to do more than a baby, except in the way of sending for a doctor when I see how bad he was, and waiting on him myself day and night, which I have done faithful, and am that worn-out in consequence, that I shake like a haspen, and can't touch a bit of victuals. I had but just slipped round to the court, while he was asleep, poor dear, to give my children their dinner; for it's a hard trial, sir, having a helpless young family depending upon one; and it would but be fair that all I have gone through should be considered; for though I says it as shouldn't, there isn't one of your hired nurses would do more; and I'm willing to continue of it, provisoed as I have help at nights, and my trouble considered in my wages."

"You need have no apprehension; you shall be paid for your trouble. Has he been long ill?"

"Well, sir, he took the cold as were the beginning of his illness a fortnight ago come next Thursday. You may remember, perhaps, as it came on awful wet in the afternoon, last Thursday week, and Mr. Saltram was out in the rain, and walked home in it,—not being able to get a cab, I suppose, or perhaps not caring to get one, for he was always a careless gentleman in such respects,—and come in wet through to the skin; and instead of changing his clothes, as a Christian would have done, just gives himself a shake like, as he might have been a New-fondling dog that had been swimming, and sits down before the fire, which of course drawed out the steam from his things and made it worse, and writes away for dear life till twelve o'clock that night, having something particular to finish for them magazines, he says; and so, when I come to tidy-up a bit the last thing at night, I found him sitting at the table writing, and didn't take no more notice of me than a dog, which was his way, though never meant unkindly—quite the reverse."

The laundress paused to draw breath, and to pour a dose of medicine from one of the bottles on the table.

"Well, sir, the next day, he had a vi'lent cold, as you may suppose, and was low and languid-like, but went on with his writing, and it weren't no good asking him not. 'I want money, Mrs. Pratt,' he said; 'you can't tell how bad I want money, and these people pay me for my stuff as fast as I send it in.' The day after that he was a deal worse, and had a wandering way like, as if he didn't know what he was doing; and sat turning over his papers with one hand, and leaning his head upon the other, and groaned so that it went through one like a knife to hear him. 'It's no use,' he said at last; 'it's no use!' and then went and threw hisself down upon that bed, and has never got up since, poor dear gentleman! I went round to fetch a doctor out of Essex Street, finding as he was no better in the evening, and awful hot, and still more wandering-like—Mr. Mew by name, a very nice gentleman—which said as it were rheumatic fever, and has been here twice a day ever since."

"Has Mr. Saltram never been in his right senses since that day?" Gilbert asked.

"O yes, sir; off and on for the first week he was quite hisself at times; but for the last three days he hasn't known any one, and has talked and jabbered a deal, and has been dreadful restless."

"Does the doctor call it a dangerous case?"

"Well, sir, not to deceive you, he ast me if Mr. Saltram had any friends as I could send for; and I says no, not to my knowledge; 'for,' says Mr. Mew, 'if he have any relations or friends near at hand, they ought to be told that he's in a bad way;' and only this morning he said as how he should like to call in a physician, for the case was a bad one."

"I see. There is danger evidently," Gilbert said gravely. "I will wait and hear what the doctor says. He will come again to-day, I suppose?"

"Yes, sir; he's sure to come in the evening."

"Good; I will stay till the evening. I should like you to go round immediately to this Mr. Mew's house, and ask for the address of some skilled nurse, and then go on, in a cab if necessary, and fetch her."

"I could do that, sir, of course,—not but what I feel myself capable of nursing the poor dear gentleman."

"You can't nurse him night and day, my good woman. Do what I tell you, and bring back a professional nurse as soon as you can. If Mr. Mew should be out, his people are likely to know the address of such a person."

He gave the woman some silver, and despatched her; and then, being alone, sat down quietly in the sick-room to think out the situation.

Yes, there was no longer any doubt; that piteous appeal to Marian had settled the question. John Saltram, the friend whom he had loved, was the traitor. John Saltram had stolen his promised wife, had come between him and his fair happy future, and had kept the secret of his guilt in a dastardly spirit that made the act fifty times blacker than it would have seemed otherwise.

Sitting in the dreary silence of that sick chamber, a silence broken only by the painful sound of the sleeper's difficult breathing, many things came back to his mind; circumstances trivial enough in themselves, but invested with a grave significance when contemplated by the light of today's revelation.

He remembered those happy autumn afternoons at Lidford; those long, drowsy, idle days in which John Saltram had given himself up so entirely to the pleasure of the moment, with surely something more than mere sympathy with his friend's happiness. He remembered that last long evening at the cottage, when this man had been at his best, full of life and gaiety; and then that sudden departure, which had puzzled him so much at the time, and yet had seemed no surprise to Marian. It had been the result of some suddenly-formed resolution perhaps, Gilbert thought.

"Poor wretch! he may have tried to be true to me," he said to himself, with a sharp bitter pain at his heart.

He had loved this man so well, that even now, knowing himself to have been betrayed, there was a strange mingling of pity and anger in his mind, and mixed with these a touch of contempt. He had believed in John Saltram; had fancied him nobler and grander than himself, somehow; a man who, under a careless half-scornful pretence of being worse than his fellows, concealed a nature that was far above the common herd; and yet this man had proved the merest caitiff, a weak cowardly villain.

"To take my hand in friendship, knowing what he had done, and how my life was broken! to pretend sympathy; to play out the miserable farce to the very last! Great heaven! that the man I have honoured could be capable of so much baseness!"

The sleeper moved restlessly, the eyes were opened once more and turned upon Gilbert, not with the same utter blankness as before, but without the faintest recognition. The sick man saw some one watching him, and the figure was associated with an unreal presence, the phantom of his brain, which had been with him often in the day and night.

"The man again!" he muttered. "When will she come?" And then raising himself upon his elbow, he cried imploringly, "Mother, you fetch her!"

He was speaking to his mother, whom he had loved very dearly—his mother who had been dead fifteen years.

Gilbert's mind went back to that far-away time in Egypt, when he had lain like this, helpless and unconscious, and this man had nursed and watched him with unwearying tenderness.

"I will see him safely through this," he said to himself, "and then——"

And then the account between them must be squared somehow. Gilbert Fenton had no thought of any direful vengeance. He belonged to an age in which injuries are taken very quietly, unless they are wrongs which the law can redress—wounds which can be healed by a golden plaster in the way of damages.

He could not kill his friend; the age of duelling was past, and he not romantic enough to be guilty of such an anachronism as mortal combat. Yet nothing less than a duel to the death could avenge such a wrong.

So friendship was at an end between those two, and that was all; it was only the utter severance of a tie that had lasted for years, nothing more. Yet to Gilbert it seemed a great deal. His little world had crumbled to ashes; love had perished, and now friendship had died this sudden bitter death, from which there was no possible resurrection.

In the midst of such thoughts as these he remembered the sick man's medicine. Mrs. Pratt had given him a few hurried directions before departing on her errand. He looked at his watch, and then went over to the table and prepared the draught and administered it with a firm and gentle hand.

"Who's that?" John Saltram muttered faintly. "It seems like the touch of a friend."

He dropped back upon the pillow without waiting for any reply, and fell into a string of low incoherent talk, with closed eyes.

The laundress was a long time gone, and Gilbert sat alone in the dismal little bedroom, where there had never been the smallest attempt at comfort since John Saltram had occupied it. He sat alone, or with that awful companionship of one whose mind was far away, which was so much more dreary than actual loneliness—sat brooding over the history of his friend's treachery.

What had he done with Marian? Was her disappearance any work of his, after all? Had he hidden her away for some secret reason of his own, and then acted out the play by pretending to search for her? Knowing him for the traitor he was, could Gilbert Fenton draw any positive line of demarcation between the amount of guilt which was possible and that which was not possible to him?

What had he done with Marian? How soon would he be able to answer that question? or would he ever be able to answer it? The thought of this delay was torture to Gilbert Fenton. He had come here to-day thinking to make an end of all his doubts, to force an avowal of the truth from those false lips. And behold, a hand stronger than his held him back. His interrogation must await the answer to that awful question—life or death.

The woman came in presently, bustling and out of breath. She had found a very trustworthy person, recommended by Mr. Mew's assistant—a person who would come that evening without fail.

"It was all the way up at Islington, sir, and I paid the cabman three-and-six altogether, which he said it were his fare. And how has the poor dear been while I was away?" asked Mrs. Pratt, with her head on one side and an air of extreme solicitude.

"Very much as you see him now. He has mentioned a name once or twice, the name of Marian. Have you ever heard that?"

"I should say I have, sir, times and often since he's been ill. 'Marian, why don't you come to me?' so pitiful; and then, 'Lost, lost!' in such a awful wild way. I think it must be some favourite sister, sir, or a young lady as he has kep' company with."

"Marian!" cried the voice from the bed, as if their cautious talk had penetrated to that dim brain. "Marian! O no, no; she is gone; I have lost her! Well, I wished it; I wanted my freedom."

Gilbert started, and stood transfixed, looking intently at the unconscious speaker. Yes, here was the clue to the mystery. John Saltram had grown tired of his stolen bride—had sighed for his freedom. Who should say that he had not taken some iniquitous means to rid himself of the tie that had grown troublesome to him?

Gilbert Fenton remembered Ellen Carley's suspicions. He was no longer inclined to despise them.

It was dreary work to sit by the bedside watching that familiar face, to which fever and delirium had given a strange weird look; dismal work to count the moments, and wonder when that voice, now so thick of utterance as it went on muttering incoherent sentences and meaningless phrases, would be able to reply to those questions which Gilbert Fenton was burning to ask.

Was it a guilty conscience, the dull slow agony of remorse, which had stricken this man down—this strong powerfully-built man, who was a stranger to illness and all physical suffering? Was the body only crushed by the burden of the mind? Gilbert could not find any answer to these questions. He only knew that his sometime friend lay there helpless, unconscious, removed beyond his reach as completely as if he had been lying in his coffin.

"O God, it is hard to bear!" he said half aloud: "it is a bitter trial to bear. If this illness should end in death, I may never know Marian's fate."

He sat in the sick man's room all through that long dismal afternoon, waiting to see the doctor, and with the same hopeless thoughts repeating themselves perpetually in his mind.

It was nearly eight o'clock when Mr. Mew at last made his evening visit. He was a grave gray-haired little man, with a shrewd face and a pleasant manner; a man who inspired Gilbert with confidence, and whose presence was cheering in a sick-room; but he did not speak very hopefully of John Saltram.

"It is a bad case, sir—a very bad case," he said gravely, after he had made his careful examination of the patient's condition. "There has been a violent cold caught, you see, through our poor friend's recklessness in neglecting to change his damp clothes, and rheumatic fever has set in. But it appears to me that there are other causes at work—mental disturbance, and so on. Our friend has been taxing his brain a little too severely, I gather from Mrs. Pratt's account of him; and these things will tell, sir; sooner or later they have their effect."

"Then you apprehend danger?"

"Well, yes; I dare not tell you that there is an absence of danger. Mr. Saltram has a fine constitution, a noble frame; but the strain is a severe one, especially upon the mind."

"You spoke just now of over-work as a cause for this mental disturbance. Might it not rather proceed from some secret trouble of mind, some hidden care?" Gilbert asked anxiously.

"That, sir, is an open question. The mind is unhinged; there is no doubt of that. There is something more here than the ordinary delirium we look for in fever cases."

"You have talked of a physician, Mr. Mew; would it not be well to call one in immediately?"

"I should feel more comfortable if my opinion were supported, sir: not that I believe there is anything more can be done for our patient than I have been doing; but the case is a critical one, and I should be glad to feel myself supported."

"If you will give me the name and address of the gentleman you would like to call in, I will go for him immediately."

"To-night? Nay, my dear sir, there is no occasion for such haste; to-morrow morning will do very well."

"To-morrow morning, then; but I will make the appointment to-night, if I can."

Mr. Mew named a physician high in reputation as a specialist in such cases as John Saltram's; and Gilbert dashed off at once in a hansom to obtain the promise of an early visit from this gentleman on the following morning. He succeeded in his errand; and on returning to the Temple found the professional nurse installed, and the sick-room brightened and freshened a little by her handiwork. The patient was asleep, and his slumber was more quiet than usual.

Gilbert had eaten nothing since breakfast, and it was now nearly nine o'clock in the evening; but before going out to some neighbouring tavern to snatch a hasty dinner, he stopped to tell Mrs. Pratt that he should sleep in his friend's chamber that night.

"Why, you don't mean that, sir, sure to goodness," cried the laundress, alarmed; "and not so much as a sofy bedstead, nor nothing anyways comfortable."

"I could sleep upon three or four chairs, if it were necessary; but there is an old sofa in the bedroom. You might bring that into this room for me; and the nurse can have it in the day-time. She won't want to be lying down to-night, I daresay. I don't suppose I shall sleep much myself, but I am a little knocked up, and shall be glad of some sort of rest. I want to be on the spot, come what may."

"But, sir, with the new nurse and me, there surely can't be no necessity; and you might be round the first thing in the morning like to see how the poor dear gentleman has slep'."

"I know that, but I would rather be on the spot. I have my own especial reasons. You can go home to your children."

"Thank you kindly, sir; which I shall be very glad to take care of 'em, poor things. And I hope, sir, as you won't forget that I've gone through a deal for Mr. Saltram—if so be as he shouldn't get better himself, which the Lord forbid—to take my trouble into consideration, bein' as he were always a free-handed gentleman, though not rich."

"Your services will not be forgotten, Mrs. Pratt, depend upon it. Perhaps I'd better give you a couple of sovereigns on account: that'll make matters straight for the present."

"Yes, sir; and many thanks for your generosity," replied the laundress, agreeably surprised by this prompt donation, and dropping grateful curtseys before her benefactor; "and Mr. Saltram shall want nothing as my care can provide for him, you may depend upon it."

"That is well. And now I am going out to get some dinner; I shall be back in half an hour."

The press and bustle of the day's work was over at the tavern to which Gilbert bent his steps. Dinners and diners seemed to be done with for one more day; and there were only a couple of drowsy-looking waiters folding table-cloths and putting away cruet-stands and other paraphernalia in long narrow closets cut in the papered walls, and invisible by day.

One of these functionaries grew brisk again, with a wan factitious briskness, at sight of Gilbert, made haste to redecorate one of the tables, and in bland insinuating tones suggested a dinner of six courses or so, as likely to be agreeable to a lonely and belated diner; well aware in the depths of his inner consciousness that the six courses would be all more or less warmings-up of viands that had figured in the day's bill of fare.

"Bring me a chop or a steak, and a pint of dry sherry," Gilbert said wearily.

"Have a slice of turbot and lobster-sauce, sir—the turbot are uncommon fine to-day; and a briled fowl and mushrooms. It will be ready in five minutes."

"You may bring me the fowl, if you like: I won't wait for fish. I'm in a hurry."

The attendant gave a faint sigh, and communicated the order for the fowl and mushrooms through a speaking-tube. It was the business of his life to beguile his master's customers into over-eating themselves, and to set his face against chops and steaks; but he felt that this particular customer was proof against his blandishments. He took Gilbert an evening paper, and then subsided into a pensive silence until the fowl appeared in an agreeable frizzling state, fresh from the gridiron, but a bird of some experience notwithstanding, and wingless. It was a very hasty meal. Gilbert was eager to return to those chambers in the Temple—eager to be listening once more for some chance words of meaning that might be dropped from John Saltram's pale parched lips in the midst of incoherent ravings. Come what might, he wanted to be near at hand, to watch that sick-bed with a closer vigil than hired nurse ever kept; to be ready to surprise the briefest interval of consciousness that might come all of a sudden to that hapless fever-stricken sinner. Who should say that such an interval would not come, or who could tell what such an interval might reveal?

Gilbert Fenton paid for his dinner, left half his wine undrunk, and hurried away; leaving the waiter with rather a contemptuous idea of him, though that individual condescended to profit by his sobriety, and finished the dry sherry at a draught.

It was nearly ten when Gilbert returned to the chambers, and all was still quiet, that heavy slumber continuing; an artificial sleep at the best, produced by one of Mr. Mew's sedatives. The sofa had been wheeled from the bedroom to the sitting-room, and placed in a comfortable corner by the fire. There were preparations too for a cup of tea, to be made and consumed at any hour agreeable to the watcher; a small teakettle simmering on the hob; a tray with a cup and saucer, and queer little black earthenware teapot, on the table; a teacaddy and other appliances close at hand,—all testifying to the grateful attention of the vanished Pratt.

Gilbert shared the nurse's watch till past midnight. Long before that John Saltram woke from his heavy sleep, and there was more of that incoherent talk so painful to hear—talk of people that were dead, of scenes that were far away, even of those careless happy wanderings in which those two college friends had been together; and then mere nonsense talk, shreds and patches of random thought, that scorned to be drawn from, some rubbish-chamber, some waste-paper basket of the brain.

It was weary work. He woke towards eleven, and a little after twelve dropped asleep again; but this time, the effect of the sedative having worn off, the sleep was restless and uneasy. Then came a brief interval of quiet; and in this Gilbert left him, and flung himself down upon the sofa, to sink into a slumber that was scarcely more peaceful than that of the sick man.

He was thoroughly worn out, however, and slept for some hours, to be awakened suddenly at last by a shrill cry in the next room. He sprang up from the sofa, and rushed in. John Saltram was sitting up in bed, propped by the pillows on which his two elbows were planted, looking about him with a fierce haggard face, and calling for "Marian." The nurse had fallen asleep in her arm-chair by the fire, and was slumbering placidly.

"Marian," he cried, "Marian, why have you left me? God knows I loved you; yes, even when I seemed cold and neglectful. Everything was against me; but I loved you, my dear, I loved you! Did I ever say that you came between me and fortune—was I mean enough, base enough, ever to say that? It was a lie, my love; you were my fortune. Were poverty and obscurity hard things to bear for you? No, my darling, no; I will face them to-morrow, if you will come back to me. O no, no, she is gone; my life has gone: I broke her heart with my hard bitter words; I drove my angel away from me."

He had not spoken so coherently since Gilbert had been with him that day. Surely this must be an interval of consciousness, or semi-consciousness. Gilbert went to the bedside, and, seating himself there quietly, looked intently at the altered face, which stared at him without a gleam of recognition.

"Speak to me, John Saltram," he said. "You know me, don't you—the man who was once your friend, Gilbert Fenton?"

The other burst into a wild bitter laugh. "Gilbert Fenton—my friend, the man who trusts me still! Poor old Gilbert! and I fancied that I loved him, that I would have freely sacrificed my own happiness for his."

"And yet you betrayed him," Gilbert said in a low distinct voice. "But that may be forgiven, if you have been guilty of no deeper wrong than that. John Saltram, as you have a soul to be saved, what have you done with Marian—with—your wife?"

It cost him something, even in that moment of excitement, to pronounce those two words.

"Killed her!" the sick man answered with the same mad laugh. "She was too good for me, you see; and I grew weary of her calm beauty, and I sickened of her tranquil goodness. First I sacrificed honour, friendship, everything to win her; and then I got tired of my prize. It is my nature, I suppose; but I loved her all the time; she had twined herself about my heart somehow. I knew it when she was lost."

"What have you done with her?" repeated Gilbert, in a low stern voice, with his grasp upon John Saltram's arm.

"What have I done with her? I forget. She is gone—I wanted my freedom; I felt myself fettered, a ruined man. She is gone; and I am free, free to make a better marriage."

"O God!" muttered Gilbert, "is this man the blackest villain that ever cumbered the earth? What am I to think, what am I to believe?"

Again he repeated the same question, with a stem kind of patience, as if he would give this guilty wretch the benefit of every possible doubt, the unwilling pity which his condition demanded. Alas! he could obtain no coherent answer to his persistent questioning. Vague self-accusation, mad reiteration of that one fact of his loss; nothing more distinct came from those fevered lips, nor did one look of recognition flash into those bloodshot eyes.

The time at which this mystery was to be solved had not come yet; there was nothing to be done but to wait, and Gilbert waited with a sublime patience through all the alternations of a long and wearisome sickness.

"Talk of friends," Mrs. Pratt exclaimed, in a private conference with the nurse; "never did I see such a friend as Mr. Fenting, sacrificing of himself as he do, day and night, to look after that poor creature in there, and taking no better rest than he can get on that old horsehair sofy, which brickbats or knife boards isn't harder, and never do you hear him murmur."

And yet for this man, whose, battle with the grim enemy, Death, he watched so patiently, what feeling could there be in Gilbert Fenton's heart in all the days to come but hatred or contempt? He had loved him so well, and trusted him so completely, and this was the end of it.

Christmas came while John Saltram was lying at death's door, feebly fighting that awful battle, struggling unconsciously with the bony hand that was trying to drag him across that fatal threshold; just able to keep himself on this side of that dread portal beyond which there lies so deep a mystery, so profound a darkness. Christmas came; and there were bells ringing, and festive gatherings here and there about the great dreary town, and Gilbert Fenton was besieged by friendly invitations from Mrs. Lister, remonstrating with him for his want of common affection in preferring to spend that season among his London friends rather than in the bosom of his family.

Gilbert wrote: to his sister telling her that he had particular business which detained him in town. But had it been otherwise, had he not been bound prisoner to John Saltram's sick-room, he would scarcely have cared to take his part in the conventional feastings and commonplace jovialities of Lidford House. Had he not dreamed of a bright home which was to be his at this time, a home beautified by the presence of the woman he loved? Ah, what delight to have welcomed the sacred day in the holy quiet of such a home, they two alone together, with all the world shut out!

CHAPTER XXXI.
ELLEN CARLEY'S TRIALS.

CHRISTMAS came in the old farm-house near Crosber; and Ellen Carley, who had no idea of making any troubled thoughts of her own an excuse for neglect of her household duties, made the sombre panelled rooms bright with holly and ivy, laurel and fir, and busied herself briskly in the confection of such pies and puddings as Hampshire considered necessary to the due honour of that pious festival. There were not many people to see the greenery and bright holly-berries which embellished the grave old rooms, not many whom Ellen very much cared for to taste the pies and puddings; but duty must be done, and the bailiff's daughter did her work with a steady industry which knew no wavering.

Her life had been a hard one of late, very lonely since Mrs. Holbrook's disappearance, and haunted with a presence which was most hateful to her. Stephen Whitelaw had taken to coming to the Grange much oftener than of old. There was seldom an evening now on which his insignificant figure was not to be seen planted by the hearth in the snug little oak-parlour, smoking his pipe in that dull silent way of his, which was calculated to aggravate a lively person like Ellen Carley into some open expression of disgust or dislike. Of late, too, his attentions had been of a more pronounced character; he took to dropping sly hints of his pretensions, and it was impossible for Ellen any longer to doubt that he wanted her to be his wife. More than this, there was a tone of assurance about the man, quiet as he was, which exasperated Miss Carley beyond all measure. He had the air of being certain of success, and on more than one occasion spoke of the day when Ellen would be mistress of Wyncomb Farm.

On his repetition of this offensive speech one evening, the girl took him up sharply:—

"Not quite so fast, if you please, Mr. Whitelaw," she said; "it takes two to make a bargain of that kind, just the same as it takes two to quarrel. There's many curious changes may come in a person's life, no doubt, and folks never know what's going to happen to them; but whatever changes may come upon me, *that* isn't one of them. I may live to see the inside of the workhouse, perhaps, when I'm too old for service; but I shall never sleep under the roof of Wyncomb Farmhouse."

Mr. Whitelaw gave a spiteful little laugh.

"What a spirited one she is, ain't she, now?" he said with a sneer. "O, you won't, won't you, my lass; you turn up that pretty little nose of yours—it do turn up a bit of itself, don't it, though?—at Wyncomb Farm and Stephen Whitelaw; your father tells a different story, Nell."

"Then my father tells a lying story," answered the girl, blushing crimson with indignation; "and it isn't for want o' knowing the truth. He knows that, if it was put upon me to choose between your house and the union, I'd go to the union—and with a light heart too, to be free of you. I didn't want to be rude, Mr. Whitelaw; for you've been civil-spoken enough to me, and I daresay you're a good friend to my father; but I can't help speaking the truth, and you've brought it on yourself with your nonsense."

"She's got a devil of a tongue of her own, you see, Whitelaw," said the bailiff, with a savage glance at his daughter; "but she don't mean above a quarter what she says—and when her time comes, she'll do as she's bid, or she's no child of mine."

"O, I forgive her," replied Mr. Whitelaw, with a placid air of superiority; "I'm not the man to bear malice against a pretty woman, and to my mind a pretty woman looks all the prettier when she's in a passion. I'm not in a hurry, you see, Carley; I can bide my time; but I shall never take a mistress to Wyncomb unless I can take the one I like."

After this particular evening, Mr. Whitelaw's presence seemed more than ever disagreeable to poor Ellen. He had the air of her fate somehow, sitting rooted to the hearth night after night, and she grew to regard him with a half superstitious horror, as if he possessed some occult power over her, and could bend her to his wishes in spite of herself. The very quietude of the man became appalling to her. Such a man seemed capable of accomplishing anything by the mere force of persistence, by the negative power that lay in his silent nature.

"I suppose he means to sit in that room night after night, smoking his pipe and staring with those pale stupid eyes of his, till I change my mind and promise to marry him," Ellen said to herself, as she meditated angrily on the annoyance of Mr. Whitelaw's courtship. "He may sit there till his hair turns gray—if ever such red hair does turn to anything better than itself—and he'll find no change in me. I wish Frank were here to keep up my courage. I think if he were to ask me to run away with him, I should be tempted to say yes, at the risk of bringing ruin upon both of us; anything to escape out of the power of that man. But come what may, I won't endure it much longer. I'll run away to service soon after Christmas, and father will only have himself to thank for the loss of me."

It was Mr. Whitelaw who appeared as principal guest at the Grange on Christmas-day; Mr. Whitelaw, supported on this occasion by a widowed cousin of his who had kept house for him for some years, and who bore a strong family likeness to him both in person and manner, and Ellen Carley thought that it was impossible for the world to contain a more disagreeable pair. These were the guests who consumed great quantities of Ellen's pies and puddings, and who sat under her festal garlands of holly and laurel. She had been especially careful to hang no scrap of mistletoe, which might have afforded Mr. Whitelaw an excuse for a practical display of his gallantry; a fact which did not escape the playful observation of his cousin, Mrs. Tadman.

"Young ladies don't often forget to put up a bit of mistletoe," said this matron, "when there's a chance of them they like being by;" and she glanced in a meaning way from Ellen to the master of Wyncomb Farm.

"Miss Carley isn't like the generality of young ladies," Mr. Whitelaw answered with a glum look, and his kinswoman was fain to drop the subject.

Alone with Ellen, sly Mrs. Tadman took occasion to launch out into enthusiastic praises of her cousin; to which the girl listened in profound silence, closely watched all the time by the woman's sharp gray eyes. And then by degrees her tone changed ever so little, and she owned that her kinsman was not altogether faultless; indeed it was curious to perceive what numerous shortcomings were coexistent with those shining merits of his.

"He has been a good friend to me," continued the matron; "that I never have denied and never shall deny. But I have been a good servant to him; ah! there isn't a hired servant as would toil and drudge, and watch and pinch, as I have done to please him, and never have had payment from him more than a new gown at Christmas, or a five-pound note after harvest. And of course, if ever he marries, I shall have to look for a new home; for I know too much of his ways, I daresay, for a wife to like to have me about her—and me of an age when it seem a hard to have to go among strangers—and not having saved sixpence, where I might have put by a hundred pounds easy, if I hadn't been working without wages for a relation. But I've not been called a servant, you see; and I suppose Stephen thinks that's payment enough for my trouble. Goodness knows I've saved him many a pound, and that he'll know when I'm gone; for he's near, is Stephen, and it goes to his heart to part with a shilling."

"But why should you ever leave him, Mrs. Tadman?" Ellen asked kindly. "I shouldn't think he could have a better housekeeper."

"Perhaps not," answered the widow, shaking her head with mysterious significance; "but his wife won't think that; and when he's got a wife he'll want her to be his housekeeper, and to pinch and scrape as I've pinched and scraped for him. Lord help her!" concluded Mrs. Tadman, with a faint groan, which was far from complimentary to her relative's character.

"But perhaps he never will marry," argued Ellen coolly.

"O, yes, he will, Miss Carley," replied Mrs. Tadman, with another significant movement of her head; "he's set his heart on that, and he's set his heart on the young woman he means to marry."

"He can't marry her unless she's willing to be his wife, any how," said Ellen, reddening a little.

"O, he'll find a way to make her consent, Miss Carley, depend upon that. Whatever Stephen Whitelaw sets his mind upon, he'll do. But I don't envy that poor young woman; for she'll have a hard life of it at Wyncomb, and a hard master in my cousin Stephen."

"She must be a very weak-minded young woman if she marries him against her will," Ellen said laughing; and then ran off to get the tea ready, leaving Mrs. Tadman to her meditations, which were not of a lively nature at the best of times.

That Christmas-day came to an end at last, after a long evening in the oak parlour enlivened by a solemn game at whist and a ponderous supper of cold sirloin and mince pies; and looking out at the wintry moonlight, and the shadowy garden and flat waste of farm-land from the narrow casement in her own room. Ellen Carley wondered what those she loved best in the world were doing and thinking of under that moonlit sky. Where was Marian Holbrook, that new-found friend whom she had loved so well, and whose fate remained so profound a mystery? and what was Frank Randall doing, far away in London, where he had gone to fill a responsible position in a large City firm of solicitors, and whence he had promised to return faithful to his first love, as soon as he found himself fairly on the road to a competence wherewith to endow her?

Thus it was that poor Ellen kept the close of her Christmas-day, looking out over the cold moonlit fields, and wondering how she was to escape from the persecution of Stephen Whitelaw.

That obnoxious individual had invited Mr. Carley and his daughter to spend New-year's-day at Wyncomb; a display of hospitality so foreign to his character, that it was scarcely strange that Mrs. Tadman opened her eyes and stared aghast as she heard the invitation given. It had been accepted too, much to Ellen's disgust; and her father told her more than once in the course of the ensuing week that she was to put on her best gown, and smarten herself up a bit, on New-year's-day.

"And if you want a new gown, Nell, I don't mind giving it you," said the bailiff, in a burst of generosity, and with the prevailing masculine idea that a new gown was a panacea for all feminine griefs. "You can walk over to Malsham and buy it any afternoon you like."

But Ellen did not care for a new gown, and told her father so, with a word or two of thanks for his offer. She did not desire fine dresses; she had indeed been looking over and furbishing up her wardrobe of late, with a view to that possible flight of hers, and it was to her cotton working gowns that she had paid most attention: looking forward to begin a harder life in some stranger's service—ready to endure anything rather than to marry Stephen Whitelaw. And of late the conviction had grown upon her that her father was very much in earnest, and that before long it would be a question whether she should obey him, or be turned out of doors. She had seen his dealings with other people, and she knew him to be a passionate determined man, hard as iron in his anger.

"I won't give him the trouble to turn me out of doors," Ellen said to herself. "When I know his mind, and that there's no hope of turning him, I'll get away quietly, and find some new home. He has no real power over me, and I have but to earn my own living to be independent of him. And I don't suppose Frank will think any the worse of me for having been a servant," thought the girl, with something like a sob. It seemed hard that she must needs sink lower in her lover's eyes, when she was so far beneath him already; he a lawyer's son, a gentleman by education, and she an untaught country girl.

CHAPTER XXXII.
THE PADLOCKED DOOR AT WYNCOMB.

THE countenance of the new year was harsh, rugged, and gloomy—as of a stony-hearted, strong-minded new year, that had no idea of making his wintry aspect pleasant, or brightening the gloom of his infancy with any deceptive gleams of January sunshine. A bitter north wind made a dreary howling among the leafless trees, and swept across the broad bare fields with merciless force—a bleak cruel new-year's-day, on which to go out a-pleasuring; but it was more in harmony with Ellen Carley's thoughts than brighter weather could have been; and she went to and fro about her morning's work, up and down cold windy passages, and in and out of the frozen dairy, unmoved by the bitter wind which swept the crisp waves of dark brown hair from her low brows, and tinged the tip of her impertinent little nose with a faint wintry bloom.

The bailiff was in very high spirits this first morning of the new year—almost uproarious spirits indeed, which vented themselves in snatches of boisterous song, as he bustled backwards and forwards from house to stables, dressed in his best blue coat and bright buttons and a capacious buff waistcoat; with his ponderous nether limbs clothed in knee-cords, and boots with vinegar tops; looking altogether the typical British farmer.

Those riotous bursts of song made his daughter shudder. Somehow, his gaiety was more alarming to her than his customary morose humour. It was all the more singular, too, because of late William Carley had been especially silent and moody, with the air of a man whose mind is weighed down by some heavy burden—so gloomy indeed, that his daughter had questioned him more than once, entreating to know if he were distressed by any secret trouble, anything going wrong about the farm, and so on. The girl had only brought upon herself harsh angry answers by these considerate inquiries, and had been told to mind her own business, and not pry into matters that in no way concerned her.

"But it does concern me to see you downhearted, father," she answered gently.

"Does it really, my girl? What! your father's something more than a stranger to you, is he? I shouldn't have thought it, seeing how you've gone again me in some things lately. Howsomedever, when I want your help, I shall know how to ask for it, and I hope you'll give it freely. I don't want fine words; they never pulled anybody out of the ditch that I've heard tell of."

Whatever the bailiff's trouble had been, it seemed to be lightened to-day, Ellen thought; and yet that unusual noisy gaiety of his gave her an uncomfortable feeling: it did not seem natural or easy.

Her household work was done by noon, and she dressed hurriedly, while her father called for her impatiently from below—standing at the foot of the wide bare old staircase, and bawling up to her that they should be late at Wyncomb. She looked very pretty in her neat dark-blue merino dress and plain linen collar, when she came tripping downstairs at last, flushed with the hurry of her toilet, and altogether so bright a creature that it seemed a hard thing she should not be setting out upon some real pleasure trip, instead of that most obnoxious festival to which she was summoned.

Her father looked at her with a grim kind of approval.

"You'll do well enough, lass," he said; "but I should like you to have had something smarter than that blue stuff. I wouldn't have minded a couple of pounds or so to buy you a silk gown. But you'll be able to buy yourself as many silk gowns as ever you like by-and-by, if you play your cards well and don't make a fool of yourself."

Ellen knew what he meant well enough, but did not care to take any notice of the speech. The time would soon come, no doubt, when she must take her stand in direct opposition to him, and in the meanwhile it would be worse than foolish to waste breath in idle squabbling.

They were to drive to Wyncomb in the bailiff's gig; rather an obsolete vehicle, with a yellow body, a mouldy leather apron, and high wheels picked out with red, drawn by a tall gray horse that did duty with the plough on ordinary occasions. Stephen Whitelaw's house was within an easy walk of the Grange; but the gig was a more dignified mode of approach than a walk, and the bailiff insisted on driving his daughter to her suitor's abode in that conveyance.

Wyncomb was a long low gray stone house, of an unknown age; a spacious habitation enough, with many rooms, and no less than three staircases, but possessing no traces of that fallen grandeur which pervaded the Grange. It had been nothing better than a farm-house from time immemorial, and had been added to and extended and altered to suit the convenience of successive generations of farmers. It was a gloomy-looking house at all times, Ellen Carley thought, but especially gloomy under that leaden winter sky; a house which it would have been almost impossible to associate with pleasant family gatherings or the joyous voices of young children; a grim desolate-looking house, that seemed to freeze the passing traveller with its cold blank stare, as if its gloomy portal had a voice to say to him, "However lost you may be for lack of shelter, however weary for want of rest, come not here!"

Idle fancies, perhaps; but they were the thoughts with which Wyncomb Farmhouse always inspired Ellen Carley.

"The place just suits its master's hard miserly nature," she said. "One would think it had been made on purpose for him; or perhaps the Whitelaws have been like that from generation to generation."

There was no such useless adornment as a flower-garden at Wyncomb. Stephen Whitelaw cared about as much for roses and lilies as he cared for Greek poetry or Beethoven's sonatas. At the back of the house there was a great patch of bare shadowless ground devoted to cabbages and potatoes, with a straggling border of savoury herbs; a patch not even divided from the farm land beyond, but melting imperceptibly into a field of mangel-wurzel. There were no superfluous hedges upon Mr. Whitelaw's dominions; not a solitary tree to give shelter to the tired cattle in the long hot summer days. Noble old oaks and patriarch beeches, tall sycamores and grand flowering chestnuts, had been stubbed up remorselessly by that economical agriculturist; and he was now the proud possessor of one of the ugliest and most profitable farms in Hampshire.

In front of the gray-stone house the sheep browsed up to the parlour windows, and on both sides of the ill-kept carriage-drive leading from the white gate that opened into the meadow to the door of Mr. Whitelaw's abode. No sweet-scented woodbine or pale monthly roses beautified the front of the house in spring or summer time. The neglected ivy had overgrown one end of the long stone building and crept almost to the ponderous old chimneys; and this decoration, which had come of itself, was the only spot of greenery about the place. Five tall poplars grew in a row about a hundred yards from the front windows; these, strange to say, Mr. Whitelaw had suffered to remain. They served to add a little extra gloom to the settled grimness of the place, and perhaps harmonised with his tastes.

Within Wyncomb Farmhouse was no more attractive than without. The rooms were low and dark; the windows, made obscure by means of heavy woodwork and common glass, let in what light they did admit with a grudging air, and seemed to frown upon the inmates of the chamber they were supposed to beautify. There were all manner of gloomy passages, and unexpected flights of half-a-dozen stairs or so, in queer angles of the house, and there was a prevailing darkness everywhere; for the Whitelaws of departed generations, objecting to the window tax, had blocked up every casement that it was possible to block up; and the stranger exploring Wyncomb Farmhouse was always coming upon those blank plastered windows, which had an unpleasant ghostly aspect, and set him longing for a fireman's hatchet to hew them open and let in the light of day.

The furniture was of the oldest, black with age, worm-eaten, ponderous; queer old four-post bedsteads, with dingy hangings of greenish brown or yellowish green, from which every vestige of the original hue had faded long ago; clumsy bureaus, and stiff high-backed chairs with thick legs and gouty feet, heavy to move and uncomfortable to sit upon. The house was clean enough, and the bare floors of the numerous bed-chambers, which were only enlivened here and there with small strips or bands of Dutch carpet, sent up a homely odour of soft soap; for Mrs. Tadman took a fierce delight in cleaning, and the solitary household drudge who toiled under her orders had a hard time of it. There was a dismal kind of neatness about everything, and a bleak empty look in the sparsely furnished rooms, which wore no pleasant sign of occupation, no look of home. The humblest cottage, with four tiny square rooms and a thatched roof, and just a patch of old-fashioned garden with a sweetbrier hedge and roses growing here and there among the cabbages; would have been a pleasanter habitation than Wyncomb, Ellen Carley thought.

Mr. Whitelaw exhibited an unwonted liberality upon this occasion. The dinner was a ponderous banquet, and the dessert a noble display of nuts and oranges, figs and almonds and raisins, flanked by two old-fashioned decanters of port and sherry; and both the bailiff and his host did ample justice to the feast. It was a long dreary afternoon of eating and drinking; and Ellen was not sorry to get away from the prim wainscoted parlour, where her father and Mr. Whitelaw were solemnly sipping their wine, to wander over the house with Mrs. Tadman.

It was about four o'clock when she slipped quietly out of the room at that lady's invitation, and the lobbies and long passages had a shadowy look in the declining light. There was light enough for her to see the rooms, however; for there were no rare collections of old china, no pictures or adornments of any kind, to need a minute inspection.

"It's a fine old place, isn't it?" asked Mrs. Tadman. "There's not many farmers can boast of such a house as Wyncomb."

"It's large enough," Ellen answered, with a tone which implied the reverse of admiration; "but it's not a place I should like to live in. I'm not one to believe in ghosts or such nonsense, but if I could have any such foolish thoughts, I should have them here. The house looks as if it was haunted, somehow."

Mrs. Tadman laughed a shrill hard laugh, and rubbed her skinny hands with an air of satisfaction.

"You're not easy to please, Miss Carley," she said; "most folks think a deal of Wyncomb; for, you see, it's only them that live in a house as can know how dull it is; and as to the place being haunted, I never heard tell of anything of that kind. The Whitelaws ain't the kind of people to come back to this world, unless they come to fetch their money, and then they'd come fast enough, I warrant. I used to see a good deal of my uncle, John Whitelaw, when I was a girl, and never did a son take after his father closer than my cousin Stephen takes after him; just the same saving prudent ways, and just the same masterful temper, always kept under in that quiet way of his."

As Ellen Carley showed herself profoundly indifferent to the lights and shades of Mr. Whitelaw's character, Mrs. Tadman did not pursue the subject, but with a gentle sigh led the way to another room, and so on from room to room, till they had explored all that floor of the house.

"There's the attics above; but you won't care to see *them*," she said. "The shepherd and five other men sleep up there. Stephen thinks it keeps them steadier sleeping under the same roof with their master; and he's able to ring them up of a morning, and to know when they go to their work. It's wearying for me to have to get up and see to their breakfasts, but I can't trust Martha Holden to do that, or she'd let them eat us out of house and home. There's no knowing what men like that can eat, and a side of bacon would go as fast as if you was to melt it down to tallow. But you must know what they are, Miss Carley, having to manage for your father."

"Yes," Ellen answered, "I'm used to hard work."

"Ah," murmured the matron, with a sigh, "you'd have plenty of it, if you came here."

They were at the end of a long passage by this time; a passage leading to the extreme end of the house, and forming part of that ivy-covered wing which seemed older than the rest of the building. It was on a lower level than the other part, and they had descended two or three steps at the entrance to this passage. The ceilings were lower too, the beams that supported them more massive, the diamond-paned windows smaller and more heavily leaded, and there was a faint musty odour as of a place that was kept shut up and uninhabited.

"There's nothing more to see here," said Mrs. Tadman quickly; "I had better go back I don't know what brought me here; it was talking, I suppose, made me come without thinking. There's nothing to show you this way."

"But there's another room there," Ellen said, pointing to a door just before them—a heavy clumsily-made door, painted black.

"That room—well, yes; it's a kind of a room, but hasn't been used for fifty years and more, I've heard say. Stephen keeps seeds there and such-like. It's always locked, and he keeps the key of it."

There was nothing in this closed room to excite either curiosity or interest in Ellen's mind, and she was turning away from the door with perfect indifference, when she started and suddenly seized Mrs. Tadman's arm.

"Hark!" she said, in a frightened, breathless way; "did you hear that?"

"What, child?"

"Did you say there was no one in there—no one?"

"Lord bless your heart, no, Miss Carley, nor ever is. What a turn you did give me, grasping hold of my arm like that!"

"I heard something in there—a footstep. It must be the servant."

"What, Martha Holden! I should like to see her venturing into any room Stephen keeps private to himself. Besides, that door's kept locked; try it, and satisfy yourself."

The door was indeed locked—a door with a clumsy old-fashioned latch, securely fastened by a staple and padlock. Ellen tried it with her own hand.

"Is there no other door to the room?" she asked.

"None; and only one window, that looks into the wood-yard, and is almost always blocked up with the wood piled outside it. You must have heard the muslin bags of seed blowing about, if you heard anything."

"I heard a footstep," said Ellen firmly; "a human footstep. I told you the house was haunted, Mrs. Tadman."

"Lor, Miss Carley, I wish you wouldn't say such things; it's enough to make one's blood turn cold. Do come downstairs and have a cup of tea. It's quite dark, I declare; and you've given me the shivers with your queer talk."

"I'm sorry for that; but the noise I heard must have been either real or ghostly, and you won't believe it's real."

"It was the seed-bags, of course."

"They couldn't make a noise like human footsteps. However, it's no business of mine, Mrs. Tadman, and I don't want to frighten you."

They went downstairs to the parlour, where the tea-tray and a pair of candles were soon brought, and where Mrs. Tadman stirred the fire into a blaze with an indifference to the consumption of fuel which made her kinsman stare, even on that hospitable occasion. The blaze made the dark wainscoted room cheerful of aspect, however, which the two candles could not have done, as their light was almost absorbed by the gloomy panelling.

After tea there was whist again, and a considerable consumption of spirits-and-water on the part of the two gentlemen, in which Mrs. Tadman joined modestly, with many protestations, and, with the air of taking only an occasional spoonful, contrived to empty her tumbler, and allowed herself to be persuaded to take another by the bailiff, whose joviality on the occasion was inexhaustible.

The day's entertainment came to an end at last, to Ellen's inexpressible relief; and her father drove her home in the yellow gig at rather an alarming pace, and with some tendency towards heeling over into a ditch. They got over the brief journey safely, however, and Mr. Carley was still in high good humour. He went off to see to the putting up of his horse himself, telling his daughter to wait till he came back, he had something particular to say to her before she went to bed.

CHAPTER XXXIII.
"WHAT MUST BE SHALL BE."

ELLEN Carley waited in the little parlour, dimly lighted by one candle. The fire had very nearly gone out, and she had some difficulty in brightening it a little. She waited very patiently, wondering what her father could have to say to her, and not anticipating much pleasure from the interview. He was going to talk about Stephen Whitelaw and his hateful money perhaps. But let him say what he would, she was prepared to hold her own firmly, determined to provoke him by no open opposition, unless matters came to an extremity, and then to let him see at once and for ever that her resolution was fixed, and that it was useless to persecute her.

"If I have to go out of this house to-night, I will not flinch," she said to herself.

She had some time to wait. It had been past midnight when they came home, and it was a quarter to one when William Carley came into the parlour. He was in a unusually communicative mood to-night, and had been superintending the grooming of his horse, and talking to the underling who had waited up to receive him.

He was a little unsteady in his gait as he came into the parlour, and Ellen knew that he had drunk a good deal at Wyncomb. It was no new thing for her to see him in this condition unhappily, and the shrinking shuddering sensation with which he inspired her to-night was painfully familiar.

"It's very late, father," she said gently, as the bailiff flung himself heavily into an arm-chair by the fire-place. "If you don't want me for anything particular, I should be glad to go to bed."

"Would you, my lass?" he asked grimly. "But, you see, I do want you for something particular, something uncommon particular; so there's no call for you to be in a hurry. Sit down yonder," he added, pointing to the chair opposite his own. "I've got something to say to you, something serious."

"Father," said the girl, looking him full in the face, pale to the lips, but very firm, "I don't think you're in a state to talk seriously of anything."

"O, you don't, don't you, Miss Impudence? You think I'm drunk, perhaps. You'll find that, drunk or sober, I've only one mind about you, and that I mean to be obeyed. Sit down, I tell you. I'm not in the humour to stand any nonsense to-night. Sit down."

Ellen obeyed this mandate, uttered with a fierceness unusual even in Mr. Carley, who was never a soft-spoken man. She seated herself quietly on the opposite side of the hearth, while her father took down his pipe from the chimney-piece, and slowly filled it, with hands that trembled a little over the accustomed task.

When he had lighted the pipe, and smoked about half-a-dozen whiffs with a great assumption of coolness, he addressed himself to his daughter in an altered and conciliating tone.

"Well, Nelly," he said, "you've had a rare day at Wyncomb, and a regular ramble over the old house with Steph's cousin. What do you think of it?"

"I think it's a queer gloomy old place enough, father. I wonder there's any one can live in it. The dark bare-looking rooms gave me the horrors. I used to think this house was dull, and seemed as if it was haunted; but it's lively and gay as can be, compared to Wyncomb."

"Humph!" muttered the bailiff. "You're a fanciful young lady, Miss Nell, and don't know a fine substantial old house when you see one. Life's come a little too easy to you, perhaps. It might have been better for you if you'd seen more of the rough side. Being your own missus too soon, and missus of such a place as this, has spoiled you a bit. I tell you, Nell, there ain't a better house in Hampshire than Wyncomb, though it mayn't suit your fanciful notions. Do you know the size of Stephen Whitelaw's farm?"

"No, father; I've never thought about it."

"What do you say to three hundred acres—over three hundred, nigher to four perhaps?"

"I suppose it's a large farm, father. But I know nothing about such things."

"You suppose it's large, and you know nothing about such things!" cried the bailiff, with an air of supreme irritation. "I don't believe any man was ever plagued with such an aggravating daughter as mine. What do you say to being mistress of such a place, girl?—mistress of close upon four hundred acres of land; not another man's servant, bound to account for every blade of grass and every ear of corn, as I am, but free and independent mistress of the place, with the chance of being left a widow by and by, and having it all under your own thumb; what do you say to that?"

"Only the same that I have always said, father. Nothing would ever persuade me to marry Stephen Whitelaw. I'd rather starve."

"And you shall starve, if you stick to that," roared William Carley with a blasphemous oath. "But you won't be such a fool, Nell. You'll hear reason; you won't stand out against your poor old father and against your own interests. The long and the short of it is, I've given Whitelaw my promise that you shall be his wife between this and Easter."

"What!" exclaimed Ellen, with a faint cry of horror; "you don't mean that you've promised that, father! You can't mean it!"

"I can and do mean it, lass."

"Then you've made a promise that will never be kept. You might have known as much when you made it. I'm sure I've been plain-spoken enough about Stephen Whitelaw."

"That was a girl's silly talk. I didn't think to find you a fool when I came to the point. I let you have your say, and looked to time to bring you to reason. Come, Nell, you're not going against your father, are you?"

"I must, father, in this. I'd rather die twenty deaths than marry that man. There's nothing I wouldn't rather do."

"Isn't there? You'd rather see your father in gaol, I suppose, if it came to that?"

"See you in gaol!" cried the girl aghast. "For heaven's sake, what do you mean, father? What fear is there of your being sent to prison, because I won't marry Stephen Whitelaw? I'm not a baby," she added, with a hysterical laugh; "you can't frighten me like that."

"No; you're a very wise young woman, I daresay; but you don't know everything. You've seen me downhearted and out of sorts for this last half-year; but I don't suppose you've troubled yourself much about it, except to worry me with silly questions sometimes, when I've not been in the humour to be talked to. Things have been going wrong with me ever since hay-harvest, and I haven't sent Sir David sixpence yet for last year's crops. I've put him off with one excuse after another from month to month. He's a careless master enough at most times, and never over-sharp with my accounts. But the time has come when I can't put him off any longer. He wants money badly, he says; and I'm afraid he begins to suspect something. Any way, he talks of coming here in a week or so to look into things for himself. If he does that, I'm ruined."

"But the money, father—the money for the crops—how has it gone? You had it, haven't you?"

"Yes," the bailiff answered with a groan; "I've had it, worse luck."

"And how has it gone?"

"What's that to you? What's the good of my muddling my brains with figures to-night? It's gone, I tell you. You know I'm fond of seeing a race, and never miss anything in that way that comes-off within a day's drive of this place. I used to be pretty lucky once upon a time, when I backed a horse or bet against one. But this year things have gone dead against me; and my bad luck made me savage somehow, so that I went deeper than I've been before, thinking to get back what I'd lost."

"O, father, father! how could you, and with another man's money?"

"Don't give me any of your preaching," the bailiff answered gloomily; "I can get enough of that at Malsham Chapel if I want it. It's in your power to pull me through this business if you choose."

"How can I do that, father?"

"A couple of hundred pounds will set me square. I don't say there hasn't been more taken, first and last; but that would do it. Stephen Whitelaw would lend me the money—give it me, indeed, for it comes to that—the day he gets your consent to be his wife."

"And you'd sell me to him for two hundred pounds, father?" the girl asked bitterly.

"I don't want to go to gaol."

"And if you don't get the money from Stephen, what will happen?"

"I can't tell you that to a nicety. Penal servitude for life, most likely. They'd call mine a bad case, I daresay."

"But Sir David might be merciful to you, father. You've served him for along time."

"What would he care for that? I've had his money, and he's not a man that can afford to lose much. No, Nell, I look for no mercy from Sir David; those careless easy-going men are generally the hardest in such a business as this. It's a clear case of embezzlement, and nothing can save me unless I can raise money enough to satisfy him."

"Couldn't you borrow it of some one else besides Stephen Whitelaw?"

"Who else is there that would lend me two hundred pounds? Ask yourself that, girl. Why, I haven't five pounds' worth of security to offer."

"And Mr. Whitelaw will only lend the money upon one condition?"

"No, curse him!" cried William Carley savagely. "I've been at him all this afternoon, when you and that woman were out of the room, trying to get it out of him as a loan, without waiting for your promise; but he's too cautious for that. 'The day Ellen gives her consent, you shall have the money,' he told me; 'I can't say anything fairer than that or more liberal.'"

"He doesn't suspect why you want it, does he, father?" Ellen asked with a painful sense of shame.

"Who can tell what he may suspect? He's as deep as Satan," said the bailiff, with a temporary forgetfulness of his desire to exhibit this intended son-in-law of his in a favourable light. "He knows that I want the money very badly; I couldn't help his knowing that; and he must think it's something out of the common that makes me want two hundred pounds."

"I daresay he guesses the truth," Ellen said, with a profound sigh.

It seemed to her the bitterest trial of all, that her father's wrong-doing should be known to Stephen Whitelaw. That hideous prospect of the dock and the gaol was far off as yet; she had not even begun to realise it; but she did fully realise the fact of her father's shame, and the blow seemed to her a heavy one, heavier than she could bear.

For some minutes there was silence between father and daughter. The girl sat with her face hidden in her hands; the bailiff smoked his pipe in sullen meditation.

"Is there no other way?" Ellen asked at last, in a plaintive despairing tone; "no other way, father?"

"None," growled William Carley. "You needn't ask me that question again; there is no other way; you can get me out of my difficulties if you choose. I should never have been so venturesome as I was, if I hadn't made sure my daughter would soon be a rich woman. You can save me if you like, or you can hold-off and let me go to prison. There's no good preaching about it or arguing about it; you've got the choice and you must make it. Most young women in your place would think themselves uncommon lucky to have such a chance as you've got, instead of making a trouble about it, let alone being able to get their father out of a scrape. But you're your own mistress, and you must do as you please."

"Let me have time to think," the girl pleaded piteously; "let me have only a little time to think, father. And you do believe that I'm sorry for you, don't you?" she asked, kneeling beside him and clasping his unwilling hand. "O father, I hope you believe that!"

"I shall know what to believe when I know what you're going to do," the bailiff answered moodily; and his daughter knew him too well to hope for any more gracious speech than this.

She bade him good-night, and went slowly up to her own room to spend the weary wakeful hours in a bitter struggle, praying that she might be enlightened as to what she ought to do; praying that she might die rather than become the wife of Stephen Whitelaw.

When she and her father met at breakfast in the dull gray January morning, his aspect was even darker than it had been on the previous night; but he did not ask her if she had arrived at any conclusion. He took his meal in sullen silence, and left her without a word.

They met again a little before noon, at which hour it was Mr. Carley's habit to consume a solid luncheon. He took his seat in the same gloomy silence that he had preserved at breakfast-time, but flung an open letter across the table towards his daughter.

"Am I to read this?" she asked gently.

"Yes, read it, and see what I've got to look to."

The letter was from Sir David Forster; an angry one, revealing strong suspicions of his agent's dishonesty, and announcing that he should be at the Grange on the fifth of the month, to make a close investigation of all matters connected with the bailiff's administration. It was a letter that gave little hope of mercy, and Ellen Carley felt that it was so. She saw that there were no two sides to the question: she must save her father by the utter sacrifice of her own feelings, or suffer him to perish.

She sat for some minutes in silence, with Sir David's letter in her hand, staring blankly at the lines in a kind of stupor; while her father ate cold roast-beef and pickled-cabbage—she wondered how he could eat at such a time—looking up at her furtively every now and then.

At last she laid down the letter, and lifted her eyes to his face. A deadly whiteness and despair had come over the bright soubrette beauty, and even William Carley's hard nature was moved a little by the altered expression of his daughter's countenance.

"It must be as you wish, father," she said slowly; "there is no help for it; I cannot see you brought to disgrace. Stephen Whitelaw must have the price he asks for his money."

"That's a good lass," cried the bailiff, springing up and clasping his daughter in his arms, a most unusual display of affection on his part; "that's bravely spoken, Nell, and you never need repent the choice that'll make you mistress of Wyncomb Farm, with a good home to give your father in his old age."

The girl drew herself hastily from his embrace, and turned away from him with a shudder. He was her father, and there was something horrible in the idea of his disgrace; but there was very little affection for him in her mind. He was willing to sell her into bondage in order to save himself. It was in this light she regarded the transaction with Stephen Whitelaw.

CHAPTER XXXIV.
DOUBTFUL INFORMATION.

THE early days of the new year brought little change in John Saltram's condition. Mr. Mew, and the physician who saw him once in every three days, seemed perhaps a shade more hopeful than they had been, but would express no decided opinion when Gilbert pressed them with close questioning. The struggle was still going on—the issue still doubtful.

"If we could keep the mind at rest," said the physician, "we should have every chance of doing better; but this constant restlessness, this hyper-activity of the brain, of which you and Mr. Mew tell me, must needs make a perpetual demand upon the patient's physical powers. The waste is always going on. We cannot look for recovery until we obtain more repose."

Several weeks had passed since the beginning of John Saltram's illness, and there were no tidings from Mr. Medler. Every day Gilbert had expected some communication from that practitioner, only to be disappointed. He had called twice in Soho, and on both occasions had been received by a shabby-looking clerk, who told him that Mr. Medler was out, and not likely to come home within any definite time. He was inclined to fancy, by the clerk's manner on his second visit, that there was some desire to avoid an interview on Mr. Medler's part; and this fancy made him all the more anxious to see that gentleman. He did not, therefore, allow much time to elapse between this second visit to the dingy chambers in Soho and a third. This time he was more fortunate; for he saw the lawyer let himself in at the street-door with his latch-key, just as the cab that drove him approached the house.

The same shabby clerk opened the door to him.

"I want to see your master," he said decisively, making a move towards the office-door.

The clerk contrived to block his way.

"I beg your pardon, sir, I don't think Mr. Medler's in; but I'll go and see."

"You needn't give yourself the trouble. I saw your master let himself in at this door a minute ago. I suppose you were too busy to hear him come in."

The clerk coughed a doubtful kind of cough, significant of perplexity.

"Upon my word, sir, I believe he's out; but I'll see."

"Thanks; I'd rather see myself, if you please," Gilbert said, passing the perturbed clerk before that functionary could make up his mind whether he ought to intercept him.

He opened the office-door and went in. Mr. Medler was sitting at his desk, bending over some formidable document, with the air of a man who is profoundly absorbed by his occupation; with the air also, Gilbert thought, of a man who has been what is vernacularly called "on the listen."

"Good-morning, Mr. Medler," Gilbert said politely; "your clerk had such a conviction of your being out, that I had some difficulty in convincing him you were at home."

"I've only just come in; I suppose Lucas didn't hear me."

"I suppose not; I've been here twice before in search of you, as I conclude you have been told. I have expected to hear from you daily."

"Well, yes—yes," replied the lawyer in a meditative way; "I am aware that I promised to write—under certain circumstances."

"Am I to conclude, then, that you were silent because you had nothing to communicate? that you have obtained no tidings of any kind respecting Mrs. Holbrook?"

Mr. Medler coughed; a cough no less expressive of embarrassment than that of his clerk.

"Why, you see, Mr. Fenton," he began, crossing his legs, and rubbing his hands in a very deliberate manner, "when I made that promise with reference to Mrs. Holbrook, I made it of course without prejudice to the interests or inclinations of my client. I might be free to communicate to you any information I received upon this subject—or I might find myself pledged to withhold it."

Gilbert's face flushed with sudden excitement.

"What!" he cried, "do you mean to say that you have solved the mystery of Marian Holbrook's fate? that you know her to be alive—safe—well, and have kept back the knowledge from me?"

"I have been compelled to submit to the wishes of my client. I will not say that I have not offered considerable opposition to her desire upon this point, but finding her resolution fixed, I was bound to respect it."

"She is safe—then all this alarm has been needless? You have seen her?"

"Yes, Mr. Fenton, I have seen her."

"And she—she forbade you to let me know of her safety? She was willing that I should suffer all the anguish of uncertainty as to her fate? I could not have believed her so unkind."

"Mrs. Holbrook had especial reasons for wishing to avoid all communication with former acquaintances. She explained those reasons to me, and I fully concurred in them."

"She might have such reasons with regard to other people; she could have none with reference to me."

"Pardon me, she mentioned your name in a very particular manner."

"And yet she has had good cause to trust in my fidelity."

"She has a very great respect and esteem for you, I am aware. She said as much to me. But her reasons for keeping her affairs to herself just now are quite apart from her personal feeling for yourself."

"I cannot understand this. I am not to see her then, I suppose; not to be told her address?"

"No; I am strictly forbidden to disclose her address to any one."

"Yet you can positively assure me that she is in safety—her own mistress—happy?"

"She is in perfect safety—her own mistress—and as happy as it is possible she can be under the unfortunate circumstances of her married life. She has left her husband for ever; I will venture to tell you so much as that."

"I am quite aware of that fact."

"How so? I thought Mr. Holbrook was quite unknown to you?"

"I have learnt a good deal about him lately."

"Indeed!" exclaimed the lawyer, with a genuine air of surprise.

"But of course your client has been perfectly frank in her communications with you upon this subject?" Gilbert said.

"Yes; I know that Mrs. Holbrook has left her husband, but I did not for a moment suppose she had left him of her own free will. From my knowledge of her character and sentiments, that is just the last thing I could have imagined possible. There was no quarrel between them; indeed, she was expecting his return with delight at the very time when she left her home in Hampshire. The thought of sharing her fortune with him was one of perfect happiness. How can you explain her abrupt flight from him in the face of this?"

"I am not free to explain matters, Mr. Fenton," answered the lawyer; "you must be satisfied with the knowledge that the lady about whom you have been so anxious is safe."

"I thank God for that," Gilbert said earnestly; "but that, knowledge of itself is not quite enough. I shall be uneasy so long as there is this secrecy and mystery surrounding her fate. There is something in this sudden abandonment of her husband which is painfully inexplicable to me."

"Mrs. Holbrook may have received some sudden revelation of her husband's unworthiness. You are aware that a letter reached her a few hours before she left Hampshire? There is no doubt that letter influenced her actions. I do not mind admitting a fact which is so obvious."

"The revelation that could move her to such a step must have been a very startling one."

"It was strong enough to decide her course," replied the lawyer gravely.

"And you can assure me that she is in good hands?" Gilbert asked anxiously.

"I have every reason to suppose so. She is with her father."

Mr. Medler announced this fact as if there were nothing extraordinary in it. Gilbert started to his feet.

"What!" he exclaimed; "she is with Mr. Nowell—the father who neglected her in her youth, who of course seeks her now only for the sake of her fortune? And you call that being in good hands, Mr. Medler? For my own part, I cannot imagine a more dangerous alliance. When did Percival Nowell come to England?"

"A very short time ago. I have only been aware of his return within the last two or three weeks. His first step on arriving in this country was to seek for his daughter."

"Yes; when he knew that she was rich, no doubt."

"I do not think that he was influenced by mercenary motives," the lawyer said, with a calm judicial air. "Of course, as a man of the world, I am not given to look at such matters from a sentimental point of view. But I really believe that Mr. Nowell was anxious to find his daughter, and to atone in some measure for his former neglect."

"A very convenient repentance," exclaimed Gilbert, with a short bitter laugh. "And his first act is to steal his daughter from her home, and hide her from all her former friends. I don't like the look of this business, Mr. Medler; I tell you so frankly."

"Mr. Nowell is my client, you must remember, Mr. Fenton. I cannot consent to listen to any aspersion of his character, direct or indirect."

"And you positively refuse to tell me where Mrs. Holbrook is to be found?"

"I am compelled to respect her wishes as well as those of her father."

"She has been placed in possession of her property, I suppose?"

"Yes; her grandfather's will has been proved, and the estate now stands in her name. There was no difficulty about that—no reason for delay."

"Will you tell me if she is in London?" Gilbert asked impatiently.

"Pardon me, my dear sir, I am pledged to say nothing about Mrs. Holbrook's whereabouts."

Gilbert gave a weary sigh.

"Well, I suppose it is useless to press the question, Mr. Medler," he said. "I can only repeat that I don't like the look of this business. Your client, Mr. Nowell, must have a very strong reason for secrecy, and my experience of life has shown me that there is very seldom mystery without wrong doing of some kind behind it. I thank God that Mrs. Holbrook is safe, for I suppose I must accept your assurance that she is so; but until her position is relieved from all this secrecy, I shall not cease to feel uneasy as to her welfare. I am glad, however, that the issue of events has exonerated her husband from any part in her disappearance."

He was glad to know this—glad to know that however base a traitor to himself, John Saltram had not been guilty of that deeper villany which he had at times been led to suspect. Gilbert Fenton left Mr. Medler's office a happier man than when he had entered it, and yet only half satisfied. It was a great thing to know that Marian was safe; but he would have wished her in the keeping of any one rather than of him whom the world would have called her natural protector.

Nor was his opinion of Mr. Medler by any means an exalted one. No assertion, of that gentleman inspired him with heart-felt confidence; and he had not left the lawyer's office long before he began to ask himself whether there was truth in any portion of the story he had heard, or whether he was not the dupe of a lie.

Strange that Marian's father should have returned at so opportune a moment; still more strange that Marian should suddenly desert the husband she had so devotedly loved, and cast in her lot with a father of whom she knew nothing but his unkindness. What if this man Medler had been, lying to him from first to last, and was plotting to get old Jacob Nowell's fortune into his own hands?

"I must find her," Gilbert said to himself; "I must be certain that she is in safe hands. I shall know no rest till I have found her."

Harassed and perplexed beyond measure, he walked through the busy streets of that central district for some time without knowing where he was going, and without the faintest purpose in his steps. Then the notion suddenly flashed upon him that he might hear something of Percival Nowell at the shop in Queen Anne's Court, supposing the old business to be still carried on there under the sway of Mr. Tulliver; and it seemed too early yet for the probability of any change in that quarter.

Gilbert was in the Strand when this notion occurred to him. He turned his steps immediately, and went back to Wardour-street, and thence to the dingy court where he had first discovered Marian's grandfather.

There was no change; the shop looked exactly the same as it had looked in the lifetime of Jacob Nowell. There were the same old guineas in the wooden bowl, the same tarnished tankards and teapots on view behind the wire-guarded glass, the same obscure hints of untold riches within, in the general aspect of the place.

Mr. Tulliver darted forward from his usual lurking-place as Gilbert went in at the door.

"O!" he exclaimed, with undisguised disappointment, "it's you, is it, sir? I thought it was a customer."

"I am sorry to disappoint your expectation of profit. I have looked in to ask you two or three questions, Mr. Tulliver; that is all."

"Any information in my power I'm sure I shall be happy to afford, sir. Won't you be pleased to take a seat?"

"How long is it since you saw Mr. Nowell, your former employer's son?" Gilbert asked, dropping into the chair indicated by the shopman, and coming at once to the point.

Mr. Tulliver was somewhat startled by the question. That was evident, though he was not a man who wore his heart upon his sleeve.

"How long is it since I've seen Mr. Nowell—Mr. Percival Nowell, sir?" he repeated, staring thoughtfully at his questioner.

"Yes; you need not be afraid to speak freely to me; I know Mr. Nowell is in London."

"Well, sir, I've not seen him often since his father's death."

Since his father's death! And according to Mr. Medler, Jacob Nowell's son had only arrived in England after the old man's death;—or stay, the lawyer had declared that he had been only aware of Percival's return within the last two or three weeks. That was a different thing, of course; yet was it likely this man could have returned, and his father's lawyer have remained ignorant of his arrival?

Gilbert did not allow the faintest expression of surprise to appear on his countenance.

"Not often since your master's death: but how often before?"

"Well, he used to come in pretty often before the old man died; but they were both of 'em precious close. Mr. Percival never let out that he was my master's son, but I guessed as much before he'd been here many times."

"How was it that I never came across him?"

"Chance, I suppose; but he's a deep one. If you'd happened to come in when he was here, I daresay he'd have contrived to slip away somehow without your seeing him."

"When did he come here last?" asked Gilbert.

"About a fortnight ago. He came with Mr. Medler, the lawyer, who introduced him formally as my master's son; and they took possession of the place between them for Mrs. Holbrook, making an arrangement with me to carry on the business, and making precious hard terms too."

"Have you seen Mrs. Holbrook since that morning when she left London for Hampshire, immediately after her grandfather's death?"

"Never set eyes on her since then; but she's in London, they told me, living with her father. She came up to claim the property. I say, the husband must be rather a curious party, mustn't he, to stand that kind of thing, and part company with her just when she's come into a fortune?"

"Have you any notion where Mrs. Holbrook or her father is to be found? I should be glad to make you a handsome present if you could enlighten me upon that point."

"I wish I could, sir. No, I haven't the least idea where the gentleman hangs out. Oysters ain't closer than that party. I thought he'd get his paw upon his father's money, somehow, when I used to see him hanging about this place. But I don't believe the old man ever meant him to have a sixpence of it."

There was very little satisfaction, to be obtained from Mr. Tulliver; and except as to the one fact of Percival Nowell's return, Gilbert left Queen Anne's Court little wiser than when he entered it.

Brooding upon the revelations of that day as he walked slowly westward, he began to think that Percival and Mr. Medler had been in league from the time of the prodigal son's return, and that his own exclusion from the will as executor, and the substitution of the lawyer's name, had been brought about for no honourable purpose. What would a weak inexperienced woman be between two such men? or what power could Marian have, once under her father's influence, to resist his will? How she had fallen under that influence so completely as to leave her husband and her quiet country home, without a word of explanation, was a difficult question to answer; and Gilbert Fenton meditated upon it with a troubled mind.

He walked westward, indifferent where he went in the perplexity of his thoughts, anxious to walk off a little of his excitement if he could, and to return to his sick charge in the temple in a calmer frame of mind. It was something gained, at the worst, to be able to return to John Saltram's bedside freed from that hideous suspicion which had tormented him of late.

Walking thus, he found himself, towards the close of the brief winter day, at the Marble Arch. He went through the gate into the empty Park, and was crossing the broad road near the entrance, when an open carriage passed close beside him, and a woman's voice called to the coachman to stop.

The carriage stopped so abruptly and so near him that he paused and looked up, in natural wonderment at the circumstance. A lady dressed in mourning was leaning forward out of the carriage, looking eagerly after him. A second glance showed him that this lady was Mrs. Branston.

"How do you do, Mr. Fenton," she cried, holding out her little black-gloved hand: "What an age since I have seen you! But you have not forgotten me, I hope?"

"That is quite impossible, Mrs. Branston. If I had not been very much absorbed in thought just now, I should have recognised you sooner. It was very kind of you to stop to speak to me."

"Not at all. I have something most particular to say to you. If you are not in a very great hurry, would you mind getting into the carriage, and letting me drive you round the Park? I can't keep you standing in the road to talk."

"I am in no especial hurry, and I shall be most happy to take a turn round the Park with you."

Mrs. Branston's footman opened the carriage-door, and Gilbert took his seat opposite the widow, who was enjoying her afternoon drive alone for once in a way; a propitious toothache having kept Mrs. Pallinson within doors.

"I have been expecting to see you for ever so long, Mr. Fenton. Why do you never call upon me?" the pretty little widow began, with her usual frankness.

"I have been so closely occupied lately; and even if I had not been so, I should have scarcely expected to find you in town at this unfashionable season."

"I don't care the least in the world for fashion," Mrs. Branston said, with an impatient shrug of her shoulders. "That is only an excuse of yours, Mr. Fenton; you completely forgot my existence, I have no doubt. All my friends desert me now-a-days—older friends than you. There is Mr. Saltram, for instance. I have not seen him for—O, not for ever so long," concluded the widow, blushing in the dusk as she remembered that visit of hers to the Temple—that daring step which ought to have brought John Saltram so much nearer to her, but which had resulted in nothing but disappointment and regret—bitter regret that she should have cast her womanly pride into the very dust at this man's feet to no purpose.

But Adela Branston was not a proud woman; and even in the midst of her regret for having done this foolish thing, she was always ready to make excuses for the man she loved, always in danger of committing some new folly in his behalf.

Gilbert Fenton felt for the poor foolish little woman, whose fair face was turned to him with such a pleading look in the wintry twilight. He knew that what he had to tell her must needs carry desolation to her heart—knew that in the background of John Saltram's life there lurked even a deeper cause of grief for this gentle impressionable little soul.

"You will not wonder that Mr. Saltram has not called upon you lately when you know the truth," he said gravely: "he has been very ill."

Mrs. Branston clasped her hands, with a faint cry of terror.

"Very ill—that means dangerously ill?"

"Yes; for some time he was in great danger. I believe that is past now; but I am not quite sure of his safety even yet. I can only hope that he may recover."

Hope that he might recover, yes; but to be a friend of his, Gilbert's, never more. It was a dreary prospect at best. John Saltram would recover, to seek and reclaim his wife, and then those two must needs pass for ever out of Gilbert Fenton's life. The story would be finished, and his own part of it bald enough to be told on the fly-leaf at the end of the book.

Mrs. Branston bore the shock of his ill news better than Gilbert had expected. There is good material even in the weakest of womankind when the heart is womanly and true.

She was deeply shocked, intensely sorry; and she made no attempt to mask her sorrow by any conventional speech or pretence whatsoever. She made Gilbert give her all the details of John Saltram's illness, and when he had told her all, asked him plainly if she might be permitted to see the sick man.

"Do let me see him, if it is possible," she said; "it would be such a comfort to me to see him."

"I do not say such a thing is not possible, my dear Mrs. Branston; but I am sure it would be very foolish."

"O, never mind that; I am always doing foolish things. It would only be one folly more, and would hardly count in my history. Dear Mr. Fenton, do let me see him."

"I don't think you quite know what you are asking, Mrs. Branston. Such a sick-bed as John Saltram's would be a most painful scene for you. He has been delirious from the beginning of his illness, and is so still. He rarely has an interval of anything like consciousness, and in all the time that I have been with him has never yet recognised me; indeed, there are moments when I am inclined to fear that his brain may be permanently deranged."

"God forbid!" exclaimed Adela, in a voice that was choked with tears.

"Yes, such a result as that would be indeed a sore calamity. I have every wish to set your mind at ease, believe me, Mrs. Branston, but in John Saltram's present state I am sure it would be ill-advised for you to see him."

"Of course I cannot press the question if you say that," Adela answered despondently; "but I should have been so glad if you could have allowed me to see him. Not that I pretend to the smallest right to do so; but we were very good friends once—before my husband's death. He has changed to me strangely since that time."

Gilbert felt that it was almost cruel to keep this poor little soul in utter ignorance of the truth. He did not consider himself at liberty to say much; but some vague word of warning might serve as a slight check upon the waste of feeling which was going on in the widow's heart.

"There may be a reason for that change, Mrs. Branston," he said. "Mr. Saltram may have formed some tie of a kind to withdraw him from all other friendships."

"Some attachment, you mean!" exclaimed the widow; "some other attachment," she added, forgetting how much the words betrayed. "Do you think that, Mr. Fenton? Do you think that John Saltram has some secret love-affair upon his mind?"

"I have some reason to suspect as much, from words that he has dropped during his delirium."

There was a look of unspeakable pain in Mrs. Branston's face, which had grown deadly pale when Gilbert first spoke of John Saltram's illness. The pretty childish lips quivered a little, and her companion knew that she was suffering keenly.

"Have you any idea who the lady is?" she asked quietly, and with more self-command than Gilbert had expected from her.

"I have some idea."

"It is no one whom I know, I suppose?"

"The lady is quite a stranger to you."

"He might have trusted me," she said mournfully; "it would have been kinder in him to have trusted me."

"Yes, Mrs. Branston; but Mr. Saltram has unfortunately made concealment the policy of his life. He will find it a false policy sooner or late."

"It was very cruel of him not to tell me the truth. He might have known that I should look kindly upon any one he cared for. I may be a very foolish woman, Mr. Fenton, but I am not ungenerous."

"I am sure of that," Gilbert said warmly, touched by her candour.

"You must let me know every day how your friend is going on, Mr. Fenton," Adela said after a pause; "I shall consider it a very great favour if you will do so."

"I will not fail."

They had returned to Cumberland-gate by this time, and at Gilbert's request Mrs. Branston allowed him to be set down near the Arch. He called a cab, and drove to the Temple; while poor Adela went back to the splendid gloom of Cavendish-square, with all the fabric of her future life shattered.

Until this hour she had looked upon John Saltram's fidelity to herself as a certainty; she knew, now that her hope was slain all at once, what a living thing it had been, and how great a portion of her own existence had taken its colour therefrom.

It was fortunate for Mrs. Branston that Mrs. Pallinson's toothache, and the preparations and medicaments supplied to her by her son—all declared to be infallible, and all ending in ignominious failure—occupied that lady's attention at this period, to the exclusion of every other thought, or Adela's pale face might have excited more curiosity than it did. As it was, the matron contented herself by making some rather snappish remarks upon the folly of going out to drive late on a January afternoon, and retired to administer poultices and cataplasms to herself in the solitude of her own apartment soon after dinner, leaving Adela Branston free to ponder upon John Saltram's cruelty.

"If he had only trusted me," she said to herself more than once during those mournful meditations; "if he had only given me credit for some little good sense and generosity, I should not feel it as keenly as I do. He must have known that I loved him—yes, I have been weak enough to let him see that—and I think that once he used to like me a little—in those old happy days when he came so often to Maidenhead. Yes, I believe he almost loved me then."

And then the thought that this man was lying desperately ill, perhaps in danger of death, blotted out every other thought. It was so bitter to know him in peril, and to be powerless to go to him; worse than useless to him were she by his side, since it was another whose image haunted his wandering brain—another whose voice he longed to hear.

She spent a sleepless melancholy night, and had no rest next day, until a commissionnaire brought her a brief note from Gilbert Fenton, telling her that if there were any change at all in the patient, it was on the side of improvement.

CHAPTER XXXV.
BOUGHT WITH A PRICE.

ELLEN Carley was not allowed any time to take back the promise given to her father, had she been inclined to do so. Mr. Whitelaw made his appearance at the Grange early in the evening of the 2nd of January, with a triumphant simper upon his insipid countenance, which was inexpressibly provoking to the unhappy girl. It was clear to her, at first sight of him, that her father had been at Wyncomb that afternoon, and her hateful suitor came secure of success. His wooing was not a very romantic episode in his commonplace existence. He did not even attempt to see Ellen alone; but after he had been seated for about half-an-hour in the chimney-corner, nestling close to the fire in a manner he much affected, being of a particularly chilly temperament, given to shiver and turn blue on the smallest provocation, he delivered himself solemnly of the following address:—

"I make no doubt, Miss Carley, that you have taken notice for some time past of my sentiments towards yourself. I have never made any secret of those sentiments, neither have I talked much about them, not being a man of many words. I used to fancy myself the very reverse of a marrying man, and I don't say but what at this moment I think the man who lives and dies a bachelor does the wisest for his own comfort and his own prosperity. But we are not the masters of our feelings, Miss Carley. You have growed upon me lately somehow, so that I've got not to care for my life without you. Ask Mrs. Tadman if my appetite hasn't fell off within this last six months to a degree that has frightened her; and a man of my regular habits must be very far gone in love, Miss Carley, when his appetite forsakes him. From the time I came to know you as a young woman, in the bloom of a young woman's beauty, I said to myself, 'That's the girl I'll marry, and no other.' Your father can bear me out in that, for I said the same to him. And finding that I had his approval, I was satisfied to bide my time, and wait till you came round to the same way of thinking. Your father tells me yesterday afternoon, and again this afternoon, that you have come round to that way of feeling. I hope he hasn't deceived me, Miss Carley."

This was a very long speech for Stephen Whitelaw. It was uttered in little gasps or snatches of speech, the speaker stopping at the end of every sentence to take breath.

Ellen Carley sat on that side of the comfortable round table most remote from Mr. Whitelaw, deadly pale, with her hands clasped before her. Once she lifted her eyes with a piteous look to her father's face; but he was smoking his pipe solemnly, with his gaze fixed upon the blazing logs in the grate, and contrived not to see that mute despairing appeal. He had not looked at his daughter once since Stephen Whitelaw's arrival, nor had he made any attempt to prepare her for this visit, this rapid consummation of the sacrifice.

"Come, Miss Carley," said the former rather impatiently, after there had been a dead silence of some minutes, "I want to get an answer direct from your own lips. Your father hasn't been deceiving me, has he?"

"No," Ellen said in a low voice, almost as if the reply were dragged from her by some physical torture. "If my father has given you a promise for me, I will keep it. But I don't want to deceive you, on my part, Mr. Whitelaw," she went on in a somewhat firmer tone. "I will be your wife, since you and my father have settled that it must be so; but I can promise no more than that. I will be dutiful and submissive to you as a wife, you may be sure—only———"

Mr. Whitelaw smiled a very significant smile, which implied that it would be his care to insure his wife's obedience, and that he was troubled by no doubts upon that head.

The bailiff broke-in abruptly at this juncture.

"Lord bless the girl, what need is there of all this talk about what she will be and what she won't be? She'll be as good a wife as any woman in England, I'll stake my life upon that. She's been a good daughter, as all the world knows, and a good daughter is bound to make a good wife. Say no more about it, Nell. Stephen Whitelaw knows he'll make no bad bargain in marrying you."

The farmer received this remark with a loud sniff, expressive of offended dignity.

"Very likely not, William Carley," he said; "but it isn't every man that can make your daughter mistress of such a place as Wyncomb; and such men as could do it would look for money with a wife, however young and pretty she might be. There's two sides to a bargain, you see, William, and I should like things to be looked at in that light between you and me."

"You've no call to take offence, Steph," answered the bailiff with a conciliating grin. "I never said you wasn't a good match for my girl; but a pretty girl and a prudent clever housekeeper like Nell is a fortune in herself to any man."

"Then the matter's settled, I suppose," said Mr. Whitelaw; "and the sooner the wedding comes off the better, to my mind. If my wife that is to be wants anything in the way of new clothes, I shall be happy to put down a twenty-pound note—or I'd go as far as thirty—towards 'em."

Ellen shook her head impatiently.

"I want nothing new," she said; "I have as many things as I care to have."

"Nonsense, Nell," cried her father, frowning at her in a significant manner to express his disapproval of this folly, and in so doing looking at her for the first time since her suitor's advent. "Every young woman likes new gowns, and of course you'll take Steph's friendly offer, and thank him kindly for it. He knows that I'm pretty hard-up just now, and won't be able to do much for you; and it wouldn't do for Mrs. Whitelaw of Wyncomb to begin the world with a shabby turn-out."

"Of course not," replied the farmer; "I'll bring you the cash to-morrow evening, Nell; and the sooner you buy your wedding-gown the better. There's nothing to wait for, you see. I've got a good home to take you to. Mother Tadman will march, of course, between this and my wedding-day. I sha'n't want her when I've a wife to keep house for me."

"Of course not," said the bailiff. "Relations are always dangerous about a place—ready to make mischief at every hand's turn."

"O, Mr. Whitelaw, you won't turn her out, surely—your own flesh and blood, and after so many years of service. She told me how hard she had worked for you."

"Ah, that's just like her," growled the farmer. "I give her a comfortable home for all these years, and then she grumbles about the work."

"She didn't grumble," said Ellen hastily. "She only told me how faithfully she had served you."

"Yes; that comes to the same thing. I should have thought you would have liked to be mistress of your house, Nell, without any one to interfere with you."

"Mrs. Tadman is nothing to me," answered Ellen, who had been by no means prepossessed by that worthy matron; "but I shouldn't like her to be unfairly treated on my account."

"Well, we'll think about it, Nell; there's no hurry. She's worth her salt, I daresay."

Mr. Whitelaw seemed to derive a kind of satisfaction from the utterance of his newly-betrothed's Christian name, which came as near the rapture of a lover as such a sluggish nature might be supposed capable of. To Ellen there was something hideous in the sound of her own name spoken by those hateful lips; but he had a sovereign right so to address her, now and for evermore. Was she not his goods, his chattels, bought with a price, as much as a horse at a fair?

That nothing might be wanting to remind her of the sordid bargain, Mr. Whitelaw drew a small canvas bag from his pocket presently—a bag which gave forth that pleasant chinking sound that is sweet to the ears of so many as the music of gold—and handed it across the hearth to William Carley.

"I'm as good as my word, you see," he said with a complacent air of patronage. "There's the favour you asked me for; I'll take your IOU for it presently, if it's all the same to you—as a matter of form—and to be given back to you upon my wedding-day."

The bailiff nodded assent, and dropped the bag into his pocket with a sigh of relief. And then the two men went on smoking their pipes in the usual stolid way, dropping out a few words now and then by way of social converse; and there was nothing in Mr. Whitelaw's manner to remind Ellen that she had bound herself to the awful apprenticeship of marriage without love. But when he took his leave that night he approached her with such an evident intention of kissing her as could not be mistaken by the most inexperienced of maidens. Poor Ellen indulged in no girlish resistance, no pretty little comedy of alarm and surprise, but surrendered her pale lips to the hateful salute with the resignation of a martyr. It was better that she should suffer this than that her father should go to gaol. That thought was never absent from her mind. Nor was this sacrifice to filial duty quite free from the leaven of selfishness. For her own sake, as much as for her father's, Ellen Carley would have submitted to any penalty rather than disgrace. To have him branded as a thief must needs be worse suffering than any life-long penance she might endure in matrimony. To lose Frank Randall's love was less than to let him learn her father's guilt.

"The daughter of a thief!" she said to herself. "How he would despise himself for having ever loved me, if he knew me to be that!"

CHAPTER XXXVI.
COMING ROUND.

POSSESSED with a thorough distrust of Mr. Medler and only half satisfied as to the fact of Marian's safety, Gilbert Fenton lost no time in seeking professional aid in the work of investigating this perplexing social mystery. He went once more to the metropolitan detective who had been with him in Hampshire, and whose labours there had proved so futile. The task now to be performed seemed easy enough. Mr. Proul (Proul was the name of the gentleman engaged by Gilbert) had only to discover the whereabouts of Percival Nowell; a matter of no great difficulty, Gilbert imagined, since it was most likely that Marian's father had frequent personal communication with the lawyer; nor was it improbable that he would have business with his agent or representative, Mr. Tulliver, in Queen Anne's Court. Provided with these two addresses, Gilbert fancied that Mr. Proul's work must needs be easy enough.

That gentleman, however, was not disposed to make light of the duty committed to him; whether from a professional habit of exaggerating the importance of any mission undertaken by him, or in perfect singleness of mind, it is not easy to say.

"It's a watching business, you see sir," he told Gilbert, "and is pretty sure to be tedious. I may put a man to hang about this Mr. Medler's business all day and every day for a month at a stretch, and he may miss his customer at the last, especially as you can't give me any kind of description of the man you want."

"Surely your agent could get some information out of Medler's clerk; it's in his trade to do that kind of thing, isn't it?"

"Well, yes, sir; I don't deny that I might put a man on to the clerk, and it might answer. On the other hand, such a gentleman's clerk would be likely to be uncommon well trained and uncommon little trusted."

"But we want to know so little," Gilbert exclaimed impatiently; "only where this man lives, and who lives with him."

"Yes," murmured Mr. Proul, rubbing his chin thoughtfully; "it ain't much, as you say, and it might be got out of the clerk, if the clerk knows it; but as to Mrs. Holbrook having got away from Hampshire and come to London, that's more than I can believe. I worked that business harder and closer than ever I worked any business yet. You told me to spare neither money nor time, and I didn't spare either; though it was more a question of time than money, for my expenses were light enough, as you know. I don't believe Mrs. Holbrook could have got away from Malsham station up to the time when I left Hampshire. I'm pretty certain she couldn't have left the place any other way than by rail; I'm more than certain she couldn't have been living anywhere in the neighbourhood when I was hunting for her. In short, it comes to this—I stick to my old opinion, that the poor lady was drowned in Malsham river."

This was just what Gilbert, happily for his own peace, could not bring himself to believe. He was ready to confide in Mr. Medler as a model of truth and honesty, rather than admit the possibility of Marian's death.

"We have this man Medler's positive assertion, that Mrs. Holbrook is with her father, you see, Mr. Proul," he said doubtfully.

"*That* for Medler's assertion!" exclaimed the detective contemptuously; "there are lawyers in London who will assert anything for a consideration. Let him produce the lady; and if he does produce her, I give him leave to say that Thomas Henry Proul is incapable of his business; or, putting it in vulgar English, that T.H.P. is a duffer. Of course I shall carry out any business you like to trust me with, Mr. Fenton, and carry it out thoroughly. I'll set a watch upon Mr. Medler's offices, and I'll circumvent him by means of his clerk, if I can; but it's my rooted conviction that Mrs. Holbrook never left Hampshire."

This was discouraging; and with that ready power to adapt itself to circumstances which is a distinguishing characteristic of the human mind, Gilbert Fenton began to entertain a very poor opinion of the worthy Proul's judgment. But not knowing any better person whose aid he could enlist in this business, he was fain to confide his chances of success to that gentleman, and to wait with all patience for the issue of events. Much of this dreary interval of perpetual doubt and suspense was spent beside John Saltram's sick bed. There were strangely mingled feelings in the watcher's breast; a pitying regret that struggled continually with his natural anger; a tender remembrance of past friendship, which he despised as a shameful weakness in his nature, but could not banish from his mind, as he sat in the stillness of the sick-room, watching the helpless creature who had once kept as faithful a vigil for him.

To John Saltram's recovery he looked also as to his best chance of restoring Marian to her natural home. The influence that he himself was powerless to bring to bear upon Percival Nowell's daughter might be easily exerted by her husband.

"She was lured away from him, perhaps, by some specious lie of her father's, some cruel slander of the husband. There had been bitter words between them. Saltram has betrayed as much in his wandering talk; but to the last there was no feeling but love for him in her heart. Ellen Carley is my witness for that; nothing less than some foul lie could have tempted her away from him."

In the meantime, pending the sick man's recovery, the grand point was to discover the whereabouts of Marian and her father; and for this discovery Gilbert was compelled to trust to the resources of the accomplished Proul. So eager was he for the result, that if be could have kept a watch upon Mr. Medler's office with his own eyes, he would have done so; but this being out of the question, and the more prudent course a complete avoidance of the lawyer's neighbourhood, he could only await the result of his paid agent's researches, in the hope that Mr. Nowell was still in London, and would have need of frequent communication with his late father's solicitor. The first month of the year dragged itself slowly to an end, and the great city underwent all those pleasing alternations, from snow to mud, from the slipperiness of a city paved with plate-glass to the sloppiness of a metropolis ankle-deep in a rich brown compound of about the consistency and colour of mock-turtle soup, which are common to great cities at this season; and still John Saltram lingered on in the shabby solitude of his Temple chambers, slowly mending, Mr. Mew declared, towards the end of the month, and in a fair way towards recovery. The time came at last when the fevered mind began to cease from its perpetual wanderings; when the weary brain, sorely enfeebled by its long interval of unnatural activity, dropped suddenly into a state of calm that was akin to apathy.

The change came with an almost alarming suddenness. It was at the beginning of February, close upon the dead small hours of a bleak windy night, and Gilbert was keeping watch alone in the sick-room, while the professional nurse slept comfortably on the sofa in the sitting-room. It was his habit now to spend the early part of the night in such duty as this, and to go home to bed between four and five in the morning, at which time the nurse was ready to relieve guard.

He had been listening to the dismal howling of the winds, threatening damage to neighbouring chimney-pots of rickety constitution, and thinking idly of the men that had come and gone amidst those old buildings, and how few amongst them all had left any mark behind them; inclined to speculate too how many of them had been men capable of better work than they had done, only carelessly indifferent to the doing of it, like him who lay on that bed yonder, with one muscular arm, powerful even in its wasted condition, thrown wearily above his head, and an undefinable look, that seemed half pain, half fatigue, upon his haggard face.

Suddenly, while Gilbert Fenton was meditating in this idle desultory manner, the sleeper awakened, looked full at him, and called him by his name.

"Gilbert," he said very quietly, "is it really you?"

It was the first time, in all his long watches by that bed, that John Saltram had recognised him. The sick man had talked of him often in his delirium; but never before had he looked his former friend in the face with one ray of recognition in his own. An indescribable thrill of pain went through Gilbert's heart at the sound of that calm utterance of his name. How sweet it would have been to him, what a natural thing it would have seemed, to have fallen upon his old friend's breast and wept aloud in the deep joy of this recovery! But they were friends no longer. He had to remember how base a traitor this man had been to him.

"Yes, John, it is I."

"And you have been here for a long time. O God, how many months have I been lying here? The time seems endless; and there have been so many people round me—a crowd of strange faces—all enemies, all against me. And people in the next room—that was the worst of all. I have never seen them, but I have always known that they were there. They could not deceive me as to that— hiding behind that door, and watching me as I lay here. You might have turned them out, Gilbert," he added peevishly; "it seems a hard thing that you could let them stay there to torment me."

"There has been no one in either of the rooms, John; no one but myself and the hired nurse, the doctors, and Mrs. Pratt now and then. These people have no existence out of your sick fancy. You have been, very ill, delirious, for a long time. I thank God that your reason has been restored to you; yes, I thank God with all my heart for that."

"Have I been mad?" the other asked.

"Your mind has wandered. But that has passed at last with the fever, as the doctors hoped it might. You are calm now, and must try to keep yourself quiet; there must be no more talk between us to-night."

The sick man took no notice of this injunction; but for the time was not disobedient, and lay for some minutes staring at the watcher's face with a strange half-vacant smile upon his own.

"Gilbert," he said at last, "what have they done with my wife? Why has she been kept away from me?"

"Your wife? Marian?"

"Yes Marian. You know her name, surely. Did she know that I was ill, and yet stayed away from me?"

"Was her place here, John Saltram?—that poor girl whom you married under a false name, whom you tried to hide from all the world. Have you ever brought her here? Have you ever given her a wife's license, or a wife's place? How many lies have you not told to hide that which any honest man would have been proud to confess to all the world?"

"Yes, I have lied to you about her, I have hidden my treasure. But it was for your sake, Gilbert; it was for the sake of our old friendship. I could not bear to lose you; I could not bear to stand revealed before you as the weak wretch who betrayed your trust and stole your promised wife. Yes, Gilbert, I have been guilty beyond all measure. I have looked you in the face and told you lies. I wanted to keep you for my friend; I could not stand the thought of a life-long breach between us. Gilbert, old friend, have pity on me. I was weak—wicked, if you like—but I loved you very dearly."

He stretched out his bony hand with an appealing gesture, but it was not taken. Gilbert sat with his head turned away, his face hidden from the sick man.

"Anything would have been better than the course you chose," he said at last in a very quiet voice. "If she loved you better than me—than me, who would have thought it so small a thing to lay down my life for her happiness, or to stand aloof and keep the secret of my broken heart while I blest her as the cherished wife of another—if you had certain reason to be sure she loved you, you should have asserted your right to claim her love like a man, and should have been prompt to tell me the bitter truth. I am a man, and would have borne the blow as a man should bear it. But to sneak into my place behind my back, to steal her away from me, to marry her under a false name—a step that might go far to invalidate the marriage, by the way—and then leave me to piece-out the broken story, syllable by syllable, to suffer all the torture of a prolonged suspense, all the wasted passion of anger and revenge against an imaginary enemy, to find at last that the man I had loved and trusted, honoured and admired beyond all other men throughout the best years of my life, was the man who had struck this secret blow—it was the conduct of a villain and a coward, John Saltram. I have no words to speak my contempt for so base a betrayal. And when I remember your pretended sympathy, your friendly counsel—O God! it was the work of a social Judas; nothing was wanted but the kiss."

"Yes," the other answered with a faint bitter laugh; "it was very bad. Once having began, you see, it was but to add one lie to another. Anything seemed better than to tell you the truth. I fancied your devotion for Marian would wear itself out much sooner than it did—that you would marry some one else; and then I thought, when you were happy, and had forgotten that old fancy, I would have confessed the truth, and told you it was your friend who was your rival. It might have seemed easy to you to forgive me under those happier circumstances, and so our old friendship might never have been broken. I waited for that, Gilbert. Don't suppose that it was not painful to me to act so base a part; don't suppose that I did not suffer. I did—in a hundred ways. You have seen the traces of that slow torture in my face. In every way I had sinned from my weak desire to win my love and yet keep my friend; and God knows the burden of my sin has been heavy upon me. I will tell you some day—if ever I am strong enough for so many words, and if you will hear me out patiently— the whole story of my temptation; how I struggled against it, and only gave way at last when life seemed insupportable to me without the woman I loved."

After this he lay quiet again for some minutes, exhausted by having spoken so long. All the factitious strength, which had made him loud and violent in his delirium, was gone; he seemed as weak as a sick child.

"Where is she?" he asked at last; "why doesn't she come to me? You have not answered that question."

"I have told you that her place is not here," Gilbert replied evasively. "You have no right to expect her here, never having given her the right to come."

"No; it is my own fault. She is in Hampshire still, I suppose. Poor girl, I would give the world to see her dear face looking down at me. I must get well and go back to her. When shall I be strong enough to travel?—to-morrow, or if not to-morrow, the next day; surely the next day—eh, Gilbert?"

He raised himself in the bed in order to read the answer in Gilbert's face, but fell back upon the pillows instantly, exhausted by the effort. Memory had only returned to him in part. It was clear that he had forgotten the fact of Marian's disappearance,—a fact of which he had seemed half-conscious long ago in his delirium.

"How did you find out that Marian was my wife?" he asked presently, with perfect calmness. "Who betrayed my secret?"

"Your own lips, in your delirious talk of her, which has been incessant; and if collateral evidence were needed to confirm your words, this, which I found the other day marking a place in your Shakespeare."

Gilbert took a scrap of ribbon from his breast, a ribbon with a blue ground and a rosebud on it,—a ribbon which he had chosen himself for Marian, in the brief happy days of their engagement.

John Saltram contemplated the scrap of colour with a smile that was half sombre, half ironical.

"Yes, it was hers," he said; "she wore it round that slim swan's throat of hers; and one morning, when I was leaving her in a particularly weak frame of mind, I took it from her neck and brought it away in my bosom, for the sake of having something about me that she had worn; and then I put it in the book, you see, and forgot all about it. A fitting emblem of my love—full of passion and fervour to-day, at the point of death to-morrow. There have been times when I would have given the world to undo what I had done, when my life seemed blighted by this foolish marriage; and again, happier moments, when my wife was all the universe to me, and I had not a thought or a dream beyond her. God bless her! You will let me go to her, Gilbert, the instant I am able to travel, as soon as I can drag myself anyhow from this bed to the railway? You will not stand between me and my love?"

"No, John Saltram; God knows, I have never thought of that."

"And you knew I was a traitor—you knew it was my work that had destroyed your scheme of happiness—and yet have been beside me, watching me patiently through this wretched illness?"

"That was a small thing to do You did as much, and a great deal more, for me, when I was ill in Egypt. It was a mere act of duty."

"Not of friendship. It was Christian charity, eh, Gilbert? If thine enemy hunger, feed him; if he thirst, give him drink; and so on. It was not the act of a friend?"

"No, John Saltram, between you and me there can never again be any such word as friendship. What little I have done for you I think I would have done for a stranger, had I found a stranger as helpless and unfriended as I found you. I am quite sure that to have done less would have been to neglect a sacred duty. There is no question of obligation. Till you are on your feet again, a strong man, I will stand by you; when that time comes, we part for ever."

John Saltram sank back upon his pillow with a heavy sigh, but uttered no protest against this sentence. And this was all that came of Gilbert's vengeful passion against the man who had wronged him; this was the end of a long-cherished anger. "A lame and impotent conclusion," perhaps, but surely the only end possible under the circumstances. He could not wage war against a feeble creature, whose hold on life was still an uncertainty; he could not forget his promise to Marian, that no harm should come to her husband through any act of his. So he sat quietly by the bedside of his prostrate foe, watched him silently as he fell into a brief restless slumber, and administered his medicine when he woke with a hand that was as gentle as a woman's.

Between four and five o'clock the nurse came in from the next room to take her place, refreshed by a sleep of several hours; and then Gilbert departed in the chill gloom of the winter's morning, still as dark as night,—departed with his mind lightened of a great load; for it had been very terrible to him to think that the man who had once been his friend might go down to the grave without an interval of reason.

CHAPTER XXXVII.
A FULL CONFESSION.

GILBERT did not go to the Temple again till he had finished his day's work at St. Helen's, and had eaten his modest dinner at a tavern in Fleet-street. He found that Mr. Mew had already paid his second visit to the sick-room, and had pronounced himself much relieved and delighted by the favourable change.

"I have no fear now," he had said to the nurse. "It is now only a question of getting back the physical strength, which has certainly fallen to a very low ebb. Perfect repose and an entire freedom from care are what we have to look to."

This the nurse told Gilbert. "He has been very restless all day," she added, "though I've done what I could to keep him quiet. But he worries himself, now that his senses have come back, poor gentleman; and it isn't easy to soothe him any way. He keeps on wondering when he'll be well enough to move, and so on, over and over again. Once, when I left the room for a minute and went back again, I found him attempting to get out of bed—only to try his strength, he said. But he's no more strength than a new-born baby, poor soul, and it will be weeks before he's able to stir. If he worries and frets, he'll put himself back for a certainty; but I daresay you'll have more influence over him than I, sir, and that you may be able to keep him quiet."

"I doubt that," answered Gilbert; "but I'll do my best. Has he been delirious to-day?"

"No, sir, not once; and of course that's a great thing gained."

A feeble voice from the inner room called Gilbert by name presently, and he went in at its bidding.

"Is that you, Gilbert? Come in, for pity's sake. I was sure of the voice. So you have come on your errand of charity once more. I am very glad to see you, though you are not my friend. Sit down, ministering Christian, sit by my side; I have some questions to ask you."

"You must not talk much, John. The doctor insists upon perfect tranquillity."

"He might just as well insist upon my making myself Emperor of all the Russias; one demand would be about as reasonable as the other. How long have I been lying here like a log—a troublesome log, by the way; for I find from some hints the nurse dropped to-day as to the blessing of my recovery, that I have been somewhat given to violence;—how long have I been ill, Gilbert?"

"A very long time."

"Give me a categorical answer. How many weeks and days?"

"You were taken ill about the middle of December, and we are now in the first week of February."

"Nearly two months; and in all that time I have been idle—*ergo*, no remittances from publishers. How have I lived, Gilbert? How have the current expenses of my illness been paid? And the children of Israel—have they not been clamorous? There was a bill due in January, I know. I was working for that when I got pulled up. How is it that my vile carcass is not in their hands?"

"You need give yourself no trouble; the bill has been taken up."

"By you, of course? Yes; you do not deny it. And you have been spending your money day by day to keep me alive. But then you would have done as much for a stranger. Great heaven, what a mean hound I seem to myself, as I lie here and think what you have done for me, and how I have acted towards you!" He turned himself in his bed with a great effort, and lay with his face to the wall. "Let me hide my face from you," he said; "I am a shameful creature."

"Believe me, once more, there is not the faintest shadow of an obligation," Gilbert responded eagerly; "I can very well afford anything I have done; shall never feel myself the poorer for it by a sixpence. I cannot bear that these things should be spoken of between us. You know how often I have begged you to let me help you in the past, and how wounded I have been by your refusal."

"Yes, when we were friends, before I had ever wronged you. If I had taken your help then, I should hardly have felt the obligation. But, stay, I am not such a pauper as I seem. My wife will have money; at least you told me that the old man was rich."

"Yes, your wife will have money, plenty of money. You have no need to trouble yourself about financial matters. You have only to consider what the doctor has said. Your recovery depends almost entirely upon your tranquillity of mind. If you want to get well speedily, you must remember this."

"I do want to get well. I am in a fever to get well; I want to see my wife. But my recovery will be evidently a tedious affair. I cannot wait to see her till I am strong enough to travel. Why should she not come to me here? She can—she must come. Write to her, Gilbert; tell her how I languish for her presence; tell her how ill I have been."

"Yes; I will write by and by."

"By and by! Your tone tells me that you do not mean what you say. There is something you are keeping from me. O, my God, what was that happened before I was ill? My wife was missing. I was hunting for her without rest for nearly a week; and then they told me she was drowned, that there was no hope of finding her. Was that real, Gilbert? or only a part of my delirium? Speak to me, for pity's sake. Was it real?"

"Yes, John; your perplexity and trouble were real, but unnecessary; your wife is safe."

"Safe? Where?"

"She is with her father."

"She did not even know that her father was living."

"No, not till very lately. He has come home from America, it seems, and Marian is now under his protection."

"What! she could desert me without a word of warning—without the faintest hint of her intention—to go to a father of whom she knew nothing, or nothing that was not eminently to his discredit!"

"There may have been some strong influence brought to bear to induce her to take such a step."

"What influence?"

"Do not worry yourself about that now; make all haste to get well, and then it will be easy for you to win her back."

"Yes; only place me face to face with her, and I do not think there would be much question as to that. But that she should forsake me of her own free will! It is so unlike my Marian—my patient, long-suffering Marian; I can scarcely believe such a thing possible. But that question can soon be put at rest. Write to her, Gilbert; tell her that I have been at death's door; that my chance of recovery hangs upon her will. Father or no father, *that* will bring her to my side."

"I will do so, directly I know her address."

"You do not know where she is?"

"Not yet. I am expecting to obtain that information every day. I have taken measures to ascertain where she is."

"And how do you know that she is with her father?"

"I have the lawyer's authority for that; a lawyer whom the old man, Jacob Nowell, trusted, whom he left sole executor to his will."

It was necessary above all things that John Saltram's mind should be set at rest; and in order to secure this result Gilbert was fain to affect a supreme faith in Mr. Medler.

"You believe this man, Gilbert?" the invalid asked anxiously.

"Of course. He has no reason for deceiving me."

"But why withhold the father's address?"

"It is easy enough to conjecture his reasons for that; a dread of your influence robbing him of his daughter. Her fortune has made her a prize worth disputing, you see. It is natural enough that the father should wish to hide her from you."

"For the sake of the money?—yes, I suppose that is the beginning and end of his scheme. My poor girl! No doubt he has told her all manner of lies about me, and so contrived to estrange that faithful heart. Will you insert an advertisement in the *Times*, Gilbert, under initials, telling her of my illness, and entreating her to come to me?"

"I will do so if you like; but I daresay Nowell will be cautious enough to keep the advertisement-sheet away from her, or to watch it pretty closely, and prevent her seeing anything we may insert. I am taking means to find them, John I, must entreat you to rest satisfied with that."

"Rest satisfied,—when I am uncertain whether I shall ever see my wife again! That is a hard thing to do."

"If you harass yourself, you will not live to see her again. Trust in me, John; Marian's safety is as dear to me as it can be to you. I am her sworn friend and brother, her self-appointed guardian and defender. I have skilled agents at work; we shall find her, rely upon it."

It was a strange position into which Gilbert found himself drifting; the consoler of this man who had so basely robbed him. They could never be friends again, these two; he had told himself that, not once, but many times during the weary hours of his watching beside John Saltram's sick-bed. They could never more be friends; and yet he found himself in a manner compelled to perform the offices of friendship. Nor was it easy to preserve anything like the neutral standing which he had designed for himself. The life of this sometime friend of his hung by so frail a link, he had such utter need of kindness; so what could Gilbert do but console him for the loss of his wife, and endeavour to inspire him with a hopeful spirit about her? What could he do less than friendship would have done, although his affection for this old friend of his youth had perished for evermore? The task of consolation was not an easy one. Once restored to his right mind, with a vivid sense of all that had happened to him before his illness, John Saltram was not to be beguiled into a false security. The idea that his wife was in dangerous hands pursued him perpetually, and the consciousness of his own impotence to rescue her goaded him to a kind of mental fever.

"To be chained here, Gilbert, lying on this odious bed like a dog, when she needs my help! How am I to bear it?"

"Like a man," the other answered quietly. "Were you as well as I am this moment, there's nothing you could do that I am not doing. Do you think I should sit idly here, if the best measures had not been taken to find your wife?"

"Forgive me. Yes; I have no doubt you have done what is best. But if I were astir, I should have the sense of doing something. I could urge on those people you employ, work with them even."

"You would be more likely to hinder than to assist them. They know their work, and it is a slow drudging business at best, which requires more patience than you possess. No, John, there is nothing to be done but to wait, and put our trust in Providence and in time."

This was a sermon which Gilbert Fenton had occasion to preach very often in the slow weary days that followed John Saltram's recovery of his right senses. The sick man, tossing to and fro upon the bed he loathed with such an utter loathing, could not refrain from piteous bewailings of his helplessness. He was not a good subject for sickness, had never served his apprenticeship to a sick-bed until now, and the ordeal seemed to him a very long one. In all that period of his delirious wanderings there had been an exaggerated sense of time in his mind. It seemed to him that he had been lying there for years, lost in a labyrinth of demented fancies. Looking back at that time, now that his reason had been restored to him, he was able to recall his delusions one by one, and it was very difficult for him to understand, even now, that they were all utterly groundless, the mere vagabondage of a wandering brain; that the people he had fancied close at hand, lurking in the next room—he had rarely seen them close about his bed, but had been possessed with a vivid sense of their neighbourhood—had been never near him; that the old friends and associates of his boyhood, who had been amongst these fancied visitors, were for the greater number dead and passed away long before this time; that he had been, in every dream and every fancy of that weary interval, the abject slave of his own hallucinations. Little by little his strength came back to him by very slow degrees—so slowly, indeed, that the process of recovery might have sorely tried the patience of any man less patient than Gilbert. There came a day at last when the convalescent was able to leave his bed for an hour or so, just strong enough to crawl into the sitting-room with the help of Gilbert's arm, and to sit in an easy-chair, propped up by pillows, very feeble of aspect, and with a wan haggard countenance that pleaded mutely for pity. It was impossible to harbour revengeful feelings against a wretch so stricken.

Mr. Mew was much elated by this gradual improvement in his patient, and confessed to Gilbert, in private, that he had never hoped for so happy a result. "Nothing but an iron constitution, and your admirable care, could have carried our friend through such an attack, sir," he said decisively. "And now that we are getting round a little, we must have change of air—change of air and of scene; that is imperatively necessary. Mr. Saltram talks of a loathing for these rooms; very natural under the circumstances. We must take him away directly he can bear the removal."

"I rather doubt his willingness to stir," Gilbert answered, thoughtfully. "He has anxieties that are likely to chain him to London."

"If there is any objection of that kind it must be conquered," Mr. Mew said. "A change will do your friend more good than all the physic I can give him."

"Where would you advise me to take him?"

"Not very far. He couldn't stand the fatigue of a long journey. I should take him to some quiet little place near town—the more countrified the better. It isn't a very pleasant season for the country; but in spite of that, the change will do him good."

Gilbert promised to effect this arrangement, as soon as the patient was well enough to be moved. He would run down to Hampton or Kingston, he told Mr. Mew, in a day or two, and look for suitable lodgings.

"Hampton or Kingston by all means," replied the surgeon cheerily. "Both very pleasant places in their way, and as mild as any neighbourhood within easy reach of town. Don't go too near the water, and be sure your rooms are dry and airy—that's the main point. We might move him early next week, I fancy; if we get him up for an hour or two every day in the interval."

Gilbert had kept Mrs. Branston very well informed as to John Saltram's progress, and that impetuous little woman had sent a ponderous retainer of the footman species to the Temple daily, laden now with hothouse grapes, and anon with dainty jellies, clear turtle-soups, or delicate preparations of chicken, blancmanges and iced drinks; the conveyance whereof was a sore grievance to the ponderous domestic, in spite of all the aid to be derived from a liberal employment of cabs. Adela Branston had sent these things in defiance of her outraged kinswoman, Mrs. Pallinson, who was not slow to descant upon the impropriety of such a proceeding.

"I wonder you can talk in such a way, when you know how friendless this poor Mr. Saltram is, and how little trouble it costs me to do as much as this for him. But I daresay the good Samaritan had some one at home who objected to the waste of that twopence he paid for the poor traveller."

Mrs. Pallinson gave a little shriek of horror on hearing this allusion, and protested against so profane a use of the gospel.

"But the gospel was meant to be our guide in common things, wasn't it, Mrs. Pallinson? However, there's not the least use in your being angry; for I mean to do what I can for Mr. Saltram, and there's no one in the world could turn me from my intention."

"Indeed!" cried the elder lady, indignantly; "and when he recovers you mean to marry him, I daresay. You will be weak enough to throw away your fortune upon a profligate and a spendthrift, a man who is certain to make any woman miserable."

And hereupon there arose what Sheridan calls "a very pretty quarrel" between the two ladies, which went very near to end in Mrs. Pallinson's total withdrawal from Cavendish-square. Very nearly, but not quite, to that agreeable consummation did matters proceed; for, on the very verge of the final words which could have spoken the sentence of separation, Mrs. Pallinson was suddenly melted, and declared that nothing, no outrage of her feelings—"and heaven knows how they have been trodden on this day," the injured matron added in parenthesis—should induce her to desert her dearest Adela. And so there was a hollow peace patched up, and Mrs. Branston felt that the blessings of freedom, the delightful relief of an escape from Pallinsonian influences, were not yet to be hers. Directly she heard from Gilbert that change of air had been ordered for the patient, she was eager to offer her villa near Maidenhead for his accommodation. "The house is always kept in apple-pie order," she wrote to Gilbert; "and I can send down more servants to make everything comfortable for the invalid."

"I know he is fond of the place," she added in conclusion, after setting out all the merits of the villa with feminine minuteness; "at least I know he used to like it, and I think it would please him to get well there. I can only say that it would make *me* very happy; so do arrange it, dear Mr. Fenton, if possible, and oblige yours ever faithfully, ADELA BRANSTON."

"Poor little woman," murmured Gilbert, as he finished the letter. "No; we will not impose upon her kindness; we will go somewhere else. Better for her that she should see and hear but little of John Saltram for all time to come; and then the foolish fancy will wear itself out perhaps, and she may live to be a happy wife yet; unless she, too, is afflicted with the fatal capability of constancy. Is that such a common quality, I wonder? are there many so luckless as to love once and once only, and who, setting all their hopes upon one cast, lose all if that be fatal?"

Gilbert told John Saltram of Mrs. Branston's offer, which he was as prompt to decline as Gilbert himself had been. "It is like her to wish it," he said; "but no, I should feel myself a double traitor and impostor under her roof. I have done her wrong enough already. If I could have loved her, Gilbert, all might have been well for you and me. God knows I tried to love her, poor little woman; and she is just the kind of woman who might twine herself about any man's heart—graceful, pretty, gracious, tender, bright and intelligent enough for any man; and not too clever. But *my* heart she never touched. From the hour I saw that *other*, I was lost. I will tell you all about that some day. No; we will not go to the villa. Write and give Mrs. Branston my best thanks for the generous offer, and invent some excuse for declining it; that's a good fellow."

By-and-by, when the letter was written, John Saltram said,—"I do not want to go out of town at all, Gilbert. It's no use for the doctor to talk; I can't leave London till we have news of Marian."

Gilbert had been prepared for this, and set himself to argue the point with admirable patience. Mr. Proul's work would go on just as well, he urged, whether they were in London or at Hampton. A telegram would bring them any tidings as quickly in the one place as the other. "I am not asking you to go far, remember," he added. "You will be within an hour's journey of London, and the doctors declare this change is indispensable to your recovery. You have told us what a horror you have of these rooms."

"Yes; I doubt if any one but a sick man can understand his loathing of the scene of his illness. That room in there is filled with the shadows that haunted me in all those miserable nights—when the fever was at its worst, and I lived amidst a crowd of phantoms. Yes, I do most profoundly hate that room. As for this matter of change of air, Gilbert, dispose of me as you please; my worthless existence belongs to you."

Gilbert was quick to take advantage of this concession. He went down to Hampton next day, and explored the neighbourhood on both sides of the Thames. His choice fell at last on a pretty little house within a stone's throw of the Palace gates, the back windows whereof looked out upon the now leafless solitude of Bushy Park, and where there was a comfortable-looking rosy-faced landlady, whose countenance was very pleasant to contemplate after the somewhat lachrymose visage of Mrs. Pratt. Here he found he could have all the accommodation he required, and hither he promised to bring the invalid early in the following week.

There were as yet no tidings worth speaking of from Mr. Proul. That distinguished member of the detective profession waited upon Gilbert Fenton with his budget twice a week, but the budget was a barren one. Mr. Proul's agent pronounced Mr. Medler's clerk the toughest individual it had ever been his lot to deal with. No amount of treating at the public-house round the corner—and the agent had ascended from the primitive simplicity of a pint of porter to the highest flights in the art of compound liquors—could exert a softening influence upon that rigid nature. Either the clerk knew nothing about Percival Nowell, or had been so well schooled as to disclose nothing of what he knew. Money had been employed by the agent, as well as drink, as a means of temptation; but even every insidious hint of possible gains had failed to move the ill-paid underling to any revelation.

"It's my belief the man knows nothing, or else I should have had it out of him by hook or by crook," Mr. Proul's agent told him, and Mr. Proul repeated to his client.

This first agent having thus come to grief, and having perhaps made himself a suspected person in the eyes of the Medler office by his manoeuvres, a second spy had been placed to keep close watch upon the house, and to follow any person who at all corresponded with the detective idea of Mr. Nowell. It could be no more than an idea, unfortunately, since Gilbert had been able to give the accomplished Proul no description of the man he wanted to trace. Above all, the spy was to take special note of any lady who might be seen to enter or leave the office, and to this end he was furnished with a close description of Marian.

Gilbert called upon Mrs. Branston before carrying John Saltram out of town; he fancied that her offer of the Maidenhead villa would be better acknowledged personally than by a letter. He found the pretty little widow sorely disappointed by Mr. Saltram's refusal to occupy her house, and it was a little difficult to explain to her why they both preferred other quarters for the convalescent.

"Why will he not accept the smallest favour from me?" Adela Branston asked plaintively. "He ought to know that there is no *arrière pensée* in any offer which I make him—that I have no wish except for his welfare. Why does he not trust me a little more?"

"He will do so in future, I think, Mrs. Branston," Gilbert answered gravely. "I fancy he has learned the folly and danger of all underhand policy, and that he will put more faith in his friends for the rest of his life."

"And he is really much better, quite out of danger? Do the doctors say that?"

"He is as much out of danger as a man can well be whose strength has all been wasted in a perilous illness. He has that to regain yet, and the recovery will be slow work. Of course in his condition a relapse would be fatal; but there is no occasion to apprehend a relapse."

"Thank heaven for that! And you will take care of him, Mr. Fenton, will you not?"

"I will do my very best. He saved my life once; so you see that I owe him a life."

The invalid was conveyed to Hampton on a bright February day, when there was an agreeable glimpse of spring sunshine. He went down by road in a hired brougham, and the journey seemed a long one; but it was an unspeakable relief to John Saltram to see the suburban roads and green fields after the long imprisonment of the Temple,—a relief that moved him almost to tears in his extreme weakness.

"Could you believe that a man would be so childish, Gilbert?" he said apologetically. "It might have been a good thing for me to have died in that dismal room, for heaven only knows what heavy sorrow lies before me in the future. Yet the eight of these common things touches me more keenly than all the glory of the Jungfrau touched me ten years ago. What a gay bright-looking world it is! And yet how many people are happy in it? how many take the right road? I suppose there is a right road by which we all might travel, if we only knew how to choose it."

He felt the physical weariness of the journey acutely, but uttered no complaint throughout the way; though Gilbert could see the pale face growing paler, the sunken cheeks more pinched of aspect, as they went on. To the last he pronounced himself delighted by that quiet progress through the familiar landscape; and then having reached his destination, had barely strength to totter to a comfortable chintz-covered sofa in the bright-looking parlour, where he fainted away. The professional nurse had been dismissed before they left London, and Gilbert was now the invalid's only attendant. The woman had performed her office tolerably well, after the manner of her kind; but the presence of a sick nurse is not a cheering influence, and John Saltram was infinitely relieved by her disappearance.

"How good you are to me, Gilbert!" he said, that first evening of his sojourn at Hampton, after he had recovered from his faint, and was lying on the sofa sipping a cup of tea. "How good! and yet you are my friend no longer; all friendship is at an end between us. Well, God knows I am as helpless as that man who fell among thieves; I cannot choose but accept your bounty."

CHAPTER XXXVIII.
AN ILL-OMENED WEDDING.

AFTER that promise wrung from her by such a cruel agony, that fatal bond made between her and Stephen Whitelaw, Ellen Carley's life seemed to travel past her as if by some enchantment. Time lost its familiar sluggishness; the long industrious days, that had been so slow of old, flew by the bailiff's daughter like the shadows from a magic-lantern. At the first, after that desperate miserable day upon which the hateful words were uttered that were to bind her for life to a detested master, the girl had told herself that something must happen to prevent the carrying out of this abhorrent bargain. Something would happen. She had a vague faith that Providence would interfere somehow to save her. Day after day she looked into her father's face, thinking that from him, perhaps, might come some sign of wavering, some hint of possible release. Vain hope. The bailiff having exacted the sacrifice, pretended to think his daughter's welfare secured by that very act. He did not hesitate to congratulate her on her good fortune, and to protest, with an accustomed oath, that there was not a sensible woman in England who would not envy her so excellent a match. Once poor Ellen, always impetuous and plain-spoken, lost all patience with him, and asked how he dared to say such things.

"You know that I hate this man, father!" she cried passionately; "and that I hate myself for what I am going to do. You know that I have promised to be his wife for your sake, for your sake only; and that if I could have saved you from disgrace by giving you my life, I should have done it gladly to escape this much greater sacrifice. Never speak to me about Stephen Whitelaw again, father, unless you want to drive me mad. Let me forget what sin I am going to commit, if I can; let me go on blindfold."

It was to be observed that from the hour, of her betrothal. Ellen Carley as far as possible avoided her father's companionship. She worked more busily than ever about the big old house, was never tired of polishing the little-used furniture and dusting the tenantless bed-chambers; she seemed, indeed, to be infected with Mrs. Tadman's passion for superhuman cleanliness. To her dairy duties also she devoted much more time than of old; anything to escape the parlour, where her father sat idle for a considerable portion of the day, smoking his pipe, and drinking rather more than was good for him. Nor did Mr. Carley, for his part, appear to dislike this tacit severance between his daughter and himself. As the foolish young woman chose to accept good fortune in a perverse spirit, it was well that they two should see as little of each other as possible. Every evening found Mr. Whitelaw a punctual visitor in the snug panelled parlour, and at such times the bailiff insisted upon his daughter's presence; she was obliged to sit there night after night, stitching monotonously at some unknown calico garment—which might well from the state of mind of the worker have been her winding-sheet; or darning one of an inexhaustible basket of woollen stockings belonging to her father. It was her irksome duty to be there, ready to receive any awkward compliment of her silent lover's, ready to acquiesce meekly in his talk of their approaching wedding. But at all other times Mr. Carley was more than content with her absence.

At first the bailiff had made a feeble attempt to reconcile his daughter to her position by the common bribe of fine clothes. He had extorted a sum of money from Stephen Whitelaw for this purpose, and had given that sum, or a considerable part of it, to his daughter, bidding her expend it upon her wedding finery. The girl took the money, and spent a few pounds upon the furbishing-up of her wardrobe, which was by no means an extensive one; but the remaining ten-pound note she laid by in a secret place, determined on no account to break in upon it.

"The time may come when all my life will depend upon the possession of a few pounds," she said to herself; "when I may have some chance of setting myself free from that man."

She had begun to contemplate such a possibility already, before her wedding-day. It was for her father's sake she was going to sell her liberty, to take upon herself a bondage most odious to her. The time might come when her father would be beyond the reach of shame and disgrace, when she might find some manner of escape from her slavery.

In the meantime the days hurried on, and Providence offered her no present means of rescue. The day of doom came nearer and nearer; for the bailiff took part with his future son-in-law, and would hear of no reasons which Ellen could offer for delay. He was eager to squeeze the farmer's well-filled purse a little tighter, and he fancied he might do this when his daughter was Stephen Whitelaw's wife. So suitor and father were alike pitiless, and the wedding was fixed for the 10th of March. There were no preparations to be made at Wyncomb Farmhouse. Mr. Whitelaw did not mean to waste so much as a five-pound note upon the embellishment of those barely-furnished rooms in honour of his bright young bride; although Mrs. Tadman urged upon him the necessity of new muslin curtains here, and new dimity there, a coat or so of paint and new whitewash in such and such rooms, and other small revivals of the same character; not sorry to be able to remind him in this indirect manner that marriage was an expensive thing.

"A young woman like that will expect to see things bright and cheerful about her," said Mrs. Tadman, in her most plausible tone, and rubbing her thin hands with an air of suppressed enjoyment. "If you were going to marry a person of your own age, it would be different, of course; but young women have such extravagant notions. I could see Miss Carley did not think much of the furniture when I took her over the house on new-year's-day. She said the rooms looked gloomy, and that some of them gave her the horrors, and so on. If you don't have the place done up a bit at first, you'll have to get it done at last, depend upon it; a young wife like that will make the money spin, you may be sure."

"Will she?" said Mr. Whitelaw, with a satisfied grin. "That's my look-out. I don't think you've had very much chance of making my money spin, eh, Mrs. Tadman?"

The widow cast up her hands and eyes towards the ceiling of the parlour where they were sitting.

"Goodness knows I've had precious little chance of doing that, Stephen Whitelaw," she replied.

"I should reckon not; and my wife will have about as much."

There was some cold comfort in this. Mrs. Tadman had once hoped that if her cousin ever exalted any woman to the proud position of mistress of Wyncomb, she herself would be that favoured individual; and it was a hard thing to see a young person, who had nothing but a certain amount of good looks to recommend her, raised to that post of honour in her stead. It was some consolation, therefore, to discover that the interloper was to reign with very limited powers, and that none of the privileges or indulgences usually granted to youthful brides by elderly bridegrooms were to be hers. It was something, too, for Mrs. Tadman to be allowed to remain beneath the familiar shelter of that gloomy old house, and this boon had been granted to her at Ellen's express request.

"I suppose she's going to turn lazy as soon as she's married, or she wouldn't have wanted to keep you," the farmer said in rather a sulky manner, after he had given Mrs. Tadman his gracious permission to remain in his service. "But if she is, we must find some way of curing her of that. I don't want a fine lady about *my* place. There's the dairy, now; we might do more in that way, I should think, and get more profit out of butter-making than we do by sending part of the milk up to London. Butter fetches a good price now-a-days from year's end to year's end, and Ellen is a rare hand at a dairy; I know that for certain."

Thus did Mr. Whitelaw devote his pretty young wife to an endless prospect of butter-making. He had no intention that the alliance should be an unprofitable one, and he was already scheming how he might obtain some indirect kind of interest for that awful sum of two hundred pounds advanced to William Carley.

Sir David Forster had not come to make that threatened investigation of things at the Grange. Careless always in the management of his affairs, the receipt of a handsome sum of money from the bailiff had satisfied him, and he had suffered his suspicions to be lulled to rest for the time being, not caring to undertake the trouble of a journey to Hampshire, and an examination of dry business details.

It was very lucky for Mr. Carley that his employer was so easy and indolent a master; for there were many small matters at the Grange which would have hardly borne inspection, and it would have been difficult for Sir David to come there without making some discovery to his bailiff's disadvantage. The evil day had been warded off, however, by means of Stephen Whitelaw's money, and William Carley meant to act more cautiously, more honestly even, in future. He would keep clear of race-courses and gambling booths, he told himself, and of the kind of men who had beguiled him into dishonourable dealing.

"I have had an uncommon narrow squeak of it," he muttered to himself occasionally, as he smoked a meditative pipe, "and have been as near seeing the inside of Portland prison as ever a man was. But it'll be a warning to me in future. And yet who could have thought that things would have gone against me as they did? There was Sir Philip Christopher's bay colt Pigskin, for instance; that brute was bound to win."

February came to an end; and when March once began, there seemed no pause or breathing-time for Ellen Carley till the 10th. And yet she had little business to occupy her during those bleak days of early spring. It was the horror of that rapid flight of time, which seemed independent of her own life in its hideous swiftness. Idle or busy, it was all the same. The days would not linger for her; the dreaded 10th was close at hand.

Frank Randall was still in London, in that solicitor's office—a firm of some standing in the City—to which he had gone on leaving his father. He had written two or three times to Ellen since he left Hampshire, and she had answered his letters secretly; but pleasant though it was to her to hear from him, she begged him not to write, as her father's anger would be extreme if a letter should by any evil chance fall into his hands. So within the last few months there had been no tidings of Ellen's absent lover, and the girl was glad that it was so. What could she have said to him if she had been compelled to tell him of her engagement to Stephen Whitelaw? What excuse could she have made for marrying a man about whom she had been wont to express herself to Frank Randall in most unequivocal terms? Excuse there was none, since she could not betray her father. It was better, therefore, that young Randall should hear of her marriage in the common course of things, and that he should think of her just as badly as he pleased. This was only one more poisoned drop in a cup that was all bitterness.

"He will believe that I was a hypocrite at heart always," the unhappy girl said to herself, "and that I value Stephen Whitelaw's money more than his true heart—that I can marry a man I despise and dislike for the sake of being rich. What can he think worse of me than that? and how can he help thinking that? He knows that I have a good spirit of my own, and that my father could not make me do anything against my will. He will never believe that this marriage has been all my father's doing."

The wedding morning came at last, bright and spring-like, with a sun that shone as gaily as if it had been lighting the happiest union that was ever recorded in the hymeneal register. There were the first rare primroses gleaming star-like amidst the early greenery of high grassy banks in solitary lanes about Crosber, and here and there the tender blue of a violet. It would have seemed a very fair morning upon which to begin the first page in the mystic volume of a new life, if Ellen Carley had been going to marry a man she loved; but no hapless condemned wretch who ever woke to see the sun shining upon the day of his execution could have been more profoundly wretched than the bailiff's daughter, as she dressed herself mechanically in her one smart silk gown, and stood in a kind of waking trance before the quaint old-fashioned looking-glass which reflected her pale hopeless face. She had no girlish companion to assist in that dismal toilet. Long ago there had been promises exchanged between Ellen

Carley and her chosen friend, the daughter of a miller who lived a little way on the other side of Crosber, to the effect that whichever was first to marry should call upon the other to perform the office of bridesmaid; and Sarah Peters, the miller's daughter, was still single and eligible for the function. But there was to be no bridesmaid at this blighted wedding. Ellen had pleaded urgently that things might be arranged as quietly as possible; and the master of Wyncomb, who hated spending money, and who apprehended that the expenses of any festivity would in all probability fall upon his own shoulders, was very well pleased to assent to this request of his betrothed.

"Quite right, Nell," he said; "we don't want any foolish fuss, or a pack of people making themselves drunk at our expense. You and your father can come quietly to Crosber church, and Mrs. Tadman and me will meet you there, and the thing's done. The marriage wouldn't be any the tighter if we had a hundred people looking on, and the Bishop of Winchester to read the service."

It was arranged in this manner, therefore; and on that pleasant spring morning William Carley and his daughter walked to the quiet village where Gilbert Fenton had discovered the secret of Marian's retreat. The face under the bride's little straw bonnet was deadly pale, and the features had a rigid look that was new to them. The bailiff glanced at his daughter in a furtive way every now and then, with an uneasy sense of this strange look in her face. Even in his brute nature there were some faint twinges of compunction, now that the deed he had been so eager to compass was well-nigh done—some vague consciousness that he had been a hard and cruel father.

"And yet it's all for her own good," he told himself, "quite as much as for mine. Better to marry a rich man than a pauper any day; and to take a dislike to a man's age or a man's looks is nothing but a girl's nonsense. The best husband is the one that can keep his wife best; and if I hadn't forced on this business, she'd have taken up with lawyer Randall's son, who's no better than a beggar, and a pretty life she'd have had of it with him."

By such reasoning as this William Carley contrived to set his conscience at rest during that silent walk along the rustic lane between the Grange and Crosber church. It was not a conscience very difficult to appease. And as for his daughter's pallid looks, those of course were only natural to the occasion.

Mr. Whitelaw and Mrs. Tadman were at the church when the bailiff and his daughter arrived. The farmer had made a scarecrow of himself in a new suit of clothes, which he had ordered in honour of this important event, after a great deal of vacillation, and more than one countermand to the Malsham tailor who made the garments. At the last he was not quite clear in his mind as to whether he wanted the clothes, and the outlay was a serious one. Mrs. Tadman had need to hold his every-day coat up to the light to convince him that the collar was threadbare, and that the sleeves shone as if purposely polished by some ingenious process.

"Marriage is an expensive thing," she told him again, with a sigh; "and young girls expect to see a man dressed ever so smart on his wedding-day."

"I don't care for her expectations," Mr. Whitelaw muttered, in reply to this remark; "and if I don't want the clothes, I won't have 'em. Do you think I could get over next Christmas with them as I've got?"

Mrs. Tadman said "No" in a most decisive manner. Perhaps she derived a malicious pleasure from the infliction of that tailor's bill upon her cousin Whitelaw. So the new suit had been finally ordered; and Stephen stood arrayed therein before the altar-rails in the gray old church at Crosber, a far more grotesque and outrageous figure to contemplate than any knight templar, or bearded cavalier of the days of the first English James, whose effigies were to be seen in the chancel. Mrs. Tadman stood a little way behind him, in a merino gown, and a new bonnet, extorted somehow from the reluctant Stephen. She was full of smiles and cordial greetings for the bride, who did not even see her. Neither did Ellen Carley see the awkward figure of her bridegroom. A mist was before her eyes, as if there had been an atmosphere of summer blight or fog in the village church. She knelt, or rose, as her prayer-book taught her, and went through the solemn service as placidly as if she had been a wondrous piece of mechanism constructed to perform such movements; and then, like a creature in a dream, she found herself walking out of the church presently, with her hand on Stephen Whitelaw's arm. She had a faint consciousness of some ceremony in the vestry, where it had taken Stephen a long time to sign his name in the register, and where the clergyman had congratulated him upon his good fortune in having won for himself such a pretty young wife; but it was all more or less like a dreadful oppressive dream. Mr. Whitelaw's chaise-cart was waiting for them; and they all four got in, and drove at once to Wyncomb; where there was another ponderous dinner, very much like the banquet of new-year's-day, and where the bailiff drank freely, after his wont, and grew somewhat uproarious towards tea-time, though Mr. Whitelaw's selections of port and sherry were not of a kind to tempt a connoisseur.

There was to be no honeymoon trip. Stephen Whitelaw did not understand the philosophy of running away from a comfortable home to spend money in furnished lodgings; and he had said as much, when the officious Tadman suggested a run to Weymouth, or Bournemouth, or a fortnight in the Isle of Wight. To Ellen it was all the same where the rest of her life should be spent. It could not be otherwise than wretched henceforward, and the scene of her misery mattered nothing. So she uttered no complaint because her husband brought her straight home to Wyncomb Farmhouse, and her wedded life began in that dreary dwelling-place.

CHAPTER XXXIX.
A DOMESTIC MYSTERY.

IT was near the end of March, but still bleak cold weather. Ellen Carley had been married something less than a fortnight, and had come to look upon the dismal old farm-house by the river with a more accustomed eye than when Mrs. Tadman had taken her from room to room on a journey of inspection. Not that the place seemed any less dreary and ugly to her to-day than it had seemed at the very first. Familiarity could not make it pleasant. She hated the house and everything about and around it, as she hated her husband, with a rooted aversion, not to be subdued by any endeavour which she might make now and then—and she did honestly make such endeavour—to arrive at a more Christian-like frame of mind.

Notwithstanding this deeply-seated instinctive dislike to all her surroundings, she endured her fate quietly, and did her duty with a patient spirit which might fairly be accepted as an atonement for those inward rebellious feelings which she could not conquer. Having submitted to be the scapegoat of her father's sin, she bore her burden very calmly, and fulfilled the sacrifice without any outward mark of martyrdom.

She went about the work of the farm-house with a resolute active air that puzzled Mrs. Tadman, who had fully expected the young wife would play the fine lady, and leave all the drudgery of the household to her. But it really seemed as if Ellen liked hard work. She went from one task to another with an indefatigable industry, an energy that never gave way. Only when the day's work in house and dairy was done did her depression of spirits become visible. Then, indeed, when all was finished, and she sat down, neatly dressed for the afternoon, in the parlour with Mrs. Tadman, it was easy to see how utterly hopeless and miserable this young wife was. The pale fixed face, the listless hands clasped loosely in her lap, every attitude of the drooping figure, betrayed the joyless spirit, the broken heart. At these times, when they were alone together, waiting Stephen Whitelaw's coming home to tea, Mrs. Tadman's heart, not entirely hardened by long years of self-seeking, yearned towards her kinsman's wife; and the secret animosity with which she had at first regarded her changed to a silent pity, a compassion she would fain have expressed in some form or other, had she dared.

But she could not venture to do this. There was something in the girl, a quiet air of pride and self-reliance, in spite of her too evident sadness, which forbade any overt expression of sympathy; so Mrs. Tadman could only show her friendly feelings in a very small way, by being especially active and brisk in assisting all the household labours of the new mistress of Wyncomb, and by endeavouring to cheer her with such petty gossip as she was able to pick up. Ellen felt that the woman was kindly disposed towards her, and she was not ungrateful; but her heart was quite shut against sympathy, her sorrow was too profound to be lightened ever so little by human friendship. It was a dull despair, a settled conviction that for her life could never have again a single charm, that her days must go on in their slow progress to the grave unlightened by one ray of sunshine, her burden carried to the end of the dreary journey unrelieved by one hour of respite. It seemed very hard for one so young, not quite three-and-twenty yet, to turn her back upon every hope of happiness, to be obliged to say to herself, "For me the sun can never shine again, the world I live in can never more seem beautiful, or beautiful only in bitter contrast to my broken heart." But Ellen told herself that this fate was hers, and that she must needs face it with a resolute spirit.

The household work employed her mind in some measure, and kept her, more or less, from thinking; and it was for this reason she worked with such unflinching industry, just as she had worked in the last month or two at the Grange, trying to shut her eyes to that hateful future which lay so close before her. Mr. Whitelaw had no reason to retract what he had said in his pride of heart about Ellen Carley's proficiency in the dairy. She proved herself all that he had boasted, and the dairy flourished under the new management. There was more butter, and butter of a superior quality, sent to market than under the reign of Mrs. Tadman; and the master of Wyncomb made haste to increase his stock of milch cows, in order to make more money by this branch of his business. To have won for himself a pretty young wife, who, instead of squandering his substance, would help him to grow richer, was indeed a triumph, upon which Mr. Whitelaw congratulated himself with many a suppressed chuckle as he went about his daily labours, or jogged slowly home from market in his chaise-cart.

As to his wife's feelings towards himself, whether those were cold indifference or hidden dislike, that was an abstruse and remote question which Mr. Whitelaw never took the trouble to ask himself. She was his wife. He had won her, that was the grand point; whatever disinclination she might have felt for the alliance, whatever love she might have cherished for another, had been trampled down and subjugated, and he, Stephen Whitelaw, had obtained the desire of his heart. He had won her, against that penniless young jackanapes, lawyer Randall's son, who had treated him with marked contempt on more than one occasion when they happened to come across each other in Malsham Corn-exchange, which was held in the great covered quadrangular courtyard of the chief inn at Malsham, and was a popular lounge for the inhabitants of that town. He had won her; her own sentiments upon the subject of this marriage were of very little consequence. He had never expected to be loved by his wife, his own ideas of that passion called love being of the vaguest; but he meant to be obeyed by her. She had begun well, had taken her new duties upon herself in a manner that gladdened his sordid soul; and although they had been married nearly a fortnight, she had given no hint of a desire to know the extent of his wealth, or where he kept any little hoard of ready money that he might have by him in the house. Nor on market-day had she expressed any wish to go with him to Malsham to spend money on drapery; and he had an idea, sedulously cultivated by Mrs. Tadman, that young women were perpetually wanting to spend money at drapers' shops. Altogether, that first fortnight of his married life had been most satisfactory, and Mr. Whitelaw was inclined to regard matrimony as a wise and profitable institution.

The day's work was done, and Ellen was sitting with Mrs. Tadman in the every-day parlour, waiting for the return of her lord and master from Malsham. It was not a market-day, but Stephen Whitelaw had announced at dinner-time that he had an appointment at Malsham, and had set out immediately after dinner in the chaise-cart, much to the wonderment of Mrs. Tadman, who was an inveterate gossip, and never easy until she arrived at the bottom of any small household mystery. She wondered not a little also at Ellen's supreme indifference to her husband's proceedings.

"I can't for the life of me think what's taken him to Malsham to-day," she said, as she plied her rapid knitting-needles in the manufacture of a gray-worsted stocking. "I haven't known him go to Malsham, except of a market-day, not once in a twelvemonth. It must be a rare business to take him there in the middle of the week; for he can't abide to leave the farm in working-hours, except when he's right down obliged to it. Nothing goes on the same when his back's turned, he says; there's always something wrong. And if it was an appointment with any one belonging to Malsham, why couldn't it have stood over till Saturday? It must be something out of the common that won't keep a couple of days."

Mrs. Tadman went on with her knitting, gazing at Ellen with an expectant countenance, waiting for her to make some suggestion. But the girl was quite silent, and there was a blank expression in her eyes, which looked out across the level stretch of grass between the house and the river, a look that told Mrs. Tadman very few of her words had been heard by her companion. It was quite disheartening to talk to such a person; but the widow went on nevertheless, being so full of her subject that she must needs talk to some one, even if that some one were little better than a stock or a stone.

"There was a letter that came for Stephen before dinner to-day; he got it when he came in, but it was lying here for an hour first. Perhaps it was that as took him to Malsham; and yet that's strange, for it was a London letter—and it don't seem likely as any one could be coming down from London to meet Steph at Malsham. I can't make top nor tail of it."

Mrs. Tadman laid down her knitting, and gave the fire a vigorous stir. She wanted some vent for her vexation; for it was really too provoking to see Ellen Whitelaw sitting staring out of the window like a lifeless statue, and not taking the faintest interest in the mystery of her husband's conduct. She stirred the fire, and then busied herself with the tea-table, giving a touch here and there where no re-arrangement was wanted, for the sake of doing something.

The room looked comfortable enough in the cold light of the spring afternoon. It was the most occupied room in the house, and the least gloomy. The glow of a good fire brightened the scanty shabby furniture a little, and the table, with its white cloth, homely flowered cups and saucers, bright metal teapot, and substantial fare in the way of ham and home-made bread, had a pleasant look enough in the eyes of any one coming in from a journey through the chill March atmosphere. Mr. Whitelaw's notion of tea was a solid meal, which left him independent of the chances of supper, and yet open to do something in that way; in case any light kickshaw, such as liver and bacon, a boiled sheep's head, or a beef-steak pie, should present itself to his notice.

Ellen roused herself from her long reverie at last. There was the sound of wheels upon the cart-track across the wide open field in front of the house.

"Here comes Mr. Whitelaw," she said, looking out into the gathering dusk; "and there's some one with him."

"Some one with him!" cried Mrs. Tadman. "Why, my goodness, who can that be?"

She ran to the window and peered eagerly out. The cart had driven up to the door by this time, and Mr. Whitelaw and his companion were alighting. The stranger was rather a handsome man, Mrs. Tadman saw at the first glance, tall and broad-shouldered, clad in dark-gray trousers, a short pilot-coat, and a wide-awake hat; but with a certain style even in this rough apparel which was not the style of agricultural Malsham, an unmistakable air that belongs to a dweller in great cities.

"I never set eyes upon him before," exclaimed Mrs. Tadman, aghast with wonder; for visitors at Wyncomb were of the rarest, and an unknown visitor above all things marvellous.

Mr. Whitelaw opened the house-door, which opened straight into a little lobby between the two parlours. There was a larger door and a spacious stone entrance-hall at one end of the house; but that door had not been opened within the memory of man, and the hall was only used as a storehouse now-a-days. There was some little mumbling talk in the lobby before the two men came in, and then Mrs. Tadman's curiosity was relieved by a closer view of the stranger.

Yes, he was certainly handsome, remarkably handsome even, for a man whose youth was past; but there was something in his face, a something sinister and secret, as it were, which did not strike Mrs. Tadman favourably. She could not by any means have explained the nature of her sensations on looking at him, but, as she said afterwards, she felt all in a moment that he was there for no good. And yet he was very civil-spoken too, and addressed both the ladies in a most conciliating tone, and with a kind of florid politeness.

Ellen looked at him, interested for the moment in spite of her apathetic indifference to all things. The advent of a stranger was something so rare as to awaken a faint interest in the mind most dead to impressions. She did not like his manner; there was something false and hollow in his extreme politeness. And his face—what was it in his face that startled her with such a sudden sense of strangeness and yet of familiarity?

Had she ever seen him before? Yes; surely that was the impression which sent such a sudden shook through her nerves, which startled her from her indifference into eager wonder and perplexity. Where had she seen him before? Where and when? Long ago, or only very lately? She could not tell. Yet it seemed to her that she had looked at eyes like those, not once, but many times in her life. And yet the man was utterly strange to her. That she could have seen him before appeared impossible. It must have been some one like him she had seen, then. Yes, that was it. It was the shadow of another face in his that had startled her with so strange a feeling, almost as if she had been looking upon some ghostly thing. Another face, like and yet unlike.

But what face? whose face?

She could not answer that question, and her inability to solve the enigma tormented her all tea-time, as the stranger sat opposite to her, making a pretence of eating heartily, in accordance with Mr. Whitelaw's hospitable invitation, while that gentleman himself ploughed away with a steady persistence that made awful havoc with the ham, and reduced the loaf in a manner suggestive of Jack the Giant-killer.

The visitor presently ventured to remark that tea-drinking was not much in his way, and that, if it were all the same to Mr. Whitelaw, he should prefer a glass of brandy-and-water; whereupon the brandy-bottle was produced from a cupboard by the fire-place, of which Stephen himself kept the key, judiciously on his guard against a possible taste for ardent spirits developing itself in Mrs. Tadman.

After this the stranger sat for some time, drinking cold brandy-and-water, and staring moodily at the fire, without making the faintest attempt at conversation, while Mr. Whitelaw finished his tea, and the table was cleared; and even after this, when the farmer had taken his place upon the opposite side of the hearth, and seemed to be waiting for his guest to begin business.

He was not a lively stranger; he seemed, indeed, to have something on his mind, to be brooding upon some trouble or difficulty, as Mrs. Tadman remarked to her kinsman's wife afterwards. Both the women watched him; Ellen always perplexed by that unknown likeness, which seemed sometimes to grow stronger, sometimes to fade away altogether, as she looked at him; Mrs. Tadman in a rabid state of curiosity, so profound was the mystery of his silent presence.

What was he there for? What could Stephen want with him? He was not one of Stephen's sort, by any means; had no appearance of association with agricultural interests. And yet there he was, a silent inexplicable presence, a mysterious figure with a moody brow, which seemed to grow darker as Mrs. Tadman watched him.

At last, about an hour after the tea-table had been cleared, he rose suddenly, with an abrupt gesture, and said,

"Come, Whitelaw, if you mean to show me this house of yours, you may as well show it to me at once."

His voice had a harsh unpleasant sound as he said this. He stood with his back to the women, staring at the fire, while Stephen Whitelaw lighted a candle in his slow dawdling way.

"Be quick, man alive," the stranger cried impatiently, turning sharply round upon the farmer, who was trimming an incorrigible wick with a pair of blunted snuffers. "Remember, I've got to go back to Malsham; I haven't all the night to waste."

"I don't want to set my house afire," Mr. Whitelaw answered sullenly; "though, perhaps, *you* might like that. It might suit your book, you see."

The stranger gave a sudden shudder, and told the farmer with an angry oath to "drop that sort of insolence."

"And now show the way, and look sharp about it," he said in an authoritative tone.

They went out of the room in the next moment. Mrs. Tadman gazed after them, or rather at the door which had closed upon them, with a solemn awe-stricken stare.

"I don't like the look of it, Ellen," she said; "I don't at all like the look of it."

"What do you mean?" the girl asked indifferently.

"I don't like the hold that man has got over Stephen, nor the way he speaks to him—almost as if Steph was a dog. Did you hear him just now? And what does he want to see the house for, I should like to know? What can this house matter to him, unless he was going to buy it? That's it, perhaps, Ellen. Stephen has been speculating, and has gone and ruined himself, and that strange man is going to buy Wyncomb. He gave me a kind of turn the minute I looked at him. And, depend upon it, he's come to turn us all out of house and home."

Ellen gave a faint shudder. What if her father's wicked scheming were to come to such an end as this! what if she had been sold into bondage, and the master to whom she had been given had not even the wealth which had been held before her as a bait in her misery! For herself she cared little whether she were rich or poor. It could make but a difference of detail in the fact of her unhappiness, whether she were mistress of Wyncomb or a homeless tramp upon the country roads. The workhouse without Stephen Whitelaw must needs be infinitely preferable to Wyncomb Farm with him. And for her father, it seemed only a natural and justifiable thing that his guilt and his greed should be so punished. He had sold his daughter into life-long slavery for nothing but that one advance of two hundred pounds. He had saved himself from the penalty of his dishonesty, however, by that sacrifice; and would, no doubt, hold his daughter's misery lightly enough, even if poverty were added to the wretchedness of her position.

The two women sat down on opposite sides of the hearth; Mrs. Tadman, too anxious to go on with her accustomed knitting, only able to wring her hands in a feeble way, and groan every now and then, or from time to time burst into some fragmentary speech.

"And Stephen's just the man to have such a thing on his mind and keep it from everybody till the last moment," she cried piteously. "And so many speculations as there are now-a-days to tempt a man to his ruin—railways and mines, and loans to Turks and Red Indians and such-like foreigners; and Steph might so easy be tempted by the hope of larger profits than he can make by farming."

"But it's no use torturing yourself like that with fears that may be quite groundless," Ellen said at last, rousing herself a little in order to put a stop to the wailing and lamentations of her companion. "There's no use in anticipating trouble. There may be nothing in this business after all. Mr. Whitelaw may have a fancy for showing people his house. He wanted me to see it, if you remember, that new-year's afternoon."

"Yes; but that was different. He meant to marry you. Why should he want to show the place to a stranger? I can't believe but what that strange man is here for something, and something bad. I saw it in his face when he first came in."

It was useless arguing the matter; Mrs. Tadman was evidently not to be shaken; so Ellen said no more; and they sat on in silence, each occupied with her own thoughts.

Ellen's were not about Stephen Whitelaw's financial condition, but they were very sad ones. She had received a letter from Frank Randall since her marriage; a most bitter letter, upbraiding her for her falsehood and desertion, and accusing her of being actuated by mercenary motives in her marriage with Stephen Whitelaw.

"How often have I heard you express your detestation of that fellow!" the young man wrote indignantly. "How often have I heard you declare that no earthly persuasion should ever induce you to marry him! And yet before my back has been turned six months, I hear that you are his wife. Without a word of warning, without a line of explanation to soften the blow—if anything could soften it—the news comes to me, from a stranger who knew nothing of my love for you. It is very hard, Ellen; all the harder because I had so fully trusted in your fidelity."

"I will own that the prospect I had to offer you was a poor one; involving long delay before I could give you such a home as I wanted to give you; but O, Nelly, Nelly, I felt so sure that you would be true to me! And if you found yourself in any difficulty, worried beyond your power of resistance by your father—though I did not think you were the kind of girl to yield weakly to persuasion—a line from you would have brought me to your side, ready to defend you from any persecution, and only too proud to claim you for my wife, and carry you away from your father's unkindness."

The letter went on for some time in the same upbraiding strain. Ellen shed many bitter tears over it in the quiet of her own room. It had been delivered to her secretly by her old friend Sarah Peters, the miller's daughter, who had been the confidante of her love affairs; for even in his indignation Mr. Randall had been prudent enough to consider that such a missive, falling perchance into Stephen Whitelaw's hands, might work serious mischief.

Cruel as the letter was, Ellen could not leave it quite unanswered; some word in her own defence she must needs write; but her reply was of the briefest.

"There are some things that can never be explained," she wrote, "and my marriage is one of those. No one could save me from it, you least of all. There was no help for me; and I believe, with all my heart, that, in acting as I did, I only did my duty. I had not the courage to write to you beforehand to tell you what was going to be. I thought it was almost better you should hear it from a stranger. The more hardly you think of me, the easier it will be for you to forget me. There is some comfort in that. I daresay it will be very easy for you to forget. But if, in days to come, when you are happily married to some one else, you can teach yourself to think more kindly of me, and to believe that in what I did I acted for the best, you will be performing an act of charity towards a poor unhappy girl, who has very little left to hope for in this world."

It was a hard thing for Ellen to think that, in the estimation of the man she loved, she must for ever seem the basest and most mercenary of womankind; and yet how poor an excuse could she offer in the vague pleading of her letter! She could not so much as hint at the truth; she could not blacken her father's character. That Frank Randall should despise her, only made her trial a little sharper, her daily burden a little heavier, she told herself.

With her mind full of these thoughts, she had very little sympathy to bestow upon Mrs. Tadman, whose fragmentary lamentations only worried her, like the murmurs of some troublesome not-to-be-pacified child; whereby that doleful person, finding her soul growing heavier and heavier, for lack of counsel or consolation, could at last endure this state of suspense no longer in sheer inactivity, but was fain to bestir herself somehow, if even in the most useless manner. She got up from her seat therefore, went over to the door, and, softly opening it, peered out into the darkness beyond.

There was nothing, no glimmer of Stephen's candle, no sound of men's footsteps or of men's voices; the merest blankness, and no more. The two men had been away from the parlour something more than half an hour by this time.

For about five minutes Mrs. Tadman stood at the open door, peering out and listening, and still without result. Then, with a shrill sudden sound through the long empty passages, there came a shriek, a prolonged piercing cry of terror or of pain, which turned Mrs. Tadman's blood to ice, and brought Ellen to her side, pale and breathless.

"What was that?"

"What was that?"

Both uttered the same question simultaneously, looking at each other aghast, and then both fled in the direction from which that shrill cry had come.

A woman's voice surely; no masculine cry ever sounded with such piercing treble.

They hurried off to discover the meaning of this startling sound, but were neither of them very clear as to whence it had come. From the upper story no doubt, but in that rambling habitation there was so much scope for uncertainty. They ran together, up the staircase most used, to the corridor from which the principal rooms opened. Before they could reach the top of the stairs, they heard a scuffling hurrying sound of heavy footsteps on the floor above them, and on the landing met Mr. Whitelaw and his unknown friend; face to face.

"What's the matter?" asked the farmer sharply, looking angrily at the two scared faces.

"That's just what we want to know," his wife answered. "Who was it that screamed just now? Who's been hurt?"

"My friend stumbled against a step in the passage yonder, and knocked his shin. He cried out a bit louder than he need have done, if that's what you mean, but not loud enough to cause all this fuss. Get downstairs again, you two, and keep quiet. I've no patience with such nonsense; coming flying upstairs as if you'd both gone mad."

"It was not your friend's voice we heard," Ellen answered resolutely; "it was a woman's cry. You must have heard it surely, Stephen Whitelaw."

"I heard nothing but what I tell you," the farmer muttered sulkily. "Get downstairs, can't you?"

"Not till I know what's the matter," his wife said, undismayed by his anger. "Give me your light, and let me go and see."

"You can go where you like, wench, and see what you can; and an uncommon deal wiser you'll be for your trouble."

And yet, although Mr. Whitelaw gave his wife the candlestick with an air of profound indifference, there was an uneasy look in his countenance which she could plainly see, and which perplexed her not a little.

"Come, Mrs. Tadman," she said decisively, "we had better see into this. It was a woman's voice, and must have been one of the girls, I suppose. It may be nothing serious, after all,—these country girls scream out for a very little,—but we'd better get to the bottom of it."

Mr. Whitelaw burst into a laugh—and he was a man whose laughter was as unpleasant as it was rare.

"Ay, my wench, you'd best get to the bottom of it," he said, "since you're so uncommon clever. Me and my friend will go back to the parlour, and take a glass of grog."

The gentleman whom Mr. Whitelaw honoured with his friendship had stood a little way apart all this time, wiping his forehead with a big orange coloured silk handkerchief. That blow upon his shin must have been rather a sharp one, if it had brought that cold sweat out upon his ashen face.

"Yes," he muttered; "come along, can't you? don't stand cawing here all night;" and hurried downstairs before his host.

It had been all the business of a couple of minutes. Ellen Whitelaw and Mrs. Tadman went down to the ground floor by another staircase leading directly to the kitchen. The room looked comfortable enough, and the two servant-girls were sitting at a table near the fire. One was a strapping rosy-cheeked country girl, who did all the household work; the other an overgrown clumsy-looking girl, hired straight from the workhouse by Mr. Whitelaw, from economical motives; a stolid-looking girl, whose intellect was of the lowest order; a mere zoophyte girl, one would say—something between the vegetable and animal creation.

This one, whose name was Sarah Batts, was chiefly employed in the poultry-yard and dairy. She had a broad brawny hand, which was useful for the milking of cows, and showed some kind of intelligence in the management of young chickens and the treatment of refractory hens.

Martha Holden, the house-servant, was busy making herself a cap as her mistress came into the kitchen, droning some Hampshire ballad by way of accompaniment to her work. Sarah Batts was seated in an attitude of luxurious repose, with her arms folded, and her feet on the fender.

"Was it either of you girls that screamed just now?" Ellen asked anxiously.

"Screamed, ma'am! no, indeed," Martha Holden answered, with an air of perfect good faith. "What should we scream for? I've been sitting here at my work for the last hour, as quiet as could be."

"And, Sarah,—was it you, Sarah? For goodness' sake tell the truth."

"Me, mum! lor no, mum. I was up with master showing him and the strange gentleman a light."

"You were upstairs with your master? And did you hear nothing? A piercing shriek that rang through the house;—you must surely have heard it, both of you."

Martha shook her head resolutely.

"Not me, mum; I didn't hear a sound. The kitchen-door was shut all the time Sarah was away, and I was busy at work, and thinking of nothing but my work. I wasn't upon the listen, as you may say."

The kitchen was at the extreme end of the house, remote from that direction whence the unexplainable cry seemed to have come.

"It is most extraordinary," Ellen said gravely, perplexed beyond all measure. "But you, Sarah; if you were upstairs with your master, you must surely have heard that shriek; it seemed to come from upstairs."

"Did master hear it?" asked the girl deliberately.

"He says not."

"Then how should I, mum? No, mum, I didn't hear nothink; I can take my Bible oath of that."

"I don't want any oaths; I only want to know the meaning of this business. There would have been no harm in your screaming. You might just as well speak the truth about it."

"Lor, mum, but it warn't me," answered Sarah Batts with an injured look. "Whatever could go to put it in your head as it was me?"

"It must have been one or other of you two girls. There's no other woman in the house; and as you were upstairs, it seems more likely to have been you. However, there's no use talking any more about it. Only we both heard the scream, didn't we, Mrs. Tadman?"

"I should think we did, indeed," responded the widow with a vehement shudder. "My flesh is all upon the creep at this very moment. I don't think I ever had such a turn in my life."

They went back to the parlour, leaving the two servants still sitting by the fire; Sarah Batts with that look of injured innocence fixed upon her wooden countenance, Martha Holden cheerfully employed in the construction of her Sunday cap. In the parlour the two men were both standing by the table, the stranger with his back to the women as they entered, Stephen Whitelaw facing him. The former seemed to have been counting something, but stopped abruptly as the women came into the room.

There was a little heap of bank-notes lying on the table. Stephen snatched them up hastily, and thrust them in a bundle into his waistcoat-pocket; while the stranger put a strap round a bulky red morocco pocket-book with a more deliberate air, as of one who had nothing to hide from the world.

That guilty furtive air of Stephen's, and, above all, that passage of money between the two men, confirmed Mrs. Tadman in her notion that Wyncomb Farm was going to change hands. She resumed her seat by the fire with a groan, and accepted Ellen's offer of a glass of spirits-and-water with a doleful shake of her head.

"Didn't I tell you so?" she whispered, as Mrs. Whitelaw handed her the comforting beverage.

The stranger was evidently on the point of departure. There was a sound of wheels on the gravel outside the parlour window—the familiar sound of Stephen Whitelaw's chaise-cart; and that gentleman was busy helping his visitor on with his great-coat.

"I shall be late for the last train," said the stranger, "unless your man drives like the very devil."

"He'll drive fast enough, I daresay, if you give him half-a-crown," Mr. Whitelaw answered with a grin; "but don't let him go and do my horse any damage, or you'll have to pay for it."

"Of course. You'd like to get the price of a decent animal out of me for that broken-kneed hard-mouthed brute of yours," replied the stranger with a scornful laugh. "I think there never was such a money-grubbing, grinding, grasping beggar since the world began. However, you've seen the last shilling you're ever likely to get out of me; so make the best of it; and remember, wherever I may be, there are friends of mine in this country who will keep a sharp look-out upon you, and let me know precious quick if you don't stick to your part of our bargain like an honest man, or as nearly like one as nature will allow you to come. And now good-night, Mr. Whitelaw.—Ladies, your humble servant."

He was gone before Ellen or Mrs. Tadman could reply to his parting salutation, had they been disposed to do so. Mr. Whitelaw went out with him, and gave some final directions to the stable-lad who was to drive the chaise-cart, and presently came back to the parlour, looking considerably relieved by his guest's departure.

Mrs. Tadman rushed at once to the expression of her fears.

"Stephen Whitelaw," she exclaimed solemnly, "tell us the worst at once. It's no good keeping things back from us. That man has come here to turn us out of house and home. You've sold Wyncomb."

"Sold Wyncomb! Have you gone crazy, you old fool?" cried Mr. Whitelaw, contemplating his kinswoman with a most evil expression of countenance. "What's put that stuff in your head?"

"Your own doings, Stephen, and that man's. What does he come here for, with his masterful ways, unless it's to turn us out of house and home? What did you show him the house for? Nigh upon an hour you were out of this room with him, if you were a minute. Why did money pass from him to you? I saw you put it in your pocket—a bundle of bank-notes."

"You're a prying old catemeran!" cried Mr. Whitelaw savagely, "and a drunken old fool into the bargain.—Why do you let her muddle herself with the gin-bottle like that, Ellen? You ought to have more respect for my property. You don't call that taking care of your husband's house.—As for you, mother Tadman, if you treat me to any more of this nonsense, you will find yourself turned out of house and home a precious deal sooner than you bargained for; but it won't be because of my selling Wyncomb. Sell Wyncomb, indeed! I've about as much thought of going up in a balloon, as of parting with a rood or a perch of my father's land."

This was a very long speech for Mr. Whitelaw; and, having finished it, he sank into his chair, quite exhausted by the unusual effort, and refreshed himself with copious libations of gin-and-water.

"What was that man here for, then, Stephen? It's only natural I should want to know that," said Mrs. Tadman, abashed, but not struck dumb by her kinsman's reproof.

"What's that to you? Business. Yes, there *has* been money pass between us, and it's rather a profitable business for me. Perhaps it was horse-racing, perhaps it wasn't. That's about all you've any call to know. I've made money by it, and not lost. And now, don't let me be bothered about it any more, if you and me are to keep friends."

"I'm sure, Stephen," Mrs. Tadman remonstrated in a feebly plaintive tone, "I've no wish to bother you; there's nothing farther from my thoughts; but it's only natural that I should be anxious about a place where I've lived so many years. Not but what I could get my living easy enough elsewhere, as you must know, Stephen, being able to turn my hand to almost anything."

To this feeble protest Mr. Whitelaw vouchsafed no answer. He had lighted his pipe by this time, and was smoking and staring at the fire with his usual stolid air—meditative, it might be, or only ruminant, like one of his own cattle.

But all through that night Mr. Whitelaw, who was not commonly a seer of visions or dreamer of dreams, had his slumbers disturbed by some unwonted perplexity of spirit. His wife lay broad awake, thinking of that prolonged and piercing cry, which seemed to her, the more she meditated upon it, in have been a cry of anguish or of terror, and could not fail to notice this unusual disturbance of her husband's sleep. More than once he muttered to himself in a troubled manner; but his words, for the most part, were incoherent and disjointed—words of which that perplexed listener could make nothing.

Once she heard him say, "A bad job—dangerous business."

CHAPTER XL.
IN PURSUIT.

JOHN Saltram improved daily at Hampton Court. In spite of his fierce impatience to get well, in order to engage in the search for Marian—an impatience which was in itself sufficient to militate against his well-being—he did make considerable progress on the road to recovery. He was still very weak, and it must take time to complete his restoration; but he was no longer the pale ghost of his former self that Gilbert had brought down to the quiet suburb.

It would have been a cruel thing to leave him much alone at such a time, or it would have seemed very cruel to Gilbert Fenton, who had ever present in his memory those old days in Egypt when this man had stood him in such good stead. He remembered the days of his own sickness, and contrived to perform his business duties within the smallest time possible, and so spend the rest of his life in the comfortable sitting-rooms looking out upon Bushy-park on the one side, and on the other upon the pretty high road before the Palace grounds.

Nor was there any sign in the intercourse of those two that the bond of friendship between them was broken. There was, it is true, a something deprecating in John Saltram's manner that had not been common to him of old, and in Gilbert Fenton a deeper gravity than was quite natural; but that was all. It was difficult to believe that any latent spirit of animosity could lurk in the mind of either. In sober truth, Gilbert, in his heart of hearts, had forgiven his treacherous friend. Again and again he had told himself that the wrong he had suffered was an unpardonable offence, a thing not to be forgiven upon any ground whatever. But, lo, when he looked into his mind to discover the smouldering fires of that burning anger which he had felt at first against the traitor, he could find nothing but the gray ashes of a long-expired flame. The wrong had been suffered, and he loved his old friend still. Yes, there was that in his heart for John Saltram which no ill-doing could blot out.

So he tended the convalescent's couch with a quiet devotion that touched the sinner very deeply, and there was a peace between those two which had in it something almost sacred. In the mind of the one there was a remorseful sense of guilt, in the heart of the other a pitying tenderness too deep for words.

One night, as they were together on opposite sides of the fire, John Saltram lying on a low sofa drawn close to the hearth, Gilbert seated lazily in an easy-chair, the invalid broke out suddenly into a kind of apology for his wrong-doing.

The conversation had flagged between them after the tea-things had been removed by the brisk little serving-maid of the lodgings; Gilbert gazing meditatively at the fire, John Saltram so quiet that his companion had thought him asleep.

"I said once that I would tell you all about that business," he began at last, in a sudden spasmodic way; "but, after all there is so little to tell. There is no excuse for what I did; I know that better than you can know it. A man in my position, who had a spark of generosity or honour, would have strangled his miserable passion in its birth, would have gone away directly he discovered his folly, and never looked upon Marian Nowell's face again. I did try to do that, Gilbert. You remember that last night we ever spent together at Lidford—what a feverishly-happy night it was; only a cottage-parlour with a girl's bright face shining in the lamplight, and a man over head and ears in love, but a glimpse of paradise to that man. I meant that it should be the last of my weakness, Gilbert. I had pledged myself to that by all the outspoken oaths wherewith a man can bind himself to do his duty. And I did turn my back upon the scene of my temptation, as you know, heartily resolved never to approach the edge of the pit again. I think if you had stayed in England, Gilbert, if you had been on the spot to defend your own rights, all would have gone well, I should have kept the promise I had made for myself."

"It was so much the more sacred because of my absence, John," Gilbert said.

"Perhaps. After all, I suppose it was only a question of opportunity. That particular devil who tempts men to their dishonour contrived that the business should be made fatally easy for me. You were away, and the coast was clear, you know. I loved you, Gilbert; but there is a passion stronger than the love which a man feels for his dearest friend. I meant most steadfastly to keep my faith with you; but you were away, and that fellow Forster plagued me to come to him. I refused at first—yes, I held out for a couple of months; but the fever was strong upon me—a restless demon not to be exorcised by hard work, or dissipation even, for I tried both. And then before you were at the end of your journey, while you were still a wanderer across the desolate sea, happy in the thought of your dear love's fidelity, my courage gave way all at once, and I went down to Heatherly. And so I saw her, and saw that she loved me—all unworthy as I was; and from that hour I was a lost man; I thought of nothing but winning her."

"If you had only been true to me, even then, John; if you had written to me declaring the truth, and giving me fair warning that you were my rival, how much better it would have been! Think what a torture of suspense, what a world of wasted anger, you might have saved me."

"Yes, it would have been the manlier course, no doubt," the other answered; "but I could not bring myself to that. I could not face the idea of your justifiable wrath. I wanted to win my wife and keep my friend. It was altogether a weak notion, that idea of secrecy, of course, and couldn't hold water for any time, as the result has shown; but I thought you would get over your disappointment quickly—those wounds are apt to heal so speedily—and fall in love elsewhere; and then it would have been easy for me to tell you the truth. So I persuaded my dear love, who was easily induced to do anything I wished, to consent to our secret being kept from you religiously for the time being, and to that end we were married under a false name—not exactly a false name either. You remember my asking you if you had ever heard the name of Holbrook before your hunt after Marian's husband? You said no; yet I think you must have seen the name in some of my old college books. I was christened John Holbrook. My grandmother was one of the Holbrooks of Horley-place, Sussex, people of some importance in their day, and our family were rather proud of the name. But I have dropped it ever since I was a lad."

"No, I don't think I can ever have seen the name; I must surely have remembered it, if I had seen it."

"Perhaps so. Well, Gilbert, there is no more to be said. I loved her, selfishly, after the manner of mankind. I could not bring myself to give her up, and pursued her with a passionate persistence which must plead *her* excuse. If her uncle had lived, I doubt whether I should ever have succeeded. But his death left the tender womanly heart weakened by sorrow; and so I won her, the dearest, truest wife that ever man was blest withal. Yet, I confess to you, so wayward is my nature, that there have been moments in which I repented my triumph—weak hours of doubt and foreboding, in which I fear that dear girl divined my thoughts. Since our wretched separation I have fancied sometimes that a conviction of this kind on her part is at the root of the business, that she has alienated herself from me, believing—in plain words—that I was tired of her."

"Such an idea as that would scarcely agree with Ellen Carley's account of Marian's state of mind during that last day or two at the Grange. She was eagerly expecting your return, looking forward with delight to the pleasant surprise you were to experience when you heard of Jacob Nowell's will."

"Yes, the girl told me that. Great heavens, why did I not return a few days earlier! I was waiting for money, not caring to go back empty-handed; writing and working like a nigger. I dared not meet my poor girl at her grandfather's, since in so doing I must risk an encounter with you."

After this they talked of Marian's disappearance for some time, going over the same ground very often in their helplessness, and able, at last, to arrive at no satisfactory conclusion. If she were with her father, she was with a bad, unscrupulous man. That was a fact which Gilbert Fenton no longer pretended to deny. They sat talking till late, and parted for the night in very different spirits.

Gilbert had a good deal of hard work in the City on the following day; a batch of foreign correspondence too important to be entrusted to a clerk, and two or three rather particular interviews. All this occupied him up to so late an hour, that he was obliged to sleep in London that night, and to defer his return to Hampton till the next day's business was over. This time he got over his work by an early hour, and was able to catch a train that left Waterloo at half-past five. He felt a little uneasy at having been away from the convalescent so long though he knew that John Saltram was now strong enough to get on tolerably without him, and that the people of the house were careful and kindly, ready at any moment to give assistance if it were wanted.

"Strange," he thought to himself, as the train approached the quiet, riverside village—"strange that I should be so fond of the fellow, in spite of all; that I should care more for his society than that of any man living. It is the mere force of habit, I suppose. After all these years of liking, the link between us is not to be broken, even by the deepest wrong that one man can do another."

The spring twilight was closing in as he crossed the bridge and walked briskly along an avenue of leafless trees at the side of the green. The place had a peaceful rustic look at this dusky hour. There were no traces of that modern spoiler the speculative builder just hereabouts; and the quaint old houses near the barracks, where lights were twinkling feebly here and there, had a look of days that are gone, a touch of that plaintive poetry which pervades all relics of the past. Gilbert felt the charm of the hour; the air still and mild, the silence only broken by the cawing of palatial rooks; and whatever tenderness towards John Saltram there was lurking in his breast seemed to grow upon him as he drew nearer to their lodgings; so that his mood was of the softest when he opened the little garden-gate and went in.

"I will make no further pretence of enmity," he said to himself; "I will not keep up this farce of estrangement. We two will be friends once more. Life is not long enough for the rupture of such a friendship."

There was no light shining in the parlour window, no pleasant home-glow streaming out upon the night. The blank created by this unwonted darkness chilled him somehow, and there was a vague sense of dread in his mind as he opened the door. There was no need to knock. The simple household was untroubled by the fear of burglariously-disposed intruders, and the door was rarely fastened until after dark.

Gilbert went into the parlour; all was dark and silent in the two rooms, which communicated with folding doors, and made one fair-sized apartment. There were no preparations for dinner; he could see that in the deepening dusk. The fire had been evidently neglected, and was at an expiring point.

"John!" he called, stirring the fire with a vigorous hand, whereby he gave it the *coup-de-grace*, and the last glimmer sank to darkness. "John, what are you doing?"

He fancied the convalescent had fallen asleep upon the sofa in the inner room; but when he went in search of him, he found nothing but emptiness. He rang the bell violently, and the brisk maid-servant came flying in.

"Oh, dear, sir, you did give me and missus such a turn!" she said, gasping, with her hand on her heart, as if that organ had been seriously affected. "We never heard you come in, and when the bell rung——"

"Is Mr. Saltram worse?" Gilbert asked, eagerly.

"Worse, poor dear gentleman; no, sir, I should hope not, though he well may be, for there never was any one so imprudent, not of all the invalids I've ever had to do with—and Hampton is a rare place for invalids. And I feel sure if you'd been here, sir, you wouldn't have let him do it."

"Let him do what? Are you crazy, girl? What, in heaven's name, are you talking of?"

"You wouldn't have let him start off to London post-haste, as he did yesterday afternoon, and scarcely able to stand alone, in a manner of speaking."

"Gone to London! Do you mean to say that my friend Mr. Saltram went to London?"

"Yes, sir; yesterday afternoon between four and five."

"What utter madness! And when did he come back?"

"Lor' bless you, sir, he ain't come back yet. He told missus as his coming back was quite uncertain, and she was not to worry herself about him. She did all she could, almost to going down on her knees, to hinder him going; but it was no use. It was a matter of life and death as he was going upon, he said, and that there was no power on earth could keep him back, not if he was ten times worse than he was. The strange gentleman hadn't been in the house much above a quarter of an hour, when they was both off together in a fly to the station."

"What strange gentleman?"

"A stout middle-aged man, sir, with gray whiskers, that came from London, and asked for you first, and then for Mr. Saltram; and those two hadn't been together more than five minutes, when Mr. Saltram rang the bell in a violent hurry, and told my missus he was going to town immediate, on most particular business, and would she pack him a carpet-bag with a couple of shirts, and so on. And then she tried all she could to turn him from going; but it was no good, as I was telling you, sir, just now. Go he would, and go he did; looking quite flushed and bright-like when he went out, so as you'd have scarcely known how ill he'd been. And he left a bit of a note for you on the chimbley-piece, sir."

Gilbert found the note; a hurried scrawl upon half a sheet of paper, twisted up hastily, and unsealed.

"She is found, Gilbert," wrote John Saltram. "Proul has traced the father to his lair at last, and my darling is with him. They are lodging at 14, Coleman-street, Tottenham-court-road. I am off this instant. Don't be angry with me, true and faithful friend; I could not rest an hour away from her now that she is found. I have no plan of action, but leave all to the inspiration of the moment. You can follow me whenever you please. Marian must thank you for your goodness to me. Marian must persuade you to forgive my sin against you—Ever yours, J.S."

Follow him! yes, of course. Gilbert had no other thought. And she was found at last, after all their suspense, their torturing anxiety. She was found; and whatever danger there might be in her association with Percival Nowell, she was safe so far, and would be speedily extricated from the perilous alliance by her husband. It seemed at first so happy a thing that Gilbert could scarcely realise it; and yet, throughout the weary interval of ignorance as to her fate, he had always declared his belief in her safety. Had he been really as confident as he had seemed, as the days had gone by, one after another, without bringing him any tidings of her? had there been no shapeless terror in his mind, no dark dread that when the knowledge came, it might be something worse than ignorance? Yes, now in the sudden fulness of his joy, he knew how much he had feared, how very near he had been to despair.

But John Saltram, what of him? Was it not at the hazard of his life that he had gone upon this sudden journey, reckless and excited, in a fever of hope and delight?

"Providence will surely be good to him," Gilbert thought.

"He bore the journey from town when he was much worse than he is now. Surely he will bear a somewhat rougher journey now, buoyed up by hope."

The landlady came in presently, and insisted upon giving Mr. Fenton her own version of the story which he had just heard from her maid; and a very close and elaborate version it was, though not remarkable for any new facts. He was fain to listen to it with a show of patience, however, and to consent to eat a mutton chop which the good woman insisted upon cooking for him, after his confession that he had eaten nothing since breakfast. He kept telling himself that there was no hurry; that he was not wanted in Coleman-street; that his presence there was a question of his own gratification and nothing else; but the fever in his mind was not to be set at rest go easily. There was a sense of hurry upon him that he could not shake off, argue with himself as wisely as he would.

He took a hasty meal, and started off to the railway station directly afterwards, though there was no train to carry, him back to London for nearly an hour.

It was weary work waiting at the little station, while the keen March wind blew sharply across the unsheltered platform on which Gilbert paced to and fro in his restlessness; weary work waiting, with that sense of hurry and anxiety upon him, not to be shaken off by any effort he could make to take a hopeful view of the future. He tried to think of those two whom he loved best on earth, whose union he had taught himself, by a marvellous effort of unselfishness, to contemplate with serenity, tried to think of them in the supreme happiness of their restoration to each other; but he could not bring his mind to the realisation of this picture. After all those torments of doubt and perplexity which he had undergone during the last three months, the simple fact of Marian's safety seemed too good a thing to be true. He was tortured by a vague sense of the unreality of this relief that had come so suddenly to put an end to all perplexities.

"I feel as if I were the victim of some hoax, some miserable delusion," he said to himself. "Not till I see her, not till I clasp her by the hand, shall I believe that she is really given back to us."

And in his eagerness to do this, to put an end to that slow torture of unreasonable doubt which had come upon him since the reading of John Saltram's letter, the delay at the railway station was an almost intolerable ordeal; but the hour came to an end at last, the place awoke from its blank stillness to a faint show of life and motion, a door or two banged, a countrified-looking young woman with a good many bundles and a band-box came out of the waiting-room and arranged her possessions in readiness for the coming train, a porter emerged lazily from some unknown corner and looked up the line—then, after another five minutes of blankness, there came a hoarse throbbing in the distance, a bell rang, and the up-train panted into the station. It was a slow train, unluckily for Gilbert's impatience, which stopped everywhere, and the journey to London took him over an hour. It was past nine when a hansom drove him into Coleman-street, a dull unfrequented-looking thoroughfare between Tottenham-court-road and Gower-street, overshadowed a little by the adjacent gloom of the University Hospital, and altogether a low-spirited street.

Gilbert looked up eagerly at the windows of Number 14, expecting to see lights shining, and some visible sign of rejoicing, even upon the house front; but there was nothing. Either the shutters were shut, or there was no light within, for the windows were blank and dark. It was a slight thing, but enough to intensify that shapeless foreboding against which he had been struggling throughout his journey.

"You must have come to the wrong house," he said to the cabman as he got out.

"No, sir, this is 14."

Yes, it was the right number. Gilbert read it on the door; and yet it could scarcely be the right house; for tied to the door-handle was a placard with "Apartments" engraved upon it, and this house would hardly be large enough to accommodate other lodgers besides Mr. Nowell and his daughter. Yet there is no knowing the capabilities of a London lodging-house in an obscure quarter, and there might be some vacant garret in the roof, or some dreary two-pair back, dignified by the name of "apartments." Gilbert gave a loud hurried knock. There was a delay which seemed to him interminable, then a hasty shuffling of slipshod feet upon the basement stairs, then the glimmer of a light through the keyhole, the removal of a chain, and at last the opening of the door. It was opened by a young person with her hair dressed in the prevailing fashion, and an air of some gentility, which clashed a little with a certain slatternliness that pervaded her attire. She was rather a pretty girl, but had the faded London look of late hours, and precocious cares, instead of the fresh bloom and girlish brightness which should have belonged to her.

"Did you please to wish to see the apartments, sir?" she asked politely.

"No; I want to see Mr. and Mrs.—the lady and gentleman who are lodging here."

He scarcely knew under what name he ought to ask for Marian. It seemed unnatural to him now to speak of her as Mrs. Holbrook.

"The lady and gentleman, sir!" the girl exclaimed with a surprised air. "There's no one lodging here now. Mr. Nowell and his daughter left yesterday morning."

"Left yesterday morning?"

"Yes, sir. They went away to Liverpool; they are going to America—to New York."

"Mr. Nowell and his daughter, Mrs. Holbrook?"

"Yes, sir, that was the lady's name."

"It's impossible," cried Gilbert; "utterly impossible that Mrs. Holbrook would go to America! She has ties that would keep her in England; a husband whom she would never abandon in that manner. There must be some mistake here."

"O no, indeed, sir, there's no mistake. I saw all the luggage labelled with my own eyes, and the direction was New York by steam-packet *Oronoco*; and Mrs. Holbrook had lots of dresses made, and all sorts of things. And as to her husband, sir, her father told me that he'd treated her very badly, and that she never meant to go back to him again to be made unhappy by him. She was going to New York to live with Mr. Nowell all the rest of her life."

"There must have been some treachery, some underhand work, to bring this about. Did she go of her own free will?"

"O, dear me, yes, sir. Mr. Nowell was kindness itself to her, and she was very fond of him, and pleased to go to America, as far as I could make out."

"And she never seemed depressed or unhappy?"

"I never noticed her being so, sir. They were out a good deal, you see; for Mr. Nowell was a gay gentleman, very fond of pleasure, and he would have Mrs. Holbrook always with him. They were away in Paris ever so long, in January and the beginning of February, but kept on the lodgings all the same. They were very good lodgers."

"Had they many visitors?"

"No, sir; scarcely any one except a gentleman who used to come sometimes of an evening, and sit drinking spirits-and-water with Mr. Nowell; he was his lawyer, I believe, but I never heard his name."

"Did no one come here yesterday to inquire for Mrs. Holbrook towards evening?"

"Yes, sir; there was a gentleman came in a cab. He looked very ill, as pale as death, and was in a dreadful way when he found they were gone. He asked me a great many questions, the same as you've asked me, and I think I never saw any one so cut-up as he seemed. He didn't say much about that either, but it was easy to see it in his face. He wanted to look at the apartments, to see whether he could find anything, an old letter or such-like, that might be a help to him in going after his friends, and mother took him upstairs."

"Did he find anything?"

"No, sir; Mr. Nowell hadn't left so much as a scrap of paper about the place. So the gentleman thanked mother, and went away in the same cab as had brought him."

"Do you know where he was going?"

"I fancy he was going to Liverpool after Mr. Nowell and his daughter. He seemed all in a fever, like a person that's ready to do anything desperate. But I heard him tell the cabman Cavendish-square."

"Cavendish-square! Yes, I can guess where he was going. But what could he want there?" Gilbert said to himself, while the girl stared at him wonderingly, thinking that he, as well as the other gentleman, had gone distraught on account of Mr. Nowell's daughter.

"Thank you for answering my questions so patiently, and good-night," said Gilbert, slipping some silver into her hand; for his quick eye had observed the faded condition of her finery, and a general air of poverty conspicuous in her aspect. "Stay," he added, taking out his card-case; "if you should hear anything farther of these people, I should be much obliged by your sending me word at that address."

"I won't forget, sir; not that I think we're likely to hear any more of them, they being gone straight off to America."

"Perhaps not. But if you do hear anything, let me know."

He had dismissed his cab on alighting in Coleman-street, believing that his journey was ended; but the walk to Cavendish-square was a short one, and he set out at a rapid pace.

The check that had befallen him was a severe one. It seemed a deathblow to all hope, a dreary realization of that vague dread which had pursued him from the first. If Marian had indeed started for America, what new difficulties must needs attend every effort to bring her back; since it was clear that her father's interests were involved in keeping her under his influence, and separating her entirely from her husband. The journey to New York was no doubt intended to secure this state of things. In America, in that vast country, with which this man was familiar with long residence, how easy for him to hide her for ever from her friends! how vain would all inquiries, all researches be likely to prove!

At the ultimate moment, in the hour of hope and rejoicing, he was lost to them irrevocably.

"Yet criminals have been traced upon the other side of the Atlantic, where the police have been prompt to follow them," Gilbert said to himself, glancing for an instant at the more hopeful side of the question; "but not often where they've got anything like a start. Did John Saltram really mean to follow those two to Liverpool, I wonder? Such a journey would seem like madness, in his state; and yet what a triumph if he should have been in time to prevent their starting by the *Oronoco*!"

And then, after a pause, he asked himself,

"What could he want with Mrs. Branston, at a time when every moment was precious? Money, perhaps. He could have had none with him. Yes, money, no doubt; but I shall discover that from her presently, and may learn something of his plans into the bargain."

Gilbert went into a stationer's shop and purchased a *Bradshaw*. There was a train leaving Euston station for Liverpool at a quarter to eleven. He might be in time for that, after seeing Mrs. Branston. That lady happened fortunately to be at home, and received Gilbert alone in her favourite back drawing-room, where he found her ensconced in that snug retreat made by the six-leaved Japanese screen, which formed a kind of temple on one side of the fire-place. There had been a final rupture between Adela and Mrs. Pallinson a few days before, and that matron, having shown her cards a little too plainly, had been routed by an unwonted display of spirit on the part of the pretty little widow. She was gone, carrying all her belongings with her, and leaving peace and liberty behind her. The flush of triumph was still upon Mrs. Branston; and this unexpected victory, brief and sudden in its occurrence, like most great victories, was almost a consolation to her for that disappointment which had stricken her so heavily of late.

Adela Branston welcomed her visitor very graciously; but Gilbert had no time to waste upon small talk, and after a hasty apology for his untimely intrusion, dashed at once into the question he had come to ask.

"John Saltram was with you yesterday evening, Mrs. Branston," he said. "Pray tell me the purpose that brought him here, and anything you know of his plan of action after leaving you."

"I can tell you very little about that. He was going upon a journey he told me, that evening, immediately indeed; a most important journey; but he did not tell me where he was going."

"I think I can guess that," said Gilbert. "Did he seem much agitated?"

"No; he was quite calm; but he had a resolute air, like a man who has some great purpose to achieve. I thought him looking very white and weak, and told him that I was sure he was too ill to start upon a long journey, or any journey. I begged him not to go, if it were possible to avoid going, and used every argument I could think of to persuade him to abandon the idea of such a thing. But it was all no use. 'If I had only a dozen hours to live, I must go,' he said."

"He came to ask you for money for his journey, did he not?"

"He did. I suppose to so close a friend as you are to him, there can be no breach of confidence in my admitting that. He came to borrow any ready-money I might happen to have in the house. Fortunately, I had a hundred and twenty pounds by me in hard cash."

"And he took that?—he wanted as much as that?" asked Gilbert eagerly.

"Yes, he said he was likely to require as much as that."

"Then he must have thought of going to America."

"To America! travel to America in his weak state of health?" cried Mrs. Branston, aghast.

"Yes. It seems like madness, does it not? But there are circumstances under which a man may be excused for being almost mad. John Saltram has gone in pursuit of some one very dear to him, some one who has been separated from him by treachery."

"A woman?"

Adela Branston's fair face flushed crimson as she asked the question. A woman? Yes, no doubt he was in pursuit of that woman whom he loved better than her.

"I cannot stop to answer a single question now, my dear Mrs. Branston," Gilbert said gently. "You shall know all by-and-by, and I am sure your generous heart will forgive any wrong that has been done you in this business. Good night. I have to catch a train at a quarter to eleven; I am going to Liverpool."

"After Mr. Saltram?"

"Yes; I do not consider him in a fitting condition to travel alone. I hope to be in time to prevent his doing anything rash."

"But how will you find him?"

"I must make a round of the hotels till I discover his head-quarters. Good night."

"Let me order my carriage to take you to the station."

"A thousand thanks, but I shall be there before your carriage would be ready. I can pick up a cab close by and shall have time to call at my lodgings for a carpet-bag. Once more, good night."

It was still dark when Gilbert Fenton arrived at Liverpool. He threw himself upon a sofa in the waiting-room, where he had an hour or so of uncomfortable, unrefreshing sleep, and then roused himself and went out to begin his round of the hotels.

A surly fly-driver of unknown age and prodigious deafness carried him from house to house; first to all the principal places of entertainment, aristocratic, family, and commercial; then to more obscure taverns and boarding-houses, until the sun was high and the commerce of Liverpool in full swing; and at all these places Gilbert questioned night-porters, and chief waiters, and head chamber-maids, until his brain grew dizzy by mere repetition of his questions; but no positive tidings could he obtain of John Saltram. There was a coffee-house near the quay where it seemed just possible that he had slept; but even here the description was of the vaguest, and the person described might just as well have been John Smith as John Saltram. Gilbert dismissed the fly-man and his vehicle at last, thoroughly wearied out with that morning's work.

He went to one of the hotels, took a hasty breakfast, and then hurried off to the offices belonging to the owners of the *Oronoco*.

That vessel had started for New York at nine o'clock on the previous morning, and John Saltram had gone with her. His name was the last on the list of passengers; he had only taken his passage an hour before the steamer left Liverpool, but there his name was in black and white. The names of Percival Nowell, and of Mrs. Holbrook, his daughter, were also in the list. The whole business was clear enough, and there was nothing more that Gilbert could do. Had John Saltram been strong and well, his friend would have felt nothing but satisfaction in the thought that he was going in the same vessel with Marian, and would without doubt bring her back in triumph. But the question of his health was a painful one to contemplate. Could he, or could he not endure the strain that he had put upon himself within the last eight-and-forty hours? In desperate straits men can do desperate things—there was always that fact to be remembered; but still John Saltram might break down under the burden he had taken upon himself; and when Gilbert went back to London that afternoon he was sorely anxious about this feeble traveller.

He found a letter from him at the lodgings in Wigmore-street; a hurried letter written at Liverpool the night before John Saltram's departure. He had arrived there too late to get on board the *Oronoco* that night, and had ascertained that the vessel was to leave at nine next morning.

"I shall take my passage in her in case of the worst," he wrote; "and if I cannot see Marian and persuade her to come on shore with me, I must go with her to New York. Heaven knows what power her father may use against me in the brief opportunity I shall have for seeing her before the vessel starts; but he can't prevent my being their fellow-passenger, and once afloat it shall go hard with me if I cannot make my dear girl hear reason. Do not be uneasy about my health, dear old friend; you see how well I am keeping up under all this strain upon body and mind. You will see me come back from America a new man, strong enough to prove my gratitude for your devotion, in some shape or other, I trust in God."

CHAPTER XLI.
OUTWARD BOUND.

THE bustle of departure was at its culminating point when John Saltram went on board the *Oronoco*, captain and officers scudding hither and thither, giving orders and answering inquiries at every point, with a sharp, short, decisive air, as of commanding powers in the last half-hour before a great battle; steward and his underlings ubiquitous; passengers roaming vaguely to and fro, in quest of nothing particular, and in a state of semi-distraction.

In this scene of confusion there was no one to answer Mr. Saltram's eager inquires about those travellers whom he had pursued to this point. He did contrive, just about ten minutes before the vessel sailed, to capture the ubiquitous steward by the button-hole, and to ask for tidings of Mr. Nowell, before that excited functionary could wrench himself away.

"Mr. Nowell, sir; upon my word, sir, I can't say. Yes, there is a gentleman of that name on board; state-rooms number 5 and 7; got a daughter with him—tall dark gentleman, with a moustache and beard. Yes, sir, he was on deck just now, on the bridge; but I don't see him, I suppose he's gone below. Better look for him in the saloon, sir."

The ten minutes were over before John Saltram had seen half the faces on board the crowded vessel; but in his hurried wanderings to and fro, eager to see that one face which he so ardently desired to behold once wore, he had met nothing but strangers. There was no help for it: the vessel would steam out seaward presently, and he must needs go with her. At the best, he had expected this. It was not likely that, even if he could have obtained speech with his wife, she could have been prevailed upon immediately to desert the father whose fortunes she had elected to follow, and return to shore with the husband she had abandoned. Her mind must have been poisoned, her judgment perverted, before she could have left him thus of her own free will; and it would need the light of calm reason to set things right again. No; John Saltram could scarcely hope to carry her off by a *coup-de-main*, in the face of the artful schemer who had evidently obtained so strong an influence over her. That she could for a moment contemplate this voyage to America with her father, was enough to demonstrate the revolution that must have taken place in her feelings towards her husband.

"Slander and lies are very strong," John Saltram said to himself; "but I do not think, when my dear love and I are once face to face, any power on earth can prevail against me. She must be changed indeed, if it can; she must be changed indeed, if anything but a lie can part us."

He had come on board the *Oronoco* prepared for the worst, and furnished with a slender outfit for the voyage, hurriedly purchased at a Liverpool clothier's. He had plenty of money in his pocket—enough to pay for his own and his wife's return passage; and the thought of this useless journey across the Atlantic troubled him very little. What did it matter where he was, if she were with him? The mental torture he had undergone during all this time, in which he had seemed in danger of losing her altogether, had taught him how dear she was—how precious and perfect a treasure he had held so lightly.

The vessel steamed put of the Mersey, and John Saltram, indifferent to the last glimpse of his native land, was still roaming hither and thither, in quest of the familiar face he longed with such a passionate yearning to see; but up to this point he sought for his wife in vain. Mrs. Holbrook had evidently retired at once to her cabin. There was nothing for him to do but to establish a channel of communication with her by means of the stewardess.

He found this official with some trouble, and so desperately busy that it was no easy matter to obtain speech with her, pursued as she was by forlorn and distracted female passengers, clamorously eager to know where she had put that "waterproof cloak," or "Maud," or "travelling-bag," or "dressing-case." He did at last contrive to enlist her services in his behalf, and extort some answer to his questions.

"Yes," she told him, "Mrs. Holbrook was on board—state-room number 7. She had gone to her room at once, but would appear at dinner-time, no doubt, if she wasn't ill."

John Saltram tore a blank leaf from his pocket-book, and wrote one hasty line:

"I am here, Marian; let me see you for God's sake.

"JOHN HOLBROOK."

"If you'll take that to the lady in number 7, I shall be exceedingly obliged," he said to the stewardess, slipping half-a-crown into her willing hand at the same time.

"Yes, sir, this very minute, sir."

John Saltram sat down upon a bench outside the ladies' cabin, in a sort of antechamber between the steward's pantry and store-rooms, strongly perfumed with the odour of grocery, and waited for Marian's coming. He had no shadow of doubt that she would come to him instantly, in defiance of any other guardian or counseller. Whatever lies might have been told her—however she might have been taught to doubt him—he had a perfect faith in the power of his immediate presence. They had but to meet face to face, and all would be well.

Indeed, there was need that things should be well for John Saltram very speedily. He had set nature at defiance so far, acting as if physical weakness were unknown to him. There are periods in a man's life in which nothing seems impossible to him; in which by the mere force of will he triumphs over impossibility. But such conquests are apt to be of the briefest. John Saltram felt that he must very soon break down. The heavily throbbing heart, the aching limbs, the dizzy sight, and parched throat, told him how much this desperate chase had cost him. If he had strength enough to clasp his wife's hand, to give her loving greeting and tell her that he was true, it would be about as much as he could hope to achieve; and then he felt that he would be glad to crawl into any corner of the vessel where he might find rest.

The stewardess came back to him presently, with rather a discomfited air.

"The lady says she is too ill to see any one, sir," she told John Saltram; "but under any circumstances she must decline to see you."

"She said that—my wife told you that?"

"Your wife, sir! Good gracious me, is the lady in number 7 your wife? She came on board with her father, and I understood they were only two in party."

"Yes; she came with her father. Her father's treachery has separated her from me; but a few words would explain everything, if I could only see her."

He thought it best to tell the woman the truth, strange as it might seem to her. Her sympathies were more likely to be enlisted in his favour if she knew the actual state of the case.

"Did Mrs. Holbrook positively decline to see me?" he asked again, scarcely able to believe that Marian could have resisted even that brief appeal scrawled upon a scrap of paper.

"She did indeed, sir," answered the stewardess. "Nothing could be more positive than her manner. I told her how anxious you seemed—for I could see it in your face, you see, sir, when you gave me the paper—and I really didn't like to bring you such a message; but it was no use. 'I decline to see him,' the lady said, 'and be sure you bring me no more messages from this gentleman;' and with that, sir, she tore up the bit of paper, as cool as could be. But, dear me, sir, how ill you do look, to be sure!"

"I have been very ill. I came from a sick-room to follow my wife."

"Hadn't you better go and lie down a little, sir? You look as if you could scarcely stand. Shall I fetch the steward for you?"

"No, thanks. I can find my way to my berth, I daresay. Yes, I suppose I had better go and lie down. I can do no more yet awhile."

He could do no more, and had indeed barely strength to stagger to his sleeping-quarters, which he discovered at last with some difficulty. Here he flung himself down, dressed as he was, and lay like a log, for hours, not sleeping, but powerless to move hand or foot, and with his brain racked by torturing thoughts. "As soon as I am able to stand again, I will see her father, and exact a reckoning from him," he said to himself again and again, during those long dreary hours of prostration; but when the next day came, he was too weak to raise himself from his narrow bed, and on the next day after that he was no better. The steward was much concerned by his feeble condition, especially as it was no common case of sea-sickness; for John Saltram had told him that he was never sea-sick. He brought the prostrate traveller soda-water and brandy, and tried to tempt him to eat rich soups of a nutritious character; but the sick man would take nothing except an occasional draught of soda-water.

On the third day of the voyage the steward was very anxious to bring the ship's surgeon to look at Mr. Saltram; but against this John Saltram resolutely set his face.

"For pity's sake, don't bore me with any more doctors!" he cried fretfully. "I have had enough of that kind of thing. The man can do nothing for me. I am knocked up with over exertion and excitement—that's all; my strength will come back to me sooner or later if I lie quietly here."

The steward gave way, for the time being, upon this appeal, and the surgeon was not summoned; but Mr. Saltram's strength seemed very slow to return to him. He could not sleep; he could only lie there listening to all the noises of the ship, the perpetual creaking and rattling, and tramping of footsteps above his head, and tortured by his impatience to be astir again. He would not stand upon punctilio this time, he told himself; he would go straight to the door of Marian's cabin, and stand there until she came out to him. Was she not his wife—his very own—powerless to hold him at bay in this manner? His strength did not come back to him; that wakeful prostration in which the brain was always busy, while the aching body lay still, did not appear to be a curative process. In the course of that third night of the voyage John Saltram was delirious, much to the alarm of his fellow-passenger, the single sharer of his cabin, a nervous elderly gentleman, who objected to his illness altogether as an outrage upon himself, and was indignantly desirous to know whether it was contagious.

So the doctor was brought to the sick man early next morning whether he would or not, and went through the usual investigations, and promised to administer the usual sedatives, and assured the anxious passenger that Mr. Saltram's complaint was in nowise infectious.

"He has evidently been suffering from serious illness lately, and has been over-exerting himself," said the doctor; "that seems very clear. We shall contrive to bring him round in a few days, I daresay, though he certainly has got into a very low state."

The doctor said this rather gravely, on which the passenger again became disturbed of aspect. A death on board ship must needs be such an unpleasant business, and he really had not bargained for anything of that kind. What was the use of paying first-class fare on board a first-class vessel, if one were subject to annoyance of this sort? In the steerage of an overcrowded emigrant ship such a thing might be a matter of course—a mere natural incident of the voyage—but on board the *Oronoco* it was most unlooked for.

"He's not going to die, is he?" asked the passenger, with an injured air.

"O dear, no, I should hope not. I have no apprehension of that sort," replied the surgeon promptly.

He would no doubt have said the same thing up to within an hour or so of the patient's decease.

"There is an extreme debility, that is all," he went on quite cheerfully; "and if we can induce him to take plenty of nourishment, we shall get on very well, I daresay."

After this the nervous passenger was profoundly interested in the amount of refreshment consumed by the patient, and questioned the steward about him with a most sympathetic air.

John Saltram, otherwise John Holbrook, was not destined to die upon this outward voyage. He was very eager to be well, or at least to be at liberty to move about again; and perhaps this impatient desire of his helped in some measure to bring about his recovery. The will, physiologists tell us, has a great deal to do with these things.

The voyage was a prosperous one. The good ship steamed gaily across the Atlantic through the bleak spring weather; and there was plenty of eating and drinking, and joviality and flirtation on board her, while John Saltram lay upon his back, very helpless, languishing to be astir once more.

During these long dreary days and nights he had contrived to send several messages to the lady in the state-cabin, feeble pencil scrawls, imploring her to come to him, telling her that he was very ill, at death's door almost, and desired nothing so much as to see her, if only for a moment. But the answer—by word of mouth of the steward or stewardess always—was unfailingly to the same effect:—the lady in number 7 refused to hold any communication with the sick gentleman.

"She's a hard one!" the steward remarked to the stewardess, when they talked the matter over in a comfortable manner during the progress of a snug little supper in the steward's cabin, "she must be an out-and-out hard-hearted one to stand out against him like that, if he is her husband, and I suppose he is. I told her to-day—when I took his message—how bad he was, and that it was a chance if he ever went ashore alive; but she was walking up and down deck with her father ten minutes afterwards, laughing and talking like anything. I suppose he's been a bad lot, Mrs. Peterson, and deserves no better from her; but still it does seem hard to see him lying there, and his wife so near him, and yet refusing to go and see him."

"I've no common patience with her," said the stewardess with acrimony; "the cold-hearted creature!—flaunting about like that, with a sick husband within a stone's throw of her. Suppose he is to blame, Mr. Martin; whatever his faults may have been, it isn't the time for a wife to remember them."

To this Mr. Martin responded dubiously, remarking that there were some carryings on upon the part of husbands which it was difficult for a wife not to remember.

The good ship sped on, unhindered by adverse winds or foul weather, and was within twenty-four hours of her destination when John Saltram was at last able to crawl out of the cabin, where he had lain for some eight or nine days crippled and helpless.

The first purpose which he set himself to accomplish was an interview with Marian's father. He wanted to grapple his enemy somehow—to ascertain the nature of the game that was being played against him. He had kept himself very quiet for this purpose, wishing to take Percival Nowell by surprise; and on this last day but one of the voyage, when he was able for the first time to rise from his berth, no one but the steward and the surgeon knew that he intended so to rise.

He had taken the steward in some measure into his confidence; and that official, after helping him to dress, left him seated in the cabin, while he went to ascertain the whereabouts of Mr. Nowell. Mr. Martin, the steward, came back after about five minutes.

"He's in the saloon, sir, reading, quite alone. You couldn't have a better opportunity of speaking to him."

"That's a good fellow. Then I'll go at once."

"You'd better take my arm, sir; you're as weak as a baby, and the ship lurches a good deal to-day."

"I'm not very strong, certainly. I begin to think I never shall be strong again. Do you know, Martin, I was once stroke in a university eight. Not much vigour in my biceps now, eh?"

It was only a few paces from one cabin to the other; but Mr. Saltram could scarcely have gone so far without the steward's supporting arm. He was a feeble-looking figure, with a white wan face, as he tottered along the narrow passage between the tables, making his way to that end of the saloon where Percival Nowell lounged luxuriously, with his legs stretched at full length upon the sofa, and a book in his hand.

"Mr. Nowell, I believe," said the sick man, as the other looked up at him with consummate coolness. Whatever his feelings might be with regard to his daughter's husband, he had had ample time to prepare himself for an encounter with him.

"Yes, my name is Nowell. But I have really not the honour to——"

"You do not know me," answered John Saltram. "No, but it is time you did so. I am your daughter's husband, John Holbrook."

"Indeed. I have heard that she has been persecuted by the messages of some person calling himself her husband. You are that person, I presume."

"I have tried to persuade my wife to see me. Yes; and I mean to see her before this vessel arrives in port."

"But if the lady in question refuses to have anything to say to you?"

"We shall soon put that to the test. I have been too ill to stir ever since I came on board, or you would have heard of me before this, Mr. Nowell. Now that I can move about once more, I shall find a way to assert my claims, you may be sure. But in the first place, I want to know by what right you stole my wife away from her home—by what right you brought her on this voyage?"

"Before I answer that question, Mr.—Mr. Holbrook, as you choose to call yourself, I'll ask you another. By what right do you call yourself my daughter's husband? what evidence have you to produce to prove that you are not a barefaced impostor? You don't carry your marriage-certificate about with you, I daresay; and in the absence of some kind of documentary evidence, what is to convince me that you are what you pretend to be—my daughter's husband?"

"The evidence of your daughter's own senses. Place me face to face with her; she will not deny my identity."

"But how, if my daughter declines to see you, as she does most positively? She has suffered enough at your hands, and is only too glad to be released from you."

"She has suffered—she is glad to be released! Why, you most consummate scoundrel!" cried John Saltram, "there never was an unkind word spoken between my wife and me! She was the best, most devoted of women; and nothing but the vilest treachery could have separated us. I know not what villanous slander you have made her believe, or by what means you lured her away from me; but I know that a few words between us would let in the light upon your plot. You had better make the best of a bad position, Mr. Nowell. As my wife's father, you know, you are pretty sure to escape. Whatever my inclination might be, my regard for her would make me indulgent to you. You'll find candour avail you best in this case, depend upon it. Your daughter has inherited a fortune, and you want to put your hand upon it altogether. It would be wiser to moderate your desires, and be content with a fair share of the inheritance. Your daughter is not the woman to treat you ungenerously, nor am I the man to create any hindrance to her generosity."

"I can make no bargain with you, sir," replied Mr. Nowell, with the same cool audacity of manner that had distinguished him throughout the interview; "nor am I prepared to admit your claim to the position you assume. But if my daughter is your wife, she left you of her own free will, under no coercion of mine; and she must return to you in the same manner, or you must put the machinery of the law in force to compel her. And *that*, I flatter myself, in a free country like America, will be rather a difficult business."

It was hard for John Saltram to hear any man talk like this, and not be able to knock him down. But in his present condition Marian's husband could not have grappled a child, and he knew it.

"You are an outrageous scoundrel!" he said between his set teeth, tortured by that most ardent desire to dash his clenched fist into Mr. Nowell's handsome dissolute-looking face. "You are a most consummate villain, and you know it!"

"Hard words mean so little," returned Mr. Nowell coolly, "and go for so little. That kind of language before witnesses would be actionable; but, upon my word, it would be mere child's play on my part to notice it, especially to a man in your condition. You'd better claim your wife from the captain, and see what he will say to you. I have told him that there's some semi-lunatic on board, who pretends to be Mrs. Holbrook's husband; so he'll be quite prepared to hear your statement."

John Saltram left the saloon in silence. It was worse than useless talking to this man, who presumed upon his helpless state, and openly defied him. His next effort must be to see Marian.

This he found impossible, for the time being at any rate. The state-room number 7 was an apartment a little bigger than a rabbit-hutch, opening out of a larger cabin, and in that cabin there reposed a ponderous matron who had suffered from sea-sickness throughout the voyage, and who could in no wise permit a masculine intruder to invade the scene of her retirement.

The idea of any blockade of Marian's door was therefore futile. He must needs wait as patiently as he might, till she appeared of her own free will. He could not have to wait very long; something less than a day and a night, the steward had told him, would bring them to the end of the voyage.

Mr. Saltram went on deck, still assisted by the friendly steward, and seated himself in a sheltered corner of the vessel, hoping that the sea-breeze might bring him back some remnant of his lost strength. The ship's surgeon had advised him to get a little fresh air as soon as he felt himself able to bear it; so he sat in his obscure nook, very helpless and very feeble, meditating upon what he should do when the final moment came and he had to claim his wife.

He had no idea of making his wrongs known to the captain, unless as a last desperate resource. He could not bring himself to make Marian the subject of a vulgar squabble. No, it was to herself alone he would appeal; it was in the natural instinct of her own heart that he would trust.

Very long and weary seemed the remaining hours of that joyless voyage. Mr. Saltram was fain to go back to his cabin after an hour on deck, there to lie and await the morrow. He had need to husband his strength for the coming encounter. The steward told him in the evening that Mrs. Holbrook had not dined in the saloon that day, as usual. She had kept her cabin closely, and complained of illness.

The morning dawned at last, after what had seemed an endless night to John Saltram, lying awake in his narrow berth—a bleak blusterous morning, with the cold gray light staring in at the port-hole, like an unfriendly face. There was no promise in such a daybreak; it was only light, and nothing more.

Mr. Saltram, having duly deliberated the matter during the long hours of that weary night, had decided that his wisest course was to lie *perdu* until the last moment, the very moment of landing, and then to come boldly forward and make his claim. It was useless to waste his strength in any futile endeavour to baffle so hardy a scoundrel as Percival Nowell. At the last, when Marian was leaving the ship, it would be time for him to assert his right as her husband, and to defy the wretch who had beguiled her away from him.

Having once arrived at this decision, he was able to await the issue of events with some degree of tranquility. He had no doubt, even now, of his wife's affection for him, no fear as to the ultimate triumph of her love over all the lies and artifices of that scheming scoundrel, her father.

It was nearly three o'clock in the afternoon when the steward came to tell him that they were on the point of arriving at their destination. The wharf where they were to land was within sight. The man had promised to give him due warning of this event, and John Saltram had therefore contrived to keep himself quiet amidst all the feverish impatience and confusion of mind prevailing, amongst the other passengers. He was rewarded for his prudence; for when he rose to go on deck, he found himself stronger than he had felt yet. He went up the companion-ladder, took his place close to the spot at which the passengers must all leave the vessel, and waited.

New York was very near. The day had been cold and showery, but the sun was shining now, and the whole scene looked bright and gay. Every one seemed in high spirits, as if the new world they were about to touch contained for them a certainty of Elysium. It was such a delicious relief to arrive at the great lively Yankee city, after the tedium of a ten-day's voyage, pleasant and easy as the transit had been.

John Saltram looked eagerly among the faces of the crowd, but neither Percival Nowell nor his daughter were to be seen amongst them. Presently the vessel touched the wharf, and the travellers began to move towards the gangway. He watched them, one by one, breathlessly. At the very last, Mr. Nowell stepped quickly forward, with a veiled figure on his arm.

She was closely veiled, her face quite hidden by thick black lace, and she was clinging with something of a frightened air to her companion's arm.

John Saltram sprang up from his post of observation, and confronted the two before they could leave the vessel.

"Marian," he said, in slow decided tone, "let go that man's arm. You will leave this vessel with me, and with no one else."

"Stand out of the way, fellow," cried Percival Nowell; "my daughter can have nothing to say to you."

"Marian, for God's sake, obey me! There is the vilest treachery in this man's conduct. Let go his arm. My love, my darling, come with me!"

There was a passionate appeal in his tone, but it produced no answer.

"Marian!" he cried, still interposing himself between these two and the passage to the landing wharf. "Marian, I will have some answer!"

"You have had your answer, sir," said Percival Nowell, trying to push him aside. "This lady does not know you. Do you want to make a scene, and render yourself ridiculous to every one here? There are plenty of lunatic asylums in New York that will accommodate you, if you are determined to make yourself eligible for them."

"Marian!" repeated John Saltram, without vouchsafing the faintest notice of this speech. "Marian, speak to me!"

And then, as there came no answer from that shrinking clinging figure, with a sudden spring forward, that brought him quite close to her, John Saltram tore the veil away from the hidden face.

"This must be some impostor," he said; "this is not my wife."

He was right. The creature clinging to Percival Nowell's arm was a pretty woman enough, with rather red hair, and a common face. She was about Marian's height; and that was the only likeness between them.

The spectators of this brief fracas crowded round the actors in it, seeing nothing but the insult offered to a lady, and highly indignant with John Saltram; and amidst their murmurs Percival Nowell pushed his way to the shore, with the woman still clinging to his arm.

CHAPTER XLII.
THE PLEASURES OF WYNCOMB.

THAT shrill anguish-stricken cry which Ellen Whitelaw had heard on the night of the stranger's visit to Wyncomb Farm haunted her afterwards with a wearisome persistence. She could not forget that wild unearthly sound; she could not help continually trying to find some solution for the mystery, until her brain was tired with the perpetual effort.

Ponder upon this matter as she might, she could find no reasonable explanation of the enigma; and in spite of her common sense—a quality of which she possessed a very fair share—she was fain to believe at last that this grim bare-looking old house was haunted, and that the agonised shriek she and Mrs. Tadman had heard that night was only the ghostly sound of some cry wrung from a bleeding heart in days gone by, the echo of an anguish that had been in the far past.

She even went so far as to ask her husband one day if he had ever heard that the house was haunted, and whether there was any record of crime or wrong that had been done in it in the past. Mr. Whitelaw seemed scarcely to relish the question; but after one of his meditative pauses laughed his wife's inquiry to scorn, and told her that there were no ghosts at Wyncomb except the ghosts of dead rats that had ravaged the granaries—and certainly *they* seemed to rise from their graves in spite of poison and traps, cats and ferrets—and that, as to anything that had been done in the house in days gone by, he had never heard tell that his ancestors had ever done anything but eat and drink and sleep, and save money from year's end to year's end; and a hard time they'd had of it to pay their way and put something by, in the face of all the difficulties that surround the path of a farmer.

If Ellen Whitelaw's life had been as the lives of happier women, full of small daily cares and all-engrossing domestic interests, the memory of that unearthly scream would no doubt have faded out of her mind ere long, instead of remaining, as it did, a source of constant perplexity to her. But there was no interest, no single charm in her life. There was nothing in the world left for her to care for. The fertile flats around Wyncomb Farmhouse bounded her universe. Day by day she rose to perform the same monotonous duties, sustained by no lofty aim, cheered by neither friendship nor affection; for she could not teach herself to feel anything warmer than toleration for her daily companion, Mrs. Tadman—only working laboriously because existence was more endurable to her when she was busy than when she was idle. It was scarcely strange, then, that she brooded upon the memory of that night when the nameless stranger had come to Wyncomb, and that she tried to put the fact of his coming and that other incident of the cry together, and to make something out of the two events by that means; but put them together as she might, she was no nearer any solution of the mystery. That her husband and the stranger could have failed to hear that piercing shriek seemed almost impossible: yet both had denied hearing it. The story of the stranger having knocked his shin and cried out on doing so, appeared like a feeble attempt to account for that wild cry. Vain and hopeless were all her endeavours to arrive at any reasonable explanation, and her attempts to get anything like an opinion out of Mrs. Tadman were utterly useless. Mr. Whitelaw's cousin was still inclined to take a gloomy view of the stranger's visit, in spite of her kinsman's assurance that the transaction between himself and the unknown was a profitable one. Horse-racing—if not parting with a farm—Mrs. Tadman opined was at the bottom of the business; and when did horse-racing ever fail to lead to ruin sooner or later? It was only a question of time. Ellen sighed, remembering how her father had squandered his employer's money on the race-course, and how, for that folly of his, she had been doomed to become Stephen Whitelaw's wife. But there did not seem to her to be anything of the horsey element in her husband's composition. He was never away from home, except to attend to his business at market; and she had never seen him spelling over the sporting-papers, as her father had been wont to do, night after night, with a perplexed brow and an anxious face, making calculations upon the margin of the print every now and then with a stump of lead pencil, and chewing the end of it meditatively in the intervals of his lection.

Although Mrs. Whitelaw did not, like Mrs. Tadman, associate the idea of the stranger's visit with any apprehension of her husband's impending ruin, she could not deny that some kind of change had arisen in him since that event. He had always drunk a good deal, in his slow quiet manner, which impressed people unacquainted with his habits with a notion of his sobriety, even when he was steadily emptying the bottle before him; but he drank more now, and sat longer over his drink, and there was an aspect of trouble and uneasiness about him at times which fairly puzzled his wife. Of course the most natural solution for all this was the one offered by the dismally prophetic Tadman. Stephen Whitelaw had been speculating or gambling, and his affairs were in disorder. He was not a man to be affected by anything but the most sordid considerations, one would suppose. Say that he had lost money, and there you had a key to the whole.

He got into a habit of sitting up at night, after the rest of the household had gone to bed. He had done this more or less from the time of his marriage; and Mrs. Tadman had told Ellen that the habit was one which had arisen within the last few months.

"He would always see to the fastenings of the house with his own eyes," Mrs. Tadman said; "but up to last autumn he used to go upstairs with me and the servants. It's a new thing for him to sit up drinking his glass of grog in the parlour by himself."

The new habit seemed to grow upon Mr. Whitelaw more rapidly after that visit of the stranger's. He took to sitting up till midnight—an awful hour in a farm-house; and Ellen generally found the spirit-bottle empty in the morning. Night after night, he went to bed soddened with drink. Once, when his kinswoman made some feeble remonstrance with him about this change in his habits, he told her savagely to hold her tongue—he could afford to drink as much as he pleased—he wasn't likely to come upon *her* to pay for what he took. As for his wife, she unhappily cared nothing what he did. He could not become more obnoxious to her than he had been from the first hour of her acquaintance with him, let him do what he would.

Little by little, finding no other explanation possible, Mrs. Whitelaw grew to believe quite firmly in the supernatural nature of that unforgotten cry. She remembered the unexplainable footstep which she had heard in the padlocked room in the early dusk of that new-year's-day, when Mrs. Tadman and she explored the old house; and she associated these two sounds in her mind as of a like ghostly character. From this time forward she shrank with a nervous terror from that darksome passage leading to the padlocked door at the end of the house. She had never any occasion to go in this direction. The rooms in this wing were low, dark, and small, and had been unused for years. It was scarcely any wonder if rats had congregated behind the worm-eaten wainscot, to scare nervous listeners with their weird scratchings and scramblings. But no one could convince Ellen Whitelaw that the sounds she had heard on new-year's-day were produced by anything so earthly as a rat. With that willingness to believe in a romantic impossibility, rather than in a commonplace improbability so natural to the human mind, she was more ready to conceive the existence of a ghost than that her own sense of hearing might have been less powerful than her fancy. About the footsteps she was quite as positive as she was about the scream; and in the last instance she had the evidence of Mrs. Tadman's senses to support her.

She was surprised to find one day, when the household drudge, Martha Holden, had been cleaning the passage and rooms in that deserted wing—a task very seldom performed—that the girl had the same aversion to that part of the house which she felt herself, but of which she had never spoken in the presence of the servants.

"If it wasn't for Mrs. Tadman driving and worrying after me all the time I'm at work, I don't think I could stay there, mum," Martha told her mistress. "It isn't often I like to be fidgetted and followed; but anything's better than being alone in that unked place."

"It's rather dark and dreary, certainly, Martha," Ellen answered with an admirable assumption of indifference; "but, as we haven't any of us got to live there, that doesn't much matter."

"It isn't that, mum. I wouldn't mind the darkness and the dreariness—and I'm sure such a place for spiders I never did see in my life; there was one as I took down with my broom to-day, and scrunched, as big as a small crab—but it's worse than, that: the place is haunted."

"Who told you that?"

"Sarah Batts."

"Sarah Batts! Why, how should she know anything about it? She hasn't been here so long as you; and she came straight from the workhouse."

"I think master must have told her, mum."

"Your master would never have said anything so foolish. I know that *he* doesn't believe in ghosts; and he keeps all his garden-seeds in the locked room at the end of the passage; so he must go there sometimes himself."

"O yes, mum; I know that master goes there. I've seen him go that way at night with a candle."

"Well, you silly girl, he wouldn't use the room if he thought it was haunted, would he? There are plenty more empty rooms in the house."

"I don't know about that, I'm sure, mum; but anyhow I know Sarah Batts told me that passage was haunted. 'Don't you never go there, Martha,' she says, 'unless you want to have your blood froze. I've heard things there that have froze mine.' And I never should go, mum, if it wasn't for moth—Mrs. Tadman's worrying and driving, about the place being cleaned once in a way. And Sarah Batts is right, mum, however she may have got to know it; for I have heard things."

"What things?"

"Moaning and groaning like, as if it was some one in pain; but all very low; and I never could make out where it came from. But as to the place being haunted, I've no more doubt about it than about my catechism."

"But, Martha, you ought to know it's very silly and wicked to believe in such things," Ellen Whitelaw said, feeling it her duty to lecture the girl a little, and yet half inclined to believe her. "The moanings and groanings, as you call them, were only sounds made by the wind, I daresay."

"O dear no, mum," Martha answered, shaking her head in a decided manner; "the wind never made such noises as *I* heard. But I don't want to make you nervous, mum; only I'd sooner lose a month's wages than stay for an hour alone in the west wing."

It was strange, certainly; a matter of no importance, perhaps, this idle belief of a servant's, these sounds which harmed no one; and yet all these circumstances worried and perplexed Ellen Whitelaw. Having so little else to think of, she brooded upon them incessantly, and was gradually getting into a low nervous way. If she complained, which she did very rarely, there was no one to sympathise with her. Mrs. Tadman had so many ailments of her own, such complicated maladies, such deeply-rooted disorders, that she could be scarcely expected to give much attention to the trivial sufferings of another person.

"Ah, my dear," she would exclaim with a groan, if Ellen ventured to complain of a racking headache, "when you've lived as long as I have, and gone through what I've gone through, and have got such a liver as I've got, you'll know what bad health means. But at your age, and with your constitution, it's nothing more than fancy."

And then Mrs. Tadman would branch off into a graphic description of her own maladies, to which Ellen was fain to listen patiently, wondering vaguely as she listened whether the lapse of years would render her as wearisome a person as Mrs. Tadman.

She had no sympathy from anyone. Her father came to Wyncomb Farm once a week or so, and sat drinking and smoking with Mr. Whitelaw; but Ellen never saw him alone. He seemed carefully to avoid the chance of being alone with her, guiltily conscious of his part in the contriving of her marriage, and fearing to hear some complaint about her lot. He pretended to take it for granted that her fate was entirely happy, congratulated her frequently upon her prosperity, and reminded her continually that it was a fine thing to be the sole mistress of the house she lived in, instead of a mere servant—as he himself was, and as she had been at the Grange—labouring for the profit of other people.

Up to this time Mr. Carley had had some reason to be disappointed with the result of his daughter's marriage, so far as his own prosperity was affected thereby. Not a sixpence beyond that one advance of the two hundred pounds had the bailiff been able to extort from his son-in-law. It was the price that Mr. Whitelaw had paid for his wife, and he meant to pay no more. He told William Carley as much one day when the question of money matters was pushed rather too far—told him in the plainest language.

This was hard; but that two hundred pounds had saved the bailiff from imminent destruction. He was obliged to be satisfied with this advantage, and to bide his time.

"I'll have it out of the mean hound sooner or later," he muttered to himself as he walked homewards, after a social evening with the master of Wyncomb.

One evening Mr. Carley brought his daughter a letter. It was from Gilbert Fenton, who was quite unaware of Ellen's marriage, and had written to her at the Grange. This letter afforded her the only pleasure she had known since fate had united her to Stephen Whitelaw. It told her that Marian Holbrook was living, and in all probability safe—though by no means in good hands. She had sailed for America with her father; but her husband was in hot pursuit of her, and her husband was faithful.

"I have schooled myself to forgive him," Gilbert went on to say, "for I know that he loves her—and that must needs condone my wrongs. I look forward anxiously to their return from America, and hope for a happy reunion amongst us all—when your warm friendship shall not be forgotten. I am waiting impatiently for news from New York, and will write to you again directly I hear anything definite. We have suffered the torments of suspense for a long weary time, but I trust and believe that the sky is clearing."

This was not much, but it was more than enough to relieve Ellen Carley's mind of a heavy load. Her dear young lady, as she called Marian, was not dead—not lying at the bottom of that cruel river, at which Ellen had often looked with a shuddering horror, of late, thinking of what might be. She was safe, and would no doubt be happy. This was something. Amid the wreck of her own fortunes, Ellen Whitelaw was unselfish enough to rejoice in this.

Her husband asked to see Mr. Fenton's letter, which he spelt over with his usual deliberate air, and which seemed to interest him more than Ellen would have supposed likely—knowing as she did how deeply he had resented Marian's encouragement of Frank Randall's courtship.

"So she's gone to America with her father, has she?" he said, when he had perused the document twice. "I shouldn't have thought anybody could have persuaded her to leave that precious husband of hers. And she's gone off to America, and he after her! That's rather a queer start, ain't it, Nell?" Mrs. Whitelaw did not care to discuss the business with her husband. There was something in his tone, a kind of veiled malice, which made her angry.

"I don't suppose you care whether she's alive or dead," she said impatiently; "so you needn't trouble yourself to talk about her."

"Needn't I? O, she's too grand a person to be talked of by such as me, is she? Never mind, Nell; don't be cross. And when Mrs. Holbrook comes back to England, you shall go and see her."

"I will," answered Ellen; "if I have to walk to London to do it."

"O, but you sha'n't walk. You shall go by rail. I'll spare you the money for that, for once in a way, though I'm not over fond of wasting money."

Day by day Mr. Whitelaw's habits grew more secluded and morose. It is not to be supposed that he was troubled by those finer feelings which might have made the misery of a better man; but even in his dull nature there may have been some dim sense that his marriage was a failure and mistake; that in having his own way in this matter he had in nowise secured his own happiness. He could not complain of his wife's conduct in any one respect. She was obedient to his will in all things, providing for his comfort with scrupulous regularity, industrious, indefatigable even. As a housekeeper and partner of his fortunes, no man could have desired a better wife. Yet dimly, in that sluggish soul, there was the consciousness that he had married a woman who hated him, that he had bought her with a price; and, being a man prone to think the worst of his fellow-creatures, Mr. Whitelaw believed that, sooner or later, his wife meant to have her revenge upon him somehow. She was waiting for his death perhaps; calculating that, being so much her senior, and a hard-working man, he would die soon enough to leave her a young widow. And then, of course, she would marry Frank Randall; and all the money which he, Stephen, had amassed, by the sacrifice of every pleasure in life, would enrich that supercilious young coxcomb.

It was a hard thing to think of, and Stephen pondered upon the expediency of letting off Wyncomb Farm, and sinking all his savings in the purchase of an annuity. He could not bring himself to contemplate selling the house and lands that had belonged to his race for so many generations. He clung to the estate, not from any romantic reverence for the past, not from any sentimental associations connected with those who had gone before him, but from the mere force of habit, which rendered this grim ugly old house and these flat shelterless fields dearer to him than all the rest of the universe. He was a man to whom to part with anything was agony; and if he loved anything in the world, he loved Wyncomb. The possession of the place had given him importance for twenty years past. He could not fancy himself unconnected with Wyncomb. His labours had improved the estate too; and he could not endure to think how some lucky purchaser might profit by his prudence and sagacity. There had been some fine old oaks on the land when he inherited it, all mercilessly stubbed-up at the beginning of his reign; there had been tall straggling hedgerows, all of a tangle with blackberry bushes, ferns, and dog-roses, hazel and sloe trees, all done away with by his order. No, he could never bring himself to sell Wyncomb. Nor was the purchase of an annuity a transaction which he was inclined to accomplish. It was a pleasing notion certainly, that idea of concentrating all his hoarded money upon the remaining years of his life—retiring from the toils of agriculture, and giving himself up for the rest of his days to an existence of luxurious idleness. But, on the other hand, it would be a bitter thing to surrender his fondly-loved money for the poor return of an income, to deprive himself of all opportunity of speculating and increasing his store.

So the annuity scheme lay dormant in his brain, as it were, for the time being. It was something to have in reserve, and to carry out any day that his wife gave him fair cause to doubt her fidelity.

In the mean time he went on living his lonely sulky kind of life, drinking a great deal more than was good for him in his own churlish manner, and laughing to scorn any attempt at remonstrance from his wife or Mrs. Tadman. Some few times Ellen had endeavoured to awaken him to the evil consequences that must needs ensue from his intemperate habits, feeling that it would be a sin on her part to suffer him to go on without some effort to check him; but her gently-spoken warnings had been worse than useless.

CHAPTER XLIII.
MR. WHITELAW MAKES AN END OF THE MYSTERY.

MRS. Whitelaw had been married about two months. It was bright May weather, bright but not yet warm; and whatever prettiness Wyncomb Farm was capable of assuming had been put on with the fresh spring green of the fields and the young leaves of the poplars. There were even a few hardy flowers in the vegetable-garden behind the house, humble perennials planted by dead and gone Whitelaws, which had bloomed year after year in spite of Stephen's utilitarian principles. It was a market-day, the household work was finished, and Ellen was sitting with Mrs. Tadman in the parlour, where those two spent so many weary hours of their lives, the tedium whereof was relieved only by woman's homely resource, needlework. Even if Mrs. Whitelaw had been fond of reading, and she only cared moderately for that form of occupation, she could hardly have found intellectual diversion of that kind at Wyncomb, where a family Bible, a few volumes of the *Annual Register*, which had belonged to some half-dozen different owners before they came from a stall in Malsham market to the house of Whitelaw, a grim-looking old quarto upon domestic medicine, and a cookery-book, formed the entire library. When the duties of the day were done, and the local weekly newspaper had been read—an intellectual refreshment which might be fairly exhausted in ten minutes—there remained nothing to beguile the hours but the perpetual stitch—stitch—stitch of an industriously-disposed sempstress; and the two women used to sit throughout the long afternoons with their work-baskets before them, talking a little now and then of the most commonplace matters, but for the greater part of their time silent. Sometimes, when the heavy burden of Mrs. Tadman's society, and the clicking of needles and snipping of scissors, grew almost unendurable, Ellen would run out of the house for a brief airing in the garden, and walk briskly to and fro along the narrow pathway between the potatoes and cabbages, thinking of her dismal life, and of the old days at the Grange when she had been full of gaiety and hope. There was not perhaps much outward difference in the two lives. In her father's house she had worked as hard as she worked now; but she had been free in those days, and the unknown future all before her, with its chances of happiness. Now, she felt like some captive who paces the narrow bounds of his prison-yard, without hope of release or respite, except in death.

This particular spring day had begun brightly, the morning had been sunny and even warm; but now, as the afternoon wore away, there were dark clouds, with a rising wind and a sharp gusty shower every now and then. Ellen took a solitary turn in the garden between the showers. It was market-day; Stephen Whitelaw was not expected home till tea-time, and the meal was to be eaten at a later hour than usual.

The rain increased as the time for the farmer's return drew nearer. He had gone out in the morning without his overcoat, Mrs. Tadman remembered, and was likely to get wet through on his way home, unless he should have borrowed some extra covering at Malsham. His temper, which of late had been generally at its worst, would hardly be improved by this annoyance.

There was a very substantial meal waiting for him: a ponderous joint of cold roast beef, a dish of ham and eggs preparing in the kitchen, with an agreeable frizzling sound, a pile of hot buttered cakes kept hot upon the oven top; but there was no fire in the parlour, and the room looked a little cheerless in spite of the well-spread table. They had discontinued fires for about a fortnight, at Mr. Whitelaw's command. He didn't want to be ruined by his coal-merchant's bill if it was a chilly spring, he told his household; and at his own bidding the fire-place had been polished and garnished for the summer. But this evening was colder than any evening lately, by reason of that blusterous rising wind, which blew the rain-drops against the window-panes with as sharp a rattle as if they had been hailstones; and Mr. Whitelaw coming in presently, disconsolate and dripping, was by no means inclined to abide by his own decision about the fires.

"Why the —— haven't you got a fire here?" he demanded savagely.

"It was your own wish, Stephen," answered Mrs. Tadman.

"My own fiddlesticks! Of course I didn't care to see my wood and coals burning to waste when the sun was shining enough to melt any one. But when a man comes home wet to the skin, he doesn't want to come into a room like an ice-house. Call the girl, and tell her to light a blazing fire while I go and change my clothes. Let her bring plenty of wood, and put a couple of logs on top of the coals. I'm frozen to the very bones driving home in the rain."

Mrs. Tadman gave a plaintive sigh as she departed to obey her kinsman.

"That's just like Stephen," she said; "if it was you or me that wanted a fire, we might die of cold before we got leave to light one; but he never grudges anything for his own comfort!"

Martha came and lighted a fire under Mrs. Tadman's direction. That lady was inclined to look somewhat uneasily upon the operation; for the grate had been used constantly throughout a long winter, and the chimney had not been swept since last spring, whereby Mrs. Tadman was conscious of a great accumulation of soot about the massive old brickwork and ponderous beams that spanned the wide chimney. She had sent for the Malsham sweep some weeks ago; but that necessary individual had not been able to come on the particular day she wished, and the matter had been since then neglected. She remembered this now with a guilty feeling, more especially as Stephen had demanded a blazing fire, with flaring pine-logs piled half-way up the chimney. He came back to the parlour presently, arrayed in an old suit of clothes which he kept for such occasions—an old green coat with basket buttons, and a pair of plaid trousers of an exploded shape and pattern—and looking more like a pinched and pallid scarecrow than a well-to-do farmer. Mrs. Tadman had only carried out his commands in a modified degree, and he immediately ordered the servant to put a couple of logs on the fire, and then drew the table close up to the hearth, and sat down to his tea with some appearance of satisfaction. He had had rather a good day at market, he condescended to tell his wife during the progress of the meal; prices were rising, his old hay was selling at a rate which promised well for the new crops, turnips were in brisk demand, mangold enquired for—altogether Mr. Whitelaw confessed himself very well satisfied with the aspect of affairs.

After tea he spent his evening luxuriantly, sitting close to the fire, with his slippered feet upon the fender, and drinking hot rum-and-water as a preventive of impending, or cure of incipient, cold. The rum-and-water being a novelty, something out of the usual order of his drink, appeared to have an enlivening effect upon him. He talked more than usual, and even proposed a game at cribbage with Mrs. Tadman; a condescension which moved that matron to tears, reminding her, she said, of old times, when they had been so comfortable together, before he had taken to spend his evenings at the Grange.

"Not that I mean any unkindness to you, Ellen," the doleful Tadman added apologetically, "for you've been a good friend to me, and if there's one merit I can lay claim to, it's a grateful heart; but of course, when a man marries, he never is the same to his relations as when he was single. It isn't in human nature that he should be."

Here Mrs. Tadman's amiable kinsman requested her to hold her jaw, and to bring the board if she was going to play, or to say as much if she wasn't. Urged by this gentle reminder, Mrs. Tadman immediately produced a somewhat dingy-looking pack of cards and a queer little old-fashioned cribbage-board.

The game lasted for about an hour or so, at the end of which time the farmer threw himself back in his chair with a yawn, and pronounced that he had had enough of it. The old eight-day clock in the lobby struck ten soon after this, and the two women rose to retire, leaving Stephen to his night's libations, and not sorry to escape out of the room, which he had converted into a kind of oven or Turkish bath by means of the roaring fire he had insisted upon keeping up all the evening. He was left, therefore, with his bottle of rum about half emptied, to finish his night's entertainment after his own fashion.

Mrs. Tadman ventured a mild warning about the fire when she wished him good night; but as she did not dare to hint that there had been any neglect in the chimney-sweeping, her counsel went for very little. Mr. Whitelaw threw on another pine-log directly the two women had left him, and addressed himself to the consumption of a fresh glass of rum-and-water.

"There's nothing like being on the safe side," he muttered to himself with an air of profound wisdom. "I don't want to be laid up with the rheumatics, if I can help it."

He finished the contents of his glass, and went softly out of the room, carrying a candle with him. He was absent about ten minutes, and then came back to resume his comfortable seat by the fire, and mixed himself another glass of grog with the air of a man who was likely to finish the bottle.

While he sat drinking in his slow sensual way, his young wife slept peacefully enough in one of the rooms above him. Early rising and industrious habits will bring sleep, even when the heart is hopeless and the mind is weary. Mrs. Whitelaw slept a tranquil dreamless sleep to-night, while Mrs. Tadman snored with a healthy regularity in a room on the opposite side of the passage.

There was a faint glimmer of dawn in the sky, a cold wet dawn, when Ellen was awakened suddenly by a sound that bewildered and alarmed her. It was almost like the report of a pistol, she thought, as she sprang out of bed, pale and trembling. It was not a pistol shot, however, only a handful of gravel thrown sharply against her window.

"Stephen," she cried, half awake and very much, frightened, "what was that?" But, to her surprise, she found that her husband was not in the room.

While she sat on the edge of her bed hurrying some of her clothes on, half mechanically, and wondering what that startling sound could have been, a sudden glow of red light shone in at her window, and at the same moment her senses, which had been only half awakened before, told her that there was an atmosphere of smoke in the room.

She rushed to the door, forgetting that to open it was perhaps to admit death, and flung it open. Yes, the passage was full of smoke, and there was a strange crackling sound below.

There could be little doubt as to what had happened—the house was on fire. She remembered how repeatedly Mrs. Tadman had declared that Stephen would inevitably set the place on fire some night or other, and how little weight she had attached to the dismal prophecy. But the matron's fears had not been groundless, it seemed. The threatened calamity had come.

"Stephen!" she cried, with all her might, and then flew to Mrs. Tadman's door and knocked violently. She waited for no answer, but rushed on to the room where the two women-servants slept together, and called to them loudly to get up for their lives, the house was on fire.

There were still the men in the story above to be awakened, and the smoke was every moment growing thicker. She mounted a few steps of the staircase, and called with all her strength. It was very near their time for stirring. They must hear her, surely. Suddenly she remembered an old disused alarm-bell which hung in the roof. She had seen the frayed rope belonging to it hanging in an angle of the passage. She flew to this, and pulled it vigorously till a shrill peal rang out above; and once having accomplished this, she went on, reckless of her own safety, thinking only how many there were to be saved in that house.

All this time there was no sign of her husband, and a dull horror came over her with the thought that he might be perishing miserably below. There could be no doubt that the fire came from downstairs. That crackling noise had increased, and every now and then there came a sound like the breaking of glass. The red glow shining in at the front windows grew deeper and brighter. The fire had begun in the parlour, of course, where they had left Stephen Whitelaw basking in the warmth of his resinous pine-logs.

Ellen was still ringing the bell, when she heard a man's footstep coming along the passage towards her. It was not her husband, but one of the farm-servants from the upper story, an honest broad-shouldered fellow, as strong as Hercules.

"Lord a mercy, mum, be that you?" he cried, as he recognised the white half-dressed figure clinging to the bell-rope "let me get 'ee out o' this; the old place'll burn like so much tinder;" and before she could object, he had taken her up in his arms as easily as if she had been a child, and was carrying her towards the principal staircase.

Here they were stopped. The flames and smoke were mounting from the lobby below; the man turned immediately, wasting no time by indecision, and ran to the stairs leading down to the kitchen. In this direction all was safe. There was smoke, but in a very modified degree.

"Robert," Ellen cried eagerly, when they had reached the kitchen, where all was quiet, "for God's sake, go and see what has become of your master. We left him drinking in the parlour last night. I've called to him again and again, but there's been no answer."

"Don't you take on, mum; master's all right, I daresay. Here be the gals and Mrs. Tadman coming downstairs; they'll take care o' you, while I go and look arter him. You've no call to be frightened. If the fire should come this way, you've only got to open yon door and get out into the yard. You're safe here."

The women were all huddled together in the kitchen by this time, half dressed, shivering, and frightened out of their wits. Ellen Whitelaw was the only one among them who displayed anything like calmness.

The men were all astir. One had run across the fields to Malsham to summon the fire-engine, another was gone to remove some animals stabled near the house.

The noise of burning wood was rapidly increasing, the smoke came creeping under the kitchen-door presently, and, five minutes after he had left them, the farm-servant came back to say that he could find no traces of his master. The parlor was in flames. If he had been surprised by the fire in his sleep, it must needs be all over with him. The man urged his mistress to get out of the house at once; the fire was gaining ground rapidly, and it was not likely that anything he or the other men could do would stop its progress.

The women left the kitchen immediately upon this warning, by a door leading into the yard. It was broad daylight by this time; a chilly sunless morning, and a high wind sweeping across the fields and fanning the flames, which now licked the front wall of Wyncomb Farmhouse. The total destruction of the place seemed inevitable, unless help from Malsham came very quickly. The farm servants were running to and fro with buckets of water from the yard, and flinging their contents in at the shattered windows of the front rooms; but this was a small means of checking the destruction. The house was old, built for the most part of wood, and there seemed little hope for it.

Ellen and the other women went round to the front of the house, and stood there, dismal figures in their scanty raiment, with woollen petticoats pinned across their shoulders, and disordered hair blown about their faces by the damp wind. They stood grouped together in utter helplessness, looking at the work of ruin with a half-stupid air; almost like the animals who had been hustled from one place of shelter to another, and were evidently lost in wonder as to the cause of their removal.

But presently, as the awful scene before them grew more familiar, the instincts of self-interest arose in each breast. Mrs. Tadman piteously bewailed the loss of her entire wardrobe, and some mysterious pocket-book which she described plaintively as her "little all." She dwelt dolefully upon the merits of each particular article, most especially upon a French-merino dress she had bought for Stephen's wedding, which would have lasted her a lifetime, and a Paisley shawl, the gift of her deceased husband, which had been in her possession twenty years, and had not so much as a thin place in it.

Nor was the disconsolate matron the only one who lamented her losses. Sarah Batts, with clasped hands and distracted aspect, wept for the destruction of her "box."

"There was money in it," she cried, "money! Oh, don't you think the men could get to my room and save it?"

"Money!" exclaimed Mrs. Tadman, sharply, aroused from the contemplation of her own woes by this avowal; "you must be cleverer than I took you for, Sarah Batts, to be able to save money, and yet be always bedizened with some new bit of finery, as you've been."

"It was give to me," Sarah answered indignantly, "by them as had a right to give it."

"For no good, I should think," replied Mrs. Tadman; "what should anybody give you money for?"

"Never you mind; it was mine. O dear, O dear! if one of the men would only get my box for me."

She ran to intercept one of the farm-labourers, armed with his bucket, and tried to bribe him by the promise of five shillings as a reward for the rescue of her treasures. But the man only threatened to heave the bucket of water at her if she got in his way; and Miss Batts was obliged to abandon this hope.

The fire made rapid progress meanwhile, unchecked by that ineffectual splashing of water. It had begun at the eastern end of the building, the end most remote from those disused rooms in the ivy-covered west wing; but the wind was blowing from the north-east, and the flames were spreading rapidly towards that western angle. There was little chance that any part of the house could be saved.

While Ellen Whitelaw was looking on at the work of ruin, with a sense of utter helplessness, hearing the selfish lamentations of Mrs. Tadman and Sarah Batts like voices in a dream, she was suddenly aroused from this state of torpor by a loud groan, which sounded from not very far off. It came from behind her, from the direction of the poplars. She flew to the spot, and on the ground beneath one of them she found a helpless figure lying prostrate, with an awful smoke-blackened face—a figure and face which for some moments she did not recognize as her husband's.

She knew him at last, however, and knelt down beside him. He was groaning in an agonized manner, and had evidently been fearfully burnt before he made his escape.

"Stephen!" she cried. "O, thank God you are here! I thought you were shut up in that burning house. I called with all my might, and the men searched for you."

"It isn't much to be thankful for," gasped the farmer. "I don't suppose there's an hour's life in me; I'm scorched from head to foot, and one arm's helpless. I woke up all of a sudden, and found the room in a blaze. The flames had burst out of the great beam that goes across the chimney-piece. The place was all on fire, so that I couldn't reach the door anyhow; and before I could get out of the window, I was burnt like this. You'd have been burnt alive in your bed but for me. I threw up a handful of gravel at your window. It must have woke you, didn't it?"

"Yes, yes, that was the sound that woke me; it seemed like a pistol going off. You saved my life, Stephen. It was very good of you to remember me."

"Yes; there's men in my place who wouldn't have thought of anybody but themselves."

"Can I do anything to ease you, Stephen?" asked his wife.

She had seated herself on the grass beside him, and had taken his head on her lap, supporting him gently. She was shocked to see the change the fire had made in his face, which was all blistered and distorted.

"No, nothing; till they come to carry me away somewhere. I'm all one burning pain."

His eyes closed, and he seemed to sink into a kind of stupor. Ellen called to one of the men. They might carry him to some place of shelter surely, at once, where a doctor could be summoned, and something done for his relief. There was a humble practitioner resident at Crosber, that is to say, about two miles from Wyncomb. One of the farm-servants might take a horse and gallop across the fields to fetch this man.

Robert Dunn, the bailiff, heard her cries presently and came to her. He was very much shocked by his master's condition, and at once agreed to the necessity of summoning a surgeon. He proposed that they should carry Stephen Whitelaw to some stables, which lay at a safe distance from the burning house, and make up some kind of bed for him there. He ran back to dispatch one of the men to Crosber, and returned immediately with another to remove his master.

But when they tried to raise the injured man between them, he cried out to them to let him alone, they were murdering him. Let him lie where he was; he would not be moved. So he was allowed to lie there, with his head on his wife's lap, and his tortured body covered by a coat, which one of the men brought him. His eyes closed again, and for some time he lay without the slightest motion.

The fire was gaining ground every instant, and there was yet no sign of the engine from Malsham; but Ellen Whitelaw scarcely heeded the work of destruction. She was thinking only of the helpless stricken creature lying with his head upon her lap; thinking of him perhaps in this hour of his extremity with all the more compassion, because he had always been obnoxious to her. She prayed for the rapid arrival of the surgeon, who must surely be able to give some relief to her husband's sufferings, she thought. It seemed dreadful for him to be lying like this, with no attempt made to lessen his agony. After a long interval he lifted his scorched eyelids slowly, and looked at her with a strange dim gaze.

"The west wing," he muttered; "is that burnt?"

"No, Stephen, not yet; but there's little hope they'll save any part of the house."

"They must save that; the rest don't matter—I'm insured heavily; but they must save the west wing."

His wife concluded from this that he had kept some of his money in one of those western rooms. The seed-room perhaps, that mysterious padlocked chamber, where she had heard the footstep. And yet she had heard him say again and again that he never kept an unnecessary shilling in the house, and that every pound he had was out at interest. But such falsehoods and contradictions are common enough amongst men of miserly habits; and Stephen Whitelaw would hardly be so anxious about those western rooms unless something of value were hidden away there. He closed his eyes again, and lay groaning faintly for some time; then opened them suddenly with a frightened look and asked, in the same tone,

"The west wing—is the west wing afire yet?"

"The wind blows that way, Stephen, and the flames are spreading. I don't think they could save it—not if the engine was to come this minute."

"But I tell you they must!" cried Stephen Whitelaw. "If they don't, it'll be murder—cold-blooded murder. O, my God, I never thought there was much harm in the business—and it paid me well—but it's weighed me down like a load of lead, and made me drink more to drown thought. But if it should come to this—don't you understand? Don't sit staring at me like that. If the fire gets to the west wing, it will be murder. There's some one there—some one locked up—that won't be able to stir unless they get her out."

"Some one locked up in the west wing! Are you mad, Stephen?"

"It's the truth. I wouldn't do it again—no, not for twice the money. Let them get her out somehow. They can do it, if they look sharp."

That unforgotten footstep and equally unforgotten scream flashed into Mrs. Whitelaw's mind with these words of her husband's. Some one shut up there; yes, that was the solution of the mystery that had puzzled and tormented her so long. That cry of anguish was no supernatural echo of past suffering, but the despairing shriek of some victim of modern cruelty. A poor relation of Stephen's perhaps—a helpless, mindless creature, whose infirmities had been thus hidden from the world. Such things have been too cruelly common in our fair free country.

Ellen laid her husband's head gently down upon the grass and sprang to her feet.

"In which room?" she cried. But there was no answer. The man lay with closed eyes—dying perhaps—but she could do nothing for him till medical help came. The rescue of that unknown captive was a more urgent duty.

She was running towards the burning house, when she heard a horse galloping on the road leading from the gate. She stopped, hoping that this was the arrival of the doctor; but a familiar voice called to her, and in another minute her father had dismounted and was close at her side.

"Thank God you're safe, lass!" he exclaimed, with some warmer touch of paternal feeling than he was accustomed to exhibit. "Our men saw the fire when they were going to their work, and I came across directly. Where's Steph?"

"Under the trees yonder, very much hurt; I'm afraid fatally. But there's nothing we can do for him till the doctor comes. There's someone in still greater danger, father. For God's sake, help us to save her—some one shut up yonder, in a room at that end of the house."

"Some one shut up! One of the servants, do you mean?"

"No, no, no. Some one who has been kept shut up there—hidden—ever so long. Stephen told me just now. O, father, for pity's sake, try to save her!"

"Nonsense, lass. Your husband's brain must have been wandering. Who should be shut up there, and you live in the house and not know it? Why should Stephen hide any one in his house? What motive could he have for such a thing? It isn't possible."

"I tell you, father, it is true. There was no mistaking Stephen's words just now, and, besides that, I've heard noises that might have told me as much, only I thought the house was haunted. I tell you there is some one—some one who'll be burnt alive if we're not quick—and every moment's precious. Won't you try to save her?"

"Of course I will. Only I don't want to risk my life for a fancy. Is there a ladder anywhere?"

"Yes, yes. The men have ladders."

"And where's this room where you say the woman is shut up?"

"At that corner of the house," answered Ellen, pointing.

"There's a door at the end of the passage, but no window looking this way. There's only one, and that's over the wood-yard."

"Then it would be easiest to get in that way?"

"No, no, father. The wood's all piled up above the window. It would take such a time to move it."

"Never mind that. Anything's better than the risk of going into yonder house. Besides, the room's locked, you say. Have you got the key?"

"No; but I could get it from Stephen, I daresay."

"We won't wait for you to try. We'll begin at the wood-yard."

"Take Robert Dunn with you, father. He's a good brave fellow."

"Yes, I'll take Dunn."

The bailiff hurried away to the wood-yard, accompanied by Dunn and another man carrying a tall ladder. The farm-servants had ceased from their futile efforts at quenching the fire by this time. It was a labour too hopeless to continue. The flames had spread to the west wing. The ivy was already crackling, as the blaze crept over it. Happily that shut-up room was at the extreme end of the building, the point to which the flames must come last. And here, just at the moment when the work of devastation was almost accomplished, came the Malsham fire-engine rattling along gaily through the dewy morning, and the Malsham amateur fire-brigade, a very juvenile corps as yet, eager to cover itself with laurels, but more careful in the adjustment of its costume than was quite consistent with the desperate nature of its duty. Here came the brigade, in time to do something at any rate, and the engine soon began to play briskly upon the western wing.

Ellen Whitelaw was in the wood-yard, watching the work going on there with intense anxiety. The removal of the wood pile seemed a slow business, well as the three men performed their work, flinging down great crushing piles of wood one after another without a moment's pause. They were now joined by the Malsham fire-escape men, who had got wind of some one to be rescued from this part of the house, and were eager to exhibit the capabilities of a new fire-escape, started with much hubbub and glorification, after an awful fire had ravaged Malsham High-street, and half-a-dozen lives had been wasted because the old fire-escape was out of order and useless.

"We don't want the fire-escape," cried Mr. Carley as the tall machine was wheeled into the yard. "The room we want to get at isn't ten feet from the ground. You can give us a hand with this wood if you like. That's all we want."

The men clambered on to the wood-pile. It was getting visibly lower by this time, and the top of the window was to be seen. Ellen watched with breathless anxiety, forgetting that her husband might be dying under the poplars. He was not alone there; she had sent Mrs. Tadman to watch him.

Only a few minutes more and the window was cleared. A pale face could be dimly seen peering out through the dusty glass. William Carley tried to open the lattice, but it was secured tightly within. One of the firemen leapt forward upon his failure, and shattered every pane of glass and every inch of the leaden frame with a couple of blows from his axe, and then the bailiff clambered into the room.

He was hidden from those below about five minutes, and then emerged from the window, somehow or other, carrying a burden, and came struggling across the wood to the ladder by which he and the rest had mounted. The burden which he carried was a woman's figure, with the face hidden by his large woollen neckerchief. Ellen gave a cry of horror. The woman must surely be dead, or why should he have taken such pains to cover her face?

He brought his burden down the ladder very carefully, and gave the lifeless figure into Ellen's arms.

"Help me to carry her away yonder, while Robert gets the cart ready," he said to his daughter; "she's fainted." And then he added in a whisper, "For God's sake, don't let any one see her face! it's Mrs. Holbrook."

CHAPTER XLIV.
AFTER THE FIRE.

YES, it was Marian. She whom Gilbert Fenton had sought so long and patiently, with doubt and anguish in his heart; she whose double John Saltram had followed across the Atlantic, had been within easy reach of them all the time, hidden away in that dreary old farm-house, the innocent victim of Percival Nowell's treachery, and Stephen Whitelaw's greed of gain. The whole story was told by-and-by, when the master of Wyncomb Farm lay dying.

William Carley and his daughter took her to the Grange as soon as the farmer's spring cart was ready to convey her thither. It was all done very quickly, and none of the farm-servants saw her face. Even if they had done so, it is more than doubtful that they would have recognised her, so pale a shadow of her former self had she become during that long dreary imprisonment; the face wan and wasted, with a strange sharpened look about the features which was like the aspect of death; all the brightness and colour vanished out of the soft brown hair; an ashen pallor upon her beauty, that made her seem like a creature risen from the grave.

They lifted her into the cart, still insensible, and seated her there, wrapped in an old horse-cloth, with her head resting on Mrs. Whitelaw's shoulder; and so they drove slowly away. It was only when they had gone some little distance from the farm, that the fresh morning air revived her, and she opened her eyes and looked about her, wildly at first, and with a faint shuddering sigh.

Then, after a few moments, full consciousness came back to her, and a sudden cry of rapture broke from the pale lips. "O God!" she exclaimed, "am I set free?"

"Yes, dear Mrs. Holbrook, you are free, never again to go back to that cruel place. O, to think that you should be used so, and I so near!"

Marian lifted her head from Ellen's shoulder, and recognised her with a second cry of delight.

"Ellen, is it you? Then I am safe; I must be safe with you."

"Safe! yes, dear. I would die sooner than any harm should come to you again. Who could have brought this cruelty about? who could have shut you up in that room?"

"My father," Marian answered with a shudder. "He wanted my money, I suppose; and instead of killing me, he shut me up in that place."

She said no more just then, being too weak to say much; and Ellen, who was employed in soothing and comforting her, did not want her to talk. It was afterwards, when she had been established in her old rooms at the Grange, and had taken a little breakfast, that she told Ellen something more about her captivity.

"O, Ellen, if I were to tell you what I have suffered! But no, there are no words can tell that. It's not that they ill-used me. The girl who waited on me brought me good food, and even tried to make me comfortable in her rough way; but to sit there day after day, Ellen, alone, with only a dim light from the top of the window above the wood-stack; to sit there wondering about my husband, whether he was searching for me still, and would ever find me, or whether, as was more likely, he had given me up for dead. Think of me, Ellen, if you can, sitting there for weeks and months in my despair, trying to reckon the days sometimes by the aid of some old newspaper which the girl brought me now and then, at other times losing count of them altogether."

"Dear Mrs. Holbrook, I can't understand it even yet. Tell me how it all came about—how they ever lured you into that place."

"It was easy enough, Ellen; I wasn't conscious when they took me there. The story is very short. You remember that day when you left the Grange, how happy I was, looking forward to my husband's return, and thinking of the good news I had to tell him. We were to be rich, and our lives free and peaceful henceforward; and I had seen him suffer so much for the want of money. It was the morning after you left when the post brought me a letter from my father—a letter with the Malsham post-mark. I had seen him in town, as you know, and was scarcely surprised that he should write to me. But I was surprised to find him so near me, and the contents of the letter were very perplexing. My father entreated me to meet him on the river-side pathway, between Malsham station and this house. He had been informed of my habits, he said, and that I was accustomed to walk there. That was curious, when, so far as I knew, he had sever been near this place; but I hardly thought about the strangeness of it then. He begged me so earnestly to see him; it was a matter of life or death, he said. What could I do, Nelly? He was my father, and I felt that I owed him some duty. I could not refuse to see him; and if he had some personal objection to coming here, it seemed a small thing for me to take the trouble to go and meet him. I could but hear what he had to say."

"I wish to heaven I had been here!" exclaimed Ellen; "you shouldn't have gone alone, if I had known anything about it."

"I think, if you had been here, I should have told you about the letter, for it puzzled me a good deal, and I knew how well I could trust you. But you were away; and my father's request was so urgent—the hour was named—I could do nothing but accede to it. So I went, leaving no message for you or for my husband, feeling so sure of my return within an hour or two."

"And you found your father waiting for you?"

"Yes, on the river-bank, within a short distance of Mr. Whitelaw's house. He began by congratulating me on the change in my prospects,—I was a rich woman, he said. And then he went on to vilify my husband in such hateful words, Ellen; telling me that I had married a notorious scoundrel and profligate, and that he could produce ample evidence of what he affirmed; and all this with a pretended pity for my weakness and ignorance of the world. I laughed his shameful slanders to scorn, and told him that I knew my husband too thoroughly to be alarmed even for a moment by such groundless charges. He still affected to compassionate me as the weakest and most credulous of women, and then came to a proposal which he said he had travelled to Hampshire on purpose to make to me. It was, that I should leave my husband, and place myself under his protection; that I should go to America with him when he returned there, and so preserve my fortune from the clutches of a villain. 'My fortune?' I said; 'yes, I see that it is *that* alone you are thinking of. How can you suppose me so blind as not to understand that? You had better be candid with me, and say frankly what you want. I have no doubt my husband will allow me to make any reasonable sacrifice in your favour.'"

"What did he say to that?"

"He laughed bitterly at my offer. 'Your husband!' he said 'I am not likely to see the colour of my father's money, if you are to be governed by him.' 'You do him a great wrong,' I answered. 'I am sure that he will act generously, and I shall be governed by him.'"

"He was very angry, I suppose?"

"No doubt of it; but for some time he contrived to suppress all appearance of anger, and urged me to believe his statements about my husband, and to accept his offer of a home and protection with him. I cannot tell you how plausible his words were—what an appearance of affection and interest in my welfare he put on. Then, finding me firm, he changed his tone, and there were hidden threats mixed with his entreaties. It would be a bad thing for me if I refused to go with him, he said; I would have cause to repent my folly for the rest of my life. He said a great deal, using every argument it is possible to imagine; and there was always the same threatening under-tone. He could not move me in the least, as you may fancy, Nell. I told him that nothing upon earth would induce me to leave my husband, or to think ill of him. And in this manner we walked up and down for nearly two hours, till I began to feel very tired and faint. My father saw this, and when we came within sight of Wyncomb Farmhouse, proposed that I should go in and rest, and take a glass of milk or some kind of refreshment. I was surprised at this proposal, and asked him if he knew the people of the house. He said yes, he knew something of Mr. Whitelaw; he had met him the night before in the coffee-room of the inn at Malsham."

"Then your father had slept at Malsham the night before?"

"Evidently. His letter to me had been posted at Malsham, you know. I asked him how long he had been in this part of the country, and he rather evaded the question. Not long, he said; and he had come down here only to see me. At first I refused to go into Mr. Whitelaw's house, being only anxious to get home as quickly as possible. But my father seemed offended by this. I wanted to get rid of him, he said, although this was likely to be our last interview—the very last time in his life that he would ever see me, perhaps. I could not surely grudge him half an hour more of my company. I could scarcely go on refusing after this; and I really felt so tired and faint, that I doubted my capability of walking back to this house without resting. So I said yes, and we went into Wyncomb Farmhouse. The door was opened by a girl when my father knocked. There was no one at home, she told him; but we were quite welcome to sit down in the parlour, and she would bring me a glass of fresh milk and a slice of bread-and-butter.

"The house had a strange empty look, I thought. There was none of the life or bustle one expects to see at a farm; all was silent as the grave. The gloom and quietness of the place chilled me somehow. There was a fire burning in the parlour, and my father made me sit down very close to it, and I think the heat increased that faintness which I had felt when I came into the house.

"Again and again he urged his first demand, seeming as if he would wear down all opposition by persistence. I was quite firm; but the effect of all this argument was very wearisome, and I began to feel really ill.

"I think I must have been on the point of fainting, when the door was opened suddenly, and Mr. Whitelaw came in. In the next moment, while the room was spinning round before my eyes, and that dreadful giddiness that comes before a dead faint was growing worse, my father snatched me up in his arms, and threw a handkerchief over my face. I had just sense enough to know that there was chloroform upon it, and that was all. When I opened my eyes again, I was lying on a narrow bed, in a dimly-lighted room, with a small fire burning in a rusty grate in one corner, and some tea-things, with a plate of cold meat, on a table near it. There was a scrap of paper on this table, with a few lines scrawled upon it in pencil, in my father's hand: 'You have had your choice, either to share a prosperous life with me, or to be shut up like a mad woman. You had better make yourself as comfortable as you can, since you have no hope of escape till it suits my purpose to have you set free. Good care will be taken of you. You must have been a fool to suppose that I would submit to the injustice of J.N.'s will.'

"For a long time I sat like some stupid bewildered creature, going over these words again and again, as if I had no power to understand them. It was very long before I could believe that my father meant to shut me up in that room for an indefinite time—for the rest of my life, perhaps. But, little by little, I came to believe this, and to feel nothing but a blank despair. O, Nelly, I dare not dwell upon that time! I suffered too much. God has been very merciful to me in sparing me my mind; for there were times when I believe I was quite mad. I could pray sometimes, but not always. I have spent whole days in prayer, almost as if I fancied that I could weary out my God with supplications."

"And Stephen; did you see him?"

"Yes, now and then—once in several days, in a week perhaps. He used to come, like the master of a madhouse visiting his patients, to see that I was comfortable, he said. At first I used to appeal to him to set me free—kneeling at his feet, promising any sacrifice of my fortune for him or for my father, if they would release me. But it was no use. He was as hard as a rock; and at last I felt that it was useless, and used to see him come and go with hopeless apathy. No, Ellen, there are no words can describe what I suffered. I appealed to the girl who waited on me daily, but who came only once a-day, and always after dark. I might as well have appealed to the four walls of my room; the girl was utterly stolid. She brought me everything I was likely to want from day to day, and gave me ample means of replenishing my fire, and told me that I ought to make myself comfortable. I had a much better life than any one in the workhouse, she said; and I must be very wicked if I complained. I believe she really thought I was a harmless madwoman, and that her master had a right to shut me up in that room. One night, after I had been there for a time that seemed like eternity, my father came———"

"What!" cried Ellen Whitelaw, "the stranger! I understand. That man was your father; he came to see you that night; and as he was leaving you, you gave that dreadful shriek we heard downstairs. O, if I had known the truth—if I had only known!"

"*You* heard me, Ellen? You were there?" Marian exclaimed, surprised. She was, as yet, entirely ignorant of Ellen's marriage, and had been too much bewildered by the suddenness of her escape to wonder how the bailiff's daughter had happened to be so near at hand in that hour of deadly peril.

"Yes, yes, dear Mrs. Holbrook; I was there, and I did not help you. But never mind that now; tell me the rest of your story; tell me how your father acted that night."

"He was with me alone for about ten minutes; he came to give me a last chance, he said. If I liked to leave my husband for ever, and go to America with him, I might do so; but before he let me out of that place, he must have my solemn oath that I would make no attempt to see my husband; that I would never again communicate with any one I had known up to that time; that I would begin a new life, with him, my father, for my sole protector. I had had some experience of the result of opposing him, he said, and he now expected to find me reasonable.

"You can imagine my answer, Ellen. I would do anything, sacrifice anything, except my fidelity to my husband. Heaven knows I would have given twenty years of my life to escape from that dismal place, with the mere chance of being able to get back to my husband; but I would not take a false oath; I could not perjure myself, as that man would have made me perjure myself, in order to win my release. I knelt at his feet and clung about him, beseeching him with all the power I had to set me free; but he was harder than iron. Just at the end, when he had the door open, and was leaving me, telling me that I had lost my last chance, and would never see him again, I clung about him with one wild desperate cry. He flung me back into the room violently, and shut the door in my face. I fancied afterwards that that cry must have been heard, and that, if there had been any creature in the house inclined to help me, there would have come an end to my sufferings. But the time passed, and there was no change; only the long dreary days, the wretched sleepless nights."

This was all. There were details of her sufferings which Marian told her faithful friend by-and-by, when her mind was calmer, and they had leisure for tranquil talk; but the story was all told; and Marian lay down to rest in the familiar room, unspeakably grateful to God for her rescue, and only eager that her husband should be informed of her safety. She had not yet been told that he had crossed the Atlantic in search of her, deluded by a false scent. Ellen feared to tell her this at first; and she had taken it for granted that John Saltram was still in London. It was easy to defer any explanation just yet, on account of Marian's weakness. The exertion of telling the brief story of her sufferings had left her prostrate; and she was fain to obey her friendly nurse.

"We will talk about everything, and arrange everything, by-and-by, dear Mrs. Holbrook," Ellen said resolutely; "but for the present you *must* rest, and you must take everything that I bring you, and be very good."

And with that she kissed and left her, to perform another and less agreeable duty—the duty of attendance by her husband's sick-bed.

CHAPTER XLV.
MR. WHITELAW MAKES HIS WILL.

THEY had carried Stephen Whitelaw to the Grange; and he lay a helpless creature, beyond hope of recovery, in one of the roomy old-fashioned bed-chambers.

The humble Crosber surgeon had done his best, and had done it skilfully, being a man of large experience amongst a lowly class of sufferers; and to the aid of the Crosber surgeon had come a more prosperous practitioner from Malsham, who had driven over in his own phaeton; but between them both they could make nothing of Stephen Whitelaw. His race was run. He had been severely burnt; and if his actual injuries were not enough to kill him, there was little chance that he could survive the shock which his system had received. He might linger a little; might hold out longer than they expected; but his life was a question of hours.

The doomed man had seemed from the first to have a conviction of the truth, and appeared in no manner surprised when, in answer to his questions, the Malsham doctor admitted that his case was fatal, and suggested that, if he had anything to do in the adjustment of his affairs, he could scarcely do it too soon. At this Mr. Whitelaw groaned aloud. If he could in any manner have adjusted his affairs so as to take his money with him, the suggestion might have seemed sensible enough; but, that being impracticable, it was the merest futility. He had never made a will; it cost him too much anguish to give away his money even on paper. And now it was virtually necessary that he should do so, or else, perhaps, his wealth would, by some occult process, be seized upon by the crown—a power which he had been accustomed to regard in the abstract with an antagonistic feeling, as being the root of queen's taxes. To leave all to his wife, with some slight pension to Mrs. Tadman, seemed the most obvious course. He had married for love, and the wife of his choice had been very dutiful and submissive. What more could he have demanded from her? and why should he grudge her the inheritance of his wealth? Well, he would not have grudged it to her, perhaps, since some one must have it, if it had not been for that aggravating conviction that she would marry again, and that the man she preferred to him would riot in the possession of his hardly-earned riches. She would marry Frank Randall; and between them they would mismanage, and ultimately ruin, the farm. He remembered the cost of the manure he had put upon his fields that year, and regretted that useless outlay. It was a hard thing to have enriched his land only that others might profit by the produce.

"And if I've laid down a yard of drain-pipes since last year, I've laid down a dozen mile. There's not a bit of swampy ground or a patch of sour grass on the farm," he thought bitterly.

He lay for some hours deliberating as to what he should do. Death was near, but not so very close to him just yet. He had time to think. No, come what might, he would not leave the bulk of his property to fall into the keeping of Frank Randall.

He remembered that there were charitable institutions, to which a man, not wishing to enrich an ungrateful race, might bequeath his money, and obtain some credit for himself thereby, which no man could expect from his own relations. There was an infirmary at Malsham, rather a juvenile institution as yet, in aid whereof Mr. Whitelaw had often been plagued for subscriptions, reluctantly doling out half-a-guinea now and then, more often refusing to contribute anything. He had never thought of this place in his life before; but the image of it came into his mind now, as he had seen it on market-days for the last four years—a bran new red-brick building in Malsham High-street. He thought how his name would look, cut in large letters on a stone tablet on the face of that edifice. It would be something to get for his money; a very poor and paltry something, compared with the delight of possession, but just a little better than nothing.

He lay for some time pondering upon this, with that image of the stone tablet before his eyes, setting forth that the new wing of this institution had been erected at the desire of the late Stephen Whitelaw, Esq., of Wyncomb Farm, who had bequeathed a sum of money to the infirmary for that purpose, whereby two new wards had, in memory of that respected benefactor, been entitled the Whitelaw wards—or something to the like effect. He composed a great many versions of the inscription as he lay there, tolerably easy as to his bodily feelings, and chiefly anxious concerning the disposal of the money; but, being unaccustomed to the task of composition, he found it more difficult than he could have supposed to set forth his own glory in a concise form of words. But the tablet would be there, of course, the very centre and keystone of the building, as it were; indeed, Mr. Whitelaw resolved to make his bequest contingent upon the fulfilment of this desire. Later in the evening he told William Carley that he had made up his mind about his will, and would be glad to see Mr. Pivott, of Malsham, rival solicitor to Mr. Randall, of the same town, as soon as that gentleman could be summoned to his bedside.

The bailiff seemed surprised at this request.

"Why, surely, Steph, you can't want a lawyer mixed up in the business!" he said. "Those sort of chaps only live by making work for one another. You know how to make your will well enough, old fellow, without any attorney's aforesaids and hereinafters. Half a sheet of paper and a couple of sentences would do it, I should think; the fewer words the better."

"I'd rather have Pivott, and do it in a regular manner," Mr. Whitelaw answered quietly. "I remember, in a forgery case that was in the papers the other day, how the judge said of the deceased testator, that, being a lawyer, he was too wise to make his own will. Yes, I'd rather see Pivott, if you'll send for him, Carley. It's always best to be on the safe side. I don't want my money wasted in a chancery suit when I'm lying in my grave."

William Carley tried to argue the matter with his son-in-law; but the attempt was quite useless. Mr. Whitelaw had always been the most obstinate of men— and lying on his bed, maimed and helpless, was no more to be moved from his resolve than if he had been a Roman gladiator who had just trained himself for an encounter with lions. So the bailiff was compelled to obey him, unwillingly enough, and dispatched one of the men to Malsham in quest of Mr. Pivott the attorney.

The practitioner came to the Grange as fast as his horse could carry him. Every one in Malsham knew by this time that Stephen Whitelaw was a doomed man; and Mr. Pivott felt that this was a matter of life and death. He was an eminently respectable man, plump and dapper, with a rosy smooth-shaven face, and an air of honesty that made the law seem quite a pleasant thing. He was speedily seated by Mr. Whitelaw's bed, with a pair of candles and writing materials upon a little table before him, ready to obey his client's behests, and with the self-possessed aspect of a man to whom a last will and testament involving the disposal of a million or so would have been only an every-day piece of practice.

William Carley had shown himself very civil and obliging in providing for the lawyer's comfort, and having done so, now took up his stand by the fireplace, evidently intending to remain as a spectator of the business. But an uneasy glance which the patient cast from time to time in the direction of his father-in-law convinced Mr. Pivott that he wanted that gentleman to be got rid of before business began.

"I think, Mr. Carley, it would be as well for our poor friend and I to be alone," he said in his most courteous accents.

"Fiddlesticks!" exclaimed the bailiff contemptuously. "It isn't likely that Stephen can have any secrets from his wife's father. I'm in nobody's way, I'm sure, and I'm not going to put my spoke in the wheel, let him leave his money how he may."

"Very likely not, my dear sir. Indeed, I am sure you would respect our poor friend's wishes, even if they were to take a form unpleasing to yourself, which is far from likely. But still it may be as well for Mr. Whitelaw and myself to be alone. In cases of this kind the patient is apt to be nervous, and the business is done more expeditiously if there is no third party present. So, my dear Mr. Carley, if you have *no* objection———"

"Steph," said the bailiff abruptly, "do *you* want me out of the room? Say the word, if you do."

The patient writhed, hesitated, and then replied with some confusion,—

"If it's all the same to you, William Carley, I think I'd sooner be alone with Mr. Pivott."

And here the polite attorney, having opened the door with his own hands, bowed the bailiff out; and, to his extreme mortification, William Carley found himself on the outside of his son-in-law's room, before he had time to make any farther remonstrance.

He went downstairs, and paced the wainscoted parlour in a very savage frame of mind.

"There's some kind of devil's work hatching up there," he muttered to himself. "Why should he want me out of the room? He wouldn't, if he was going to leave all his money to Ellen, as he ought to leave it. Who else is there to get it? Not that old mother Tadman, surely. She's an artful old harridan; and if my girl had not been a fool, she'd have got rid of her out of hand when she married. Sure to goodness *she* can never stand between Stephen and his wife. And who else is there? No one that I know of; no one. Stephen wouldn't have kept any secret all these years from the folks he's lived amongst. It isn't likely. He *must* leave it all to his wife, except a hundred or so, perhaps, to mother Tadman; and it was nothing but his natural closeness that made him want me out of the way."

And at this stage of his reflections, Mr. Carley opened a cupboard near the fire-place and brought therefrom a case-bottle, from the contents of which he found farther solace. It was about half-an-hour after this that he was summoned by a call from the lawyer, who was standing on the broad landing-place at the top of the stairs with a candle in his hand, when the bailiff emerged from the parlour.

"If you'll step up here, and bring one of your men with you, I shall be obliged, Mr. Carley," the attorney said, looking over the banisters; "I want you to witness your son-in-law's will." Mr. Carley's spirits rose a little at this. He was not much versed in the ways of lawyers, and had a notion that Mr. Pivott would read the will to him, perhaps, before he signed it. It flashed upon him presently that a legatee could not benefit by a will which he had witnessed. It was obvious, therefore, that Stephen did not mean him to have anything. Well, he had scarcely expected anything. If his daughter inherited all, it would be pretty much the same thing; she would act generously of course.

He went into the kitchen, where the head man, who had been retained on the premises to act as special messenger in this time of need, was sitting in the chimney-corner smoking a comfortable pipe after his walk to and from Malsham.

"You're wanted upstairs a minute, Joe," he said; and the two went clumping up the wide old oaken staircase.

The witnessing of the will was a very brief business. Mr. Pivott did not offer to throw any light upon its contents, nor was the bailiff, sharpsighted as he might be, able to seize upon so much as one paragraph or line of the document during the process of attaching his signature thereto.

When the ceremony was concluded, Stephen Whitelaw sank back upon his pillow with an air of satisfaction.

"I don't think I could have done any better," he murmured.

"It's a hard thing for a man of my age to leave everything behind him; but I don't see that I could have done better."

"You have done that, my dear sir, which might afford comfort to any death-bed," said the lawyer solemnly.

He folded the will, and put it into his pocket.

"Our friend desires me to take charge of this document," he said to William Carley. "You will have no reason to complain, on your daughter's account, when you become familiar with its contents. She has been fairly treated—I may say very fairly treated."

The bailiff did not much relish the tone of this assurance. Fair treatment might mean very little.

"I hope she has been well treated," he answered in a surly manner. "She's been a good wife to Stephen Whitelaw, and would continue so to be if he was to live twenty years longer. When a pretty young woman marries a man twice her age, she's a right to expect handsome treatment, Mr. Pivott. It can't be too handsome for justice, in my opinion."

The solicitor gave a little gentle sigh.

"As an interested party, Mr. Carley," he said, "your opinion is not as valuable as it might be under other circumstances. However, I don't think your daughter will complain, and I am sure the world will applaud what our poor friend has done—of his own accord, mind, Mr. Carley, wholly and solely of his own spontaneous desire. It is a thing that I should only have been too proud to suggest; but the responsibility of such a suggestion is one which I could never have taken upon myself. It would have been out of my province, indeed. You will be kind enough to remember this by-and-by, my dear sir."

The bailiff was puzzled, and showed Mr. Pivott to the door with a moody countenance.

"I thought there was some devil's work," he muttered to himself, as he watched the lawyer mount his stiff brown cob and ride away into the night; "but what does it all mean? and what has Stephen Whitelaw done with his money? We shall know that pretty soon, anyhow. He can't last long."

CHAPTER XLVI.
ELLEN REGAINS HER LIBERTY.

STEPHEN Whitelaw lingered for two days and two nights, and at the expiration of that time departed this life, making a very decent end of it, and troubled by no thought that his existence had been an unworthy one.

Before he died, he told his wife something of how he had been tempted into the doing of that foul deed whereof Marian Saltram had been the victim. Those two were alone together the day before he died, when Stephen, of his own free will, made the following statement:——

"It was Mrs. Holbrook's father, you see," he said, in a plausible tone, "that put it to me, how he might want his daughter taken care of for a time—it might be a short time, or it might be rather a longish time, according to how circumstances should work out. We'd met once before at the King's Arms at Malsham, where Mr. Nowell was staying, and where I went in of an evening, once in a way, after market; and he'd made pretty free with me, and asked me a good many questions about myself, and told me a good bit about himself, in a friendly way. He told me how his daughter had gone against him, and was likely to go against him, and how some property that ought in common justice to have been left to him, had been left to her. He was going to give her a fair chance, he said, if she liked to leave her husband, who was a scheming scoundrel, and obey him. She might have a happy home with him, if she was reasonable. If not, he should use his authority as a father.

"He came to see me at Wyncomb next day—dropped in unawares like, when mother Tadman was out of the way—not that I had asked him, you see. He seemed to be quite taken with the place, and made me show him all over the house; and then he took a glass of something, and sat and talked a bit, and went away, without having said a word about his daughter. But before he went he made me promise that I'd go and see him at the King's Arms that night.

"Well, you see, Nell, as he seemed to have taken a fancy to me, as you may say, and had told me he could put me up to making more of my money, and had altogether been uncommonly pleasant, I didn't care to say no, and I went. I was rather taken aback at the King's Arms when they showed me to a private room, because I'd met Mr. Nowell before in the Commercial; however, there he was, sitting in front of a blazing fire, and with a couple of decanters of wine upon the table.

"He was very civil, couldn't have been more friendly, and we talked and talked; he was always harping on his daughter; till at last he came out with what he wanted. Would I give her house-room for a bit, just to keep her out of the way of her husband and such-like designing people, supposing she should turn obstinate and refuse to go abroad with him? 'You've a rare old roomy place,' he said. 'I saw some rooms upstairs at the end of a long passage which don't seem to have been used for years. You might keep my lady in one of those; and that fine husband of hers would be as puzzled where to find her as if she was in the centre of Africa. It would be a very easy thing to do,' he said; 'and it would be only friendly in you to do it."'

"O, Stephen!" cried his wife reproachfully, "how could you ever consent to such a wicked thing?"

"I don't know about the wickedness of it," Mr. Whitelaw responded, with rather a sullen air; "a daughter is bound to obey her father, isn't she? and if she don't, I should think he had the power to do what he liked with her. That's how I should look at it, if I was a father. It's all very well to talk, you see, Nell, but you don't know the arguments such a man as that can bring to bear. I didn't want to do it; I was against it from the first. It was a dangerous business, and might bring me into trouble. But that man bore down upon me to that extent that he made me promise anything; and when I went home that night, it was with the understanding that I was to fit up a room—there was a double door to be put up to shut out sound, and a deal more—ready for Mrs. Holbrook, in case her father wanted to get her out of the way for a bit."

"He promised to pay you, of course?" Ellen said, not quite able to conceal the contempt and aversion which this confession of her husband's inspired.

"Well, yes, a man doesn't put himself in jeopardy like that for nothing. He was to give me a certain sum of money down the first night that Mrs. Holbrook slept in my house; and another sum of money before he went to America, and an annual sum for continuing to take care of her, if he wanted to keep her quiet permanently, as he might. Altogether it would be a very profitable business, he told me, and I ought to consider myself uncommonly lucky to get such a chance. As to the kindness or unkindness of the matter, it was better than shutting her up in a lunatic asylum, he said; and he might have to do that, if I refused to take her. She was very weak in her head, he said, and the doctors would throw no difficulty in his way, if he wanted to put her into a madhouse."

"But you must have known that was a lie!" exclaimed Ellen indignantly. "You had seen and talked to her; you must have known that Mrs. Holbrook was as sane as you or I."

"I couldn't be supposed to know better than her own father," answered Mr. Whitelaw, in an injured tone; "he had a right to know best. However, it's no use arguing about it now. He had such a power over me that I couldn't go against him; so I gave in, and Mrs. Holbrook came to Wyncomb. She was to be treated kindly and made comfortable, her father said; that was agreed between us; and she has been treated kindly and made comfortable. I had to trust some one to wait upon her, and when Mr. Nowell saw the two girls he chose Sarah Batts. 'That girl will do anything for money,' he said; 'she's stupid, but she's wise enough to know her own interest, and she'll hold her tongue.' So I trusted Sarah Batts, and I had to pay her pretty stiffly to keep the secret; but she was a rare one to do the work, and she went about it as quiet as a mouse. Not even mother Tadman ever suspected her."

"It was a wicked piece of business—wicked from first to last," said Ellen. "I can't bear to hear about it."

And then, remembering that the sinner was so near his end, and that this voluntary confession of his was in some manner a sign of repentance, she felt some compunction, and spoke to him in a softer tone.

"Still I'm grateful to you for telling me the truth at last, Stephen," she said; "and, thank God, there's no harm done that need last for ever. Thank God that dear young lady did not lose her life, shut up a prisoner in that miserable room, as she might have done."

"She had her victuals regular," observed Mr. Whitelaw, "and the best."

"Eating and drinking won't keep any one alive, if their heart's breaking," said Ellen; "but, thank heaven, her sufferings have come to an end now, and I trust God will forgive your share in them, Stephen."

And then, sitting by his bedside through the long hours of that night, she tried in very simple words to awaken him to a sense of his condition. It was not an easy business to let any glimmer of spiritual light in upon the darkness of that sordid mind. There did arise perhaps in this last extremity some dim sense of remorse in the breast of Mr. Whitelaw, some vague consciousness that in that one act of his life, and in the whole tenor of his life, he had not exactly shaped his conduct according to that model which the parson had held up for his imitation in certain rather prosy sermons, indifferently heard, on the rare occasions of his attendance at the parish church. But whatever terrors the world to come might hold for him seemed very faint and shapeless, compared with the things from which he was to be taken. He thought of his untimely death as a hardship, an injustice almost. When his wife entreated him to see the vicar of Crosber before he died, he refused at first, asking what good the vicar's talk could do him.

"If he could keep me alive as long as till next July, to see how those turnips answer with the new dressing, I'd see him fast enough," he said peevishly; "but he can't; and I don't want to hear his preaching."

"But it would be a comfort to you, surely, Stephen, to have him talk to you a little about the goodness and mercy of God. He won't tell you hard things, I'm sure of that."

"No, I suppose he'll try and make believe that death's uncommon pleasant," answered Mr. Whitelaw with a bitter laugh; "as if it could be pleasant to any man to leave such a place as Wyncomb, after doing as much for the land, and spending as much labour and money upon it, as I have done. It's like nurses telling children that a dose of physic's pleasant; they wouldn't like to have to take it themselves."

And then by-and-by, when his last day had dawned, and he felt himself growing weaker, Mr. Whitelaw expressed himself willing to comply with his wife's request.

"If it's any satisfaction to you, Nell, I'll see the parson," he said. "His talk can't do me much harm, anyhow." Whereupon the rector of Crosber and Hallibury was sent for, and came swiftly to perform his duty to the dying man. He was closeted with Mr. Whitelaw for some time, and did his best to awaken Christian feelings in the farmer's breast; but it was doubtful if his pious efforts resulted in much. The soul of Stephen Whitelaw was in his barns and granaries, with his pigs and cattle. He could not so much as conceive the idea of a world in which there should be no such thing as sale and profit.

His end came quietly enough at last, and Ellen was free. Her time of bondage had been very brief, yet she felt herself twenty years older than she had seemed before that interval of misery began.

When the will was read by Mr. Pivott on the day of Stephen Whitelaw's funeral, it was found that the farmer had left his wife two hundred a year, derivable from real estate. To Mrs. Rebecca Tadman, his cousin, he bequeathed an annuity of forty pounds, the said annuity to revert to Ellen upon Mrs. Tadman's death should Ellen survive. The remaining portion of his real estate he bequeathed to one John James Harris, a distant cousin, who owned a farm in Wiltshire, with whom Stephen Whitelaw had spent some years of his boyhood, and from whom he had learned the science of agriculture. It was less from any love the testator bore John James Harris than from a morbid jealousy of his probable successor Frank Randall, that the Wiltshire farmer had been named as residuary legatee. If Stephen Whitelaw could have left his real estate to the Infirmary, he would have so left it. His personal estate, consisting of divers investments in railway shares and other kinds of stock, all of a very safe kind, was to be realized, and the entire proceeds devoted to the erection of an additional wing for the extension of Malsham Infirmary, and his gift was to be recorded on a stone tablet in a conspicuous position on the front of that building. This, which was an absolute condition attached to the bequest, had been set forth with great minuteness by the lawyer, at the special desire of his client.

Mr. Carley's expression of opinion after hearing this will read need not be recorded here. It was forcible, to say the least of it; and Mr. Pivott, the Malsham solicitor, protested against such language as an outrage upon the finer feelings of our nature.

"Some degree of disappointment is perhaps excusable upon your part, my dear sir," said the lawyer, who wished to keep the widow for his client, and had therefore no desire to offend her father; "but I am sure that in your calmer moments you will admit that the work to which your son-in-law has devoted the bulk of his accumulations is a noble one. For ages to come the sick and the suffering among our townsfolk will bless the name of Whitelaw. There is a touching reflection for you, Mr. Carley! And really now, your amiable daughter, with an income of two hundred per annum—to say nothing of that reversion which must fall in to her by-and-by on Mrs. Tadman's decease—is left in a very fair position. I should not have consented to draw up that will, sir, if I had considered it an unjust one."

"Then there's a wide difference between your notion of justice and mine," growled the bailiff; who thereupon relapsed into grim silence, feeling that complaint was useless. He could no more alter the conditions of Mr. Whitelaw's will than he could bring Mr. Whitelaw back to life—and that last operation was one which he was by no means eager to perform.

Ellen herself felt no disappointment; she fancied, indeed, that her husband, whom she had never deceived by any pretence of affection, had behaved with sufficient generosity towards her. Two hundred a year seemed a large income to her. It would give her perfect independence, and the power to help others, if need were.

CHAPTER XLVII.
CLOSING SCENES.

IT was not until the day of her husband's funeral that Ellen Whitelaw wrote to Mr. Fenton to tell him what had happened. She knew that her letter was likely to bring him post-haste to the Grange, and she wished his coming to be deferred until that last dismal day was over. Nor was she sorry that there should be some little pause—a brief interval of ignorance and tranquillity—in Marian's life before she heard of her husband's useless voyage across the Atlantic. She was in sad need of rest of mind and body, and even in those few days gained considerable strength, by the aid of Mrs. Whitelaw's tender nursing. She had not left her room during the time that death was in the darkened house, and it was only on the morning after the funeral that she came downstairs for the first time. Her appearance had improved wonderfully in that interval of little more than a week. Her eyes had lost their dim weary look, the deathly pallor of her complexion had given place to a faint bloom. But grateful as she was for her own deliverance, she was full of anxiety about her husband. Ellen Whitelaw's vague assurances that all would be well, that he would soon be restored to her, were not enough to set her mind at ease.

Ellen had not the courage to tell her the truth. It was better that Gilbert Fenton should do that, she thought. He who knew all the circumstances of Mr. Holbrook's journey, and the probabilities as to his return, would be so much better able to comfort and reassure his wife.

"He will come to-day, I have no doubt," Ellen said to herself on the morning after her husband's funeral.

She told Marian how she had written to Mr. Fenton on the day before, in order to avoid the agitation of a surprise, should he appear at the Grange without waiting to announce his coming. Nor was she mistaken as to the probability of his speedy arrival. It was not long after noon when there came a loud peal of the bell that rang so rarely. Ellen ran herself to the gate to admit the visitor. She had told him of her husband's death in her last letter, and her widow's weeds were no surprise to him. He was pale, but very calm.

"She is well?" he asked eagerly.

"Yes, sir, she is as well as one could look for her to be, poor dear, after what she has gone through. But she is much changed since last you saw her. You must prepare yourself for that, sir. And she is very anxious about her husband. I don't know how she'll take it, when she hears that he has gone to America."

"Yes, that is a bad business, Mrs. Whitelaw," Gilbert answered gravely. "He was not in a fit state to travel, unfortunately. He was only just recovering from a severe illness, and was as weak as a child."

"O dear, O dear! But you won't tell Mrs. Holbrook that, sir?"

"I won't tell her more than I can help; of course I don't want to alarm her; but I am bound to tell her some portion of the truth. You did her husband a great wrong, you see, Mrs. Whitelaw, when you suspected him of some share in this vile business. He has shown himself really devoted to her. I thank God that it has proved so. And now tell me more about this affair; your letter explains so little."

"I will tell you all, sir."

They walked in the garden for about a quarter of an hour before Gilbert went into the house. Eager as he was to see Marian, he was still more anxious to hear full particulars of that foul plot of which she had been made the victim. Ellen Whitelaw told him the story very plainly, making no attempt to conceal her husband's guilty part in the business; and the story being finished, she took him straight to the parlour where he had seen Marian for the first time after her marriage.

It was a warm bright day, and all three windows were open. Marian was sitting by one of them, with some scrap of work lying forgotten in her lap. She started up from her seat as Gilbert went into the room, and hastened forward to meet him.

"How good of you to come!" she cried. "And you have brought me news of my husband? I am sure of that."

"Yes, dear Mrs. Holbrook—Mrs. Saltram; may I not call you by that name now?—I know all; and have forgiven all."

"Then you know how deeply he sinned against you, and how much he valued your friendship? He would never have played so false a part but for that. He could not bear to think of being estranged from you."

"We are not estranged. I have tried to be angry with him; but there are some old ties that a man cannot break. He has used me very ill, Marian; but he is still my friend."

His voice broke a little as he uttered the old familiar name. Yes, she was changed, cruelly changed, by that ordeal of six months' suffering. The brightness of her beauty had quite faded; but there was something in the altered face that touched him more deeply than the old magic. She was dearer to him, perhaps, in this hour than she had ever been yet. Dearer to him, and yet divided from him utterly, now that he professed himself her husband's friend as well as her own.

Friendship, brotherly affection, those chastened sentiments which he had fancied had superseded all warmer feelings—where were they now? By the passionate beating of his heart, by his eager longing to clasp that faded form to his breast, he knew that he loved her as dearly as on the day when she promised to be his wife; that he must love her with the same measure till the end of his existence.

"Thank God for that," Marian said gently; "thank God that you are still friends. But why did he not come with you to-day? You have told him about me, I suppose?"

"Not yet, Marian; I have not been able to do that. Nor could he come with me to-day. He has left England—on a false scent."

And then he told her, in a few words, the story of John Saltram's voyage to New York; making very light of the matter, and speaking cheerily of his early return.

"He will come back at once, of course, when he finds how he has been deceived," Gilbert said.

Marian was cruelly distressed by this disappointment. She tried to bear the blow bravely, and listened with a gentle patience to Gilbert's reassuring arguments; but it was a hard thing to bear.

"He will be back soon, you say," she said; "but soon is such a vague word; and you have not told me when he went."

Gilbert told her the date of John Saltram's departure. She began immediately to question him as to the usual length of the voyage, and to calculate the time he had had for his going and return. Taking the average length of the voyage as ten days, and allowing ten days for delay in New York, a month would give ample time for the two journeys; and John Saltram had been away more than a month.

Gilbert could see that Marian was quick to take alarm on discovering this.

"My dear Mrs. Saltram, be reasonable," he said gently. "Finding such a cheat put upon him, your husband would naturally be anxious to bring your father to some kind of reckoning, to extort from him the real secret of your fate. He would no doubt stay in New York to do this; and we cannot tell how difficult the business might prove, or how long it would occupy him."

"But if he had been detained like that, he would surely have written to you," said Marian; "and you have heard nothing from him since he left England."

"Unhappily nothing. But he is not the best correspondent in the world, you know."

"Yes, yes, I know that. Yet, in such a case as this, he would surely have written, if he were well." Her eyes met Gilbert's as she said this. She stopped abruptly, dismayed by something in his face.

"You are hiding some misfortune from me," she cried; "I can see it in your face. You have had bad news of him."

"Upon my honour, no. He was not in very strong health when he left England, that is all; and, like yourself, I am naturally anxious."

He had not meant to admit even as much as this just yet; but having said this, he found himself compelled to say more. Marian questioned him so closely, that she finally extorted from him the whole history of John Saltram's illness. After that it was quite in vain to attempt consolation. She was very gentle, very patient, troubling him with no vain wailings and lamentations; but he could see that her heart was almost broken.

He left her at the end of a few hours to return to London, promising to go on to Liverpool next day, in order to be on the spot to await her husband's return, and to send her the earliest possible tidings of it.

"Your friendship for us has given you nothing but trouble and pain," she said; "but if you will do this for me, I shall be grateful to you for the rest of my life."

There was no occasion for that journey to Liverpool. When he arrived in London that night, Gilbert Fenton found a letter waiting for him at his Wigmore-street lodgings—a letter with the New York post-mark, but *not* addressed in his friend's hand. He tore it open hurriedly, just a little alarmed by this fact.

His first feeling was one of relief. There were three separate sheets of paper in the envelope, and the first which he took up was in John Saltram's hand—a hurried eager letter, dated some weeks before.

"My dear Gilbert," he wrote, "I have been duped. This man Nowell is a most consummate scoundrel. The woman with him is not Marian, but some girl whom he has picked up to represent her—his wife perhaps, or something worse. I was very ill on the passage out, and only discovered the trick at the last. Since then I have traced the scoundrel to his quarters, and have had an interview with him—rather a stormy one, as you may suppose. But the long and short of it is that he defies me. He tells me that my wife is in England, and safe, but will admit no more. I have consulted a lawyer here, but it seems I can do nothing against him—or nothing that will not involve a more complicated and protracted business than I have time or patience for. I don't want this wretch to go scot-free. It is evident that he has hatched this plot in order to get possession of his daughter's money, and I have little doubt the lawyer Medler is in it. But of course my first duty, as well as my most ardent desire, is to find Marian; and for this purpose I shall come back to England by the first steamer that will convey me, leaving Mr. Nowell's punishment to the chances of the future. My dear girl's property, as well as herself, will be best protected by my presence in England."

There was a pause here, and the next paragraph was dated two days after.

"If I have strength to come, I shall return by the next steamer; but the fact is, my dear Gilbert, I am very ill—have been completely prostrate since writing the above—and a doctor here tells me I must not think of the voyage yet awhile. But I shan't allow his opinion to govern me. If I can crawl to the steamer, which starts three days hence, I shall come."

Then there was another break, and again the writer went on in a weak and more straggling hand, without any date this time.

"My dear Gil, it's nearly a week since I wrote the last lines, and I've been in bed ever since. I'm afraid there's no hope for me; in plain words, I believe I'm dying. To you I leave the duty I am not allowed to perform. Marian is living, and in England. I believe that scoundrelly father of hers told me the truth when he declared that. You will not rest till you find her, I know; and you will protect her fortune from that wretch. God bless you, faithful old friend! Heaven knows how I yearn for the sight of your honest face, lying here among strangers, to be buried in a foreign land. See that my wife pays Mrs. Branston the money I borrowed to come here; and tell her that I was grateful to her, and thought of her on my dying bed. To my wife I send no message. She knows that I loved her; but how dear she has been to me in this bitter time of separation, she can never know.

"You will find a bulky MS. at my chambers, in the bottom drawer on the right side of my desk. It is my Life of Swift—unfinished as my own life. If, after reading it, you should think it worth publishing, as a fragment, with my name to it, I should wish you to arrange its publication. I should be glad to leave my name upon something."

In a stranger's hand, and upon another sheet of paper, Gilbert read the end of his friend's history.

"Sir,—I regret to inform you that your friend Mr. Saltram expired at eleven o'clock last night (Wednesday, May 2nd), after an illness of a fortnight's duration, throughout which I gave him my best attention as his medical adviser. He will be buried in the Cypress-hill Cemetery, on Long Island, at his own request; and he has left sufficient funds for the necessary expenses, and the payment of his hotel bill, as well as my own small claim against him. Any surplus which may be left I shall forward to you, when these payments have been made. I enclose a detailed account of the case for your satisfaction, and have the honour to be, sir,

"Yours very obediently,
"SILAS WARREN, M.D.
"113 Sixteenth-street, New York,
"May 3, 186—."

This was all.

And Gilbert had to carry these tidings to Marian. For a time he was almost paralyzed by the blow. He had loved this man as a brother; if he had ever doubted the strength of his attachment to John Saltram, he knew it now. But the worst of all was, that one bitter fact—Marian must be told, and by him.

He went back to the Grange next day. Again and again upon that miserable journey he acted over the scene which was to take place when he came to the end of it—in spite of himself, as it were—going over the words he was to say, while Marian's face rose before him like a picture. How was he to tell her? Would not the very fact of this desolation coming to her from his lips be sufficient to make him hateful to her in all the days to come? More than once upon that journey he was tempted to turn back, and to leave his dismal news to be told in a letter.

But when the fatal moment did at last arrive, the event in no manner realized the picture of his imagination. Time was not given to him to speak those solemn preliminary words by which he had intended to prepare the victim for her deathblow. His presence there, and his presence alone, were all sufficient to prepare her for some calamity.

"You have come back to me, and without him!" she exclaimed. "Tell me what has happened; tell me at once."

He had no time to defer the stroke. His face told her so much. In a few moments—before his broken words could shape themselves into coherence—she knew all.

There are some things that can never be forgotten. Never, to his dying day, can Gilbert Fenton forget the quiet agony he had to witness then.

She was very ill for a long time after that day—in danger of death. All that she had suffered during her confinement at Wyncomb seemed to fall upon her now with a double weight. Only the supreme devotion of those who cared for her could have carried her through that weary time; but the day did at last come when the peril was pronounced a thing of the past, and the feeble submissive patient might be carried away from the Grange—from the scene of her brief married life and of her bitter widowhood.

She went with Ellen Whitelaw to Ventnor. It was late in August before she was able to bear this journey; and in this mild refuge for invalids she remained throughout the winter.

Even during that trying time, when it seemed more than doubtful whether she could live to profit by her grandfather's bequest, her interests had been carefully watched by Gilbert Fenton. It was tolerably evident to his mind that Mr. Medler had been a tacit accomplice in Percival Nowell's fraud; or, at any rate, that he had enabled the pretended Mrs. Holbrook to obtain a large sum of ready money with greater ease than she could have done had he, as executor, been scrupulously careful to obtain her identification from some more trustworthy person than he knew Percival Nowell to be.

Whether these suspicions of Gilbert's were correct, whether the lawyer had been actually deceived, or had willingly lent himself to the furtherance of Nowell's design, must remain, unascertained; as well as the amount of profit which Mr. Medler may have secured to himself by the transaction. The law held him liable for the whole of the moneys thus paid over in fraud or error; but the law could do very little against a man whose sole earthly possessions appeared to be comprised by the worm-eaten desks and shabby chairs and tables in his dingy offices. The poor consolation remained of making an attempt to get him struck off "the Rolls;" but when the City firm of solicitors in whose hands Gilbert had placed Mrs. Saltram's affairs suggested this. Marian herself entreated that the man might have the benefit of the doubt as to his complicity with her father, and that no effort should be made to bring legal ruin upon him.

"There has been enough misery caused by this money already," she said. "Let the matter rest. I am richer than I care to be, as it is."

Of course Mr. Medler was not allowed to retain his position as executor. The Court of Chancery was appealed to in the usual manner, and intervened for the future protection of Mrs. Saltram's interests.

About Nowell's conduct there was, of course, no doubt; but after wasting a good deal of money and trouble in his pursuit, Gilbert was fain to abandon all hope of catching him in the wide regions of the new world. It was ascertained that the woman who had accompanied him in the *Orinoco* as his daughter was actually his wife—a girl whom he had met at some low London dancing-rooms, and married within a fortnight of his introduction to her. It is possible that prudence as well as attachment may have had something to do with this alliance. Mr. Nowell knew that, once united to him in the bonds of holy matrimony, the accomplice of his fraud would have no power to give evidence against him. The amount which he had contrived to secure to himself by this plot amounted in all to something under four thousand pounds; and out of this it may fairly be supposed that Mr. Medler claimed a considerable percentage. The only information that Gilbert Fenton could ever obtain from America was, of a shabby swindler arrested in a gambling-house in one of the more remote western cities, whose description corresponded pretty closely with that of Marian's father.

There comes a time for the healing of all griefs. The cruel wound closes at last, though the scar, and the bitter memory of the stroke, may remain for ever. There came a time—some years after John Saltram's death—when Gilbert Fenton had his reward. And if the woman he won for his wife in these latter days was not quite the fresh young beauty he had wooed under the walnut-trees in Captain Sedgewick's garden, she was still infinitely more beautiful than all other women in his eyes; she was still the dearest and best and brightest and purest of all earthly creatures for him. In that happy time—that perfect summer and harvest of his life—all his fondest dreams have been realized. He has the home he so often pictured, the children whose airy voices sounded in his dreams, the dear face always near him, and, sweeter than all, the knowledge that he is loved almost as he loves. The bitter apprenticeship has been served, and the full reward has been granted.

For Ellen Whitelaw too has come the period of compensation, and the farmer's worst fears have been realized as to Frank Randall's participation in that money he loved so well. The income grudgingly left to his wife by Stephen has enabled Mr. Randall to begin business as a solicitor upon his own account, in a small town near London, with every apparent prospect of success. Ellen's home is within easy reach of the river-side villa occupied by Mr. and Mrs. Fenton; so she is able to see her dear Marian as often as she likes; nor is there any guest at the villa more welcome than this faithful friend.

The half-written memoir of Jonathan Swift was published; and reviewers, who had no compunction in praising the dead, were quick to recognize the touch of a master hand, the trenchant style of a powerful thinker. For the public the book is of no great value; it is merely a curiosity of literature; but it is the only monument of his own rugged genius which bears the name of John Saltram.

Poor little Mrs. Branston has not sacrificed all the joys of life to the manes of her faithless lover. She is now the happy wife of a dashing naval officer, and gives pleasant parties which bring life and light into the great house in Cavendish-square; parties to which Theobald Pallinson comes, and where he shines as a small feeble star when greater lights are absent—singing his last little song, or reciting his last little poem, for the delight of some small coterie of single ladies not in the first bloom of youth; but parties from which Mrs. Pallinson keeps aloof in a stern spirit of condemnation, informing her chosen familiars that she was never more cruelly deceived than in that misguided ungrateful young woman, Adela Branston.

Printed in the United Kingdom
by Lightning Source UK Ltd.
118012UK00001B/82